D1503627

ISBN 9781518638374

Cover Design by Paul Casson

April Elaine

A Novel by April Elaine

To Richard and Elaine with love.
Your positivity eclipses all negativity.

Mid pleasures and palaces, though we may roam,
Be it ever so humble, there's no place like home.
--John Howard Payne

ONE

> You cannot run away from weakness; you must sometimes
> fight it out or perish. And if that be so,
> why not now, and where you stand?
> -Robert Louis Stevenson

I can't believe it's been over two years since Todd broke down my front doors and dragged me out to Le Château. Back then, Josie Fleming didn't want to go. She didn't want to leave the quiet refuge of her home. It took Todd, her older brother, over an hour to coerce her out of her house and onto the courts of Le Château Saint Emillion Spa and Club, or Le Château for short.

Josie tucks a loose chestnut-brown wave behind her ear and sighs. *A lot has changed since then.* She steers her black Mini Cooper convertible east on Glades Road towards the club. *I had gained so much weight so quickly that I couldn't run for more than a few steps.* The rising sun sits just above the horizon, causing her hazel eyes to squint. *It took a lot of hard work, but now I can actually run for the ball, and last three sets if I have to.* As she reaches for her shades, she recalls that fateful day.

She remembers how Todd stood in the middle of her foyer with a crowbar in his hand and a more-than-worried look upon his face. He yelled over her blaring television, "What's wrong with you! Why didn't you answer the door?" He ranted about the stacks of mail piled by her door, and her overgrown yard. He mumbled, "And judging from that emanating odor, your lack of personal hygiene is equally neglected." She heard him.

She remembers how annoyed she felt by his intrusion. Josie ignored her brother, turned back around, and switched channels.

Todd ran towards her, stepped in something, and dragged it along. He grabbed the remote and said, "Give me that! Did it ever occur to you that someone might be worried sick about you? None of your neighbors have seen you!"

Still, Josie did not respond. She snatched the remote back.

Todd looked down, kicked an empty chip bag off his foot and glared at her, "Look at me! Say something!"

Josie increased the volume.

Todd shook her by the shoulders and said, "Josie, I pictured you lying on the floor, half dead or worse! You could have at least returned my calls, and let me know that you were OK."

She remembers thinking, *But that's just it, I'm not OK.* Instead of saying so, she said, "Your wild imagination is not my problem."

So much has changed since that day. I've changed. Josie clicks her left blinker. *That was a lifetime ago.* As she turns into Le Château and queues at the gate, her memory continues. She had winced as she watched Todd take it all in: the missing furniture, the littered food cartons, and her drastic weight gain. Silence enveloped the room. Finally, she cracked first by saying, "I-I have been, you know, meaning to clean up and all."

Todd said, "I don't care about your house; I care about you." After heated back-and-forth bickering, he eventually dragged Josie out of her house and onto the tennis court. He reasoned, "You need to get moving, get out, reclaim your life." He said that he planned to use tennis to help her do just that.

She nudges her car up in line. *I would never tell him this, but he was right. Tennis has helped me reclaim parts of my life I didn't even know were missing.* Josie hands the gate attendant her identification and waits for the brass gates to open. As they do, the scrolled words split into two; "Le" splits to the left while "Château" splits to the right. As she drives through the middle, she remembers the rest of that day.

Todd held up a tennis ball and said, "Picture The Big Loser's face on it."

She remembers thinking, *How stupid is that? It's a tennis ball, not a face. And can you please not mention him anymore.* She didn't want to think about her ex-husband, and she certainly didn't want to see his face. She hit a lackluster forehand and replied, "Look, I just really don't want to be here. I want to go home."

Todd said, "Why? So you can hide away in your Pit of Despair and swallow your problems with food."

She put her hands on her hips and yelled, "Since when did you become such an expert on my life?" She ripped a crosscourt winner, "I'm handling things just fine!"

He argued, "No, you're not!"

"Yes, I am!" She crushed a backhand and said, "How can you possibly understand?" She took a high bouncing ball and nailed an overhead from the midcourt.

Todd said, "Oh, I understand all right, but it doesn't give you the excuse to become a recluse or give up normal daily habits, like brushing your teeth."

She pointed her racquet at him and yelled, "Shut Up! You know what? Just shut up!" She slapped at a backhand.

Todd said, "Tighten up your backswing."

She remembers thinking, *Tighten up? I'd like to tighten up my fist into a ball and—*

Todd added, "You call that a swing? Don't baby it!"

Before she finished her thought, something unexpected happened: the arrival of her ex-husband, Roger Fleming, in the shape of one small, yellow, tennis ball. She shouted, 'Go away,' and pounded the ball with all of her might. However, the next ball bore his face, as did the next, and the next. Each spoke as they sailed across the net towards her; *You're a worthless piece of fat blubber*, and *There's simply no reason for you to exist*, and *You're the only human being I've ever met who truly is unloveable*. She silenced ball after ball as she unleashed a fury of blistering groundstrokes.

Unexpectedly, Todd said, "It's time to go."

Josie said, "Wait. Go? Why? We just got here!"

With a sheepish grin, he said, "Because, that was the last ball. You hit the rest over the fence and into the lake."

"Oh, sorry."

He walked around the net post and tousled her hair, "No apologies in tennis...at least not when you're with me."

She nodded and helped carry his ball cart to the trunk of his car. As she left the parking lot, she remembers looking back as the ground's crew already smoothed out the divots and pockmarks on their court's surface. The sprinklers kicked on, further smoothing out the clay and creating an unblemished court, ready and waiting for a new day.

Josie parks her car under one of the banyan trees lining the parking lot. The tree looks as if it houses ten trunks rolled into one. She edges closer to its mammoth trunk to shade her car from the sweltering sun. However, the tree provides limited shade. All of its branches have been extensively trimmed to resemble a puffy, narrow Q-tip top.

Josie walks across the old brick, herringbone sidewalk and through the pink mandevilla enlaced arbor. She walks up the white stone steps to the entryway of the three-story, white, Mission Revival style clubhouse. Today, she will do something that she hasn't done since college: try out for a tennis team.

The glass doors automatically open as she enters into a two-story foyer flanked by two grand staircases on either side. A blast of refreshingly cool air sends her hair and tennis skort into brief turmoil before the doors shut behind her. She smoothes down her skort, signs in at the main desk, shows her identification, and takes the tennis towel offered.

She avoids the bustling locker room and walks to the quiet indoor pool area. As she applies sunscreen, the balmy indoor air instantly sends her hair into frizzy flyaways.

Josie pulls her shoulder-length wavy locks into a ponytail, puts on a tennis hat, and tucks some errant waves underneath. She fills her cup with ice at the end of the pool area, avoiding the long lines by the tennis court's ice machine.

She inhales a slow, deep breath and exits. *Here goes.* She walks down the wide central sidewalk canopied by interlocking, fifty-year-old, oak tree branches. She squints, studying the rays of light filtering through the yellow and dark green leaves as she peers into the cloudless sky.

The central walkway, called The Breezeway, bisects the entire tennis facility. It provides the complex's main artery from which all other paths lead. The Breezeway--paved with the same herringbone pattern as the parking lot--stretches ten feet wide. Similar to a shopping mall, various points along The Breezeway and around the complex, display "You are Here" signs. The signage provides necessary orientation for the foot traffic passing through. The tennis facility encompasses twenty-seven sprawling acres.

Josie consults the map. She's played here many times, but never on the team's practice courts. As she walks to her court, a voice catches up to her.

The girl says, "Hi, are you the new tryout?"

Josie says, "Yes, I'm Josephine Fleming, but you can call me Josie."

The girl extends her hand and says, "OK, Josie. Nice to meet you. I'm Marni Schoppelmann." Marni enthusiastically shakes Josie's hand and then pulls it, saying, "Go this way! It's a shortcut."

With Josie in tow, Marni cuts straight through a court as four older gentlemen play a crucial point. She yells, "Let!" narrowly dodging a ball sailing over the net.

One of the older gentlemen throws his racquet to the ground and yells, "Marni! That was game point!"

Marni smiles sweetly and says, "Sorry boys, duty calls!" She says to Josie as they cut across yet another court, "That's J. Paul Mooney. He's the most influential member of the club. He helped the pro who founded Le Château get the funding for it. He has a hand in everything. His wife, Monica, plays for our team. She's, uh, how to say this politely, reptilian by nature."

"What does that mean?"

"It means she would eat her own children if she had any."

"What? Does--"

"Shh. That's her right over there by the ice machine. You're skinny."

"I am?"

"Yeah. I heard you were fat. You're not fat. You're skinny."

"I was, uh, heavy for a time."

"How'd you do it?"

"Do what?"

"Loose the weight?"

"Tennis."

"Oh. Yeah. Tennis is great for that. When I go three sets in a single's match, I can pretty much eat whatever I want for the rest of the day. Plus, it's just fun."

"Eating whatever you want?"

6

"No, playing tennis. You nervous?"

"A little."

"I was, too. Tryouts are a bear! I tried out three times before I made the team."

"Geez, I didn't know tryouts would be so, uh, strenuous. This your first year?"

"Fourth. But I'll bet Mitch goes easier on you."

"Why would he do that?"

Marni stops and queues in the line for ice. She says, "Well, for one thing, you're getting to tryout when the team is already full."

"Nobody told me that the team was full."

"Yep. It is. People wait for years to get on this team. I guessed you had some sorta clout."

"Zero. I have zero clout."

"Really? Mitch had to petition the board to request your tryout and potentially adding you to our team."

Great. No pressure. "I hope it wasn't too much trouble."

Marni laughs, "Don't feel bad; Mitch is used to trouble. He coaches us for God's sake! Monica, this is Josie Fleming. Josie, Monica."

Monica looks familiar, but Josie can't place her face right away. They exchange civilities as a man's hand lands on Josie's shoulder. She turns to see a handsome, tall, deeply tanned tennis player. His short razor stubble is neatly groomed, and his dark hair pulls back into a short low ponytail with a white bandana tied on top. He extends his arms wide, hugs her, and says, "Brace Face! Welcome to the madhouse!"

Josie says, *"Brace Face?* No one has called me that since I was in high school."

"Don't you remember me? Come on! It's me, Mitch Garvey."

"Oh my gosh, Mitch? Todd's best friend growing up?" *And the biggest heartthrob in my high school.* "What did Todd used to call you? Mr. Silverspoon? You haven't aged a bit!"

—

7

"Thank you." He rubs his beard and says, "Except now I can grow one of these, and the spoon is more of a rusty tin than silver."

She laughs and says, "When Todd told me to meet with Mitch I had no idea he was talking about you. I didn't know you were in Boca. I thought you were working on Wall Street or something."

From a few feet away, Monica mumbles a little too loudly, "So that's how she got this tryout. He's an old family friend."

Josie glances awkwardly at Monica and says quietly to Mitch, "Is she talking about me? I don't want any special treatment."

Mitch ignores Monica for once, and says loudly, "You're looking at the former number one junior's player in Florida, ladies. This is my Elite Division. You don't play here just by knowing somebody." He looks directly at Monica and says, "Although, who you know has helped some in the past." Monica sticks her tongue out at him.

Josie says, "Todd didn't tell me you were here. I can't believe you left New York. I thought you loved it!"

"I thought I loved it too, but something was missing."

"But the financial stuff? That's your thing, your gift as Todd called it. You're so good at it."

"Turns out, there's a lot of people good at it."

"Yeah, but you were really good at it. Or, so I heard."

"It lost its charm. After twelve years, I found I could use my mad genius at something else, something I truly love."

"Tennis?"

"Yeah."

"But tennis is so, uh, different."

"Not really."

"Come on, Le Château is not exactly Wall Street."

"The similarities might surprise you."

"Really?"

"Yeah. For example, I still work stats. It's just that here I work a different set of stats. I still crunch numbers all day, every day."

"Wait, you're not the coach? You work in accounting here?"

"Me? Ha-ha. I'm no bean counter. No way! I'm not a complete loser!"

Josie winces. *Um, I'm an accountant, or bean counter as you say.*

Mitch continues, "Tennis has an unbelievable amount of math in it. You wouldn't believe it! As a matter of fact, I would go so far as to say tennis *is* math. From the mechanics of each movement to the player stats, it's math. It's all math."

Monica rolls her eyes and mimics the words, "Tennis is math."

Mitch says, "I saw that, Monica."

Monica says, "Honestly Mitch, you're such a nerd!"

Mitch says, "Ignore her. It's really kind of fascinating. I'll have to show you the files on player stats on my iPad sometime."

Josie manages to sound enthusiastic and says, "Great! Well. Anyway, it's been a long time. It's great to see you."

"You, too." Then, he yells down to Court One, "Ceridwin, warm Brace Face--I mean Josie--up, please."

Josie says, "I'm sorry, who?"

Monica imposes herself into the conversation by standing between Mitch and Josie. She says with added droll, "Well Chatty-Cathy, it's Ceridwin. Kah-REED-win. Got it? Cuz she's gonna whip your butt. That is, if you can tear yourself away from your scintillating 'math rocks' conversation."

Josie's heard of Ceridwin before. She watches Monica pull a face. She doesn't know what to make of this Monica character. *Is she kidding?*

Monica says, "Not so chatty now, huh. Typical. Talk about initiation by fire. Too bad your cute little tennis number isn't made out of asbestos."

Marni says, "Oh, don't listen to her. Ceridwin is such a sweetheart. You'll be fine. Don't worry. Just play the percentages and don't be a hero. Just have fun."

Monica says, "No. She's right. Don't be a hero. Although, you could use a superhero, maybe even Hercules on your side of the net. Ceridwin is not only the best tennis player in South Florida, but she used to play for the Scottish LTA and was ranked number fifty-two in the world. So yeah, just have *fun* getting clocked."

Marni says, "Stop it, Monica. Josie, don't let her psyche you out. Like I said, just have fun. This little game Monica plays is the reason I didn't make the team the first couple of times. She purposely made me choke. Don't let her get you riled up."

Josie smiles weakly and nods. *Geez. Who let the crazies out?*

Monica says, "Yeah, have fun and don't feel bad if you blow your tryout and lose Mitch's job for him. After all, he did put it on the line so you could have your own special made-up spot." She smiles sweetly and says, "Go have fun!" She twinkles her fingers goodbye.

He can't really lose his job, can he?

TWO

We cannot control the evil tongues of others;
but a good life enables us to disregard them.
-Cato the Elder

Josie walks slowly to her court. Marni waits until Josie is out of earshot and says, "Monica, I know what you're trying to do."

Monica says, "Power down, Sparky. It's all in good fun. Josie knows I'm only joking." She laughs and yells after Josie, "Right, Josie?"

Unsure of what to make of Monica, Josie keeps walking and doesn't answer.

Monica adds for good measure, "Josie, just be sure to keep your racquet in front of your face. That is, if you like where your nose is."

Josie tries to good-naturedly laugh off the comment, but what comes out of her mouth sounds more like a horsey wheeze, and less like a laugh. Josie covers her mouth. *Did that just come out of me?*

Swallowing a smile, Monica raises her eyebrows in response, but says nothing.

Mitch yells down The Breezeway to Josie, "This should only take half an hour or so. OK?"

Josie gives him the thumb's-up sign. However, with each advancing step to Court One, it becomes clear that everything is not OK. Something within Josie changes. Unannounced, butterflies arrive with a tingling, twirling, fluttery feeling deep in the pit of her stomach.

As she rounds the corner and views her open court, her stomach lurches. She loudly belches. Embarrassed, she tries swallowing the next belch, but manages to amplify it somehow. *Sigh.* The horsey voice, butterflies, and now the acid reflux take her completely by surprise.

Josie rolls her neck to loosen the muscle tension. The absurdity of the moment catches her off guard. Again, she laughs, producing another horsey guffaw. *God help me, I'm turning into Mr. Ed!*

Attempting to shrug off the nerves, she peps herself up. *OK. A little bit of the jitters. Normal. No big deal. I can handle this. Everything is fine.* The opposite proves true. *I can't believe Mitch can really lose his job over my performance today.* Her body continues on a course for mutiny. She belches again. *Great. A horse in my throat and a lurching stomach, what's next?* She doesn't have to wonder long. Josie sees Ceridwin using the net post to stretch out her calves.

Ceridwin points and says, "You can put your bag on the rack there, next to mine."

"OK, thanks." When Josie places her bag next to Ceridwin's, she reads Ceridwin's multiple bagtags: *Player of the Year; Voted Best South Florida Tennis Player; Number One - Regional Champ; Number One - State; MVP*; and the list goes on. *Ugh. Are you kidding me?*

As Josie joins Ceridwin on the court, she struggles to push thoughts of Ceridwin's multiple bagtags and Mitch's job away. *OK, let's go. Time for some fun.* However, fun is not exactly what her nerves have in mind. Her shoulder muscles tighten to the point that her right shoulder sits a good inch higher than normal. She stops and stares at her shoulder as if it were an alien being. Unable to release the tension in it, she begins to panic. *What is going on?*

Ceridwin says "Everything all right?"

"No. I mean, yes. Of course." She pushes her shoulder downward with her palm, but it won't budge. *Is this a cramp? Hmm. No, it's less of a cramp and more of a frozen, freeze-dried, locked into place sort of thing.* Her arm resembles a coat hanger dangling on her shoulder.

Confused, Josie scrambles for some idea of what to do next. She takes another deep, calming breath. However, calming herself down proves more and more difficult, as does regaining control of her racquet arm.

This is new. She laughs and quickly covers her mouth. *Oh my gosh, I really am Mr. Ed!* Never before has her body decided to give up on her and do its own thing. It feels as though every nerve connecting her mind to her arm runs into a roadblock at her shoulder before abruptly U-turning back to her brain, never fully reaching its intended destination. Her brain speaks, but nothing listens: a complete and total disconnect. *I might be able to play with a hoarse voice and butterflies in my stomach, but I can't play without my racquet arm.*

Nervous and frustrated, she tries loosening her shoulders with a circular motion to regain control of her racquet arm. *OK, I can do this! Loosen up!* However, instead of loosening, the opposite occurs. The tightness grips her shoulder with added vice. Her shoulder refuses to roll or listen. *Oh come on!* Again, she tries rolling her shoulders. *But coat hangers don't roll!*

She yells out, "Roll, damn it!" She looks up to see a confused Ceridwin looking over the net.

Ceridwin says, "Um, OK. Let's *roll*. Shall we? Ready?"

Blushing, Josie meekly replies, "Sure." However, her shoulder's opinion differs greatly. A standoff occurs. Josie's mind and body stare each other down, both refusing to give an inch. *This is ridiculous!* Panicking, her mind quickly shouts commands at her body, particularly at her racquet arm. More physical in nature than verbal, her body flips her mind the finger in response.

Making matters worse, Josie hears Monica from the adjacent court laugh and say, "Classic textbook choke if you ask me. And Mitch petitioned the board for that? He'll be out of a job by the end of the day. That train wreck just blew his career."

What Monica doesn't say--and even Ceridwin sympathizes with--is that every tennis player experiences this helpless feeling of choking sooner or later. And any player will tell you, there is only one thing worse than choking: watching someone else choke. It's cringeworthy to witness another player fall to pieces right before your eyes. Unless, of course, you're Monica. Then, watching the unraveling brings pure entertainment.

Ceridwin understands that every player chokes once in a while, and the memories of those chokes don't fade easily. Even the best tennis players in the world are not immune. Ceridwin looks away. Knowing that to be true doesn't make it any easier to watch. Ceridwin wants to say something to help Josie. Stymied, she thinks of nothing to say.

Josie tries, but her shoulder won't release enough tension for her arm to swing fluidly.

Ceridwin grimaces before finally offering, "Don't worry, Josie. Everyone chokes." She laughs and adds, "It's like being served liver and onions at your boyfriend's parents' house. You can't refuse your helping. You simply have to sit and swallow bite after miserable bite while wearing a plastered smile on your face. Right?"

Josie says, "I'm not choking. This isn't a choke. Besides, I like liver. I'm fine. Really." *Why'd I say that? I hate liver.*

Ceridwin shrugs and feeds Josie solid, medium-paced balls: the kind Josie would normally eat for lunch. Josie swings, but the muscles in her racquet arm won't work. The swing jerks short of the oncoming ball, briskly stopping mid-motion on her follow through. Josie cannot believe her eyes. Devastated and humiliated, she shanks ball after ball, not finding the court once. *I should just admit it. I'm choking! I cannot believe I cannot hit one decent ball. Not one.*

She would like to apologize, but she can't offer an explanation: just as she can't offer Ceridwin one measly, decent ball to hit. After a few minutes, Ceridwin gives up chasing down ball after ball and wheels a fully loaded cart onto the court as backup.

Only five-year-olds need a ball cart for backup. Josie starts laughing at the gesture and then crying. She follows Ceridwin's uneasy glance to Mitch standing courtside. He types something on his iPad. Mitch types something more and begins walking away.

On the court next to her, she overhears Monica laugh and say, "I think they should send that one back. It's defective. Bye-bye, Mitch. Bye-bye, Mitch's job."

Besides the sudden onset of butterflies, another arrival surprises Josie: Roger Fleming spontaneously appears in the form of one little, yellow ball after another. Josie watches a round Roger Fleming--with "Penn 4" written across his forehead--sail over the net directly toward her. He speaks. As he glides closer, she hears his words. He says, "What do we have here?" Josie aims for the little yellow head and whiffs. He sneers and says, "Hello, Fatso-Jo!"

Josie yells out loudly enough that surrounding courts hear, "I am *NOT* fat anymore!" She sets up her forehand and decides to step in, instead of hitting open stance. She doesn't wait. She takes the ball early on the rise. She flattens it out and rips an eighty-five miles per hour bullet to Ceridwin's backhand.

Caught off guard by the sudden well-targeted missile, Ceridwin stumbles backwards, but manages a slice in a last-ditch response. The ball lands short in front of Josie. She rushes in, gets her racquet back early, changes her grip, gives the ball a lot of whip, and angles it off the court for a winner that makes Ceridwin whistle.

Ceridwin glances at Mitch once more. This time, she smiles. Mitch walks back to their court. Still smiling, Ceridwin pushes the ball cart off of the court. One-half hour later, a small audience forms on their courtside steps as the rallying heats up. Mitch continues taking stats and notes, when suddenly a familiar voice interrupts. He doesn't need to look up to know who approaches. He smelled her expensive perfume long before her actual arrival.

He says, "Hello, Monica. Shouldn't you be on your own court?"

Monica tips her Pilla sunglasses down her button nose and looks over the rim at Josie. She dismisses his small talk with the wave of her hand and says, "I don't have time for chitchat." She hasn't taken her eyes off the big forehand dueling with Ceridwin for the last half hour. Salivating, she says, "Please tell me Josie made the cut."

Her heavy perfume bristles the hair inside his nostrils. He sneezes and says, "Starts today, and no thanks to you." He takes two steps forward, standing upwind of her. He makes a note for almost every stroke of Josie's. He smiles, already planning her year and projecting her win/loss ratio.

Monica also makes plans. She squints, but unsuccessfully reads Mitch's notes. She plots to ditch her current partner and claim Josie as her own. With Josie's forehand on her court, Monica envisions a year-end score line by her name: 18:0. She licks her lips. She would like to run onto Josie's court and pee a circle around her into the chalky HarTru.

Monica mumbles, "If only that were socially acceptable."

Mitch says, "What?"

"Nothing. For now, Plan B will have to do."

Mitch says, "I'm sorry, what's Plan B?"

She quickly says, "Duh! Something you do when Plan A won't work."

Josie notices Monica intently watching her every move. She sees Monica whisper something into Mitch's ear while emphatically pointing to her.

All at once, it hits Josie. *I know Monica! I've played tennis with her before. It's been a while, but I'm sure of it. It was right after my divorce. Todd dragged me out for a doubles match.*

Josie yells across the net to Ceridwin, "That girl, Monica, standing by Mitch, does she play mixed doubles here?"

Ceridwin says, "Monica Mooney? Yeah. Well, she did. Why?"

"I think I might have played against her. She looks familiar. Does she play with her husband?"

"She did, but he, uh, retired from mixed doubles. He plays tennis only with the guys now."

"I can understand why."

"What?"

"Nothing. Her husband plays the old serve and volley style? Continental grip?"

"Yep."

"OK. Then, I played them before." *Yeah, I thought I recognized her all right. Not surprisingly, she doesn't recognize me.*

. They met on the courts of Le Château when Todd dragged the unwilling and newly divorced Josie onto the courts for a mixed doubles match. Josie vividly remembers what transpired next. Monica and her husband—twenty-four years her senior--played in the club's social mixed doubles round robin. *That match was supposed to be one of those hit-and-a-giggle events. For fun.* She and Todd were paired against them. *During warm-up Monica realized I couldn't run. Yeah, I remember her all right.*

For the rest of the match Monica exploited Josie's weakness, her lack of mobility. She snickered at every short ball that Josie couldn't reach. Josie remembers a couple of Monica's tasteless jokes, too: *Fat chance of getting to that one,* and *I would weigh your options on that shot, but you broke the scale.* Monica laughed mercilessly.

Continually, Monica hit the ball short, angling it just out of reach. Josie labored, but failed miserably each time. With cool calculation, Monica unfolded her plan, and her strategy paid off. She and J. Paul went up early in the first set, 4:1. If the match were anything other than social, Monica's tactic might have been better received. However, her rude behavior left Todd fuming.

Todd put his own plan into action. Monica became too predicable with her repeated dropshots. Quickly, Todd began reading Monica's plays early, tracking down the balls Josie couldn't reach. Josie and Todd closed out the first set with a 6:4 lead.

Never gracious at losing even a singular set, Monica lashed out at all around, including her own husband. Her snide comments became almost unbearable, making the play more than unpleasant well into the second set.

At one point, Monica blasted Josie, "Josie, maybe you should go sit down and let Todd play the whole court. He practically already is anyway. And if you want to know why you missed that last point, look no farther than over your shoulder and at that enormous ass of yours."

That was the last straw for Todd. He shared more than a few choice words with Monica. J. Paul broke up the back-and-forth bickering. He asked both players to tone it down. Surprisingly, they did. Everything went along civilly until match point.

It is that last point that stands out in Josie's mind. *It was an easy point. Too easy to miss, costing J. Paul dearly.* J. Paul played the net, and Monica ran down everything. She set him up through a series of solid groundstrokes, expertly drawing a short ball from Todd.

Todd's weak reply somehow landed squarely on J. Paul's racquet. J. Paul needn't so much as move an inch to simply smash the perfectly set-up winner. However, instead of smashing what should have been a gimme at Josie, J. Paul softly angled the ball off court with a short finesse shot, avoiding Josie altogether.

The angle was well executed. However, a short ball needs to be near perfect against Todd. Todd speedily tracked down the ball, pushing it up the line for a winner and for match point.

J. Paul's chivalrous act was not lost on Josie. When they met at the net to shake hands, Josie said, "I know the right shot for your overhead was right at me. Thank you for reconsidering."

J. Paul laughed and said, "It's only tennis, right? No sense taking someone's head off. Besides, I'd be lying if I didn't say my shot was made to set a precedent."

"Precedent? What do you mean?"

"I mean now that I've avoided hitting you--and especially after I've seen your wicked overhead--I hope you'll consider doing the same for me next time."

"I see. Angle it away from you?"

J. Paul winked at her.

"You got it!"

Not sharing his same sentiment, Monica furiously stormed over, grabbed J. Paul's balls and said, "Did you just wink at her? Don't wink at the Fatso-Jo! More of these! Use more of these!" Monica squeezed hard until J. Paul bent over. "Hit it at her! Not some crazy dropshot! At her! You hear me? Right at her!" She looks directly at Josie and spits the words, "Take her head off! And don't ever wink at Fatso-Jo again!"

Josie watches Monica leave Mitch's side and resume her place on her practice court. She says to Ceridwin, "I've definitely played against her and her husband. It's an experience I'll likely never forget."

Ceridwin says, "Well, that must have been a long time ago, since J. Paul no longer plays tennis with his wife and hasn't for some time. He says he prefers watching her instead."

Josie mumbles, "Arguably, from a safe distance."

Ceridwin says, "What was that?"

"Nothing."

THREE

Self-confidence is the first requisite to great undertakings.
-Samuel Johnson

Josie arrives at Le Château for the season's first match. She carries her three-pack tennis bag down The Breezeway's long corridor. She smiles and waves to a few passers-by. She checks the lineup on the bulletin board. Mitch paired her with Vivian Bendler, the veteran on the team.

To avoid any surprises, Mitch phoned earlier to explain that two players were out, making the lineup changes necessary. No longer would Josie be playing with her practice partner, Marni. He said that playing with Vivian would only be a temporary fix.

What Mitch didn't say is that Monica cornered him and gave him another one of her ultimatums. She insisted on seeing her name next to Josie's on today's lineup. That is until she learned that Josie—like all new players-- would be starting at the bottom of the lineup. Then, Monica insisted on playing with Marni instead. This left Mitch with some last minute rearranging.

Josie sees Monica in the distance applying lipstick in the ice machine's metallic reflection. *Maybe Monica won't notice me and I won't have to chat. Wish I were playing with Marni. That would be fun.*

What Mitch also didn't tell Josie is that he paired her with Vivian for yet another reason. Vivian needs a partner; no one wants to play with her. Since Marni is newly taken, Josie fits the bill.

Mitch spent no small amount of time pondering Josie's predicament. He had much to consider. He contemplated the effects of a guy like Roger Fleming, and, of course, her divorce. Mitch remembers the old confident Josie, the one long before Roger. He makes a note in his iPad and hatches a plan to bring her back. Happy with his decision, Mitch changes screens and enters information for today's match.

Mitch watches Josie take to the court with Vivian. He crosses his fingers and hopes they gel as a team. He glances over Josie's profile on his iPad one last time. He frowns. He knows tennis and he knows the stats. He hopes Josie will fit in as Vivian's partner.

Mitch watches Vivian and Josie shake hands. Vivian says something that makes Josie throw her head back with laughter. Mitch smiles and thinks, *So far, so good.* He knows that Vivian has been playing tennis longer than Josie has been alive. She's seen it all. He thinks, *If anyone can help Josie work through her troubles and build confidence, Vivian can. I can't have Josie choking like she did in tryouts. That's no fun for anybody.*

Mitch hasn't seen them play together yet, but he plans to pair them for weeks to come. With any luck, Josie will take lessons learned on the court from the wise old Vivian and generously apply them to other parts of her life as well. It's a given that on the tennis court partners talk about more than just tennis. He's counting on that to be true.

Mitch thinks back to the old Josie again as he watches her rally. It is difficult for him not to compare. He sees her rounded shoulders, and the way she slumps. It breaks his heart to see this new Josie. He looks away, takes more notes in his iPad, and moves to another court.

Josie unloads her tennis gear on the chair next to Vivian. After decades of playing tennis, Vivian has developed an unwavering routine.

Josie watches as Vivian spreads her towel on the back of her chair, inching it back and forth until it rests evenly. Next, Vivian opens her tennis bag and places it on another towel laid to the right of her chair just so. Then, she eats a pre-game homemade granola snack--the same one as one hundred times before--and asks Josie to hit with her on a practice court before the actual warm-up begins.

Once on an adjacent practice court, Vivian performs a series of lunges and stretches, all methodically tailored to render her old bones ready for action. Next, she asks Josie to hit short balls at the service line: left then right, until her spine moves fluidly. Lastly, she moves back to the baseline and asks Josie to hit groundstrokes, alternating between back and forehands again.

On the adjacent practice court, the sprinklers sputter before producing a steady stream and transforming the day's marks into a clean, grayish-green surface. A gentle spray rises atop the sprinklers and wafts onto Vivian's practice court.

The fine mist bathes Josie in welcomed coolness. She closes her eyes, opens her mouth, and takes in the refreshingly cool spray.

Vivian says, "Let's move back to our court."

"One sec."

"Josie, the water is non-potable."

Puh, puh, puh. "Yeah. OK, no problem."

As Josie and Vivian finish and walk back to their court, Josie asks, "Ready?"

Vivian says, "Almost." She drops her tennis bag where she stands, holds her chin with one hand, and the back of her head with the other and cracks her neck twice.

Josie says, "Whoa! That was loud! Are you sure that's good for you?"

"Not sure, but it feels wonderful. Besides, at my age, everything that can get hurt already does anyhow."

It's hard not to like Vivian. Even so, and with more than a tinge of guilt, Josie doesn't want to play with her.

As if reading her mind, Vivian says, "Josie, we're different players here. I know your game. I get it. I'm not gonna gloss things over. I know Monica calls my type of tennis 'little old lady tennis'. And guess what…I don't mind."

Josie wipes her brow. *But that's just it; I don't want to play little old lady tennis.*

Vivian thumps her chest and continues, "This little old lady manages to do pretty well on the scoreboard when it's all said and done."

Josie says, "Yeah, your record is amazing!"

Vivian laughs, adjusts her oversized visor, and continues, "Whoa! I took myself way too seriously there for a second! Anyhow, back to reality. I lob more in one game than you lob in a lifetime. And dropshots? When I'm not lobbing, I'm hitting dropshots the remainder of the time."

Josie frowns. *Great. But I prefer real tennis.*

Vivian laughs again and then grows serious, "I know you prefer to rally or go in for the big put-a-way. I get it! I really do! Look, all I want to do is end the point quickly, maybe too quickly for your taste. I just hope playing with me doesn't drive you bonkers. I just have to ask. Are you OK with this?"

Josie can't find it in her heart to tell Vivian that she doesn't want to play with her. She can't tell her that playing at Vivian's pace is like waiting for water to boil. Instead, she says, "Hey, this is supposed to be fun, right? So, let's have some fun."

Vivian says, "All right! Agreed. Fun is important! At my age, it's what I live for."

"I am not sure how this is going to go down."

"Well, you can count on me to tell it like it is. You do the same, OK? Anyway," Vivian laughs an easy laugh and continues, "whatever happens, it looks like you're stuck with me today. Just be patient and pick your moments."

"Sounds good."

"You can yell at me, tell me the ball is yours, change a play mid-point if it suits you, and make a few mistakes. It's all-good. Just know that. OK, partner?"

"OK."

Vivian extends her hand to Josie. Already, Vivian takes the pressure off.

Josie smiles broadly, shaking hands.

Vivian says, "When I'm out here chasing that darn little yellow ball around, I just try to remember one thing—you mentioned it earlier--have fun. That's my motto. I mean if we don't have fun, then what the heck are we doing out here anyway, right? It's not like anyone's paying us."

As a team, they decide who serves first, which side each will play, and what strategies to employ. They discuss the newly discovered weaknesses in their opponents and form a plan. Vivian knows how to work a strategy, and she knows how to work as a team.

However, the first few points don't go their way. Immediately, their opponents exploit perceived weaknesses in Vivian's game. They sized her up by age and instantly decided to target her presumed lack of mobility. They repeatedly drop the ball short, making her run. Once Vivian is on the run, they hit the ball to the open court, dropping the ball behind her and out of Josie's reach. They win the first few points this way.

Under labored breath, Vivian laughs and says quietly to Josie, "They're like a pair of hungry little squirrels hunting for their next nut to hoard. I think they found it in my range!"

Next, they work over Josie, picking apart her game. They have seen enough of her forehand during warm-up to know they don't like it one bit. So, they look elsewhere for their next nut. On the following point, they test Josie's running backhand. In response, Josie nails a down-the-line winner. After the point, they heatedly strategize in the back of the court for a lengthy minute. Finally, their argument ends, and they resume moving Vivian around, poking and prodding until they find their next nut. Josie and Vivian go down quickly on the scoreboard at 0:3.

Josie says to Vivian, "Let's dig ourselves out of this hole before it gets any deeper. How about we change up our formation? You know, give them a different look?"

"Uh, like, uh, what?"

"I don't know. They're killing us. Maybe you play net, and I play back?"

Vivian, still catching her breath from the string her opponents have been pulling her on, says, "Good, uh, counter-strategy, but do you, uh, mind if we wait a few more games to put it into, uh, play? I think they've shown us everything, uh, they've got. Now that I, uh, know what's coming, I can read their dropshots and, uh, their lobs much better. I'm, uh, getting used to seeing it come off of their racquets. With a little luck and, uh, anticipation, I think I can get there in time from now, uh, on, OK? I know our start doesn't look so, uh, good, but don't you worry."

Josie says, "Catch your breath. We have thirty seconds between points. Might as well use them all."

"Thanks."

Josie waits until Vivian's breath steadies. She says, "You sure about not changing formation?"

Vivian says, "Yeah, for now."

"OK."

"Come on. Time to kick some butt... little-old-lady style!"

Josie smiles and says, "Let's do it!"

"Oh, and one more thing. I saw the shorter one doesn't have an overhead. Guessing a shoulder injury. And the taller one has great groundies, but not so great volleys, especially on the backhand side. I'm guessing she is more of a singles player."

Josie says, "Yeah. Look. She's rubbing her shoulder. So, you want to pull the shorter one in and then lob her?"

Vivian, says, "Exactly what I was thinking. Normally, I wouldn't invite a doubles player into the net. Ha-ha. You know, since that is where doubles *is* won. Maybe that is what they are counting on, but I think what you said just might work!"

After a few points, Josie and Vivian decide to target the taller opponent's--Cynthia is her name--backhand at the net.

After a few more points, Josie says, "I think we struck a gold vein there."

Vivian nods and says, "She's very generous."

"Yeah. Her backhand volley is a gift that keeps giving."

"Um, she looks like she wants to take her gifts back."

Josie says, "Yeah. Let's give it a rest. Let her calm down."

"Are you kidding me?"

"No. She's frustrated. I almost feel guilty."

Cynthia lunges for a low backhand at the net. She doesn't move her feet to the ball, bending at the waist instead. In doing so, she can't generate enough pace to hit the volley back over the net. The backspin on the ball fizzles on her racquet and drops to the ground. She hocks a stringy wad of spit in Vivian's direction and throws her racquet down.

Vivian says to Josie, "Come on Josie. When you have a winning strategy, you don't go changing it. Name one sport where a player stops employing a winning strategy because their opponent looks mad. Besides, the one thing her backhand volley needs, we are giving her."

"What? Practice?"

"Yes."

"Well. When you put it that way, it's down right philanthropic!"

"Darn right. We might even get community service hours for this."

"We should."

"Absolutely."

Josie looks at yet another white glob of spittle forming in the corner of Cynthia's mouth. She thinks she sees tiny red veins protruding in the whites of Cynthia's eyes. She says to Vivian, "I don't know. Maybe we should rethink this."

"Come on. She should be thanking us."

"Don't expect her to be thanking us anytime soon. I mean look at her. She's pretty mad. Maybe we should give her backhand volley a break before she goes completely insane."

Vivian winks at Josie, "Don't worry. I'll ask the kitchen to hide all the knives from the buffet afterwards."

Josie says, "I'm serious."

Vivian says, "Oh, don't take things so seriously, Josie. She'll be all right. It's just a game. It's not life or death. Perspective."

Josie looks at Cynthia's beet-red face and grimaces. *Maybe you could ask Cynthia to get some more perspective.*

Vivian and Josie take the first set 6:3. They continue their winning strategy well into the second set. Up a break, they set their sites on the finish line.

Vivian whispers to Josie, "She's building a mausoleum."

Josie looks confused before it clicks in. She says, "Uh-huh. One brick at a time?"

"Exactly."

Down 3:1 in the second set, their opponents intensify their tactics. Desperate, they continue isolating Vivian. Now red-faced and breathing like a locomotive, Cynthia unleashes her fury, trying to burrow a hole through Vivian's head. She seethes from utter frustration. She's lost the last nine out of ten games, mainly due to her backhand volley. She's tried staying back, but Vivian and Josie won't let her. They keep pulling her to the net, forcing her to volley.

Cynthia gets an idea and smiles with anticipation. She changes her net positioning, standing so close to the net that she must take care not to touch it. Her intention: to shorten the ball's travel time between her racquet and Vivian's head. The ball speed and her aim aggressively bombard Vivian repeatedly at the net. Vivian holds her ground and boldly takes the pounding, never flinching. Maintaining her composure, Vivian brushes off several direct hits. Although they'll likely bruise, she makes no fuss. While disruptive as these low-blows may be, they aren't enough to bring their opponents' score back up. Still, Cynthia's bloodthirsty enthusiasm grows. She smiles with each new impact.

Vivian also changes tactics. Readying herself for the barrage, she effortlessly begins deflecting Cynthia's bullets for volley winners, using the pace to her advantage.

Cynthia loses control and yells, "Arggghhh!"

We've created a pirate. Josie helplessly watches Vivian fight to keep her racquet between her body and the speeding ball. Finally, Josie walks over and says, "Like you said before, it's just tennis. Why don't you come back to the baseline with me and get out of that hotseat, at least until they become more civil? They're aiming right for your face."

"I'm fine."

"I don't want you to get hurt! Come on."

Vivian gives her a mischievous grin and says, "What? And miss out on all of this fun? No way!" She laughs, but the next point doesn't go well. With clenched teeth, Cynthia gives up trying to punch her backhand volleys and unleashes a swinging volley directly to Vivian's head. The volley unloads off of Cynthia's racquet with such tremendous velocity that Vivian hardly manages to turn her face before impact. The ball hits squarely on the solid bone behind Vivian's ear, producing a loud thud.

Josie rushes over and says, "Oh my gosh, Vivian! Are you all right?"

Josie notices Cynthia raise her hand as if to say she is sorry. Josie also notices Cynthia no longer clenches her teeth, but displays a more relaxed, satiated look instead.

In truth, Vivian feels lightheaded from the blow, but refuses to say so. She doesn't want to alarm Josie, and she doesn't want to give her opponents an edge. Vivian gives Josie a wry smile and promises, "Of course. I'm fine, but she'll pay for that."

Cynthia looks disappointed. The blow seems ineffectual as Vivian casually takes her position for the next point. At the very least, she expected Vivian to feel woozy.

With a new fire in her eyes, Vivian makes good on her promise. She pulls her opponents left then right, up then back, and at times completely off of the court. Vivian carves out point after point with the deft-like precision of a master surgeon, running her opponents ragged.

At the end of the next game, Josie and Vivian find themselves up for a score of 4:1 and at the business end of the second set. Both of their opponents find themselves using their racquets as stooping posts, leaning over, and catching their breath.

Josie says to Vivian, "I see you take your promises seriously."

"I prefer to let my racquet do the talking."

"Well, it's eloquent."

Vivian twirls her racquet and says, "She."

"She?"

"Yes, not it, but *she*. I always enjoy hearing what Clara has to say."

"You named your racquet?"

"Of course. I always name my racquets."

"Clara, huh? Nice name. Means clear?"

"Yep. What she has to say truly is Clara, or clear."

Josie looks at their opponents leaning over their racquets and says, "I'll say."

In the next point, Josie finally receives a forehand: one of the few given to her the entire match. She sets up and hits an eighty-three miles per hour inside-out forehand deep up the middle. The shorter girl lunges and frames the ball for a miss-hit short lob that happens to fall directly above Vivian's head.

Josie envisions what happens next. *About time! Now, Vivian can finally smash her back! Aaah, justice!* With bated breath, Josie secretly celebrates. *Cynthia has been asking for this!* She yells out, "Crush it, Vivian!"

Vivian takes tiny adjustment steps, steadying herself for the overhead. She readies her racquet and uses her free hand to point, tracking the ball so she doesn't lose it in the sun. She makes contact and angles the ball short to the open court for the easy winner.

FOUR

Anger is wind which blows out the lamp of the mind.
-Robert Ingersoll

Josie rushes over, "Vivian! What happened? You had your chance to take her head off! Why'd you hit the ball to the side?"

"I didn't want to hit her."

"How could you not want to hit her?"

"I didn't. I won't."

"B-but Cynthia's been asking for it with the way she's been trying to maim you! You should have hit her! Hard!"

Vivian walks back to the baseline with Josie and says quietly, "Let me ask you something."

Exasperated, Josie says, "What?"

"Is she nice?"

"Who? Cynthia? Well, no."

"Is she somebody you would ask to join in a friendly weekend game?"

"Not a chance."

"Would you ask her to be on your team? Or go to lunch after the match?"

"Lunch? You mean besides the team lunch? No and no."

Vivian says, "Exactly. Then just because I can be like her, doesn't mean I should. You see? Why would I want to? Look at her. Her behavior is a disgrace."

"But what she did was wrong!"

"I know. And make no mistake; it doesn't mean that I have to take her crap either, or that I won't make her atone for that crap. What it means is that I will simply make her pay in a reasonable more respectable manner."

"By running her ragged?"

"Yes, and by winning. Besides, I think she ran enough today to prove my point. Don't you?"

"Yeah. I guess."

"I won't lower myself, and you shouldn't either. I'm not playing civilly for her sake, but for mine. See? Besides, it's just plain bad karma. Imagine what the rest of her day is like. Or what her life is like for that matter. I'd hate to be her cat."

On the next point, Vivian hits a short touch volley with added spin. She pulls Cynthia off of the court, and then sends her rushing back in to reach a deep volley. Cynthia scurries, managing to get a racquet on the ball, but only for a weak reply. Vivian takes two steps cutting the ball off, and hitting a short angled shot again. Cynthia rushes in, shortening the gap to the net. She stabs at the ball just before the bounce, popping it up. Vivian takes the ball out of the air, lobbing it over Cynthia at the net.

Cynthia drops her racquet to her side, leans on both knees, gasps for breath, and growls, "Yours!" never bothering to look back to see how her partner fares.

With extraordinary haste, Cynthia's partner covers for her, reaching the ball. She can't get there in time to set up, so she throws up a defensive lob. It's the best she can offer at this point. Vivian lightly bounces on the balls of her feet, waiting for the short lob at the net. She gets it. Cynthia flinches, expecting Vivian to smash her with an overhead. She knows that she deserves it.

Again, Vivian expertly hits to the open court. Surprised again by no impact, Cynthia turns back around in time to see Vivian taking her place for the next point. However, Vivian is too quick to do so. The point is not quite over. Cynthia's partner, reading the play in the backcourt, runs wide and hits the ball up the line. Caught flatfooted, Vivian didn't expect Cynthia's partner to make a play on the ball. Luckily, the ball floats long by a slight margin.

Vivian yells, "Out!"

Their opponents, short on energy and high on frustration, explode. No one likes to be schooled by someone twice her age, especially so ruthlessly. Both yell simultaneously, "That ball was in!"

Cynthia approaches the net, leaning over for a closer view of the mark and says, "Vivian! That ball was in and you know it!"

Her partner yells, "Cheater!"

Cynthia yells, "That's right! Cheater! Go ahead! Call the ball out! That's the only way you can win against us, isn't it!"

As more barbs fly, Josie and Vivian examine the mark. Unruffled, Vivian takes an extra ball from her pocket and places it squarely on the mark. Visually, it's obvious the ball was out with a good two-inch margin between the mark and the line.

Vivian confirms, "Out." She invites her opponents over to her side of the net to see for themselves. They rush over, egging each other on. As they race closer, they suddenly slow down.

Looking unsure, one finally says, "I suppose it could be out."

Vivian says with a wry smile, "Yes. It's hard to believe you hit a ball out."

Cynthia says, "No sense being sarcastic. I usually do hit the ball in. It's just an off day for me. That's all."

Her partner nods and says with a huff, "Well, it is windy."

The rest of the match plays out on Vivian's racquet. She controls every single point. Josie chuckles as she watches Vivian school their opponents as to what a master class truly is. Their opponents grumble and curse under labored breath.

Cynthia says to her partner, "I've had root canals more pleasant."

Cynthia's partner says, "Lucky old coot! I've never seen her play so well!"

Cynthia says, "Yeah. She's playing out of her mind."

Their opponents rack up the mileage as Vivian racks up the points. Their skirts flap from lunging for ball after ball as each lands just out of reach. Loose hair strands fall into sweaty tufts around their puffing faces. No matter how great their efforts, they continually fall two steps behind Vivian. Seething, they glare at her. Vivian remains civil and all smiles.

Their opponents' anger reaches epic proportions as they lose the next game at love for a score of 5:2. As they switch sides, Cynthia bumps Vivian with her shoulder in passing.

Cynthia says, "About time you wiped that smile off of your face."

Josie says to Cynthia, "Oh, that's really mature!"

Vivian says quietly to Josie, "Don't worry about her. Let it go."

Josie says to Vivian, "How can I?"

Vivian replies, "Stay focused. One more game to go."

As Josie and Vivian take to the other side of the court-- the side their opponents have just been playing upon--Vivian points. She says, "Josie, look at the clay. It tells a story. What do you see?"

Josie looks at the deep gouges and divots from where their opponents have overworked the court's surface. All of the switching directions and sudden stops have taken a toll on the greenish-gray clay surface. Hardly a smooth patch remains.

Josie says, "Looks like WWIII happened here."

Vivian says, "Now, look back to our side of the court."

Josie looks over the net at the side of the court she was just playing on. She counts only two long gouges and a handful of small divots. Mostly, the playing surface remains in tact and smooth.

Vivian says, "See the disparity?"

Josie says, "Yes. It looks like two completely different matches are being played on the same court."

Vivian says, "Exactly. Doesn't it look as if they have been using a shovel to dig their way out of this match?"

Josie laughs and says, "Yes."

Pleased to see Josie laugh, Vivian says, "Now you are getting it. We stay focused and don't get sucked into the drama. We can still have fun even in the midst of other women behaving badly."

"Yeah, but not when they're behaving this badly."

"Yes, we can. You will learn--and it's important--that you can still have a good day in the midst of other people behaving poorly. Just don't let it in. Don't let it bother you. Simple, really."

"I don't know if I can do that."

"Sure you can. And it will change your life when you start. I promise. Besides, I know these girls. This might be the way they play, but it's not the norm. Most girls you meet in this league keep their competitive behavior in check."

"I hope so."

"I know your first couple of experiences at Le Château have been, uh, let's say challenging. But you didn't cause Monica's rude behavior and you certainly didn't ask for it."

"But I got it."

"Yes, and it's how you choose to live with it and not let it ruin your day that matters."

"That's impossible."

"It's entirely possible. I do it all the time, although it took years for me to learn how. You can, too."

"OK. But how?"

"Start by making them keep their bad karma on their side of the net, and don't be so porous."

"Porous?"

"Yeah. Don't absorb their junk. Ignore it, in a dignified way."

"I can try. But some of what they are doing is just so, so very rude! It leaves little room for dignity."

"Rude happens. Don't let it bother you. And it's worth pointing out again that if you think I am letting Cynthia off the hook, then just look at the court's surface a second time."

"Clara has spoken."

"Ha-ha-ha. Loud and clear."

Josie laughs and says, "Remind me never to tick off Clara."

"Yeah. I wouldn't recommend it."

Josie says, "You give me hope, Vivian. I was beginning to think justice never happens. Well, maybe in the movies."

"Justice does happen. It happens in the movies, and it definitely happens in tennis."

"I hope so."

"It does, especially when Clara serves it up."

One game away from defeat, Cynthia and her partner employ stall tactics, desperately hoping for a second wind or a momentum shift. They tie shoes, change racquets, and take an extraordinary length of time discussing strategy in the backcourt. They ask for a bathroom break, though a break is not allowed at this stage in the match.

Vivian, the quintessential queen of calm, consents. Vivian uses this time to fetch the grate. Pulling the grate along by its rope handle, she drags it across the HarTru's surface, smoothing out the divots behind her. Their opponents return from the bathroom to face a newly smoothed out court. They pretend not to notice, looking already defeated and mad as hornets.

Josie says, "Do you think it's possible that they actually look even angrier than before?"

Vivian says, "Yeah. I imagine their tanks are running on fumes."

"I'd definitely say they're fuming."

One game from defeat, their opponents don't change their tactic. If anything they hit harder and harder at Vivian. Vivian takes it all in stride. As she controls point after point, she looks amused rather than ruffled. With merciless precision, she hits junk balls, disrupting their rhythm further, and bringing her team to match point at 40:15.

As Josie serves for match point, Cynthia yells out, "Don't double fault!"

Josie says, "Hey! You can't yell while I'm serving."

Cynthia looks to her partner for confirmation and says, "I didn't see her serve yet. Did you?"

Her partner says, "Nope."

Josie says, "Yes, you did. You can't yell and distract me while I am serving! That's gamesmanship! You know, you're nothing but a--"

Vivian walks back to the service line and intercepts Josie mid-sentence. She says, "Don't let them rattle you. One more point. Focus and take your time."

Josie hits a one hundred and three miles per hour ace down the "T". She and Vivian walk to the net to shake hands.

Extending her hand, Vivian says, "Nice match, ladies."

Before she reaches the net, Cynthia yells, "Out!"

Vivian and Josie stop in their tracks.

Josie says incredulously, "What!"

Vivian repeats, "What!"

Cynthia's partner says, "That ball was definitely out." She gathers the ball and puts it on an older mark, a foot out.

Josie says, "That's not--"

Vivian intercepts her again. She says to Josie, "It's their call. Don't let it rattle you. Just hit a safe kicker right smack in the middle of the box. OK?"

"OK." Josie takes a deep breath, bounces the ball, and hits a kick serve that bounces squarely in the middle of the box. *Can't call that out!*

The ball hits the clay and takes off, jumping over the receiver's head when Cynthia's partner yells, "Let!"

Josie rolls her eyes and says, "You're kidding, right?"

Cynthia's partner says, "Nope. See that ball in the backcourt. It distracted me."

Josie says, "Yeah. I see it. That came onto the court after Cynthia missed. You can't call a 'let'."

Cynthia says, "I just did."

Vivian says, "It doesn't matter. That was unreturnable. Also, not that I'm counting, but that should have been the second match point, and you know it."

Cynthia says, "I saw it coming. It distracted me. Let, let, let, let, let. LET!"

As her voice shakes, Josie's yells, "40:15, second serve." She feels her right shoulder tightening up. She hits the next serve at half-pace. Cynthia, excited to finally receive a sitter to her forehand, unleashes all of her pent up aggression into a rocket-like return deep into the middle of the court. Josie can't get there in time.

Josie says, "40:30." Clearly going for another ace, Josie misses her first serve by an inch out wide. She begins her service motion again. However, in the corner of her eye she catches motion that distracts her. It's meant to do so. As Josie serves to Cynthia's partner, Cynthia lunges in and out of the service box.

Josie lets her toss drop and says, "Hey! What are you doing? I'm serving."

Cynthia says, "Yeah, so. So serve."

"OK, but stop jumping into the service box like that. You can't do that."

Cynthia's partner says in a singsong tone, "Someone didn't read her rulebook!"

Cynthia says, "I can jump into the service box, and I will." To prove a point, she does so again.

Vivian rolls her eyes and says discreetly, "I feel as if I am playing with my five-year-old great-grandson."

"I don't know. He would probably be more mature."

"And infinitely more enjoyable."

Josie begins her service motion once again. *So be it. You asked for this.* She aims right at Cynthia. She knows enough about the rules to know that if she hits Cynthia while in the box, the point is hers. In the middle of her service motion, Josie takes her eyes off of Cynthia for a split second and looks directly up at her ball toss. At that precise moment, Cynthia steps back out of the box. The serve, which would have hit Cynthia directly, misses her and sails long.

Cynthia and her partner belly laugh and high five each other. A snort erupts from Cynthia as she snickers, "Rookie mistake!"

Now, at 40:40, or deuce, Josie's voice proves shakier while announcing the score.

Vivian hears the tension in Josie's voice and whispers, "Remember, it's just tennis."

Josie takes a deep breath. *Right. It's just tennis. One point at a time. One point at a time.* Josie nods, but even as she does so her shoulder tightens. She hits a wild serve, a good ten feet wide.

Cynthia says, "Whoa! What was that?"

Vivian says, "Like you've never hit a wide serve before." However, even as she speaks, Vivian walks back to the baseline and whispers, "Everything all right?"

Josie says, "I am tight. I can't move my shoulder well. I don't think I can serve."

Vivian says loudly, "OK!" and then softly, "OK." It would be a pity for them to lose now, especially when they are so close. Vivian says, "You just get it in. I'll do the rest."

Losing more shoulder control by the second, Josie frames the next serve. Miraculously, it bounces off the frame and somehow goes in. Cynthia hits a big forehand return. Vivian poaches like a woman half her age, intercepts Cynthia's shot, and blocks the volley deep into the middle for a winner.

Josie announces, "Our Ad." She serves, but the ball hits the HarTru on her side of the court before it even reaches the net.

Vivian turns to Josie with her eyebrows raised. She says, "Hangin' in there OK?"

Josie hangs her head and confides, "I can't serve."

A little panicky, Vivian says, "OK. Don't panic. Just hit the ball underhand. You can hit underhand, can't you?"

"Yeah. I mean I think so."

"OK. Go for it!"

Josie serves the next ball underhand with junk on it. It drops soft and short into the service box with unexpected backspin.

Shell-shocked, her opponent stands flatfooted, never responding to the ball. She says, "What was that?"

Josie doesn't answer. Cynthia answers for her. She says, "Pathetic. That's what that was. Pa-the-tic!"

Vivian says, "Well ladies, that was a pa-the-tic match point. See you next time." She shakes hands at the net with her opponents. Vivian notices Josie hovering around her tennis bag putting her racquets away. She walks over and says, "Josie, go shake hands."

Josie says, "With those cheaters? No way."

Vivian says, "Go shake hands, Josie. You will play these girls many times over the next few years. You don't want to get a reputation."

Josie doesn't reply, but she shakes hands. Vivian swings her tennis bag over her shoulder. When she does, the shift in weight sends her off-balance. She catches herself, throwing her weight into the opposite direction. However, she overcompensates and falls. Josie catches Vivian and helps her to regain her footing.

Josie says, "Are you OK?"

"Of course! Nothing a little gin and tonic can't solve. I'll ask Mitch to spike my drink at lunch." She winks.

Together they walk toward the clubhouse.

Ceridwin catches up from behind. She puts an arm around each of their shoulders and says, "Good timing! We just finished, too. By the way, nice win! I've played those girls before. Tough customers." Ceridwin pulls her arm away and says, "Hey! What's this? Is this blood?"

Only Josie looks. Vivian doesn't bother; she already knows.

Ceridwin continues, "It is. It is blood! Where is this coming from?"

Vivian frowns. She was hoping to avoid a scene. She felt woozy the last few games, but didn't say anything. The nasty mark--behind her ear where Cynthia hit her--throbs. She felt the blood trickling down inside her shirt, and she noticed the blood on her tennis towel several games ago. Until now, her red tennis shirt camouflaged the dripping wound. Her wavy hair covered the rest.

Vivian says, "It's no big deal. The ball brushed me behind the ear. I'm fine. Really."

Josie says, "Let me have a look at that."

"No, it's nothing."

Josie says, "Hold still." She lifts a section of Vivian's gray waves. Underneath sits a red matted section of hair with an inch-long oozing wound in the middle.

Ceridwin says, "That is not nothing."

Josie frowns and says, "That's a lot of blood."

Vivian laughs and says, "You should see what the other guy looks like." No one joins in her laughter.

Ceridwin frowns and says, "Looks like a clean split to the skin where the ball hit your bone. Hate to say it, but I think you need stitches."

Vivian scoffs, "I don't need stitches, just a stiff drink. Now stop fussing over me."

Josie motions for Mitch to come over.

Mitch says, "Nice win ladies. What's all the commotion?" Josie shows him the injury. He says, "Another war wound, Vivian? Yuck. This one looks nasty. Come on. I've got bandages in my office. Let's clean it up and see how bad it really is."

Vivian says, "Naw. Thanks, but I'm going home."

Mitch says, "Not before I have a look at that."

"Fine. If I must go, I'll settle for a shot of tequila too then."

Mitch laughs an easy laugh as he grabs her tennis bag and shoulders it for her. He says, "No tequila in the office, but I might be able to spare an Ibuprofen or two."

Back in his office, Mitch dials the kitchen. He orders Vivian's lunch sent directly to his office. He says, "Josie says you were woozy. You're not going to faint on me, are you?"

"It depends. Will it get me a shot of tequila?"

"No, but lunch is on the way. We'll get you fed while I bandage you up."

Vivian says, "Oww."

"Sorry. Is it tender?"

"*Yeeees.*"

Mitch cleans the wound and expertly applies a butterfly bandage, closing the two pieces of flesh over the wound. Over the years, he's become an expert at patching up players. He announces, "You'll live, but you do need stitches."

"I'm not getting stitches and I'm not leaving 'til you give me something stiffer than aspirin. I'm not a baby."

"Fine."

Vivian's food arrives. Mitch pulls open his desk drawer and lifts a book. Under the book sits an embossed stainless steel flask. He pours brandy into her coffee and says, "You really do need to see a doctor. I can drive you if you wait twenty minutes."

Vivian remembers how Mitch missed her last tournament because his car broke down. She says, "I appreciate the offer, but I'm fine. I'll just go home and take a nap." She grabs the flask and pours more.

Mitch quickly caps the flask and says, "That's enough. If you are driving yourself, then no more of this." Vivian frowns. He says, "Look, if you don't get stitches, a wound like that could keep opening and take forever to heal."

Vivian says, "Fine. I'll go."

"Good. Now, why won't anybody let me drive them anywhere?"

She says, "I've seen the way you drive and besides, I like having my own car, thank you."

"Fine."

"Fine? OK. Ask."

"Ask what?"

"Ask what it is you want to know, but are too polite to ask on account of this wound."

"Your wound is more important."

"Ask."

"Fine. What's the bottom line?"

"I'll tell you, but if I didn't know any better, I'd say you were sweet on her."

"On Josie? No way! I care, but I care about her like I am responsible for her. She's practically family."

"I didn't know you two were related."

"Related? Yes, and no. I grew up with her. Her brother is my best friend."

"Oh. Family. I see."

"Yeah."

"Just curious, did something happen to her?"

"What do you mean?"

"I mean she has no confidence. Zero. Zilch. She falls off the deep end with the slightest push."

"Nasty divorce. Asshole Ex."

"Poor kid."

"Yeah, her whole family hated him from the beginning."

Vivian shakes her head, "Always a man, isn't it? Well, he's crazy, cuz she is a keeper. Wish I had a grandson to set her up with! Anyway, she needs a confidence-building partner."

"You're hired."

"Me? Why me? I don't need another job."

"OK. How long before *someone* helps her, mentally, to get where she needs to be?"

"Seeing as tennis is ninety percent mental, that's up to her. Not me. I don't want to play with her."

"What? Why not? It looked like you two connected out there."

"We did. Such a sweetheart, really. But we are on two different playing levels. The disparity is too great. So much so that practically every ball is hit to me. When I play with her, I am the weaker player. You see? I get isolated. It's like I'm playing singles out there, not doubles. And I'm too old for singles. My body won't hold up through the course of the whole season if I play with her."

Mitch rubs the stubble on his chin and says, "Hold that thought. I may be able to work something out."

"I am not taking any illegal performance-enhancing drugs."

He looks incredulous.

Vivian explains, "Yes, I know about Monica."

"Then you know her drugs weren't performance enhancing; they were recreational, and I had nothing to do with them. It cost J. Paul a pretty penny to send her to one of those fancy rehab centers. Drugs are not allowed on the premises here. Now, like I said, I have a plan. Just leave it to me."

Mitch takes out his iPad and types. Vivian doesn't snoop or ask what he writes. She doesn't want to know. She touches her bandage and winces. She stands, pats Mitch on the shoulder, and says, "You're a good kid, Mitch. Even if you want me to take performance-enhancing drugs."

"Vivian! Nobody is taking any drugs here."

"If you say so. Anyway, I will answer the other question that is on your mind."

He doesn't look up, continues typing notes, and says, "What's that?"

She points to her bandage and says, "This little old thing isn't going to keep me away from practice or the match next week."

Mitch stops typing, looks up, and says, "What would I do without you, Vivian?"

"And more importantly, my 18:0 record every season. I know you need me."

He laughs, rushes to hold the door, and hugs her with his free arm. She winces again. He says, "Oh, sorry."

"It's OK. It just hurts to bend my neck."

"Promise you'll see the doctor today?"

"Promise." Before leaving his office, she turns and says, "Don't worry so much. Everything is going to work out just fine. You'll see."

Vivian understands the pressures of Mitch's job. While he may love his job, certain things must happen for him to keep it. Taking home the year-end trophy for the Elite Division certainly wouldn't hurt. He counts on her and her customary 18:0 season ending record to pad his team's ranking. The more successful that his teams perform, the more players aspire to play at Le Château and--according to Mitch's boss-- aspire to buy homes in Le Château. Fundamentally, winning translates into income for the club and job security for Mitch.

Mitch says, "Good. I don't want this to turn into something like that three-thousand-dollar hamstring last year."

It's not a great joke, but she laughs anyway and says, "Hey, you can't blame me for the fact that you missed maxing out on your bonus because you couldn't find a better sub for me." Vivian is the only player on the team whom he can joke with like this. She gets the business side of tennis.

He smiles and says, "That's because you truly are irreplaceable."

Vivian says, "And don't you forget it. Now, stop buttering me up."

"Who's buttering anybody up?"

"I see what you're trying to do."

He says, "Really? Then explain it to me, please. I'd like to know."

"Fine. I'll play with Josie. But if I injure myself trying to keep up and act like I'm twenty again, it's on your conscience. Got it? I'm an old woman for Pete's sake."

FIVE

Nothing happens to anybody which
he is not fitted by nature to bear.
-Marcus Aurelius Antoninus

Today marks the eighth match for Vivian and Josie as partners. After their pregame warm-up, Josie takes to the court as the player introductions begin.

Vivian whispers, "They look like Mutt and Jeff."

Josie nods. The taller opponent, Allison, stands six feet tall, towering over her partner by a good ten inches. The shorter one looks as if she is less ready for a tennis match and more ready for a photo shoot. Her blown-out blonde waves secure in two loosely pigtailed sections, pushed to either sides of oversized breasts on her tiny frame. She wears full makeup: something most tennis players don't bother with since it usually sweats off within minutes. Her shoulders and cleavage shimmer with heavy bronzer. Her bright white pleated skirt fits a good size too small. It shows the edges of her rear-end as she walks. Her hot pink tank top plunges past where a bra should be, but isn't. She bends over to tie her shoe and her thin, neon yellow, French-cut tennis bloomers show the black lacy thong underneath. She says her name is Dixie. Her southern drawl turns her name into three syllables.

The warm-up begins. Josie hits Dixie several baseline rally balls, before feeding her volleys at the net.

Dixie abruptly stops the warm-up and announces, "Oh, sorry. I forgot to sunscreen the girls." Josie and Vivian look around for small children, but see none. Dixie runs over to her tennis bag and lathers up her cleavage with SPF 50.

47

Allison says to Vivian and Josie, "I know what you are thinking, but she has an I.Q. of 145. As a matter of fact, she is in her last term interning to become a lawyer."

Vivian shrugs and says, "We didn't say anything."

Dixie hustles back onto the court and says, "Sorry to make y'all wait, but my boyfriend just bought me these and I don't want them to burn." She points to her enormous bosom and begins volleying as if they were merely talking about the weather.

Vivian changes the subject. She says, "How did you talk your law firm into giving you time off to play tennis? I thought those internships were supposed to be grueling."

Dixie laughs and says, "My boyfriend also happens to be my boss."

Vivian discretely smirks to Josie, and says, "Convenient."

Overhearing her, Dixie says, "Not really. Tennis is his idea. He doesn't want me to get fat. He often sings some silly song about how fat people have no reason to live."

Vivian shoots Josie another look, but says, "Lovely. A musician and a lawyer."

ళ~ళ

The first few games pass unceremoniously. Josie begins serving at 3:3 in the first set, when she sees a visitor quickly approaching. She instantly recognizes the familiar walk as he saunters down The Breezeway to her court. She watches the carefree swing of his arms and the thick strands of light brown bangs that slightly sway with each step.

This visitor enters their court's seating area between the bougainvillea-entwined fences. He momentarily stands under the vine-wrapped arbor next to the court. He stands, framed by vibrant fuchsia flowers. Knowingly, he avoids the bamboo chairs reserved for the players and pulls up a collapsible plastic chair. He sits, facing Josie's court. In the bright Florida sun, his hair shines a glossy chocolate brown.

Josie remembers the feel of those silky strands between her fingers. She also remembers the name of the salon where she used to book his hair glossing appointments. She watches as he leans forward, clasping his hands together, and resting his elbows on his knees.

Today, he wears her favorite light blue polo shirt. *He knows that is my favorite shirt. Is he wearing that for me?* She blushes. She gave it to him for his birthday two years ago. He takes off his aviators. *It shows off his crystal blue eyes.* She feels a pang in her stomach so intense that she grabs her midsection. *Why is he here?* She bounces the ball and prepares to serve.

She smokes an ace on her first serve, 15:0. He looks her way and mouths, "Wow." She smiles at him. She aces her second serve, 30:0.

Vivian turns and says, "Is this the zone that everyone talks about? If so, I'd like to move there or at least visit."

Josie giggles and shrugs, "I'm not thinking of my serve right now."

Vivian says, "Well, whatever works!

On the third serve, Josie hits a kicker out wide. Dixie moves in, takes the ball early, and rips the return flat, taking it off of the court. Josie gets there in time and hits the ball down the line for a winner, 40:0. Josie glances over at the visitor in the chair.

Roger claps his hands and shouts, "Nice point, ladies!"

Flustered, Josie adjusts her hair and straightens her skort. *Is he clapping for me?* She feels like a giddy schoolgirl. *He's never cared enough before now to come to any of my matches!* She smiles broadly at him again. *He knows that's my favorite shirt.*

Flattered, Josie yells, "Thank you," to Roger Fleming.

In response, Roger wrinkles his nose, and gives her a quizzical look.

On the next point, Allison hits a deep return and follows it in to the net. Josie replies, making Allison hit a tough volley. Josie anticipates a weak reply--which she receives-- and rips the ball up the middle for a swinging volley winner.

Dixie lunges for the ball, but can't quite reach it. When she lunges, one of her boobs pops out of her top. Dixie giggles and apologizes profusely to all, quickly replacing her runaway breast. She again apologizes as she takes her position, "Sorry, but I am still getting used to these."

As they exit the court for the changeover, Vivian mutters to Josie, "I thought I had seen everything there is to see on a tennis court. I stand corrected. *Now*, I have seen everything. Did she ever hear of a bra? She needs to harness those girls in place."

Josie doesn't hear Vivian. She can't take her eyes off of Roger. She positively beams at him. He seems ruffled by her stare. *He's sitting right behind my tennis bag. He must recognize it.*

At the changeover, all players sit in their chairs for the full two minutes allowed. Josie towels off and searches for the right words, and well, really, anything to say. She hasn't seen Roger for some time. Her tongue is tied. *What does he want? What should I say?*

While Josie clamors for the right words, Dixie says, "I hope you girls don't mind if my boyfriend sits here. If it bothers y'all in the least bit, it wouldn't be any trouble at all to ask him to sit further down. You just holler, OK?" Then, she turns to Roger and motions, "This is my boyfriend, Roger Fleming. Roger this is Vivian."

Roger shakes hands with Vivian. Dixie continues, "And this is Josie. You've already met Allison."

Roger extends his hand to Josie before abruptly stopping. His jaw drops. Finally, he regains composure and says, "I didn't recognize you, Jo. I mean I didn't know that was you. The last time I saw you, you were…well, you were…you know."

Suddenly, it all makes sense. She gets why Roger is here, and it's not for her. *I am such an idiot!* She looks at Dixie, the blonde pint-sized bombshell.

Dixie leans over to fix her sock and her boob practically falls out again. Josie watches Roger's reaction. *Yes. Of course. Well, at least now I can stop wondering what the other woman looks like.*

Josie says, "What? Fat? Is that the word you are looking for?"

"Yes, fat. I mean no. Wait. That's not what I mean--what I meant. Fat. That is?"

She covers her face and runs between the chairs to the corridor. She squeezes past Allison and brushes past Dixie. She can't clear the space between the table and Dixie. Dixie's oversized breasts narrow the passage. Josie knocks into the table before ricocheting off of Dixie. Josie blurts out, "I am sorry to both you and the girls!"

Josie bawls, running past the locker room, and into the pool area. She fills the elastic pockets in her tennis skort with small landscaping rocks and jumps in the pool. She cannonballs with one enormous pounding splash. Both feet firmly hit the bottom. Disappointed, she sees the water level stop just below her chin.

Breathless, Vivian, Ceridwin, and Marni catch up to her. Violet says, "There she is!"

Marni says, "Are you OK?"

Vivian takes in the scene and knowingly says, "This end of the pool stands only five feet deep."

Ceridwin says, "Anyway, perhaps Virginia Woolf was shorter." All three begin laughing.

Josie says through hiccupped tears, "I am s-such a fool! I am so glad y-you think it s-s-so funny. I am glad m-my life is such a b-big joke!"

Ceridwin says, "Oh, Josie. We're sorry. It was only a bit of a joke meant to lighten your load." All three girls laugh at the unintended pun. Josie's chin trembles above the water. Ceridwin jumps in and hugs her. She says, "Sorry. Sorry. Sorry. It was a stupid joke."

Vivian says, "Come on Josie. It's going to be all right. You're not the first person to get a broken heart you know."

Vivian jumps in the water and joins in the hug, "And, by the way, no one ever died from a broken heart."

Josie wipes away her tears and insists, "People do die from a broken heart. They do. Haven't you ever seen *Somewhere in Time* with Christopher Reeves and Jane Seymour? Christopher Reeves most certainly does die from a broken heart. He does!"

Vivian says, "Oh, come on. That was just a movie. I know it's tough, but it will get better in time. I promise."

Marni says, "No. She's right. You can die from a broken heart."

Josie releases a guttural sob.

Ceridian shoots Marni a sideways look that says, "Shut up." The look obviously doesn't register.

Marni continues, "My dad's a cardiothoracic surgeon, and I've heard him talk about a patient that did just that. It's called Broken Heart Syndrome." Ceridwin shoots Marni another look that also doesn't register.

Marni continues, "He called it something else though. Something that begins with a 'T', Takotsubo, I think. Anyway, your heart swells due to a surge in stress hormones and it doesn't pump well. It can be life threatening. I mean his patient did die. But it usually isn't. Life threatening that is. Most people make a full recovery on their own. I think they mend within a few weeks without ever even having to do anything. They just get better."

Ceridwin says, "Thank you, Doctor Schoppelmann. You are not helping."

Marni says, "Sorry. But, what was I supposed to say? It's true. Anyway, my point is that you're going to get better, Josie, without having to do anything. It's going to just mend for you. You'll see. It's going to be OK." Marni jumps into the water and joins in the hug. She adds, "Besides, we all hate him."

Again, they all three laugh. Their tennis skirts flare out like tutus in the water. A rock from Josie's skort falls and sinks, just like one of Punchinello's gray dots. The rock glistens on the pool's shimmery bottom beneath their tennis shoes.

SIX

Mistake not. Those pleasures are not pleasures that trouble the quiet and
tranquility of thy life.
-Jeremy Taylor

Monica slams through the pool's swinging gate with a loud
metal clang and stands before them. She glares at her
teammates in the pool. She says, "Has the world gone
crazy?" She places her hands firmly on her hips, and says,
"Do you not realize we are in the middle of a tennis match?
This is so typical! Did you even think of anyone besides
yourselves?"

Vivian mumbles under her breath, "That's calling the
kettle black."

Monica continues, "I hope you're happy! Now, we're
going to have to forfeit three lines because of your little
synchronized swim here. Do you even realize we were tied
for first place?"

Josie says, "Wow! We're in first place?"

For Monica, nothing matters more. She says,
"Correction. We were tied for first place. Now, we'll be
lucky to be in third! You really messed everything up!"

Ceridwin says, "Some things are more important than
rankings."

Monica says, "Is that so, Crazy Ladies? I mean what did
you put in your coffee this morning? You can't just waltz off
the court like that! This is so, so, uh, unprofessional. What
am I supposed to say to the other captain? Huh? What about
your opponents who you just left standing on the court?"

Speechless, Vivian, Ceridwin, Marni, and Josie look up at
her.

Monica says, "What? No answer?"

Ceridwin speaks up, "Tell them we decided to join the swim team instead!" She splashes Monica. Marni, Vivian, and Josie join in.

Backing up, Monica yells, "Stop! Stop it! I don't want the chlorine to get on my highlights!" She throws her hands up in the air and says, "Honestly! I think I am playing with a bunch of two-year-olds." She storms off.

Monica grumbles expletives the entire walk to Mitch's office. She slams through Mitch's office door, rattling the glass. As she throws a tantrum, people walk by his office. None dare to knock. They stop and stare before moving on.

Mitch says, "OK. OK, slow down. I caught only about half of that."

She breathes in slowly and says, "Do you know that right now you have four players from my team in the club's pool? They're swimming in their tennis clothes! And they're not on the courts, like they're supposed to be!"

Mitch opens his mouth to speak, but Monica doesn't wait. She plows on, "No? How could you know! You're busy taking a nap at your desk. If you can't get a handle on my team, then I will! Put your big boy pants on and do your job!"

Mitch says into the speakerphone, "Bill, hold my order. I'll call you back in a few minutes."

The voice on the other end says, "No problem, I hear that you are, uh, busy."

Mitch glances through his window at the courts. He notices a couple of the courts aren't playing. Surprised, he says, "Did you say 'in the club pool'?"

"Yes. In the pool."

He laughs and says, "Well now, that's a first."

"It's no laughing matter! And I don't care if it is a second, third, or a one hundredth. You have to stand in and reprimand them. This cannot be allowed to happen again! We may lose our ranking. Repercussions must be swiftly delivered in full force. Do you hear me?"

Mitch holds up his hands and says, "Whoa, Monica. I am sure there is a logical explanation."

Monica says, "No! No, there is not! I've worked--I mean we've worked so hard to be number one!"

He thinks, *Please run out of steam so I can get back to work.* He sighs when Monica takes in another deep breath, winding up again. For a brief moment, he contemplates throwing her in the pool. He smiles at the thought.

Monica leans over his desk, digging her knuckles in among his papers and files. Mitch leans back in his chair, settling in for what he expects to be the duration. Not surprisingly, Monica plays the same old card.

She demands, "Why are you smiling? Wipe that silly smile off of your face! This is serious!" Mitch manages to look serious. Monica continues, "Look, my husband helped build this very office you are sitting in with his goodwill and charity. It's his vision and monetary donation that brought this state-of-the-art tennis facility into reality. His vision didn't include girls irresponsibly leaping off of courts mid-match and into pools." She leans over his desk for emphasis, "Now, what are you going to do about it?"

Mitch momentarily shuts his eyes and counts to ten. He can't see her, but he smells her Creed Acqua Fiorentina parfume. She shakes his chair. He opens his eyes to see her angular blonde bob swishing with each emphatic shake. Her diamond earrings catch the window's light, briefly reflecting bright rays on the opposite wall. She crosses her perfectly toned arms and waits for his reply.

Mitch says, "Well, I'm not sure what to say."

Monica takes in another deep breath and says, "That's your answer? Ok, Mr. President of Tennis and Spa Services? You want to keep that title?"

Mitch kicks his feet up onto the desk and jokes, "Suits me, doesn't it?"

She knocks his feet off and says, "Then, do as I say! Reprimand all four swimmers. Today. And don't think I won't take that title from you if you don't. It would be easy, you know! Think about it. I could even have you fired. Like that!" She snaps her fingers.

Mitch stands and says, "Now, Monica, I know you're angry, but let's just calm down for a second."

She shoves him back into his seat and says, "No, you calm down! You wouldn't make half as much teaching on the city's public courts as you do here, and you know it! Plus, you would be on your feet all day: not at this cushy desk, napping."

She turns before leaving to add an afterthought. She says, "How much further can you stray from that silver spoon you were born with? I mean doesn't it hurt that you had to turn in that BMW your parents gave you for that piece of crap you drive now? What other concessions are you willing to make?"

"Back off, Monica."

"Everyone has his breaking point, you know. Even you. Imagine what you would be driving if you were fighting five other tennis pros for private lessons at the city tennis center; lessons that will bring in half of what you make here. Can you say 'scooter'?"

"I think you should leave."

"Well, you know what I think? I think of what those hard courts would do to that bum knee of yours."

Mitch stands to open the door for Monica. He says, "Look Monica, there is no need to get personal. I'm willing to hear what you have to say, but you can't come in here every time you don't like something and make idle threats. Why don't you calm down and come back in a few minutes, once you've had a chance to think things through? I am sure there is a reasonable explanation for all of this. We can talk about it. In the meantime, I will take care of the swimmers." He holds the door for her to leave. He'd like to kick her out with the heel of his shoe, but restraint is an art form he's perfected over the years when dealing with Monica.

Monica--never liking to be told what to do--grabs his collar and says, "Idle? You think my threats are idle?" She throws her head back and laughs.

He hears his own heart beat as his anger escalates.

She says, "Your job is to listen. I've said what I need to say."

"Finished?"

"No."

"Can't wait to hear the rest."

"Also, don't put me with Marni anymore. We've lost the last three matches together. It's not working. I need a new partner." She tightens her grip on his collar, pulling him slightly off balance. She smiles, lets go, and says in a suddenly sugary-sweet tone, "Okeydokey?"

Mitch doesn't take the time to wonder why the sudden change in her tone. He's given up trying to understand what goes on in her head. He says, "Monica, you can't grab me like that and make threats. For one thing, it's unprofessional. Secondly, I am pretty sure it's illegal."

"Legal, schmegal. Who cares? We just lost my--I mean our number one ranking and what are you doing about it?"

"You are taking things way too seriously. Remember, tennis is a game. It's supposed to be fun."

"That's your answer? Nothing! I knew it! You're going to do nothing!"

"I told you I would address it. And as for the new partner, I don't have one for you. You've gone through three so far, and it is not even mid-season. I can't keep coming up with new partners for you. Stick with what you've got and we will work on a new partner next season for you. And, remember to have fun."

"First of all, tennis is not fun. It is a serious mega-million-dollar business here in South Florida, and you should treat it as such. Second, you want me to wait?"

"Yes. You and Marni are making strides together. Winning is just a matter of time."

Monica crosses her arms. He watches as she contemplates something. Finally, she says, "Have it your way." She never gives up this easily: too easily for his liking.

ও⊷ও

Monica finds the four swimmers toweling off in the locker room. She leans against the wall and crosses her arms again. She waits for an apology or a chance to engage someone in a heated argument. She wants to vent. When no opportunity occurs, she tires from boredom, until she sees Ceridwin's cell phone sitting on the sink counter. She smiles. Quietly, she drops it into Marni's open tennis bag. Next, Monica takes her own wallet and nonchalantly drops it into Marni's bag. Monica smiles as she watches Marni exit the bathroom and zip her bag without so much as looking inside. Next, Monica walks out, plants herself in a plush leather chair, and waits.

Marni, Ceridwin, Josie, and Vivian exit the locker room together. When Monica sees them, she dials Ceridwin's cell phone number. She watches from a distance as Ceridwin reacts to her ringtone. Ceridwin checks her pockets and then her purse. Finally, everyone stops walking. Ceridwin says, "Where is that coming from? I know that's my ringtone. Isn't it?"

Marni says, "Yeah. Sounds like it."

Ceridwin says, "But I can't find it. It's not in my bag."

Vivian says, "Marni, it's coming from you. There. Your bag."

Marni plops her tennis bag down in the middle of the tile floor, and unzips it. To her surprise, Ceridwin's ringing cell phone sits on top of her tennis clothes. Marni picks up the phone. Embarrassed, she hands it to Ceridwin and says, "That's weird. Not sure how that got in there."

Monica instantly materializes and interrupts. She says, "Ceridwin, there you are. I have been trying to call you. I can't find my wallet. I wanted to see if maybe I left it in the locker room." Monica looks down into Marni's open bag. She says, "There it is. What a surprise! Marni, what are you doing with my wallet in your bag?" Next, Monica picks up Marni's hand towel from the bag. She holds it for all to see. She says, "This sure is cute. Where did you get this?"

Marni stammers, "Fr-fr-from t-t-tennistowels.com."

Monica displays the towel for all to see again before replacing it slowly. She says, "I really like the bright yellow tennis ball color and your pink embroidered name. Too cute! Well, gotta run! See you girls later." She resists the urge to skip to her car.

Ceridwin, Vivian, Violet, and Josie say nothing. They stare at Marni. None of them can believe it. Marni breaks the silence first and says, "Er, go me! Closet klepto and I didn't even know it. Ha-ha! Hide the silverware!"

Josie zips Marni's bag, hands it to her, and says, "Here you go, Miss Sticky Fingers. Don't forget your loot!"

Ceridwin chimes in, "If you've got a watch in there, can I have it? Mine broke."

Violet says, "My blender broke. Got one of those in there?"

Vivian says, "Can you steal my husband? He's driving me crazy. He'll fit. He's tiny."

Marni mutters sarcastically, "Very funny."

Monica lies in wait behind her steering wheel in the parking lot. She anticipates heated confrontation: Ceridwin, Vivian, Violet, and Josie sharing choice words with Marni. She envisions all three demanding to see what else is in Marni's bag. She envisions a scuffle leading to some hair pulling. She adjusts her rearview mirror and says to her reflection while applying lipstick, "Yes, hair-pulling. That would be splendid."

Monica sees all four girls enter the parking lot. She says to the mirror, "Shoooow time!" She giggles, blots her lips, but what happens next disappoints. Everyone hugs before driving off. Monica speaks to her reflection again, "Are they hugging? That's it? Where's the fighting? But Ceridwin, she took your cell phone! A-a-and she took my wallet! Don't you see? Marni needs to go!"

Deep in thought, Monica thumps her finger on the steering wheel for several minutes. Suddenly, she stops thumping, smiles, and drives away. She catches her own reflection again, winks, and says, "Time for another Plan B."

She follows Marni out of the parking lot, keeping a safe, undetected distance. Marni drives her scooter off of the road, onto the golf course's sidewalk, and past the sign reading "Cart Path Only". Marni looks both ways before she drives farther, making sure no one is around. She adjusts the tennis bag strapped to her back, and guns the engine around a bunker, green-side, for home.

Monica knows this is a shortcut for Marni. She also knows only golfers are allowed on the course. She says to her reflection, "A scooter on the golf course spells a big No-No! You can't ride across the grass! Marni, if you were to be caught, there could be trouble. Hmmmm. How much trouble? I wonder."

Monica knows Le Château's bylaws state only golfers may use the course. Furthermore, only golfers scheduled to play that particular day may access the grounds. In short, no tee time means no access.

Monica mumbles, "You can't go for a jog, take the dog for a walk, or so much as touch a blade of perfectly manicured grass without permission."

Groundskeeping ranks top priority at the club and for good reason. Annually, thousands of travelers from around the globe visit Boca Raton specifically to play on what is considered to be one of the most prestigious courses in North America. The course and its superb maintenance keep those visitors coming back year after year. Driving a scooter through it, even the cart path, is not advisable.

Monica mumbles, "At the very least it would be frowned upon. I will have to think of what the very most might be." She gets another idea and says, "*Tsk-tsk.* Marni, Marni, Marni."

৵৹৵

It's been three weeks since Monica's talk with Mitch. She grows impatient as each impending match approaches. Monica reapplies her lipstick in the locker room's mirror.

She says to her reflection, "Today's the day. Enough philanthropy. I've given Mitch plenty of time! He should've taken me seriously when he had the chance. I said I didn't want to play with Marni, and I meant it." She blots her lips and continues, "Whatever happens is his own fault! I simply can't be held responsible for what happens next."

Monica and Marni have lost the last three matches together. Their record together is now 1:7. Monica mumbles, "She's ruining my career. We'd better not be paired again today!"

Monica fumes when she hears she is paired with Marni yet again. Monica cares more about her year-end win/loss record than she does about anyone or anything. Her ranking is the most important measuring stick in her life. She grumbles as she picks up her tennis bag and slings it over her shoulder, "Enough is enough. Time to take matters into my own hands." Monica pretends she twists an ankle on the steps to The Breezeway and goes home.

Monica spends the next three weeks working out the logistics of Plan B. She considers those three weeks as a grace period of sorts for Mitch: buying him time to come to his senses and finally dissolve her partnership with Marni. She feels that this generous allowance of time qualifies her as kind, almost righteous in her actions.

She sighs and mumbles, "I guess I do have a heart under all of these scales after all."

The next morning, Monica decides she can't wait any longer. Edgy with excitement, she feels butterflies. She dries her hair in the mirror, points her brush for inflection, and says, "Grace period over. I didn't want to have to do this. However, Mitch, you leave me with no choice. If you won't take care of this, then I will. So be it, Mr. President of Tennis and Spa Services. You made me do this! Remember that!"

Monica telephones the golf club course and schedules the last tee-time of the day. She knows the course will be empty in the late afternoon's heat. She won't have to worry about bystanders or someone playing through. At that time, she also knows that her teammate, Violet Anderson, will be driving her kids to soccer practice and won't be home for several more hours.

Monica putters along in her golf cart across the green, counting the houses as she goes: *seven, eight, nine.* It's necessary to count since house after house looks much the same: a kidney shaped pool, a wrought iron fence, palm trees, and a tiled deck. From the back and with few distinguishable features, telling the houses apart proves nearly impossible. She parks her cart and approaches Violet's house: the ninth one on the right.

Monica puts on her disposable gloves. Ensuring that no one is in sight, she totes a black plastic bag to Violet's back door. She uses a box cutter to slice through the screen. Next, she takes a brick paver and throws it through the door behind the screen. Glass shatters everywhere. With the alarm now blaring, she glances at her watch, knowing the clock is ticking. She feels a rush of adrenaline, giggles, and bolts for Violet's bathroom.

Knowing where Violet keeps her jewelry box, Monica grabs the contents along with Violet's husband's antique watch collection. She shakes all of it into the black garbage bag. Remembering to grab the brick as she exits, she throws it in the bag along with the box cutter and valuables, tying it shut. A shrill scream escapes her as she hears the sirens quickly approaching Violet's street.

Briefly, Monica hesitates at the back gate to drop the yellow tennis towel with the name "Marni" embroidered on it. She laughs, "Marni, Marni, Marni. You naughty girl!" She ties her plastic gloves to the end of the garbage bag and throws the whole thing into the water hazard, watching it sink from the weight of the brick and precious content.

Giggling most of the way, Monica drives through the remaining holes, carefully filling out her golf card as if she played each one. She speeds to the Putter's Paradise Bar and Grill, and finds an empty barstool. She orders a split of champagne and three chocolate cake bonbons.

The bartender places her order in front of her and says, "Here's your champagne, ma'am. Are you celebrating something?"

Monica says, "Yes, thank you. I guess you could say that was the most exciting game of golf I've ever played." She takes a bit of a bonbon and thinks, *Mmmm. Smothered in mint buttercream icing and dipped into more chocolate. Decadent.* She savors each mouth-watering bite, almost as much as she savors pulling off the heist.

SEVEN

From the lightest of words sometimes the direst of quarrel springs.
-Cato the Elder

Marni packs her gear into her tennis bag for the day's match. She adjusts her visor in the hallway mirror and grabs her scooter's key. The doorbell rings. She looks at her watch and wonders whom that can be this early. She opens the door.

Surprised, she sees a police investigator. After a brief introduction, he flashes his identification badge and asks questions, demanding answers immediately. His tone is curt. He wants to know whether the pink embroidered yellow tennis towel with the name 'Marni' on it is hers. He holds out the clear plastic baggie with the towel in front of her.

Marni says, "I guess so. It looks like mine. I am the only Marni I know."

The investigator says, "A simple 'yes', or 'no' please ma'am."

Annoyed at this last minute intrusion, Marni says, "Yes. Now if you'll excuse me, I am in a hurry." She doesn't bother to wonder where he got her towel. She doesn't care. Quickly, she looks at her watch again. She has twenty-two minutes to get to her tennis match.

He asks, "Is it true that you had a cell phone belonging to Ceridwin Drummond Collier along with a wallet belonging to Monica Mooney in your possession three weeks ago?"

She thinks, *So that must be what this is all about! He sure does want to know a lot of stupid things.* Marni answers all of his questions quickly and as best as she can before excusing herself.

Now, with six minutes left to get to her match, she wonders why he wastes so much of her time. She zones out during his next question and thinks, *I can't believe someone sent this stupid, stupid man here to ask me stupid questions about the stupid cell phone and wallet incident! This is such a stupid waste of time!* She can't explain how those items made it into her tennis bag that day, but she has long since moved on. She wonders, *Why can't he? Whatever happened, it was no big deal: a simple accident.*

"Look," she finally says, "I have to go. I don't know how you got my towel, and right now I don't care. I also don't know how the wallet and cell phone got into my tennis bag that day, but it's no big deal. My friends were separated from their belongings for what, ten whole minutes? So, why do you care? Why should you care? What are you even doing here? This is a waste of taxpayers' money. I have to go!"

He doesn't like being shrugged off. He says, "I assure you, Miss Schoppelmann, nothing I do is a waste of taxpayers' money. They get their money's worth."

Marni laughs and says, 'Oh, I see. You are working on the earth shattering case of the wallet and cell phone that went missing for ten minutes before being unceremoniously reunited with their owners. Good for you." She brushes past him to her scooter. He grabs her wrist.

He says, "Not so fast."

"Hey! Let go of me!" She jerks her arm free and starts her scooter.

A slight spray of spit escapes his mouth when he speaks. He says, "Were you aware that Ms. Violet Anderson's home was broken into yesterday afternoon?"

Marni cuts the engine and stares at him. She blinks, speechless.

He delivers his next question with more venom. He says, "Do you often drive your scooter on the restricted golf path contrary to club policy? And when you do, are you able to get a good look at the back of many fine homes along the way?"

She wonders, *What is going on?* She tries to piece the puzzle together, but it doesn't make any sense. She asks, "Am I being charged with something?"

He doesn't answer the question directly. Instead, he says, "We are just beginning our investigation."

She thinks, *Investigation? Holy Crap!* Marni says, "Then, I will not be answering any more questions without my lawyer." Unnerved, she drives off in the direction of the courts. Shaken, she arrives five minutes late. She finds Mitch in the bleachers.

She yells up to him, "Sorry I'm late. I got hung up."

Surprised to see her, Mitch yells down, "Hey! What are you doing here? Monica said you wouldn't be playing this morning."

That piece of information doesn't sit well with Marni. She mumbles to herself, "Now how would Monica know that?" Marni yells back, "Well, here I am in the flesh. Which court am I on?"

Mitch says, "You were on Three with Monica, but Monica brought her own sub today since you were out."

Marni gives Mitch a curious look. She asks, "Did Monica say why I would be out?"

"No, just that you were out. You feeling OK?"

Marni doesn't answer the question. She yells back, "You said 'Three'?"

"Yeah, but you can't play. The match hasn't started yet, but we already exchanged lineups. So, you can't play."

"I've known the other captain for years. I'll get her OK first, but she'll be fine with it. I'm sure she'll let me play. See you in an hour or two."

Caught off guard, Monica drops her racquet as Marni approaches the court. The racquet lands on the court with a loud clang. Several decorative Swarovski crystals fall off the racquet's frame from the jolt.

Marni stands in front of Monica and cuts to the chase. She says, "How did you know I would be hung up this morning?"

Monica takes in a deep breath, and carefully chooses her words. She says, "An investigator came by asking me all kinds of questions this morning. Gosh, he took forever with his questioning! Anyway, he asked for your address. I am sorry I didn't call you first to give you a heads-up, but I was on the phone trying to find a last minute substitute."

"So, he visited you first?"

"Yes. I knew if he asked you half as many questions, you wouldn't make the match." Monica doesn't mention that she was the one who called the investigator in the first place, or that she shared more than a little information concerning Marni with him.

Marni looks relieved. She says, "Oh, Ok. I guess that makes sense. He did ask a ton of questions. So, he asked you a lot of questions, too?"

"Yes, he sure did. A real pain in the butt, if you ask me!"

Marni says, "Yeah, no kidding! Sorry for you, but glad it wasn't just me then. That guy could use a little help in the manner's department. He grabbed my arm."

"Really?"

"Yeah. Jerk. Hopefully, he was nicer to Violet. Poor Violet. I guess her home got broken into yesterday. I see she's here on Court One. So, I guess she is OK."

"Yes. She was out with her boys when it happened. Some stuff was taken, but they are all fine."

"Thank God!"

"Yeah, absolutely. Her well-being was my first concern, too. Uh, did the investigator say they found the burglar?" Monica swallows a delicious smile and says, "Or if they have a suspect, yet?"

Marni says, "No. Well, I am not sure. I think he might have been pointing the finger at me."

Feigning surprise, Monica says, "No! Really? I can't believe it! You're kidding!"

"I can't say for sure. It's all too surreal right now, but he did lay into me. I think he thinks I did it."

"Oh, no! I can't believe that! Look, you've been through a lot today already. Why not take the day off? Forget the match. Go home, and relax by the pool. See, I have a sub already, and you don't need the extra worry being out here."

Monica wants her scheming ways to pay off immediately. She doesn't want to play with Marni. She wants to play with her new ringer. With her plan in place, Monica hopes to rid herself of Marni once and for all; something she thinks Mitch should've done weeks earlier. She wants her record to improve starting today.

Marni says, "That's very thoughtful, Monica. Thank you for trying to look out for me. But, what worry? I didn't do anything wrong. I am sure everything will pan out. Besides, I wouldn't leave my partner!" She hugs Monica.

Monica hugs her back, pushing away a twinge of guilt. Monica's smile dissolves, but she still manages to sound enthusiastic, "Great! Well, if I can do anything, anything at all for you, you just let me know. You hear?"

Marni plays the match with a new lease on life, hitting the ball with a newfound aggression. Every inch of stress from this morning's encounter fuels the beast within. Her groundstrokes blister the clay. Her net game ramps up a level with heated, pinpoint accuracy. She poaches and nails one stinging volley after another.

She turns to Monica and says, "Ahh. Therapy."

Monica nods and says, "Like only tennis can give."

Marni says, "Exactly. Too bad I can't hit the actual person responsible instead of this innocent, little, yellow ball."

Monica swallows hard, but manages a smile.

Marni loudly grunts the morning away, wielding heavy blow after heavy blow. Her opponents weaken. Marni snuffs out every last bit of their hope and momentum. She hits them where it counts and pushes them onto their back feet. They crumble, utterly obliterated by the whirling brutal force of Marni.

As not much is required of her, Monica spectates most of the match. She watches Marni run. She watches Marni jump. She watches Marni smash the little yellow ball to smithereens. Never one to perspire much anyhow, Monica never breaks a sweat. She doesn't have to; Marni does all of the work.

She tirelessly watches Marni's best performance ever on a tennis court. She can't believe Marni's level of play. She wonders where Marni has been hiding it. Suddenly, she frowns guiltily. Now, she wishes that she had never dropped the embroidered yellow towel at Violet's house. She wishes she could bring back the cell phone and the hidden wallet in Marni's bag. She wishes she never planted any of it. More importantly, she wishes she could take back everything she said to the investigator. She knows it is too late. She'll never play with Marni ever again. Marni is going to jail.

Monica says, "You should've shown me this brand of tennis before now."

Marni, "Yeah. Too bad we can't have that rude investigator show up at my door before every match."

Monica shrugs, "Oh, well. There is little to be done now."

Marni says, "What do you mean?"

Monica quickly says, "Uh, well, what I mean is that our, uh, match is almost over. Literally, there is little left to be done."

The final score reads 6:1, 6:0. They finish in a record forty-one minutes. Monica and Marni greet their opponents at the net.

Monica says, "Nice match, ladies."

One opponent says, "I am sorry we didn't give you more of a match today. It just went by too quickly."

Her partner says, "To tell you the truth, it's all a blur. I am not sure what happened."

Monica says, "Marni happened."

Marni says, "I am a little embarrassed. I should apologize. I was hitting and grunting and hitting and grunting like a fiend. Sorry."

One opponent laughs and says, "I'm glad you brought that up! I wasn't going to say anything, but those weren't just grunts. Those were shrieks!"

Monica says, "Yep, that's our Marni today, our own little Shreikapova!"

One opponent laughs and says, "Yeah, you were so loud and intimidating. Did you do that to distract us?"

Marni says, "Not at all. Sorry. I needed that today. Nothing personal, but if you knew the morning I had then you would understand. Let's just say that I had some aggression to let out." Marni doesn't take the time to explain further. She has more pressing issues on her mind.

Monica and Marni finished so quickly that they decide to eat lunch early, leaving well before their teammates complete their matches. Normally, Marni would stay to cheer on her teammates, but not today. Marni's phone rings incessantly throughout her lunch.

Monica says, "Wow. Somebody really needs to talk with you!"

Marni listens to the messages and frowns. Monica raises an eyebrow, but says nothing. Marni leaves in such a rush that she forgets her racquet on the table.

When Josie finishes her match and arrives to the lunch buffet area, she finds no Marni, only her racquet. *That's unusual. Marni normally stays to watch the end of everyone's matches.* She phones to tell Marni that she found her racquet. Marni sounds distracted. Josie tells her that she'll drop off her racquet on the way home.

When Josie arrives at Marni's townhouse, the front door sits ajar. *Odd.* A police car-- parked widthwise across Marni's driveway—blocks the double garage doors. *Very odd.* Marni's scooter stands idle on the sidewalk with the engine still running. Josie walks up the driveway and turns off Marni's scooter.

Josie carries Marni's racquet up the white paver driveway, past the bright pink begonias, and around the stately grand palm. She pushes the overhead palm fronds out of the way and walks around the stonemason pillars set on either side of the garage door. She hears a noise and looks up. The balcony doors over Marni's garage suddenly shut and lock. *Beyond odd!*

Josie walks under the covered stucco entryway and knocks on the already opened door. As she raps on the thick, wooden door, she says, "Hello? Knock, knock. Anybody home?"

Marni stands in the center of the foyer's round tile mosaic. One policeman handcuffs Marni as another recites her Miranda rights.

Still, unsure of what to do, Josie knocks again. No one acknowledges her presence. She knocks more loudly and says, "Hello. Um, hellooo? Excuse me, but can anyone tell me what is going on here?"

Marni does her best to explain through tears. Too upset to think straight, she jumbles the facts. She says, "My house was broken into and Violet is being arrested."

Josie says, "What? Violet? Violet Anderson? Why would Violet break into your home? And why are you being handcuffed?"

Desperately trying to unscramble her already-confused thoughts, Marni stammers, "She didn't! I did. N-n-not my house. Violet's house. And I didn't! I mean they think I did. But I didn't! You know, break into Violet's house."

Stunned, Josie doesn't know what to say.

The same police detective from earlier this morning ushers Marni through her front door and says, "Still in a rush to go play tennis, Ms. Schoppelmann? Not so cocky now, are we?"

The policemen drive Marni to the local precinct. They photograph and fingerprint her before confiscating all of her belongings. She makes one allowable phone call. Afterwards, she sinks into the corner of her cell and cries. This is all foreign to her: the handcuffs, the arrest, and the cold steel bars in front of her. Marni has never felt so lost or so alone.

Marni brushed off the police investigator this morning. Now, she regrets her mistake. She shakes her head. The idea of her as a criminal is preposterous. She mutters, "Or so it was a few hours ago." Now, suddenly the idea--no longer preposterous--is her real life. Her life has completely changed, perhaps forever.

She looks around at the chipped paint, the scribbling on the walls, and the cold steel bars holding her here. She ponders this impossibility; how she got here. She thinks of her future and everything she holds dear. She feels suddenly uncertain. Her first encounter with a life-altering injustice makes her question the true safety and sanctity of an ordinary life. She sobs. She worries. Feeling helpless, she clutches her knees, buries her head against them, and cries harder.

Josie is not made of money. The divorce left her struggling to pay bills and to make ends meet. She reads the bail amount again and can't believe the size of the sum. *It's not like she's a murdering fugitive or something!* Still, she can't focus on money right now. Marni needs her. She refuses to let Marni stay overnight in jail. She posts the bail and insists that Marni stay in her guest room until things blow over.

Josie takes one look at Marni. From firsthand experience, she recognizes a basket case when she sees one. No one understands the state of despair better than she. She won't leave Marni alone, not until she is certain that Marni will be OK.

࿐

Marni plops down on Josie's couch. She points the remote at the television screen and surfs until she finds a tennis channel. She asks Josie for something alcoholic before sinking further into the couch.

Josie says, "No way! I am making you something, but it is definitely not alcoholic. Sorry, but right now, alcohol is not what you need."

"Yes, it is."

"It's a depressant you know. Not exactly what you need at a time like this. Here." She hands Marni a cup of Sleepy Time tea.

"Thank you, Nanny McPhee, but where's the hard stuff."

"Just try it. Hungry?"

Marni says, "No. I don't have much of an appetite. I just feel like drinking alcohol like a fish."

"Fish don't drink alcohol."

"Go with it."

"I'll try. I have wine, but try that tea first. Maybe your appetite will pick up. I've got Beef Daube Provencal cooking. It's simmering, so it's ready whenever you are. You can help yourself when you're hungry. It's impossible not to feel better after a bowl of that."

"Is that what I smell? Maybe I will try a bowl, a small bowl. I know comfort food when I smell it!"

"Ok, one sec. I'll get you some. Listen Marni, when you are ready we need to talk about today and about what your options are. We need to put some plans in place. Have you thought about having your parents come in from New York? I think it's a good idea. You need support right now. Family. Don't you think?"

Tears stream down Marni's face again. She says, "I can't tell my parents. I just can't. My Dad is in bad shape right now. He's recovering from a heart attack. It was a close call that really scared us. This might be too much for him. I'm afraid it might push him over the edge."

Josie hugs her and says, "Oh Marni, I didn't know. I'm so sorry."

"It's OK. I just didn't feel like telling anybody." She wipes the tears away and continues, "You see? Just mentioning it and look what happens."

"Completely understandable. You OK?"

"Yeah. I mean no. I mean I don't know."

"Have you thought about what you are going to do?"

"I suppose I'll need to hire a lawyer, a good one; one who can get me out of this mess. I know. I know. Things don't look too good. And I don't know how they got to this point. Honestly, I don't."

"It's a tough situation for you to be in. Well, for anyone to be in, but we'll get you out of this mess."

"Thanks Jo. You're a true friend."

Josie hugs her again. "Anytime."

Josie rinses the pan in the sink and realizes something: both positive and negative. She already knows the best lawyer in South Florida. *He is also the biggest jerk in South Florida. But professionally speaking, I can't think of a better lawyer for Marni. He is the best.* Roger Fleming has more than earned all of the accolades, success, and press that made him who he is: President of the Florida Bar Association and partner to the biggest law firm in Florida.

Josie says, "I'll call Roger in the morning. Don't worry. He will set things straight. You can sleep well tonight. Roger never loses a case. Ever."

Marni says, "I don't want you to have to call Roger for me. I know how hard that would be for you."

"Nonsense. It won't be personal. Strictly business."

"You know I am innocent, right?"

Josie grabs her hand, pats it, and says, "Anyone who knows you, knows that you didn't do it. I have never been more sure about anything in my life."

❧

Josie doesn't wait until morning. That night she calls Roger.

Roger answers on the third ring. He says, "Jo, what are you doing calling me this late?"

Josie wants to say, "You forget that I lived with you for the better part of a decade. I knew you would be awake." Instead she says, "It couldn't wait." She explains Marni's situation in detail.

Roger says, "Doesn't sound good. The towel will be the fatal blow used by the prosecution."

"Prosecution? You think it will go that far?"

"Distinct possibility."

"But you know Marni. She didn't do it!"

"Whether she did or didn't, it doesn't matter. It sounds like the evidence could be built to say that she did."

Josie says, "But that's not fair."

"Don't be naïve. I've built a career on not being fair. Get a good lawyer."

"That's why I called you. I know you will find a way to make this right and to get her out of this mess."

Roger says, "Whoa! I've got my own cases. I'm booked into next year already. I couldn't possibly take on another case right now. Not even for a friend."

Neither one speaks. Finally, Josie says, "What's it going to take?"

Roger loves looking at life from the driver's seat. It's his favorite view. He runs through a mental list of things he could possibly ask for from her. Finally, he says, "No more alimony and consider it done."

Josie says, "But Roger, I can barely make the house payments now. How am I supposed to make them if you cut my alimony completely off? As it is, you're already behind. Pick something else."

Roger has been paying her less than half of what the settlement dictates. A fact that doesn't sit well with Josie, but she knows better than to take the best lawyer in Florida to court.

"No."

She says, "Look! I need every penny. You know how much I make."

Roger says, "That's the deal. One get-out-of-jail-free card in exchange for no more alimony. Take it or leave it. It's up to you."

Josie bites her lip and says, "Half. You can reduce alimony by half."

Roger laughs at her bargaining chip. He says, "I'm already paying less than half. You made the call. You want me, or not?"

She hears Dixie's voice in the background. Dixie says in her drawl, "Who on earth are ya' talkin' to this late?"

Roger says, "No one important. Go back to bed." He walks across the hall to his office and shuts the door.

Josie resists the urge to slam the phone down. *No one important? Really? That pretty much sums up our entire marriage.* She will be glad when Marni's case is over. When it is, she vows never to speak with Roger Fleming again. She says, "Fine."

Roger twirls in his desk chair. He sings, "Fine it is!" He makes a note on a sticky pad that reads no more alimony. He folds it into an airplane and shoots it across the room. He says, "I will send over the alimony paperwork for you to sign tomorrow. In the meantime, send Marni's contact information to my email address or text it to me."

"OK. I am texting it now. Good night, Roger."

"Wait."

"What?"

"No 'thank you'? You know I don't have to take this case. I am going to have to ruffle a few feathers to do so. Where are your manners? Let's hear it, Jo."

"Setting a decent and innocent woman free should be thanks enough." Josie hangs up.

EIGHT

The argument is at an end.
-Saint Augustine

La Château's tennis courts buzz with the spread of the morning's news about Marni Schoppelmann's arrest. Walking the short distance from the parking lot to the clubhouse, Josie overhears Marni's name repeatedly in various conversations. It's as if she follows a gunpowder fuse lit with Marni's story as it snakes its way through the tennis facility. Josie reaches a boiling point when she passes two women seated at the juice bar. She's never seen these two women before, yet they talk about Marni as if they play tennis with her everyday.

One says, "Oh, I knew it was Marni all along. You see it by the way she handles herself on the court. She's a bad egg that one. She has always had that edgy side to her. It all comes down to character you know."

The other woman replies, "Yes, it absolutely does. Marni, poor thing, has none. I've heard her HOA dues are late."

"No! Really?"

"Yes. Five months."

"Should have known. You know how Marni is. Never good with her finances."

"Late on her HOA. *Tsk-tsk.*"

"Yes, that's why she's always wearing tennis outfits from last season."

"Yes, late, late, late. Again."

"Again? Well now, there's your motive right there."

Holding her tongue, Josie walks past. Thinking better, she stops, backtracks and says, "No. You know what? That's it! The fuse stops here before it reaches the dynamite!"

The two women look at Josie and one says, "I'm sorry, what? Dynamite?"

Josie continues, "I am not going to listen to your crap!"

"What crap?"

I'll bet you don't even know her. Josie gets to the point, "How exactly do you know Marni Schoppelmann?"

She says, "I'm sorry. And you are?"

"One of Marni's best friends. Now, answer the question."

The other woman says, "Well, you don't have to be so abrupt!"

"Well?"

"We're members of the same club, aren't we?" Her friend nods enthusiastically.

Josie says, "Well, we're members of the same club, and I don't know you two."

The other woman says, "Oh, you know. I've seen her on our courts."

"Right. And which courts might that be? Have you ever played tennis with Marni?"

"Well, technically, no. But, then again, she's never asked us to. She plays Elite and we play the Bronze Division, you see."

Her partner proudly adds, "We play line one for the Bronze Division. I know we are only 2.5 players, and she is a 5.0, but we're much better than our ranking." She nudges her partner.

Her partner says, "That's right! We could give anyone a run for their money!"

Josie says, "Yeah, right. You can't compete with Marni: not with her caliber of tennis, and certainly not with her caliber of character."

One of the ladies shuffles her beverage napkins suddenly looking busy. The other one says, "You don't have to be so rude about it. We do so know her! We speak on good authority."

Josie says, "Oh, OK. What color hair does she have?"

She looks at her partner for help. Receiving none, she says, "Uh, blonde?"

Josie says, "I thought so. Marni has auburn hair. You don't even know what she looks like. Do you? And it's not rude when it's true."

One of the ladies says, "Yeah, so?"

Josie says, "*So?* So, stop your petty small talk and stop spreading hurtful rumors about Marni that aren't true."

"Why are you defending a criminal anyway?"

"Marni is not a criminal! If you really did know her, you would at least know that much. And is this what you do with your spare time? Stand around and irresponsibly gossip, not giving a second thought to the good names you tarnish? Obviously, what you say speaks more about yourselves than it does about Marni."

The women let out a huff.

Josie adds, "Volumes."

The ladies slam their wheat grass shots and stand to leave. One turns to Josie and says, "Honestly, I don't know what your problem is! We were just talking. You should leave well enough alone!"

"I would if there were anything well about it!"

"It's all well. It's just idle conversation."

"It's the opposite of well. It's sickening."

"Sickening? Hardly! It's not like we're spreading some illness."

"What you're spreading is worse. The harmful filth you and your friend are spewing is damaging the good name of a great person; not to mention, it's totally and completely false. You should be ashamed!"

❧

Josie arrives to practice a few minutes late due to her run-in with the Gossip Ladies. Mitch waves her over and says, "Josie, go to the end court with Vivian today."

Josie changes direction and walks down to Court Five. *Guess I am with Vivian again. Mitch promised playing with Vivian was only temporary. Marni and I should be partners, but it sure hasn't worked out that way. Sigh.* She wonders if she'll ever play tennis with Marni again. *This is Monica's fault.*

First, Monica imposed herself as Josie's partner, before abruptly dropping her before their first match. Then, Monica imposed herself as Marni's partner. Now, Josie has been stuck with Vivian for the last several matches. While she loves Vivian, it's not exactly a perfect pairing. Their opponents target Vivian, leaving Josie standing idly by. Vivian winds up playing too much tennis, and Josie plays too little.

What Josie doesn't know is that Mitch isn't happy with the mismatch either. He had planned to put Vivian and Josie together just until Josie started winning again. But lately, everything has changed. Even though Marni is out on bail, Mitch must consider playing Josie with Vivian long-term. Starting today, he has to do so. Marni may have posted bail, but she is suspended from play until all charges are cleared. Mitch had no weight in the matter. That directive came from well above him via e-mail. He scrolls down on his iPad to finish reading the e-mail:

> We cannot allow a potential criminal on the fine courts of Le Château Saint-Emillion Country Club and Spa. It is our duty as Board Members to carefully consider those individuals whom crimes have been committed against. In particular, their rights and their safety come first and foremost. Community perception must also be considered and is paramount to the welfare of the club. By almost unanimous decision, Miss Marni Schoppelmann is hereby suspended from all club privileges until further notice.

The "almost unanimous" reference reflected Mitch's solitary vote in favor of keeping Marni in good standing. Not only confident in her innocence, he still believes in the concept that someone should remain innocent until proven guilty. Unfortunately for Marni, the rest of the board didn't see it Mitch's way.

Now short a player, Mitch needs Josie to settle in to line five for the duration. Mitch lightly thumps his chin with his stylus, planning how to best equalize play between Josie and Vivian. Quickly, he decides what he must do.

After the practice session starts, Mitch stands in the backcourt behind Josie. He waits. Josie steps in, takes the ball on the rise and hits repeated winner after winner. She uses her movement, sneaks in and puts the slower paced balls away with one punishing volley after another. Josie runs down the lobs and counter-hits with blistering topspin shots just out of reach.

Mitch watches Josie and thinks, *Josie: the one-woman show.* Outplaying the line five players, it's readily apparent that she has no business playing with them. She outruns, out-jumps, and out-hits them. She sticks out like a sore thumb. Mitch thumps his chin again. He knows what to do with a sore thumb. He goes to work, implementing his plan.

Mitch says, "Josie, don't hit the ball so hard."

Josie looks confused and says, "Really?"

"Yeah. You'll cut down on unforced errors if you take twenty, maybe thirty percent off." The other players on the court look at each other as if to say, "What errors?"

Ever the pleaser, Josie says, "Oh, OK. Like this?" She hits a ball at half-pace and with more arc. In short, she trusts Mitch.

Mitch says, "Yeah. That's it! That's the one. You can hit that all day without making a single mistake. Nice net clearance and spin for added margin."

The other players don't fully comprehend what is going on, but they don't question it. These new slower-paced balls from Josie prove much easier to retrieve and much easier to return. They don't complain.

After Mitch levels the playing field between Vivian and Josie, he adds one finishing touch. He says, "Josie, throw in some more lobs. A lot of players can't run like you can to track them down. Mix it up. You don't want to give them the same look every time. They will know what's coming. Tennis is about surprise. You should lob a minimum of thirty percent of the time. Maybe fifty."

Josie prefers taking the cover off of the ball. *Fifty? Wow.* Lobbing slows down play: something that dulls her interest. Even so, she complies with Mitch's instructions; she throws in several lobs. She grimaces. *Ugh. Definitely not my thing.* At most, she lobs fifteen percent of the time. It's definitely not her style. She may throw in a chip lob return to bail out of trouble, or dissuade a poacher, or a player who's hugging the net too closely. However, rarely does she use lobbing as an integral part of her game. *Lob, lob, lob. Call me a lobster.*

Josie says, "I don't know Mitch. In general, I am not a lobster. Er, I mean lobber."

"It's Ok. Just try it." Remembering something, Mitch performs one last tweak. He says, "Oh, and Josie, don't punch your volleys so hard. It's not about velocity. It's about finesse: touch, feel. It's about placement."

Josie fidgets with her strings, straightening them. *I thought I was placing them.* She takes in a deep breath. *Fine.* She does everything asked of her without hesitation.

The other players can't believe their luck. The beat down Josie delivered just a few minutes before, transforms before their eyes into tennis they understand. In one fell swoop; Mitch turns Josie into a line five player, not to mention a fulltime partner for Vivian.

Mitch reasons that his plan does both Josie and Vivian some good. Josie will help Vivian by being the legs of the team. In return, Vivian will continue to build Josie's confidence. He smiles. He surmises that his solution is nearly perfect.

Josie sighs. *This new brand of tennis will take some getting used to.* She wants to let loose and rip the ball. She doesn't say so. Instead, she holds back, and Vivian--understanding everything all too well--holds her tongue.

NINE

Who has a harder fight than he who is striving to overcome himself.
-Thomas a Kempis

Surprised to see Roger courtside, Josie excuses herself from practice. She approaches Roger and says, "What are you doing here?"

Roger says, "Well, nice to see you, too!"

"Well?"

"Well, what?"

"Well, you're not just going to stare at me, are you?"

He says, "Maybe. Nice, white hotpants. I think I can see through them."

"They're not hotpants. They're tennis shorts and keep your imagination to yourself. What do you want?"

He leans back into the bougainvillea and says, "No imagination needed Miss Black Lace Bikini Cut." The bougainvillea-entwined fence immerses him in bright fuchsia flowers.

"Nice try, but I am not wearing any underwear."

Roger raises his eyebrows and suppresses a grin.

Embarrassed, Josie blushes and stammers, "That's not what I mean. It's just that I-I-I have built-in shorties under the shorts. It's a tennis thing." Mad at herself for getting sucked into another one of Roger's lewd conversations, she says, "You might want to step out of the bougainvillea. Don't you know those things have thorns? Look, I need to get back to practice."

Roger laughs, steps forward out of the vine and says, "Thorns have never really bothered me. I prefer prickly things. Where's the excitement if there isn't a bit of danger involved."

"I don't really think of bougainvillea as dangerous."

"You should. Especially, when you're with me."

"Roger, I have practice now."

"I know. One sec. That's why I am here. I need to talk."

Exasperated, she sees the other players standing and waiting on her. She says, "OK. Spit it out already."

Never before has she used this tone with him. He likes it. Roger says, "I went by Marni's house. She wasn't there. I need her to sign these papers today. I need to change her arraignment date. We don't have a lot of time. The prosecution is ahead of us. Do you know where she is?"

Josie says, "She is at our, uh, I mean my house." She blushes again.

Amused, Roger says, "I see. *Our*? You still think of me when you're padding around the hallways in your bare feet?"

"What I think about is none of your business. Now, back to Marni."

Roger clears his throat, stands a little closer, and inhales slowly. She's wearing the perfume he likes. He says, "I thought she was on your tennis team."

"She is."

"Then why isn't she here practicing?"

Stomping on the brick pavers, Josie shakes pieces of the dark green clay loose from her shoes. Next, she hits the sides of her shoes with her racquet to further loosen the clay. She says, "The board won't allow her to play until all charges clear."

Roger says, "That's not legal. She hasn't been convicted of any crime. Is she still paying dues?"

Vivian walks up from behind and chimes in, "You can't very well expect Violet to play if Marni is around."

Josie quips, "You can't very well expect Marni to have committed Violet's burglary."

Vivian raises her hands and says, "Sorry. Don't bite my head off!"

Roger says, "OK. First, yes, I can expect Marni to play. She is a member of this club. Second, she should be able to exercise her full rights as a member and use the facility just as before."

Vivian quickly realizes she picks a fight with the wrong guy, and retreats back to the court.

Roger says, "Jo, where is Marni's partner. I need to talk with her." Roger looks down at his paper and says, "Uh, Monica Mooney."

Josie says, "Monica? Why do you need to speak with Monica?"

"She gave an unusually lengthy statement to the investigating officer."

"OK." Josie points to Monica's court. She says, "That one. Wearing the chandelier earrings."

Roger says, "Whoa. Can't miss those earrings, even from this distance." As he walks off, he winks at Josie and says, "Thanks, and maybe we can talk about those black lace undies another time."

"I told you I'm not wearing any--" *Ugh!* She wants to scream. She walks back to her court, but she can still hear Roger chuckle all the way to Monica's court. Josie rolls her eyes and repeats an increasingly common mantra in her head that soon this will all be over and she will never have to talk with Roger again.

❧❧

Roger approaches the back fence behind Monica's court. An older man watches the practice. Roger stands beside him. The older man reaches into his tennis bag, grabs a towel, and dries off his arms and neck.

Roger says, "Just get off the courts?"

The older man says, "Yeah. Three setter."

Roger says, "Geez! In this heat? Did you pull it out?"

"Yeah. Barely. Third set tiebreaker."

"Now, that's a workout! Gotta feel good to pull it out though. You know makes the extra set worth it."

The older man holds onto the fence and stretches his back left, then right. He says, "That's what I am trying to convince my back of."

Roger laughs, points, and says, "I don't suppose you know if that is Monica Mooney?"

The older man eyes Roger and says, "Who wants to know?"

"Forgive me. Allow me to introduce myself. I am Roger Fleming." He shakes hands with the older man and says, "I am the legal representation for Marni Schoppelmann."

The older man says, "Good kid, that Marni. I know Monica will want to help." He loosely holds the chain link fence between his fingers and stretches his calf muscles out. He says, "I'm J. Paul Mooney, Monica's husband."

Roger coughs, "Oh. Excuse me."

"Yeah. It's OK. I know what you're thinking. What's a hot young thing like that doing with an old geezer like me? Well, damned if I know. You'll have to ask her that." J. Paul laughs.

Monica bends over to pick up a ball. Underneath her skirt, she flashes a pair of tiny, lace, hot red underwear.

Roger thinks, *Nice butt,* but says, "I like the, uh, uniforms."

J. Paul says, "You mean what's underneath, right? Well, sorry, but that's for me."

"What's for you?"

"The panties. The red panties."

"Uh, huh."

"That's for me. Not you."

"Should I look away?" Roger thinks, *Fat chance.*

"Probably. That would be the gentlemanly thing to do. Anyway, Monica sat on a melted chocolate bar left on my car seat. So, she had to take off her tennis bloomers. Now, she is only wearing what was underneath."

"I see."

"Yeah. I bought her a new pair in the clubhouse, but I haven't had a chance to give them to her yet."

"But you can't be too upset. This mistake isn't all bad; it comes with some added spice."

"Any spicier and I'll have a heart attack."

"Come on. That's a bonus."

"Not really."

"You don't like that?"

"It's not that I don't like it. It's that I don't need it. You see, I'd wrap her up in a full-length parka if I could get away with it." He laughs an easy laugh again.

Roger, never a moral champion, thinks, *Whatever makes you happy, grandpa, but the red hot under thingy just made my day.* Again, instead of saying what he thinks, he says, "I hope to be in your same boat one day."

"What? Old-fashioned or maybe just old?"

"Nah. I mean I get it. I look at her, and I look at you. And I think why waste your time with fat, old, gray mares when you can drive a red hot Ferrari?" He nudges J. Paul with his elbow.

J. Paul instinctively moves his arm away. Already, he doesn't like this guy. He says, "I hope she's still with me when she's an old gray mare. Otherwise, I wouldn't have married her. What'd you say your name was?"

"Roger Fleming."

J. Paul says, "Ah. OK." Now, he remembers the name. This is Josie's ex-husband. J. Paul knows everything about the club, including much about the lives of its members. Roger's less than flattering reputation precedes him.

"OK. Well, I was going to ask Monica some questions, but I can come back another time. I wouldn't want to interfere with Red Panty Time." Again, he nudges J. Paul.

J. Paul doesn't laugh. He says, "I'll take your number. This clinic will last at least another forty-five minutes. Save you the trouble of waiting."

Roger says, "Uh-huh. Thanks. I appreciate that."

"Sure. Anything for Marni. We all know she didn't do it. Poor kid."

Roger catches another glimpse of the red underwear and leaves feeling aroused.

∽∾

Monica meets Roger at his office, per his request. Roger could have discussed matters over the phone, but his curiosity got the better of him. He wanted a closer look at the owner of the hot red underwear. When she arrives, he is not disappointed.

Monica remains all business. She answers Roger's questions succinctly. She avoids returning his lingering gaze. She derails his many attempts to poke holes in her story. Like her tennis game, Monica arrives well prepared. She effortlessly deflects Roger's shots and counterpunches with a few of her own.

Roger sits back in his black leather chair, assessing this fair beauty. He likes what he sees: the blonde angled bob, the fair skin, and the pale piercing eyes. In return, she assesses him: cocky, self-absorbed.

The light from the wall of windows directly behind Roger's chair casts an elongated shadow that darkens his face, but illuminates his back and all else in the office. A shadow cutout of his torso paints the surface of the dark wooden desk in front of him.

Roger rests his hands firmly on his desk. He listens intently. He can't place her accent. It's slight. He wonders if her accent faded from time or if she purposely rid herself of its distinct origin. To him, it sounds Northern European, but he can only guess. He waits for certain words to give her away, but they elude him.

He kicks his feet up on his desk and reclines. As she continues talking, his mind wanders. He can't get the picture of her red underwear out of his head. She shifts in her chair. He strains to catch a glimpse up her dress. Unsuccessful and disappointed, he resumes his questioning.

Monica thinks, *J. Paul was right. He's a scumbag.* She answers his next question, "I am not sure my birth year and city have anything to do with your investigation, Mr. Fleming."

Roger can't stop himself from thinking, *This is my kind of woman: wicked smart, sassy, and in control.* He ignores her comment and says, "As I mentioned on the phone, we need to know what you were doing by the water hazard behind Violet Anderson's house at the time of burglary. These and all questions pertain to the investigation."

Monica says, "Of course, they do. I told you before, Mr. Fleming--"

"Roger, please." He knows more information than he lets on, but he plans to play out his hand over time, savoring the tidbits and hoping for the chance to see the red hot underwear. He holds his cards close.

"Mr. Fleming, is it illegal to play golf on a course that I am a member of?"

Again, he ignores her question. He desperately wants to see her squirm. He tries a different tactic and says, "Interesting new developments are always popping up in this particular case."

Monica can't decide if he knows something that he isn't letting on or if he is just an idiot. She decides on the latter, but intends to play a card of her own just in case. She shifts in her chair again. Again, he strains. He frowns and thinks, *Nothing. Not a peep.*

As if reading his mind, she says, "Did you like my choice in underwear earlier today, Mr. Fleming?"

"I don't know what you mean?"

"I mean instead of the customary tennis shorties under my skirt, I wore something, shall we say, more eye-catching?"

His mouth drops open. He bites immediately and says, "Choice? It depends. By choice, you mean there is an alternative? I suppose I would have to evaluate the alternative first before I, uh, give an accurate opinion."

Monica sees exactly where this is going. In her experience, guys like Roger Fleming are too numerous to count. Already bored, she says, "I am a one-man woman, Mr. Fleming. I get propositioned all of the time."

He has no problem believing that. She adds for her own amusement, "I understand why. I am a good fuck." She lingers on the 'f'.

His mouth drops open again. On a whim and for some unknown reason, she lifts up her dress and shows him her underwear. "Blue satin with a bow is the alternative," she says. She thinks, *Why did I just do that? Like this wolf needs any more temptation.*

He slowly runs his finger along the edge of his desk with one hand. He wonders whether or not he should throw everything off of it. He doesn't want to seem too eager, but he also doesn't want to waste time. He licks his lips. He bought this oversized desk with women like her in mind.

Monica says, "Well, Mr. Fleming?"

He cannot focus, "Well, what?"

"Which is it?"

Too busy with anticipation to answer, he stares at the nipples suddenly protruding from her pale yellow knit dress. He says, "Which is what?" She crosses her arms.

Quickly, he closes the blinds behind him. Confident of what is to follow, he says, "I prefer none." He closes the short gap between them in three giant steps, quickly crossing over the copper and maroon Oriental rug.

In one move and with impeccable timing, Monica stands and grabs her chair's back. She flicks it to the ground, blocking his path. He stumbles, hitting his lip on the wooden trim of the fallen chair. She sees the scant red trace of blood on his lower lip and suddenly desires to kiss him. Instead, she picks up her purse and says, "Well, Mr. Fleming. I think I've answered enough questions for today. Like I said, I am a one-man woman. I don't mess around. Good luck with your case."

It is true, even if nothing else was. Monica prides herself in the fact that she never cheats on J. Paul. Not once in all of the years they've been together has she strayed. Today will prove no different. She walks to the elevator and presses the button. As she waits, she adjusts her hair in the metal door's reflection and mumbles, "Not going to happen. Especially not with a bottom feeder like you, Roger."

She considers Roger to be half of the man that J. Paul is, not by height, but by virtue. Over the years, J. Paul has proven to be the most decent human being she has ever met, not to mention the only man tough enough to handle her.

Where few men would take on the task, J. Paul not only expertly handles her, but he perfectly balances her as well. She's never been happier. Monica would never throw away her life with J. Paul for the likes of someone like Roger Fleming. She knows a fling would ruin her marriage. To Monica, some stakes just aren't worth the risk. She frowns at the mere thought of losing J. Paul. She knows he is the "good" that keeps her "bad" in check. Without him, the dark depths to which she would descend terrify even her.

Delivering a file, Dixie enters Roger's office. She abruptly stops and surveys the room. She observes the toppled chair, the closed blinds, and Roger's bleeding lip. She looks back through the doorway at the million-dollar baby putting on her shades in front of the elevator. She quickly adds the sum of the pieces. Dixie throws the file at Roger. The papers fan out into the air like huge white pieces of confetti.

Dixie yells, "Anything else, Mr. Fleming?" She doesn't wait for an answer.

Roger doesn't chase after her. Instead, he opens the blinds and peers into the parking lot. He watches Monica step into her white convertible Continental GTC. She carefully wraps a white scarf around her sleek blonde tresses. She ties the scarf around her neck and tucks the ends into the collar of her dress. He thinks about that yellow dress and all of its bumps and curves.

Roger mumbles, "I think I'm in love."

TEN

The greatest of faults, I should say, is to be conscious of none.
-Thomas Carlyle

Monica arrives earlier than usual on game day. She peers through the glass door of Mitch's office. It looks empty. She tries the handle. It's locked. She hears vacuuming and follows the sound down the hall and around the corner. She finds a woman vacuuming an area rug. After a brief exchange, she convinces her to open Mitch's office.

Watching the clock, Monica rifles through Mitch's filing cabinet. Bored with her findings, she digs through Mitch's desk, waiting for him to arrive. She mumbles, "Nothing interesting: bill, bill, bill, line-up, bill, tournament information, more bills, vendor information, and wait. What's this?" Monica guides her hand along under the glass desktop until it reaches contact with the object. She retrieves the tiny box and opens it, pulling out a small figurine.

Under the lamp, Monica holds up a miniature porcelain tennis racquet. She turns the figurine over and over. Finally, she pulls on its minute handle and out pops a flash drive. Excitedly, she mumbles, "Ooh, interesting." She ponders its possibilities and adds, "Very interesting."

Mitch arrives at 7:30 a.m. sharp. Surprised to see her sitting behind his desk, he says, "Monica. What are you doing here? The match doesn't start for another two hours." Perturbed, he notices his papers strewn across the desk and his disheveled open cabinet drawers. He says, "Find anything interesting?"

"Not at all. Your life in these four walls is positively boring." Monica discreetly tucks the tiny porcelain racquet under her leg and sits on it, chiding herself for not bringing her purse inside.

Mitch says, "Come on, Monica. You can't just rummage through my office like this. It's not right. What if I came over to your house and started going through your drawers? How would you like that?"

"Oooh. Sounds kinky."

Mitch ignores the comment and says, "Who let you in?"

"Housekeeping."

"Well?"

"Well, what?"

"Well, what are you doing in my office this early in the morning?"

"Ah, yes. The reason? The reason I am here is it is my third match with Tasha today."

"I am aware of that."

"Then, you are also aware that club policy states she can only sub three times. Today will be her third match."

"You said that already."

"Yes. Well. Worth repeating. Anyway, I brought her paperwork. She is joining the team." Monica shoves the papers toward Mitch and says, "Sign here."

Mitch says, "Look Monica, you don't decide who plays on this team. I do." He hands the papers back.

With one swipe, Monica knocks all of the papers from his desk onto the floor and places Tasha's papers neatly in the middle. She says, "This is top priority. Tasha stays. She is joining the team. With Marni gone, I need a steady partner. Tasha and I are 2:0 so far. I only won one match before she got here. Not gonna play without her. With her, I just might be able to eke out a decent season ending record." She hands Mitch a check and says, "Here. J. Paul wrote you a check for her dues. It's all here. Done."

Mitch says, "It's not done. And why is J. Paul writing her check?"

"Tasha works in her Dad's bakery. She can't possibly afford to play here, and I need her. It's that simple. J. Paul wants me happy. This will make me happy. Don't question it. Just deposit it."

"I can't take this. Monica, you know how things work around here. I already have girls waiting to come on the roster. They've paid their dues and have worked hard to move up. They would be happy to play with you. As a matter of fact, I have two players who have been on our wait list for months, and they're good. Really good. They deserve a chance. Why don't you save J. Paul his money?"

Monica looks at him as if he is joking. She says, "Tasha plays slightly above me, but not enough for opponents to isolate me. It's perfect. And I know the two girls you are speaking of. Believe me, I've been scouting them longer than you have. Both are a good level below me. Please. I couldn't possibly play with a weaker player. You owe me!"

"I *owe* you?"

"Yes."

Mitch imagines pushing Monica out of his chair and watching her land on her behind. He pictures throwing Monica out of his office by the scruff of her neck.

Monica says, "Hellooo? Earth to Mitchell Garvey. Did you hear anything that I just said?"

"What? I was just--"

"For heaven's sake. Stop spacing out! I said I want the paperwork to go through today. I'm tired of being the person who does everything. I swear this place would fall apart without me."

"I already let Tasha sub for you. I have been more than fair. Now, it's time for you to do the right thing. I'm moving a girl up. It takes years to do what these girls have done. They've earned a spot on this team. Again, you should at least give them a chance and save J. Paul his money. Do the right thing."

"Mitch, Mitch, Mitch. When do I ever do the right thing? Besides, what's a couple grand to J. Paul? He doesn't care. To tell you the truth, I am surprised you do. If I didn't know any better, I'd say you were falling out of love with me." She pats his cheek and continues, "I mean, this fills a neat little hole for you, doesn't it? And you can keep your two wait-listers on their current teams."

"They're ready. You'll see."

She walks around the desk, fixes her hair in the reflection of his glass door, and continues, "Obviously, they're doing well, or you wouldn't want to move them up. So, keep them as ringers where they are and make more bonus money at the end of the season."

"No."

She rolls her eyes and says, "Duh! It's called padding! As for Tasha, I'll make sure she fills the money pot and then some. I will book clinics, lessons, and lunches for her. Not to mention, she'll have to have matching gear with me as well. That is if she plans to be my partner. So, I will be dropping some serious dough at the pro shop for all kinds of matching stuff."

"Monica, why can't you just let things happen the way they're meant to?"

Suddenly, remembering the miniature racquet on the chair, she walks back and sits on it, concealing it from view once again. She says, "Don't be such a party pooper. This could work out very well for you, financially. Don't think 'poor Platinum Division girls'. Instead, think 'happy Mitch and happy Monica'."

Mitch says, "I'm not happy at all with this, and I'm surprised J. Paul is."

"Silly Mitch, didn't anyone ever tell you 'if Mama ain't happy, ain't nobody happy'? You know, you really should be thanking me. I know how much an empty spot on this team costs you."

"It's not always about the money, Monica. Besides, I can fill the spot. And what happens if you and Tasha start losing? What then, huh?"

"Won't happen."

"It might. Will I be stuck with a girl who doesn't belong on this team? And J. Paul, will he be stuck with a hefty and unnecessary bill? I know you. If things go awry, you'll be the first to blame her. You will insist that I find you a new partner. Will J. Paul keep paying for her then? Let's be realistic. You will have created a messy predicament; one I'd rather avoid now."

She laughs at him. She says, "Don't be ridiculous. Really. That's why I play doubles. I already know I'll blame her. Of course, I'll blame her. I always blame the other person. If I wanted to own up to anything, I would just play singles."

Despite himself, he chuckles and says, "You really are impossible, Monica."

"What's your point? Just do the paperwork on your end and I will see you on the courts." She stands, again forgetting what she sits upon. The miniature racquet falls to the floor. Mitch picks it up.

Mitch says, "Forgetting something?" He holds up the tiny piece of porcelain.

"Mitch, I was going to give it back. Honest. I just wanted to take a little look-see."

"I will save you the trouble. Nothing of interest is on here. Sandra, our CEO, wants a profile of all tennis players at Le Château. With the compiled information on this USB, she'll access information in order to expand public relations in the community, pinpoint potential donors, and better understand voting tendencies. The latter will prove extremely useful for next year's proposed twenty court expansion."

Monica says, "So scientific. You and your little data gathering. Wait. Let me get this straight. You have individual profiling on all members? On that!"

"Uh, yes."

Monica clasps her hands together and says, "Goodie! Where do I get one?"

Mitch tucks the miniature racquet in his pocket and pats it. He says, "You don't. If this got into the wrong hands, it could be a litigious nightmare for the club."

She looks at him and thinks, *He really is so sweet and innocent.*

He says, "Why are you looking at me like that?"

She says, "Your car could use some new tires. Your shoes are worn out. You need a new haircut: a month in the making. I could have you working on the public courts in no time. Don't think I won't! The pay-cut might be the tipping point for an Ivy Leaguer like yourself. Now give me the file!" She extends her open hand.

He stalls, "I am not saying 'no'. Just give me time to think about it. A day or two. That's all."

"Fair enough. I will have it, or I will have your job. Don't take too long to think." She smiles, fixes her hair in the glass door's reflection again and walks toward the gym for her pre-game workout.

Mitch yells after her, "Oh, and you won't be in the lineup today unless you pick up all of my papers you threw on the ground."

Monica turns, reenters, smiles sweetly, picks up the papers, and shoves them all into the trashcan. She says, "There. Picked up and put away. See you on the courts."

❧

Mitch wonders if he could get fired for giving Monica the USB device. However, that's not what worries him the most. If she gets a hold of it, he has little doubt many people's reputation would suffer at her hands. He thought this cushy tennis job would prove less stressful than his Wall Street job. He mutters, "I couldn't have known there would be a Monica Mooney lurking in the midst."

He takes a deep breath, and says, "I won't lose my job. Not for some bored Boca housewife."

He may have lucked into this job--thanks to his friend Todd--but he hasn't stayed here over the past three years on luck alone. His record speaks for itself. Mitch tripled tennis membership in that short amount of time. He brought seven losing teams to division titles, and some to repeat wins. He increased tennis revenue by over twenty percent per year. He's brought high profile tennis celebrities in for club exhibitions. He's booked multinational million dollar fundraisers, all helping to fund next year's expansion.

He's even improved the courts and grounds with better materials and award-winning landscaping. It didn't hurt that he acquired the best grounds keeper in all of South Florida. It took superior negotiating skill and more than a little bribery, but the tennis facility looks picture-perfect most every day. It's commonly featured on the front cover of tennis magazines, a bonus that boosts exposure and increases membership to the club. In short, Mitchell Garvey has built a heavily sought after reputation for himself. One in which he receives almost weekly calls from headhunters.

Most new Le Château residents state on their application that tennis is the number one draw to the club. That was not always the case. The club golf course used to be the main attraction, but not any longer. Tennis ranks number one thanks to Mitch's improvements and finely honed business skills.

Mitch kicks his feet up onto the glass desktop, relaxes, and takes in an easy breath. Monica is wrong about him. He might be an Ivy Leaguer, but that is not what drives him. Contrary to Monica's belief, not everyone is motivated by money, especially Mitch. Sure, he misses the old lifestyle, but he willingly made the sacrifice. He could do without the day-to-day worrying about bills, but he considers that a minor nuisance for the freedom his job offers. Other than dealing with the likes of Monica Mooney, his job brings him much enjoyment and satisfaction.

Mitch adjusts his chair and moves closer to his desk. Starting his computer, he mumbles, "Monica."

He will never go back to doing what he did before. Divine intervention brought him here, and it will take divine intervention to make him go. Mitch stares out of his window overlooking the grounds and the courts. He works in a tropical paradise and plays tennis for a living. He thinks, *There's nothing better.* He likes wearing tennis shoes everyday. He doesn't have to shave if he doesn't want to do so. He rubs his razor stubble and thinks, *Yeah, I like this job.*

Chance might have brought him here, but he will not risk leaving by chance. He looks at the porcelain racquet, and holds it up to the light. He muses, *It's a good thing Monica didn't read what is on here about her.*

Mitch swivels his chair and scans the wall behind him. He studies each picture and plaque. He's done a lot in three years. The last frame makes him stop and smile. It houses an old photograph of Todd, Mitch, and their college teammates winning the NCAA tennis championship. Like his job here at Le Château, he was handed a place on that team. He might have been given that tennis scholarship, but in the end, he earned every penny. His dad acquired the necessary letters and made the right telephone calls, but it was Mitch who made good on the investment, just as he's done here.

Mitch stands and holds the frame in his hand. Every year his team ended the season in the top ten. His last year, they won the title. His coach told him that Mitch was the main reason they won it.

After five years of not just tennis, but also academic success, Mitch graduated with a finance degree. He went on to work for a fortune one hundred investment firm on Wall Street. His parents had never been so proud, and he had never been so bored.

In a rash decision--and after a near mental breakdown-- he quit his job, moved to Florida, and never looked back. He began working for one of the top tennis training facilities. Mitch found passion on the courts that he missed trading stocks. He loved being out-of-doors, working with aspiring new talent, partying with friends at night, and occasionally traveling for tournaments. It was his dream job. A dream his parents didn't share. A couple of months into his new life in Florida, Mitch received this letter:

> Dear Mitchell,
>
> You've had your fun. Now, it is time to get back to work. I talked with Donaldson. He is willing to give you your old job back. Call him Monday at 9:00 a.m. sharp. Your mother and I are not willing to support this lifestyle change. Call me Monday afternoon.
>
> Yours Truly,
>
> Dad (and Mom)

Mitch mentally translated his Dad's letter. "You've had your fun." Really meant: *You can't be serious? Tennis? Really?*

"Now it's time to get back to work." Really meant: *Your mother and I cannot brag about you anymore.*

"I talked with Donaldson." Meaning: *You couldn't possibly get your old job back by yourself.*

"Call him at 9:00 a.m. sharp." Meaning: *I've arranged everything, so do what I say.*

"Call me Monday afternoon." Meaning: *I want to know that it is done.*

"Yours Truly." Meaning: *No love at the moment.*

Mitch crumpled the letter into a ball and threw it into the wastebasket. Come Monday, Mitch went to work as usual. No telephone calls. Come Tuesday, Mitch received an overnight envelope with a new letter. He was disinherited.

Mitch wasn't willing to give up the job he loved then, and he isn't willing to give it up now: not for Wall Street, not for his parents, and certainly not for the likes of Monica Mooney.

Mitch will play Monica's game, but only because he has to do so. He might be under Monica's thumb, but he will make sure that everyone else in the club doesn't have to be in his same predicament.

Mitch holds up the miniature racquet again. He knows if she gets a hold of this information, there will be hell to pay. Mitch opens his desk drawer and reaches for the small plastic case that housed the USB drive. He opens the top of the case, and pushes back the foam packing and flips it over. Luckily for him, this gift came as a matching pair.

He puts the empty flash drive into his computer and starts typing. *Emily Sinclair is an excellent piano player. She is allergic to shellfish. Maria and Don Martin are avid travelers and like cricket. Roy and Cecilia Fontaine live here half of the year and have three children.* He nearly puts himself to sleep with the stale entries. The more generic and boring the entries are, the better. Mitch makes sure Monica has nothing worth sinking her teeth into. *William Wagner's middle name is Oliver.*

Due to multiple interruptions, it's well after midnight before Mitch finishes the fake computer file and backs it up onto the USB's identical twin. He writes Monica's name across a small envelope and drops the USB drive into it, sealing it for good.

ELEVEN

You can discover more about a person in an hour of play
than in a year of conversation.
-Plato

Monica passes by Josie's court. She pauses to watch. Josie hits three moonballs in a row. Next, Josie lobs four out of the five shots hit to her. The fifth shot, Josie meekly volleys back into play instead of going for it.

Monica rolls her eyes and mumbles, "Ugh. I loathe little old lady tennis. I can't believe I ever wanted to play with Josie. What was I thinking?"

Mitch walks up from behind and says, "Hey Monica, I believe this is for you." He hands her the envelope with the USB drive and says, "What are you doing?"

"What do you mean 'what am I doing?' I'm watching your new recruit. The one that you spent so much time petitioning the board for."

"Yeah, she's good, right?"

"Very good. At pat-a-cake that is. If she babies the ball anymore she'll need to burp it."

"I don't know. I wouldn't say she babies it."

"Uh, yeah, she does."

"You're looking at it all wrong. It's more about how consistent she is. She hasn't missed one yet, right?"

Monica scoffs, "She doesn't belong in the Elite Division. Not if she hits the ball like that! I wouldn't even put her in the Platinum or Gold. As a matter of fact, she belongs much lower: in our lowest division, the Bronze division. Yes, that's exactly where she belongs. Bronze."

At that precise moment, Josie stops warming up and says to the other court players, "Sorry, I forgot to put on sunscreen. Just one second." She pulls out the SPF 45 from her bag and lathers on the lotion.

Monica can't help herself. She yells through the fence, "Yeah, that's right Josie! Lather it up, because you are looking more and more Bronze everyday!"

Josie looks over. She sees Monica and Mitch standing behind the fence. Monica smiles broadly and waves. Mitch stares at his shoes. Josie waves back with a confused look.

∽∾

A few yards away, Todd arrives at the clubhouse for lunch. He valet parks under the porte-cochere and walks through the main entrance. He enters under the grand staircases bookending either side of the foyer and checks in at the hostess stand. The hostess says that his party already waits. He meets his three golf buddies at a table overlooking the eighteenth hole. They eat, chat, and watch player after player putt their last hole of the day. During lunch, their conversation fades from golf to tennis and from tennis back to golf.

Suddenly, Todd remembers today is Josie's match day. He stands and says, "This has been fun, but if you'll excuse me gentlemen, I have a little sister to annoy. We should do this again soon."

Before they let him leave, the men check their calendars and set another date and time for lunch. Todd takes the shortcut through the tennis pro shop and down The Breezeway. He easily picks out Josie's brown wavy ponytail from yards away. He finds an empty seat and watches her match. He spectates a measly three games, when he can take no more. Stunned at her new brand of tennis, he sets out in search of Mitch.

He sees Mitch walking behind the match courts with his iPad in hand, taking notes as he goes. Todd catches up to Mitch, matching stride for stride.

Walking in sync, Todd says, "Let me see that." He grabs Mitch's iPad and scrolls until he finds Josie's profile.

Mitch grabs for the iPad and says, "Hey! Give me that back."

Todd blocks and pulls up Josie's statistics. He says, "Only two errors, but zero winners. And you're OK with that?"

Mitch says, "Sure. Two errors? Why shouldn't I be?"

Todd says, "Because she has weapons for one thing. What happened?"

"Nothing happened."

"Really? Because normally, I would be happy to see only two errors. But wow! Come on! Doesn't it bother you that Josie is at the business end of her second set and she has zero winners?"

"No."

"With a forehand weapon like hers, she should have winners in the double digits by now. Don't you think?"

Mitch says, "No, I don't. I try not to think. You should try it. Give me that. I'm busy."

"You're not worried?"

"About what?"

Todd watches Josie moonball another shot, and says, "About that! If that doesn't worry you, then something is wrong with you."

Next, Josie hits a lob from an offensive position. Todd says, "And that! Holy Crap! What did you do with my sister?"

Mitch says, "Calm down."

Josie rushes the net, but instead of stabbing her volley she dinks a short angled dropshot her opponent easily runs down.

Todd says, "What kind of shot making is that? I'm not even sure that is Josie. I mean it looks like her, but it sure doesn't play tennis like her."

"I don't know what you are talking about."

Todd gives Mitch a knowing look and says, "Yeah, right." Mitch looks quickly down at his iPad.

Todd says, "OK. What is going on?"

Mitch says, "I'm serious. I don't know what you are talking about. Again, why would I be worried? I am definitely not worried."

"Well, I am." Todd watches Josie receive another easy volley. Instead of putting it away, she softly pushes it deep. It's well placed, but her opponents run it down again and rip it up the line for a winner.

Todd says, "I take that back. I am not worried. I'm downright terrified."

'Oh, come on."

"Seriously, what have you done with her?"

Josie moves back for an overhead. Instead of smashing it, she takes fifty percent power off of her swing and angles the ball to the side. It's the right placement, but the pace proves too slow. Her opponent gets to the ball in plenty of time and hits a hard, deep ball down the middle for yet another winner.

Todd covers his mouth. Finally, he says, "Wow. If that doesn't worry you then I need to check your pulse."

Mitch says, "I think you're overreacting. She has a winning record. Besides, it doesn't worry me. Why should it? Stats change from match to match. It looks like she figured out she needs to play defense today."

Todd says, "Defense? Is that what you're calling that? What's offense? Using a walker to reach your overhead? How many lobs does she have?" Todd grabs the iPad again.

Mitch says, "We don't keep up with those."

Todd says, "I can see why. You'd run out of storage space on your app. It's a regular lobfest out there!"

Mitch attempts to change the subject. He says, "When are you getting back on the courts? I haven't seen you out here in a while."

Todd changes the subject right back. He says, "Saturday. Mixed doubles. I was going to ask Josie to sub in with me, but not if she is going to play moonball tennis like that! My grandma plays more exciting tennis!"

Mitch says, "I know your grandma, and she doesn't play tennis at all. Besides, I don't know what you mean."

Todd says, "Uh-huh. OK. Fine. I'll be right back." Todd walks to the locker room, grabs the duffle bag out of his locker, and hurriedly changes into his tennis gear. Forgetting to change his socks, he wears an all white tennis ensemble with black work socks. He arrives at the courts just as Josie finishes.

Josie towels off and puts an icepack on her neck. She peels off her wet socks and puts on her sandals. Her feet look like raisins. She says to her brother, "Hi stranger! I saw you watching. How'd we do?"

Todd doesn't answer the question. He says, "Hey Jo, got a minute to hit?"

"What? Now? I just got off the court."

"It won't take long. Maybe fifteen minutes."

"I was going to eat lunch with my teammates."

"You still can. Like I said, just a few minutes."

"I would, but I don't have any dry socks." She holds up the soggy pair she just took off and says, "No way I'm putting these back on. Another time?"

Todd grabs a clean pair of white socks out of his bag and says, "Here."

She sits back down, puts on his socks, and says, "Don't you have work or something?" The white socks come up to her shins.

"Yeah. So hurry up."

"Geez. Nice to see you, too."

Todd hits medium-paced groundstrokes. Josie moonballs the returns with heavy topspin. She lobs roughly every third shot.

Todd says, "Why are you lobbing me?"

"What do you mean?"

"I am on the baseline. Why would you lob somebody on the baseline?"

She says, "Oh, you know, to mix things up."

He doesn't like that answer or what he sees. This brand of tennis is not Josie. He wonders where she hides her monster forehand. He hits her volleys at the net. Like always, her footwork remains impeccable. However, instead of punching her volleys, Josie hits soft finesse angles.

Todd says, "Do you mix it up? You know, punch it sometimes? Or only finesse?"

"Mitch says that placement is key. I rarely miss now. I take some off and just place it. It's incredibly effective."

"Effective for what? Lulling your opponents to sleep?"

"Are you here just to insult me?"

'Sorry." Todd says, "OK, but all the time? What about power?"

"Tennis is a game of control."

Unimpressed, Todd says, "Yeah, of course it is. And calculated risk; otherwise, we really would all fall asleep." He mumbles, "And, if I have to watch you play like this any longer, I will."

"What?"

"Nothing, just talking to myself."

"That's a sign of insanity."

"No, it's not. Only if I start answering."

Todd feeds Josie some overheads. She pushes all of them back. He wonders if some possible reason exists why she won't hit the ball. Todd says, "Is your shoulder hurting you?"

"What? No! Why would my shoulder be hurting me?"

"I dunno. You just seem to be hitting differently."

"Yeah. OK. It's my neck."

Todd looks relieved, "Aah. Your neck. Ok. Did you pull a muscle? Pinch a nerve?"

Josie loses her patience and yells, "No! I've got a pain in the neck right across the net from me that just won't go away. Are you trying to drive me crazy? I just played two hours of tennis in one-hundred-degree heat. All I want to do is get off of the court!"

Josie walks off of the court and puts her racquet away. She says, "My friends are all happily chatting and eating and having a good time. And you! You're torturing me for no apparent reason. Honestly, I feel as if I am getting a checkup at the doctor's office."

"The doctor's office?"

"Yes! *Check out Josie's overhead. Check out Josie's groundstrokes. Check out Josie's volleys.* Really? Now, tell me. What are you up to?"

Todd decides to dodge the bullet until he speaks with Mitch first. He says, "OK, go ahead and meet up with your friends. I just needed a break from work. That's all."

Instantly, Josie changes her tone, "Oh, OK. I'm sorry. I didn't realize you were having a bad day. Is everything all right?"

"Yes. Fine. Just needed to get out for a minute."

She hugs him, "OK. Sorry for yelling at you. You're not a pain in the neck. Well, not today anyway."

Todd has seen enough to understand where the source of Josie's sudden transformation originates. He walks to Mitch's office and finds Mitch sitting alone behind his desk, eating and working.

Todd knocks on the open door and says, "Nice team victory today. Congratulations, coach!"

Using the back of his hand, Mitch wipes mustard from his mouth. He says, "Thanks. It's been a good day."

Todd says, "I gotta get back to work, so I'll make this quick. I don't want Josie playing little old lady tennis anymore. She looks miserable even if she says she isn't. She needs to swing out on the ball and be challenged. You forget that this is therapy for her. Challenge her."

Mitch says, "I don't know what you are talking about."

Todd says in a deadpan tone, "Right."

Mitch chews another bite of his Reuben sandwich, chasing it down with a gulp of electrolyte water. He brushes the crumbs off of his desk and out of his well-manicured, dark razor stubble. Because Todd is an old friend, Mitch decides to come clean. He says, "I don't have a partner for Vivian. She deserves one. She's a great lady, and she knows her tennis. I couldn't run this team without her. I wouldn't want to. But, no one at this level wants to play with her for exactly the reason you just mentioned. They don't want to play little old lady tennis."

"So bring someone on board."

Mitch sits on the edge of his desk and continues, "Hear me out. Josie, as you know, is coming off of a tough divorce and mentally is not in a great place. She's got to toughen up for match play. Her confidence is shot. You know you need confidence to win, and not just that; tennis isn't fun if you constantly get beat up, not physically, but emotionally."

"Josie isn't going to gain confidence by playing down a level. She's going to gain confidence by being challenged and overcoming those challenges. You, better than anyone, should know that."

Mitch looks at the remnants of his sandwich and suddenly loses his appetite. He says, "Look, Josie gets knocked down everyday. She lets it happen. Heck, she almost asks for it. I don't know what else to do. Right now, she needs a mother figure to help her through this, uh, rough patch, and to, uh, transition so to speak."

Todd says, "I agree she needs a good partner, but I don't agree with your choice."

Mitch says, "Vivian, in my opinion, is the best person for that job. Vivian nurtures. She is easy on her partner and will help build up Josie's confidence. You'll see. The only wrench is that they don't play at the same level. When I put them together, the opponents isolate Vivian."

"What's wrong with that?"

"They are scared of Josie and her big forehand. So, Vivian plays most of the match on her racquet. The match is way too lopsided. Josie maybe plays twenty percent of the points to Vivian's eighty. So, I had to, uh, change the dynamics so to speak. To make it more, uh, even."

Todd shakes his head.

Mitch says, "Come on. If you were in my shoes, you would do the same exact thing and you know it. Ask Josie if she is happy. I'll bet the answer will surprise you."

Todd says, "I don't have to ask."

"This is confidence building."

"No, this is padding."

"Give me a break."

"This is better for everyone except Josie. Fix it, Mitch. She deserves better, and you know it."

"Does everyone have to come in here making demands?"

"Fix it."

"Great! *Fix it, Mitch. Fix it, Mitch.* That's all I hear. I should pour a giant bottle of Gorilla Glue over the club sticking people into their proper places."

"Gorilla glue?"

"That'll fix it!"

"You're not making any sense."

Mitch says, "Fine. I'll fix it."

"Uh, thanks."

Mitch says, "Yeah. No problem. Nice socks." Todd still wears his black work socks with his white tennis clothes.

Todd replies, "Nice bandana."

Mitch adjusts the bandana and says, "What? Bandanas are cool."

"Correction. They were cool. Back in the nineties."

"At least, I'm not wearing my Dad's work socks." Mitch raises an eyebrow.

Todd says, "Maybe you should. You could wrap them around your head instead of that stupid bandana. It would look better."

They both laugh.

Mitch stops laughing. With a concerned look he says, "We good?"

Todd says, "Only if you let me borrow your Grandma's bandana." Todd exaggerates rubbing his chin and says, "Maybe I'll join you in the nineties and grow out a 90210 mini-beard, too. Are you Brandon or Dylan? With the highlights, I am guessing Dylan. I could be Brandon."

Despite himself, Mitch chuckles. They bump fists, lock grips, and bump shoulders. It's the closest they'll ever get to a hug.

Todd steals Mitch's bandana, wraps it around his own head, and runs down the hall yelling, "Mitch is my idol! I love the nineties! Mitch is my idol!" They cannot see it from opposite ends of the corridor, but they both smile at the same time.

Mitch mumbles, "It's good to have things back to normal."

People stop what they are doing and watch Todd run down the corridor past their glass cubicles. One of Mitch's spa managers exits her cubicle and enters Mitch's office. She asks, "Can you sign this for me, please?"

Mitch says, "Sure."

She says, "That guy running down the hall, was that a diaper on his head?"

Mitch says, "Yes."

ॐॐ

Mitch is not looking forward to telling Vivian she is without a partner once again. He looks at his half-eaten sandwich. After losing his appetite, he can't stomach the rest and throws it away. He takes the stairs and approaches the team's luncheon. As he arrives, he finds the entire Elite team laughing, eating, and reliving a few key points in the matches. Josie sits in the middle of the uproar.

Mitch thinks, *This is what it is all about. Who cares if you moonball or not?* Instead of saying how he feels, he says, "Josie, finish up and meet me on Grandstand Red in five minutes. Ceridwin, you too."

Ceridwin gathers her gear and mumbles to Josie, "Miss Popular. It seems that everyone wants to hit with you today."

Josie says, "Yep. Something is definitely up. I just don't know what."

Once on the court, Mitch feeds ball after ball into play as he stands behind Josie. Ceridwin moves Josie left, then right, and throws in a few drop shots. Josie runs. A lot. Ceridwin rushes in and takes Josie's rollers out of the air with swinging volleys, crushing winner after winner. Josie's lower paced balls prove too juicy for Ceridwin. Ceridwin tees off on almost every shot.

Mitch coaches Josie through the rallies. Mitch says, "Josie, prepare early. You don't have time for that big backswing with Ceridwin. See. It's on you too quickly. Adjust. Adjust. Feet. Feet. Feet. That's it. More load. More. No. Don't decelerate. Racquet head speed. More. That's it. Turn. Turn. Turn. Load. More load. Follow all the way through. Don't hesitate. Hit out earlier. Yes, that's it, but earlier."

It takes an hour and some change to fix what he broke. Mitch plans to see Josie a couple of more times before next week's match. He will need to reinforce today's work and prepare her for playing a couple of lines up, where she belongs. Now, if only he can find her--and now Vivian--a willing partner. No one wants to play with either.

Mitch packs up his gear, and heaves a heavy sigh. However, his goodwill didn't go unnoticed. Ceridwin waits until Josie leaves the court and is well out of earshot. She approaches Mitch and says, "Don't second guess yourself. You did the right thing."

TWELVE

When I see the elaborate study and ingenuity displayed by women in the pursuit of trifles, I feel no doubt of their capacity for the most herculean undertakings.
-Julia Ward Howe

Monica tells Mitch, "You can forget it if you think I'm playing with Josie! You'll have to find someone else! Good luck!"

Mitch wants to tell Monica this whole predicament is her fault. If she hadn't pushed to play with Josie, Marni, and then with Tasha, the lineup wouldn't be messed up in the first place. Mitch says, "More demands? You can't leave well enough alone, can you?"

Monica laughs and says, "Well enough alone? Save your idioms. I am not interested in anything well. Haven't you realized by now that I am unsatisfied unless a wall of fire follows me wherever I go?"

Mitch imagines Monica sprouting a wall of fire, and then it turning on her.

Monica says, "Wipe that silly look off of your face! Did you hear me? I asked you if you added Tasha, yet?"

Mitch says, "What? Oh. You have to play with Josie. Just this once. I am out two players this week. Next week I'll have a full roster. I will play you with Natasha then."

Monica says, "Did you add her to the team or not?"

Mitch concedes, "If you play with Josie today, I will. I'll call today to make sure she is eligible for next week's play."

Monica says, "Oh, she's eligible! Very well, then. Normally, I wouldn't bother bargaining with you, but since you are being a good boy and doing as I say, I'll do it. But only just this once. So, don't get used to my graciousness. And if today doesn't go well, then I'll fake an injury and get off of the court as soon as possible."

Mitch takes in a deep breath and lets it out slowly, counting to ten. He reminds himself that dealing with the Monicas of the world takes up only a small portion of his day. He says, "Don't do that Monica. Give it your all, win or lose. It's just one match. Most importantly, have fun."

Monica says, "Rah, rah," and walks out.

Tennis is more than a game to Monica. She has spent thousands of dollars per year over the last eleven years improving her game. She dedicates much of her week to improving her skill level. Tennis isn't part of her life; it is her life. She considers her identity justified by each and every performance. Not only does she feel that each win verifies her self-worth, but so does each designer bag or custom outfit. Her self-worth wraps tightly around her Swarovski encrusted racquet. Self-branding is her preoccupation. Monica intends to dominate, whether with her tennis or with her in-your-face style. She doesn't care whom she takes down along the way or what it costs.

Monica slings her navy racquet bag with its fine caning trim over her shoulder. She finds Josie in the indoor pool area filling her cup with ice. Monica grabs her arm viciously. Ice flings everywhere.

Josie says, "Hey! What are you doing?"

Monica says, "We need to talk. Let's go. I've played these girls before. I've got my strategy."

Josie pulls her arm away. She says, "Stop! That hurts."

Monica says, "Don't be such a baby, Josie. I barely touched you. Now come on!"

She leads Josie into the locker room. Monica pushes open the swinging locker room door. She ushers Josie across the mosaic tiles, past the shower stalls, through the locker area, and into the sauna. She slides the glass door closed behind them. Monica points to a teak serenity chair and pulls out of her bag a twelve-inch, dry-erase board. She motions for Josie to sit.

Josie cannot believe her eyes. *Is she kidding? A dry-erase board? Really? Who does she think she is? Pete Carroll?* Josie gets up to leave. She says, "This is too much Monica, even for you."

Monica shoves her back into her seat. Josie says, "Monica stop! You're hurting me!"

Monica says, "Sit down and shut up! We have only a few minutes before we meet the other team. I want to go over some plays. Stop wasting time."

They hear a locker door slam. Ceridwin walks around the corner. She opens the sliding door and sees Josie. Surveying the newly pressed fingernail marks on Josie's arm, Ceridwin says, "What's all of this about? Is there a problem here?"

Josie begins to speak, but Monica cuts her off and talks over her. Monica says, "No. We were just going over a few, uh, plays. Right, Josie?"

Josie takes the last remaining piece of ice out of her cup and applies it to the red mark swelling on her arm. She says, "No! We were not!" She walks out with Ceridwin.

Monica hurls her dry-erase board against the wall, shattering it into pieces. She lets out a shriek and then says under her breath, "You should have listened. You'll regret that!"

Monica catches up to Ceridwin and Josie on The Breezeway. She says to Josie, "Fine. Have it your way. See you on Court Three."

Josie arrives on the court. Without looking at her, Monica announces, "They've already warmed up. Josie, you'll have to start without a warm-up."

Josie says, "Fortunately, I already warmed up with Mitch."

Monica mimics, "Fortunately, I already warmed up with Mitch. Good. You'll need it!"

Josie asks Monica, "Do you mind if I play the deuce side?"

Monica says, "These are things to settle before you get on the court, Josie. If you wanted to talk strategy or formation adjustments, then you should have spent time talking with your partner, pre-game. You had your chance. Now, get on the Ad side."

Josie says, "But we both play deuce, and you got to play deuce last time. It's only fair."

Monica laughs and says, "Fair? Who said anything about fair?" Monica walks to the deuce side to return the first serve of the match.

Josie gives up, turns to her opponents and says, "Nice match ladies. Have fun!"

Monica wrinkles her nose and mocks her again, "*Nice match ladies. Have fun!*"

Whenever she can, Monica feeds medium-paced high sitters to her opponents' forehands at the net. Each sitter comes with its own personal invitation to cream Josie at the net. The net person wastes no time accepting and slamming one volley winner after another repeatedly at Josie's head and torso. Josie stands helplessly across the net. Too numerous, she gives up counting the newly emerging bruises.

Monica laughs to herself, "This is more fun than I ever imagined!" Less than halfway through the first set Josie has been hit twelve times. Monica knows. She's been counting. She smiles and says under her breath, "That must be some sort of new record."

Monica may want to win most days, but not today. Today, she wants to lose big. As a matter of fact, she wants to make the match such a painful disaster that she will never be asked to play with Josie again. Ever. She smiles, certain that after today's match, Mitch will never again ask her to do so. Monica surmises that Josie will back up that sentiment. Monica calculates the loss, its ramifications, and considers today a monumental victory of sorts.

Monica feels a tingle tickle up her spine just thinking about what else she will do during today's match to put Josie in harm's way. Giddily, she watches as her opponents close in on the feeding frenzy. Daringly, Monica grows bolder with her set-ups. She begins hitting short lobs. The opponents don't need to move a foot. The short lobs fall perfectly onto their racquets. They nail overhead after overhead directly at Josie, the net person.

It never occurs to Josie that Monica intentionally does this. She chalks Monica's poor shot-making performance to her merely having an off day. Josie says nothing to Monica. She cuts her some slack. *Everyone has a bad day every now and then.* Monica hits another sitter that Josie takes in the stomach. *Ouch. Even Monica.*

Neither does Josie blame her opponents for their barrage of stinging hits. Although it would be politer for them to hit an angle off of the court or at her feet, Josie reasons they are only doing as they are taught. When you have an overhead, you put it away. That means taking out the net person. She doesn't take the barrage personally.

Nearing the end of the first set, Monica finally loses count of how many times Josie takes a hit. The epic beat down continues. Monica lost count somewhere after thirty-two strikes. She thinks, *It's like trying to count points on a pinball machine: 8, 9, 10-11, 12-13-14-15, 16, 17, 18-19-20-21-22. Ping. Ping. Ping-ping. Ping-ping-ping-ping. Ping. Ping. Ping-ping-ping-ping. Delicious.*

Monica relishes every hit as if she delivered it herself. She never knew losing could be so enjoyable. She thinks, *Josie will be back to the ice machine before she knows it. This time the ice won't be for her cup.* A giggle escapes her. She disguises it with a cough.

Josie watches as bruises transform from vague circular marks into delineated round hues of red, purple, and a tinge of blue. Still, it doesn't occur to her that Monica coolly calculates each of those marks. Josie would never accuse her own partner of setting her up for such a beat down. She simply doesn't think like that.

Josie finally gives up and says, "Monica, I don't feel as though I am much help at the net. Maybe we should play two back for a bit." She doesn't say it, but she'd like a break from the barrage.

Monica says, "No, no. You stay up. Let's not give up more territory. Stand your ground! Keep your racquet out in front. I know you're not playing well today, but just think 'reflex volley'. Try harder. They're just better than you."

Josie detects a smile on Monica's face. In a flash, the smile disappears. Josie asks, "Did you just smile?"

"No. Why would I smile? We're losing."

Chalking Monica's smile up to her imagination, Josie shrugs it off. She hustles back to the net, takes her position, and tries her best to reflex volley.

Monica watches Josie's earnest efforts and thinks, *Gawd! What a total dodo! In the wild she would be extinct.* Monica hits another short lob. The opponent pounds a swinging volley right into Josie's thigh, leaving Josie hopping. The opponent raises her hand in apology.

Monica rolls her eyes, and thinks, *What an idiot! Josie deserves to be extinct. Mankind would be better off!* Monica can't believe the blind level of trust Josie so freely gives out to seemingly anyone, especially her. She feels no pity for Josie, quite the opposite. Monica mumbles, "If she can't take care of herself, she might as well paint a target on back."

Mitch walks behind their court. He doesn't need to consult his iPad to understand exactly what's going on. He gets it. He's not allowed to give coaching advice during a match, but this is the one time he is willing to risk the penalty. Mitch yells, "Josie, get out of the hotseat. Play two back for the rest of the match."

Josie says, "OK."

Monica yells to Mitch, "I don't want to give up the net."

Mitch yells, "I can see why. Play two back. Now!"

One opponent yells, "Hey! No coaching."

Mitch holds up a hand in apology.

Monica seethes under her breath. She shoots Mitch a steely glare. In essence, he stole her prey, and she wasn't done devouring it. Monica says to Josie, "This is a mistake. Stay where you are."

Mitch overhears and says, "Two back the rest of the match, period. We'll talk about the mistake later."

Monica shoots him another look and mumbles, "Just when I was having fun!"

Josie stays back. The opponents have isolated Josie for so long that they continue to do so out of habit. Practically every ball goes to her, though she no longer sits at the net.

Josie puts to work the practice sessions Mitch ran her through over the previous week. With her confidence shaken from the beating, she reminds herself of Mitch's words. *Don't think. Just hit.* She pumps herself up remembering that Mitch was so pleased with the week's work that he renamed her forehand: Jo's Mojo. *Come on, Jo's Mojo.*

She steadies her nerves and unleashes Jo's Mojo again and again. She pulls her opponents off court with inside out forehands, and then rips down-the-line winners. Josie does come to the net, but this time on her own terms and to put away the ball. She controls the rest of the set from the back of the court: the opposite of what she has been taught for doubles, but Josie's weapons are enough. Down 1:5, Josie and Monica close the first set out at 7:5.

Monica lays her trap and says, "I guess you didn't get the memo. Club players don't win doubles from the baseline, even Elite players. You need to get back to the net again."

Josie smiles and says, "Tell that to Jo's Mojo?"

"Who?"

"Never mind."

"I really think you should move up to the net."

"Nope. Just doing what Mitch said."

It takes their opponents a while to remove the target on Josie's back and place it onto Monica's. At 3:1 in the second set, they tire of Josie's blistering groundstrokes. Suddenly, they change tactics and isolate Monica. Though she and Josie are up a break and have a real chance to win, Monica—still bent on this match going down in flames--continues to intentionally miss-hit the ball. She strings together error after error.

Instead of growing angry at Monica's poor performance, Josie sympathizes. *This has to be Monica's worst day ever.* She imagines Monica must feel humiliated and, at the very least, completely frustrated.

Josie--assuming Monica is down in the dumps--says, "Come on, Monica. You can do it!" Josie hears Monica mumble, but can't decipher what she says.

Put off by Josie's incessant positive encouragement, Monica purposely shanks the next ball over the fence. Their opponents stop and stare at the wild miss-hit.

Under her breath, Monica mumbles, "What do you have to say about that, Josie? What? No 'almost Monica' or 'good try, Monica'?"

Josie says, "What?"

Monica says, "I said 'oopsy'."

Neither Josie nor the opponents say anything as they watch the ball roll into The Breezeway. Monica smirks and mumbles under her breath again, "I thought so. You've got nothing to say about that one now, do you!"

Josie says, "What was that?"

"I said 'go team go'!"

Josie says, "That's the attitude! Just focus on the ball, Monica. You'll find your rhythm. Hang in there."

Monica rolls her eyes and mumbles, "Saint Josie."

Josie says, "What?"

"Nothing." Monica continues to throw the match. She hits everything out. That is until a pivotal moment occurs.

One opponent says, "That's it! Hit everything to Monica." She wags her finger toward Monica.

The other opponent says, "Yeah. She can't handle our pace."

The first opponent says, "Yeah, or our superior shot making!"

Monica smiles at their assessment until she hears one of her opponents whisper too loudly, "Yeah, she shouldn't even be in this division. She sucks."

The words sting and are meant to send her game further into the toilet, but the opposite proves true. Monica grows angry. Very, very angry.

The words fuel energy from every part of Monica's body, culminating into a central powerhouse of what can only be described as frenetic tennis fury. Fantastically, she transforms before their eyes. She hits approach shot after approach shot, following the ball in to the net. She's not content with just putting the ball away. Instead, she makes them pay.

Monica places the volley to the opponent's weakest point and waits patiently for the weak reply. Then, she unleashes a smashing overhead to their stomach, or hip, or in the last case, the face. She wants to hurt them, and make them pay for ever questioning her ability.

Josie says, "Geez Monica, you don't have to get back at them for targeting me earlier."

"You think I'm doing this for you?"

"Aren't you?"

"Think again."

Josie, erroneously, thinks Monica sticks up for her. Also incorrect, she thinks Monica's big turnaround is due in part to her unwavering support. Josie knows that everyone has a bad day from time to time. *It's important, as a partner, to stay positive in order to help her out of the slump. Positivity: that's what she needs.*

She claps as Monica threads the needle down the middle for yet another winner. Josie says, "Great shot, Monica!"

Monica says, "Please, shut up."

Their opponents walk off of the courts hanging their heads. They commiserate loudly enough for Monica to hear. One says, "They got the momentum in the end. If we rode it out a little bit longer, we would have gotten it back."

Her partner says, "Yeah. Just like we did after the first set."

Monica dislikes an ungracious loser, even more than she hates a cheerleader for a partner. She wants her opponents to roll over and die graciously. So, she in turn says loudly enough for them to hear, "I hope their momentum is enough to carry them through the parking lot and to their cars." They both shoot her a nasty look.

Monica sits courtside. She tells Josie not to wait for her. Monica folds her sweaty tennis towel into a plastic bag and packs it into her navy tennis bag. She never sweats this much, but the last few games proved unusually laden with hard work. She smiles. She more than made up for lost ground.

She checks her makeup in a hand mirror and fixes her blonde bob just so. Monica pulls off her tennis shoes and sticks in her custom-made shoe deodorizers. She shoves the deodorizers--made to look like yellow, squishy tennis balls— deep into the toe box of each shoe. Next, she peels off the wet socks that cling like slippery banana skins. She places them inside the plastic bag with her shoes. She takes out her one hundred dollar flip-flops and slides her French pedicured feet into the openings. She mutters, "Aaah, better."

Embarrassed to admit it, battling foot fungus continues to plague her in these humid, sweaty conditions. The moisture in the South Floridian heat creates the perfect breeding ground for germs inside her moist tennis shoes. Per her dermatologist's recommendation, airing them out immediately after each match helps, but not entirely. She waits until no one is around and applies the prescribed antifungal foot cream. At that precise moment, Mitch leans over the back of her chair.

She jumps and says, "Oh. Mitch! I didn't see you there."

Mitch says, "Don't ever do that again."

Monica knows exactly what he is talking about. Instead of saying so, she says, "What? Win?"

Undeterred, Mitch says, "Not to Josie and not to anyone else on this team." He waits for eye contact and says, "Do I make myself clear?"

For the first time in the three years since she has known Mitchell Garvey, she is speechless. Something in Mitch's tone catches her off guard. She gets the impression that Mitch will win this argument at any cost. Monica only likes to play games where she can win. She nods agreeably.

THIRTEEN

Whenever evil befalls us, we ought to ask ourselves, after the first suffering, how can we turn it into good. So shall we take occasion, from one bitter root, to raise perhaps many flowers.
-Leigh Hunt

Josie rotates the ice pack, icing different bruises throughout the team luncheon. She can't decide which bruise hurts worse. Consequently, she can't decide which spot to ice.

Ceridwin says, "That's a lot of bruising for just one match."

"Tell me about it. Not my lucky day."

"What happened?"

"We started out slowly. We didn't hit the ball like we should. They took advantage. We were tentative. It's almost as if we were feeding them." She laughs and shrugs, "Anyway, I got a few reminders of what not to do next time."

Ceridwin says, "I see. How may bruises did Monica get?"

Josie says, "I don't know. Not sure. Maybe none. Yeah. I think none. Lucky her!" She laughs again.

Ceridwin eyes Monica at the end of the table. Monica hasn't missed a word of their conversation. Ceridwin says to Josie, but looks directly at Monica while speaking, "Yes, a little too lucky if you ask me."

Monica blushes.

Ceridwin dings her crystal goblet with the end of a long, silver iced-tea spoon. She looks around the table as her colleagues quiet down. Each person sets her polished silverware down in its respective place, wipes her mouth, and drops her napkin back into her lap, waiting.

Ceridwin picks up the oversized white and blue hydrangea centerpiece and moves it off of the pressed linen tablecloth and onto a side buffet. She smiles and says, "Much better. Now, I can see everyone." She stands in front of her chair and begins an announcement.

She says, "Ladies, Violet and I have been talking. Most of us have known Marni Schoppelmann for years. I don't need to speak as to what a great person she is. I think we all know that. And we know that she didn't steal anyone's wallet or cell phone. And we certainly know that she didn't break into Violet's home and steal her belongings."

Violet stands next to Ceridwin and says, "That's right!"

Nods in agreement spread around the table. Ceridwin holds up a piece of paper with signatures scribbled on it. She continues, "So, per Violet's request, I have written a petition asking for Marni to be reinstated to all club activities at Le Château, including tennis."

Ceridwin looks around the table. She says, "If anyone here is uncomfortable with that, please speak up. I don't mean to put you on the spot, but this petition needs to be unanimous in order for our board to accept it. So, if you feel like you cannot sign the petition, please let us know. We certainly don't want to pressure anyone into doing anything they're not comfortable with doing."

Ceridwin passes around the paper. Everyone signs. That is everyone except for Monica Mooney.

Monica looks at the petition written on Marni's behalf and frowns. She grows sicker by the moment as she stares at the paper. She doesn't want a nagging reminder--namely Marni Schoppelmann--around the club. She wants Marni to go away, disappear, forever. Monica thinks, *I already got rid of Marni once. Do I have to do it again?*

In truth--and granted not a strong one--Monica does have a conscience. She doesn't want Marni around for one simple fact. She can't stand being reminded of the horrible thing she has done to such a sweet person.

Like all things unsavory in Monica's past, she shuts the door instead of dealing with the issues head-on. Monica thinks that having Marni around will be much like having a stain in the carpet. No matter how beautiful a room may look, her eyes will always drift back to the blemish, staining her beautiful surroundings. She mumbles, "I like my carpet the way it is." She doesn't want Marni back.

The woman seated to her right says, "There's no carpet here on the veranda. Tile. It's all tile."

Monica ignores the woman, and holds the petition in her trembling hands. She mumbles, "Many think I'm ruthless, but I'm not immune to the pang of guilt."

The woman seated next to her says, "I'm sorry, what?"

Monica replies, "Mind your own business." She pushes away her momentary hesitation and mumbles, "It has to be done. Time to move on."

The woman next to her says, "Move where?"

Monica says, "I thought I told you to mind your own business."

"You did."

"Well then, mind your own business."

Monica pings her water goblet with her knife. She stands, waves the petition and says, "This is all well and good. And don't think I don't appreciate charity when I see it. By all means, I do, but in good conscience I cannot sign this. Consider what the community will think." Monica pushes her chair back and walks around the table, forming her words pensively as she walks.

Ceridwin whispers to Violet, "Who does she think she is?"

"Dunno. Perry Mason?"

Monica's soggy feet squish-squash in her flip-flops as she circles slowly around the ten-person table. She brushes her hand along the tops of the tall ladder-back chairs. Today, the clubhouse dining room overscheduled with three major events, pushing the tennis team luncheon onto the third floor veranda.

Monica doesn't mind. The view from the veranda sweeps along the golf course greens below. She positions herself between two pink flowered hanging baskets. She leans against the white stone railing under the navy and white striped awning. Beyond the table, she catches a glimpse of her reflection in the double glass doors leading from the veranda into the building. She turns. Standing here, she sees through the veranda's stucco arches and onto the greens below. Turning back, she sees her own reflection again. Yes, she likes this spot. The view suits her. While Monica addresses the women seated at the table, she keeps her eyes focused on her own reflection.

An overhead cloud moves away. The clay barrel tile roof from above juts slightly over the edge of the building, casting a long shadow over part of the table. Many seated in the sun put their visors back on.

Monica hears a door shut. She looks over the railing to see golfers exiting the story below before riding their carts to their first hole. The wind suddenly sweeps across the golf course green, up the back of the building, and billows through the navy and white awning overhead. The gust sweeps Monica's blonde silken tresses, brushing them into her face at sharp angles. She pushes her platinum strands to the side using one bright red fingernail as a barrette.

The waiters clear the table and set a three-tiered doily-lined dessert tray in the middle. Distracted by the tray laden with confectionery treasures, she briefly stops speaking. Everyone knows to leave the chocolate peppermint bark for Monica. Monica is a peppermint fanatic. It's the one culinary vice in which she allows herself to heartily indulge.

Monica says, "As I was saying, I can already hear what the other competing clubs in Boca Raton will be saying if we let complete criminals roam our facilities freely. It will affect membership, not to mention housing value. I'm sorry. I hate to sound like a killjoy, but we must think of the welfare of the club, despite our obviously dear feelings for Marni."

Ceridwin stands again, but Monica plows on, "The petition is simply a bad idea for all of us. We need to protect the club's best interest and ours as well. Really. I say Marni goes."

Violet takes off her white tennis hat, causing the gathered cornrows of braids to loosely fall around her shoulders. She says, "If I don't have a problem with Marni, then nobody else should either, including you!" She shoots Monica a look. Violet continues, "Especially you! You were her partner. How could you say that? You know her better than most anyone here. Marni Schoppelmann is not a thief! Everyone knows that. And you, of all people, should be standing up for her. N-n-not condemning her!"

Ceridwin says, "I'm with Violet. Is there some other reason you don't want Marni back here? Some reason you're not telling us?"

Monica sits down abruptly. Ceridwin thinks she detects fear in Monica's eyes. By chance, Ceridwin rides on her hunch and says, "Monica, tell us what you know."

Monica feels a prickly sensation roll up the back of her neck as beads of sweat form along her brow. She says, "What? Nothing! Sorry. Call it a moment of weakness. Call me paranoid! I would do anything for Marni." Monica signs the petition and sits down quietly.

Violet says, "Good. Now that everyone has signed, I don't think I am abusing this information. I know I am not supposed to say anything yet, but the investigator thinks he found new evidence proving Marni didn't do it. There. Cat's outta the bag. But we don't need an investigator to tell us that, do we?"

Monica chokes on her peppermint bark. She swallows hard and follows with a gulp of sparkling water. She clears her throat and says, "Why? What type of evidence is it?"

Everyone looks at her.

She continues, "Is everyone forgetting about the wallet and cell phone found in Marni's tennis bag?"

Ceridwin speaks up, "Maybe I put those items in Marni's bag by accident. We were so busy chatting in the locker room that day that I might have dropped your phone and my wallet in the wrong bag. I wasn't paying attention. I saw Marni's bag open and just plopped them in there."

Monica knows this to be a lie since she was the one who put the cell phone and wallet in Marni's bag. She wants to scream, "Liar!" but she can't. Instead, she seethes silently. This unforeseen development alters her plan. She had planted the wallet and mobile phone to bring progress to her Plan A. She had hoped the progress would lead to the permanent removal of Marni Schoppelmann as her tennis partner. She thinks, *Yes. Permanent removal. Never to be heard from again.*

Ceridwin says, "I mean if I didn't mistakenly put those items in Marni's bag, then who did?" She looks directly at Monica.

Monica bristles. She finds this turn of events unsatisfactory to say the least. She needs time to clear her mind and think about this new piece added to the puzzle. Unsure of how or where this new piece fits, she chews on the rough cuticle surrounding her right thumbnail. She wonders, *What could Ceridwin possibly hope to gain by lying?* It never occurs to Monica that Ceridwin lies not for personal gain, but to protect someone else. Someone Ceridwin wholeheartedly believes to be wronged. Monica doesn't comprehend this type of selflessness.

Monica says to Ceridwin, "Even if you made that mistake, you have to be careful." She returns the knowing look and adds, "One bad apple can spoil the whole bunch."

Ceridwin says, "I was thinking the same exact thing."

Monica stands again and shouts, "Are you calling me a bad--"

Ceridwin cuts her off and says, "We are trying to have Marni's back. What are you trying to do?"

"But--"

"But what? This can't be easy for her. She could use a friend-- *friends*, right now."

Monica silently curses Ceridwin and her do-gooder motives. She notices Ceridwin and Violet whisper something before looking at her. Certain they know something, she thinks, *But I've been so meticulously careful. Ugh! I'm too exhausted to think any more*. She pulls out her phone and books a massage for later in the afternoon. Monica waits until everyone leaves. She follows Violet to the mudroom by the lockers.

Violet cleans the clay from the bottom of her shoes. She places one tennis shoe on the low bristled rack and pushes the lever down until the spray hits the bottom of her shoe. As the water washes the excess clay away, she waits for the stream to run clear before switching feet. Next, Violet releases the lever and brushes her shoes against the tough bristles on the mounted shoe rack by the door, freeing any remaining debris

Monica says, "I forgot to do that."

Violet turns to see Monica opening her tennis bag and says, "I didn't hear you come in."

Monica says, "Snuck up on you, did I? Ha-ha!"

She takes the deodorizers out and puts the shoes back on her feet. She places one foot in the tray and begins spraying the debris away.

Monica says, "Nothing worse than leaving a trail of clay in your car."

Violet adds, "Through your garage."

Monica says, "Down your hallway."

Violet concludes, "And onto your bedroom carpet."

Monica smiles, acting chummily. She says, "I am not sure what happened back there, but I want you to know I have Marni's back, too."

Violet hugs her and says, "I am so relieved to hear you say that. I have to admit that I thought you were being kinda heartless. You know, not signing the petition and making that big stink and all. I mean we've known Marni for years."

"Don't read too much into that. It was just talk."

"She's our friend. How could you think those things? Let alone say them?"

"That wasn't me talking. I've got a lot on my plate right now."

"Oh, sorry. I didn't know. Anything you want to talk about?"

"No, thanks though. I'll figure it out. I always do. Anyway, I hope I didn't sound too callous back there."

"Maybe a little. Marni needs us right now."

Monica says, "Oh, absolutely! And we'll be there. All of us. Including me. I think the world of Marni. There's nothing I wouldn't do for her. I guess I just got caught up in the small talk. I mean I try not to, but it is a country club after all." Monica picks her next words carefully. She says, "I know the evidence doesn't do her a bit of good. I guess I should just trust my instincts, and the evidence is, well, the evidence. It could change any day."

Violet says, "I don't think evidence can change. I wouldn't say that. What I would say is Roger Fleming told Marni that he came across new evidence proving Marni didn't do it. I think Roger knows who really did do it."

Monica tastes bile rising in the back of her throat. She swallows the rancid taste and manages to produce an eager smile. She says, "Oh, how wonderful for Marni! It's nice when good things happen to good people. Isn't it?"

Violet says, "Yes, and just in the nick of time. Marni's arraignment hearing is next week."

Suddenly silent, Monica looks out of the window.

Violet says, "Is everything OK?"

Monica says, "Yes, of course. Better than OK. How could it not be? Our little Marni is going to be all right. Wonderful. Really."

"I know. I am so happy for her."

"Me, too. Obviously!"

"I am not sure why she had to go though all of this, but knowing Marni, she'll make something good out of it."

"Oh, I'm sure." Monica wants to say, "Enough with the small talk. You are a nonsensical string of rambles. Tell me what Roger said!" Instead, Monica says, "What is the new evidence?"

Violet says, "Oh, I couldn't tell you that."

"I won't tell anybody."

"It's not that. I just don't know. Roger wouldn't say. He came by yesterday to inspect the property again, and he asked more questions. He went onto the club course behind my house."

"Weird. The golf course?"

"Yeah."

"Did he say why?"

"Nope. But I'm sure he had a reason. Josie says he might be the biggest jerk on the planet, but he is positively a genius at his job. I can see why Josie bit the bullet and hired him for Marni."

"Yes, yes. Are you sure he didn't say what he was doing on the golf course?"

"Just that he was on to something. He said he is keeping things under wraps until he can blow the lid off this thing. He wouldn't say anything more, but he seemed pleased."

"He must have said something else?"

"Oh, just that Marni was never going to have to go to that arraignment hearing. That much he was sure of. He was so secretive. I guess he has to be, but something is definitely brewing. Something big. That is for sure."

"Is that all? You're sure you don't know any more?"

"Even if I did, I wouldn't be able to say anything."

"So, are you just not saying anything, or do you really not know anything more."

"I really don't know more."

"Oh, I see. Well, it's all so very exciting. Hard to not get caught up in it all. I am so very happy for our little Marni!"

"Me, too."

Monica finishes cleaning her shoes and puts them back in the plastic bag. She doesn't wash the extra dirt down the sunken drain as Violet did. Instead, she leaves the mess for someone else to clean up.

Monica says, "OK. Well, I have to run." She kisses Violet on both cheeks. Before she leaves the parking lot, she phones Roger Fleming and leaves a voicemail message.

৵৵

Roger and Dixie eat lunch together. They kiss and eat, touch and eat, then kiss some more. The waitress avoids their table and all eye contact. Roger's cell phone rings. He reads the caller I.D. It is Monica. He sends the call directly to voicemail.

He thinks, *I've been waiting for her to call. Finally.* He smiles and sticks his tongue deeper into Dixie's mouth, in a deep rolling motion. He won't call Monica back right away. He intends to make her wait. If there is one thing Roger understands, it's how to string a woman along. He massages Dixie's thigh under the table.

Monica leaves an almost monotone message on his voicemail. She doesn't want Roger to detect her sense of urgency. She wants to fuel Roger with as little ammunition as possible. She may want to pump him for information right away, but she knows she can't play into his hand. She plots what to say when he phones back. She wants to know--needs to know--what he knows. As her restlessness builds, she bites her cuticles, one by one. She bites and bites until the skin around her cuticles festers and bleeds. It burns, but she can't stop biting until the skin lies smooth and raw. She drives home in a daze and stays that way for most of the evening.

At 2:37 in the morning, Monica pops up out of bed much like a piece of toast too light for the toaster. The movement startles J. Paul. She rubs his back until he falls asleep again. Carefully, she eases out of bed so as not to wake him again. She knows what she must do. It came to her in a dream.

FOURTEEN

A woman is like a teabag; you never know how strong she is until she gets into hot water.
-Eleanor Roosevelt

Monica puts on her fuzzy, pink, high-heeled slippers. A vent's overhead blast of air conditioning chills her through. She reaches for her matching, pink, silken robe. Quietly, she walks while tying the robe's belt into a knot. She gently shuts the double doors to her bedroom and tiptoes across the marble tile. She kneels next to her antique blue bureau. She reaches underneath and pulls out an aged, wooden box. Gingerly, she carries the box into the kitchen and places it on the dark granite countertop.

She turns on an under-the-cabinet light, and carefully sifts through the box's contents. She stops on one of her favorites pieces: a family picture of herself, her parents, and her older brother. They all smile broadly on the snowy Christmas day. She runs her finger over their faces and kisses all three.

She files the photograph and pulls out the next: an image of the wooden sleigh, her family seated proudly, and their quarter horse, Svay at the helm. Svay is poised, ready to lead the family across an icy bridge. Monica blows off the dust from the photographs and remembers that fateful day. She notices the woolen caps covering their ears and that her smile perfectly resembles her mother's.

A tear lands on the image of her mother's golden hair. Monica quickly brushes the tear from the photograph and then the ones from her own cheeks. She hadn't realized that she was crying.

She holds the photograph, savoring one last look. The intricately colored details on Svay's bridle have faded to a sepia tone. However, Monica vividly remembers the details, especially the hand-painted green and gold bells hanging from the bridle. She helped her father paint and hang each one on the Christmas-red harness.

She remembers how quietly the snow fell that day. The only sounds heard for miles across the valley were the jingle of Svay's bells and the *swish, swish, swish* of the sleigh's steel runners brushing through the fresh snow. Svay guided the sleigh toward their small stone church at the bottom of the valley beyond the snow-laden pines.

It was her father's idea to ride the old sleigh on that snowy Christmas day instead of driving their car. It had been her great-grandfather's sleigh used for a long forgotten family Christmas tradition of riding to mass.

She doesn't blame her father for that fateful decision, or what happened that day. She kisses the photograph again. How she misses them, and the quiet days of her early youth. The images from the photograph might have faded, but she remembers them as if it were just yesterday. She closes her eyes and sees her family again now. She sees the rich red and gold hues of the woolen blankets her mother had tucked across their laps. How warm her mother made her feel. Another teardrop escapes.

These are the only pictures Monica has left of her family. She doesn't want to part with them and put them into the bag along with the other relics. Reluctantly, she does. It hurts to remember. She looks at the remaining pictures. The ones she would rather forget: the adolescent years in foster care long before she found her way to America, and the life she once only dreamt about.

She gathers the mementos and gently places them along with other reminders of her past life into a black plastic bag. She ties the ends closed with duct tape and the rubber gloves, exactly resembling the bag already sitting at the bottom of a water hazard.

Quietly, she punches in the alarm code and slips into the golf cart-sized garage. She changes into her wetsuit and loads her golf cart with the necessary equipment. She drives to the golf course behind Violet Anderson's house. A dim streetlight on the edge of the course guides her way. Bats fly in and out of its hazy, radiating illumination.

She parks the cart behind a purple royal robe tree, concealing it from any possible passersby. At this hour, she expects none. She looks at her wristwatch and mumbles, "The maintenance crew shouldn't arrive for another one and a half hours."

She surmises from her recent weeks of surveillance that security most likely sleeps in their cart or in front of the monitors at the gate's entrance. Not much happens at this hour.

She carries her tank, gear, and bag to the water hazard. Her dive watch reads 3:37 a.m. Again, she looks around. She sees no one. Causing barely a ripple, she slips into the lukewarm murkiness of the man-made lake. The water might feel lukewarm, but Monica is grateful to be wearing a full wetsuit. Before she puts her regulator in she mumbles, "No telling what germs and pesticide runoff lurk in this watery hole."

Monica brushes through the mossy bottom of the lake with her gloved hands, looking for the black garbage bag with the brick inside it. The reeds sway underneath her touch. She hears the loud suction from her underwater breathing apparatus as she slowly inhales and exhales. Eighteen feet below the surface, it's the only noise that she hears.

Monica sifts through a wide array of golf balls, many with their logos long faded. She sees a flash. She takes in a quick breath. She sees it's only a nine iron.

She continues sweeping back and forth, brushing through the muddy murk for the bag. The narrow, conical beam from her flashlight provides the only reprieve from the solitary darkness enveloping her. The flicker of light and the sound of her underwater breathing offer the only comforting signs of life in the eerie, underwater stillness.

Unaware, she is not the only life form to produce a trail of emerging bubbles along the water's surface. The other set of bubbles emerges closer to hers, and prove considerably larger.

At last, Monica sees the black plastic bag. Pleased, she smiles. She grabs the end and doubly ties it around her wrist to avoid the risk of dropping it. She takes the decoy bag and drops it in the exact spot where the original one sat.

Monica smiles again as she thinks, *Out with the old and in with the new. Done. This has to be it. This has to be the only loose end.* How Roger found out about this, she hasn't a clue. Now, it doesn't matter. Finally at peace, Monica feels certain that after tonight, she will have no links to the burglary. She thinks, *Roger will have nothing on me now.*

Satisfied, Monica heads to shore. Suddenly, she stops, frozen with fear. A chill runs down her spine. A flash of green and a mouthful of jagged teeth appear before her in the conical light streaming from her flashlight. Then, it is gone. She swerves. Her flashlight catches the flip of a heavy tail. She screams, but from this deep below the surface no one can hear. She drops the flashlight. The falling light casts violent shadows as it sinks to the soft, silty bottom. Monica raises her arm to block her face. The reptile, attracted by the sudden movement, swings its massive head, and clamps down mightily on the bag still attached to Monica's wrist.

The beast thrashes back and forth, swinging Monica as if she were a rag doll. She frantically yanks on the ties to release the bag, but she can't get a solid grip. The ten-foot reptile pulls Monica helplessly into deeper water and then rolls with tremendous velocity. The ties suddenly snap from the hulking force of the death roll. Monica is free. The reptile eats the bag in three giant, punctuated gulps. Bits of gold, colored stone, and shimmery silver spill from the bag as the alligator engulfs the remainder and swallows.

Monica wastes no time. The poor visibility in the murky water offers her little comfort. She sprints to shore, kicking wildly. She knows at any moment a greater force—one more powerful than she--may sweep her back into the murky depths against her will. Terrified, she scrambles for the shoreline. She reaches shallow water. Flailing, she rips off her mask and tries to run. Hindered by her gear, she cannot. She claws, climbing the sandy embankment and propelling herself onto the grass. She gains little ground under the heaviness of her tank and weight belt. Her fins further restrict her progress. To move, she must kick out widely with each step.

Her hands shake as she unhooks her weight belt and slips off her tank, dragging both behind her and away from the shoreline. She turns, peddling backwards in her fins. It's faster this way. She slips, scrambles to regain her balance, and makes up more ground. At quick glance, she judges fifteen or twenty feet separate her from the water's edge. It's not enough.

She rips off her fins and throws them in the direction of her cart. As she stands, she catches sudden movement at the water's edge. She stifles a scream.

The alligator opens its gigantic mouth and releases an unearthly noise: something between a vicious growl and a deafening hiss. Monica sees enough of its white sharp jagged teeth in the dim light to make her cry.

She falls backwards. She hugs her equipment and scoots along the ground as best she can. Finally, she stands and turns to run. The weight of her equipment continues to thwart her every stride.

She considers dropping everything to run. She can't. She knows she cannot leave a shred of evidence behind. With great effort, she loads her cart. Frantically, she gasps for air. Through bleary eyes, she drives home. Her hyperventilation subsides, but leaves in its wake a sharp case of hiccups.

She checks the cart's rearview mirror. She stops crying as the lake completely recedes into the night's blackness. She wheels a hard right into her cul-de-sac, lifting two wheels briefly off of the ground. She cries again, this time with relief, as her home comes into full view.

She presses the remote button as she nears her pale straw-colored, stucco home. The wooden garage door automatically lifts. She parks, hauling her equipment onto the garage floor.

She drags her equipment across the slate stepping-stones, through the iron gate, and into the backyard. Shivering, Monica turns on the outside cabana shower. She doesn't wait for the water to heat.

Still in full wetsuit, she meticulously rinses each piece of equipment, starting with the tank. She intended to ditch the original black garbage bag--along with all of its contents-- permanently over the causeway bridge a few miles away. Now, that plan--along with the bag--is long gone.

She shudders at the thought of the alligator. She hopes the beast ate the entirety of the bag's contents, leaving no trace. The outside light flips on. Monica doesn't have time to hide her equipment. *J. Paul!* Quickly, she takes her wedding ring off and throws it by the planter next to the pool.

J. Paul opens the door. Sleepily, he rubs his eyes and says, "Monica? Is that you?"

She doesn't answer.

He sees her, steps through the doorway and says, "I thought I heard something. What on earth are you doing out here at this time of night?" Concerned, he pads across the stone pavers in his bare feet and approaches her shivering body.

He says, "Are you all right?"

Monica doesn't like lying to him. She avoids eye contact, looking at her feet, and says, "I woke up in the middle of the night and realized my wedding ring was missing. I remembered we went swimming yesterday. I didn't take it off before I went to bed. So, I knew it must be in the pool. I thought I would look for it."

J. Paul says, "In the middle of the night? In a wetsuit?"

Monica swallows a heavy hiccup. She says, "I-I-I was submerged for a long time." Obviously, Monica has been crying.

J. Paul hurries inside, returning with an oversized towel. He wraps her in it and says, "Monica, you're shivering. For heaven's sake, this is pure madness. Leave your equipment here. Come inside. I will take care of this." Touched by how much his ring obviously means to her, he hugs her tenderly and gently ushers her inside. She melts into him. The warmth of him comforts her.

He says, "No ring is worth all this. It's just a material thing. Don't worry about it. I will look for it. Just get some sleep. I am cancelling your tennis for today. You look as though you've just seen a ghost. We'll get a hot tea in you, stop this shivering, and get you to sleep." J. Paul unzips her wetsuit and gasps, "What is that?"

Through the commotion, Monica hadn't noticed. She didn't feel anything. She winces. Now, as the adrenaline fades, she feels it. The alligator's tooth tore a two-inch gash through her wetsuit, leaving a nasty wound down to the wrist bone. Her glove caught most of the blood. Still, blood dots a trail through the backyard.

Spontaneously, Monica makes up something about catching her arm on the fencepost while carrying her equipment around to the backyard. She takes off her gloves, sees the quantity of blood trapped inside, and faints.

Four hours later, a very groggy Monica Mooney awakes. Through heavy eyelids she surveys the room. J. Paul is gone. She smells before she actually sees the fresh lavender and bright daffodils neatly placed on her bedside table. She smiles, *My favorite.*

She fumbles for the note on the vibrant bouquet. She reads it aloud, "I am bringing lunch home. You took several stitches to your wrist. You have been given a sedative. You should feel better. I will be home soon to make sure of it. Love, J. Paul." She smiles and folds the card back into the envelope before replacing it.

Monica vaguely recalls a concierge doctor visiting and stitching her wrist. She shuts her heavy eyelids and vividly sees the green scaly reptile before her. It opens its jagged-toothed mouth for her. She screams a bloodcurdling shriek, shivers, and tightly pulls the covers up to her chin. The medicine kicks in again. She sleeps soundly well past noon.

FIFTEEN

Friends are born, not made.
-Henry Adams

Due to the nasty wrist injury, Monica misses tennis for the next two weeks. When she finally returns to the tennis courts, she bandages her wrist well, and hides the bandage under an oversized terry wristband.

Mitch says, "Glad to see you back. J. Paul said you weren't feeling well."

Monica smiles. She knows J. Paul is a vault when it comes to her private information. Mitch will know nothing of the ring, injury, or doctor visits. That much, she is sure. She says, "Yes, thank you. I am feeling much better. Who am I playing with today?"

"Natasha."

"You got her on the roster?"

"She's on."

Monica hugs him, almost knocking him over. "Who's Josie playing with?"

"Whoa! Hey! Um, Marni."

"What! Are you joking?"

"Why would I be joking?"

"She broke into Violet's home and stole her valuables. That's why!"

Mitch walks over to his filing cabinet and thumbs through a drawer. He pulls out a file and opens it. He holds up a copy of the petition papers and waves them.

He says, "If you had a problem, you shouldn't have signed this. Marni Schoppelmann is one hundred percent reinstated to all club activities. No one believes she committed those crimes. And according to your signature, not even you."

Monica mumbles to herself the entire way to the courts, "That Mitchell Garvey is getting too big for his britches. That's exactly it. Someone needs to take him down a notch or two. He had better watch his step or it might just be me." Monica sees Tasha waiting for her on Court Three, and suddenly forgets about Mitch altogether.

She says, "Thank God," and hugs Tasha.

Tasha says, "I wish everyone was this happy to see me." She smiles.

Monica continues, "Ha! It's just great to see another sane person like me! This place is filled to the brim with lunatics! We understand each other: you and I. You have no idea how hard it's been here without you." Tasha smiles again. She thinks as Monica does. Or, so Monica thinks.

୧୦୶

Today is a homecoming of sorts for Marni. All of the surrounding courts buzz with the news that she is back. Crowds encircle her, waiting their turn to welcome and hug her. Violet waits her turn. Marni positively beams from the outpouring of love and support, albeit slightly uncomfortable with all of the attention.

Monica watches. Outwardly, Monica exudes charm and calmness as she surveys the scene. Inside is different. Monica almost bursts with anger. She thinks, *Marni, Marni, Marni. It's the Marni Schoppelmann show. Where's my remote? I need to change the channel.* She chews on her cuticle until it's tender and puffs with swelling.

Seemingly obsessed, Monica watches Marni's every move while she should be watching the ball. She continues mumbling, "Perfect Marni. Everyone loves Marni."

Monica frames the next ball. It bounces awkwardly off her racquet and pops over the fence. She says to Tasha, "I'll get it." She leaves her court, crosses through Marni's court, and gains access to the back gate that leads to the grounds. She searches through the shrubbery for the lost tennis ball.

Josie says, "Monica, it rolled that way." Josie points toward a lake.

Monica says, "By the lake? Right. OK. Thanks." Monica walks, but a sudden flashback halts her. She mumbles, "Why are there so many lakes in Florida?" She looks at the ball by the lake, and freezes in place. The sun shines on the lake, making it impossible to see past its reflective surface and into the water beneath. Her imagination runs wild with vivid possibilities. She sees an underwater world with sunrays-- filtering down from the surface--illuminating objects of green, brown, and silver that shimmer from the sparkling light above. She takes one step closer and freezes again. She imagines something else in its depths; something slithering among the reeds and fish; something with a large, scaly, green tail.

Although the lake appears placid, Monica knows first hand that such tranquil appearances can deceive. She subconsciously rubs the wrist where her stitches once held her skin together. In a lake shaped not too dissimilar from this one and not too far away, it happened. She remembers the alligator more than four times her size. She shivers. Yes, she knows first hand what lurks.

Monica stands and stares at the bright yellow tennis ball, still unable to move forward. She closes her eyes and sees a flash of the teeth, and the swing of a massive tail. The beast swings its massive head and opens its mouth for her. She shrieks. Everyone stops playing to look. She leaves the ball where it lies and hurries back to the courts.

Aware that all eyes are on her, she says, "A bee! There was a bee."

As Monica passes through the gate, Josie says, "You OK? Did you get stung?"

"I'm fine. No."

Marni points and says, "That's good! But over there, Monica. Look. See it? The ball. It's right there. By that lake."

Monica yells in a shrill tone, "I don't see it!"

Josie says, "The ball was right in front of you. Didn't you see it?"

"Nope. I didn't see it at all!" Monica turns sharply and passes through to her court, avoiding all eye contact. She tries sounding nonchalant by saying, "I'll just open a new can. No big deal." She hurriedly opens the new can and starts hitting before anyone says more.

Josie looks at the bright yellow ball sitting plainly in sight and looks at Marni. They both shrug.

༄ঌ

Josie's court finishes their warm-up early, in ten short minutes. She takes the extra time to readjust the tongue in her shoe before re-lacing tightly. As she pulls the bow tightly, she sees a familiar face approach her court. He waves. In response, she waves and her stomach suddenly feels queasy.

Josie stands and smoothes down her skort. She chides herself that Roger Fleming can still make her stomach flip after all of these years. She should hate him. She has a right to and part of her does. But somewhere, deep in the back corner of her heart, sits a switch that she cannot fully turn off.

Roger sits in the shared seating area between courts. He takes off his aviators and hangs them in his polo shirt's collar. He slightly pulls up and creases his seersucker golf pants and sits. His side bangs flop forward as he glances at his Breitling and adjusts its red, white, and blue Army band. He straightens up and runs a hand through his hair, pushing the loose strands away from his face. He looks at her and smiles. Josie would never admit it to anyone, but he looks good. *Sigh. Really good.*

As if reading her mind, Marni walks over and whispers, "He's looking hot."

"Yeah, but--"

Marni finishes her sentence and says, "But he's still Roger Fleming on the inside."

"Exactly."

"Sorry. That was mean. I shouldn't have said that. Especially, after he has been so nice to help me out and all."

Josie thinks of the alimony deal Roger struck with her before he would agree to take on Marni's case. She says, "Nice?"

"Well, yeah. He's working his butt off to clear my name."

"Is it possible to admire someone professionally, but not personally?"

"I guess so. You could admire their work and not them, especially if you didn't have to talk with them much."

"If you worked with them, wouldn't you have to talk with them?"

"Maybe, maybe not. You know, like if you both had a job riveting concrete or something."

Roger waves to Marni.

She waves back and yells, "You should get a job riveting concrete!"

He yells, "Can't hear you. What about concrete?"

Josie yells, "It would look good on you!"

Roger says, "What? It looks what?"

Marni yells, "She didn't mean that."

Josie says, "Yes, I did."

"Shhh, he'll hear you."

Roger yells, "I'm missing some of that! Anyway, Marni, good to see you back on the courts! 'Bout time!" The petition was originally his idea.

Josie bends over to pick up a ball. When she tucks it neatly into her shorties, Roger whistles and thinks, *I don't remember Josie having legs like that.* She wears a white tank dress that shows off not just her legs, but her entirely tanned, toned physique. With little real interest, he casually notes, *She is more fit now than when we first met.*

Roger turns his head in the direction of his true interest, and the real reason he is here today. On the next court, Monica hogs the ball during the first few games. Tasha takes a step back, remaining the "steady" behind the baseline. Monica repeatedly runs out of position, hitting balls that aren't hers. Their error to winner ratio racks up.

Tasha keeps track, but says nothing. Instead, she scrambles to make up for lost ground. She plays the percentages, as she can't afford to make any errors. Monica spends them all too frivolously with her uncharacteristically flashy play.

Tasha notices the handsome man sitting courtside. She surmises he must be why Monica puts on the big show. In truth it is, but Monica herself doesn't know why she performs for Roger. It makes no sense. She doesn't like him. She despises him. So, why the show? She thinks, *This is idiotic. Why do I care what that loser thinks?* Still, she can't stop herself from showing off.

Tasha says discreetly, "You play well in front of him." She gestures toward Roger.

Monica says, "Him? Oh, he's just some guy. That fleabag full of testosterone doesn't motivate me. Winning does." She takes a high topspin roller to her backhand and jumps with a scissor kick to meet the ball at its apex--and in the middle of her sweet spot--ripping a cross-court return.

Tasha says, "Yeah. Right. Just some guy, huh? Nice *scissor kick.*"

Monica follows the ball in and closes the net, anticipating a weak reply. She gets it. The ball sits high in the air. Monica could easily hit a simple, high forehand, volley winner. Instead, she hits a swinging volley with such crushing pace that her feet lift off the ground, making her grunt on contact.

Tasha says, "Nice grunt, too. Who exactly is that guy?"

Monica says, "Just some jerk, typical Neanderthal male. Trust me, I don't like his type."

Tasha raises an eyebrow and says, "Hmm. Really?"

"Yeah. Really."

However, Monica lingers a little longer than usual at the changeover, toweling off to give Roger his chance. He sees this opportunity and has no trouble seizing it.

Roger licks his lips and says, "They are dredging the water hazard behind Violet's house today." He waits for her response and is disappointed when he receives none.

Now, Monica knows she has the upper hand. She smiles and thinks, *Good. Let them dredge. The bag is gone. Replaced. My alibi is rock solid.* She watches Roger try to leer down her shirt. She holds her racquet in front of her cleavage and thinks, *Creep. He's playing his cards way too early. Unbelievable! Idiot!*

Monica doesn't wonder how Roger knew about the bag filled with Violet's loot, or that she threw the bag into the water hazard. She thinks, *It doesn't matter now; the loot is gone, buried in the belly of a giant green beast.* Unexpectedly, a flashback occurs. She sees the flash of teeth, the thrashing tail, and hears the deafening hiss. She shivers, but not for the reason Roger thinks.

Roger misinterprets Monica shiver, thinking that he's unnerved her. Spurred on, he moves in for the kill. "It turns out we have a red-cockaded woodpecker on our golf club course."

"Is that a bird?"

"A very rare bird."

"I'll alert the Audubon Society."

"You won't have to. An avid birder in the neighborhood excavated an artificial nest for the endangered bird. After waiting for nearly three years, he finally saw his efforts come to fruition. A female red-cockaded woodpecker made her nest and produced four eggs, all in that cluster of pines behind Violet's house."

"Scintillating. Groundbreaking. Truly. Why didn't I read about this in the paper?"

Undeterred by her sarcasm, Roger says, "He was filming the nest at the exact date and time Violet's home was broken into. He was hoping to get a better look at the nest so that he might start making a restrictor plate for it." He thinks he detects a flicker of fear in her eyes.

"All of this talk of nesting is making me hot under the collar."

He leans in closer and whispers, "Really?"

"No."

Momentarily deterred, he says, "We, uh, have great footage."

Monica falters, but only briefly, wondering, *Of me,* but says nothing.

Roger says, "Well?"

She stutters, having trouble getting her sentence out. Then once going, she gains confidence and never looks back. Monica says, "L-l-l-let me guess. He videotaped the whole burglary, and the crime is solved. Your job is done."

"Not exactly. He began videotaping the back of Violet's home just before the alarm stopped."

Aahhh. Now, knowing that Roger doesn't have footage of her actually leaving Violet's house, she thinks, *And this guy is some hotshot lawyer? Please. He can't keep his trap shut.* Realizing that Roger's line of interrogation is more of a fishing expedition than anything else, she thinks, *If he is looking for me to bite, he's a bigger idiot than I previously thought.* She gives up nothing. Monica dislikes being toyed with, but mostly she dislikes Roger Fleming.

She says, "Make your point, if you've got one."

Roger smiles. He likes this woman. She's bold, wicked smart, and sassy. He imagines in bed she would be the same. He leans closer so he can smell her perfume. She changed her perfume from last time: Bulgari Pour Femme. He is certain. He prides himself on being somewhat of a connoisseur on the artificially enhanced scents of women.

Sure of himself, Roger laughs and says, "No point, just idol conversation between two bird lovers. Or should I say lovebirds?"

"No, you shouldn't. Now, speak plainly."

Roger says, "OK. I will. About the same time as Violet's burglary, you are seen on video." Roger detects another flicker of fear. Excitedly, he continues, "Our avid birder seems to have caught his bird and our cat, so to speak, on the same day." He pauses for dramatic affect and to let his wry humor sink in.

Monica crosses her arms and resists the temptation to punch him squarely in the nose.

Roger continues, "As Violet's alarm blares, you are seen on the tape, throwing a black bag into the water hazard." He licks his lips again and says, "Care to come down to my office to talk about signing a full confession?"

Monica sizes him up and thinks, *That's it? Wow, he really is an idiot! He doesn't even have the bag yet. I can't believe he's compromising his entire investigation by giving me all of this info. This should be classified, privileged at the very least. Ahh.* She realizes what he is doing. He's using the info as leverage to get her back to his office. Instinctively, she stands, stretches, and crosses one foot in front of the other. Eagerly, he leans in, smelling her perfume. Monica thinks, *Roger, Roger, Roger, always thinking with your penis.*

Now, she knows her plan will work, and she needs nothing more of him. To her, he is disposable. She doesn't need to waste any more time kowtowing to the likes of him. She thinks, *Poor Roger: good-looking, but not too bright.*

Monica takes her time, and says slowly, "Confession to what? That I'm in the presence of an utter and complete idiot?" She turns on her heel, leaving him with his mouth gaping open. She resumes her place on the court.

Josie loses all concentration. *What are Roger and Monica talking about? Definitely looks heated.* Unable to focus, she misses the next three balls that come to her. *I know I shouldn't care if Monica piques Roger's interest.*

Still, Josie can't help herself. She recognizes Roger's body language. She also recognizes the way he looks at Monica. *He wants her.* She can tell. It shouldn't, but it hurts.

Josie feels squeamish. Her stomach churns, but there is little she can do about it. *Roger is not my problem anymore.* She thinks about Dixie. Although not a big fan, she sympathizes with her. She knows all too well what will become of Dixie should Roger begin to satisfy that thirst in his eyes with Monica. She knows that feeling firsthand.

Marni watches Roger, too. She asks Josie, "What's Roger doing here? Do you think he needs to speak to me about my case?" Marni watches Roger's body language as Monica walks away and says, "Er, or maybe to Monica?"

Josie rolls her eyes and says, "Maybe."

"But why would he need to speak to Monica about my case?"

Josie says, "Your case? No, I think he has a different agendum today." She leaves it at that. She's a grown-up. She's not going to whinge over Roger Fleming's bad behavior any longer. Josie watches Roger saunter off toward the clubhouse.

Once in the clubhouse, Roger waits by the door for Monica to exit the locker room. As she does, he pulls out a clear plastic bag from inside a brown paper one. It contains Monica's yellow underwater flashlight. She reads what he points out: her initials inscribed in red Sharpie at the flashlight's base.

Crap! She forgot about the flashlight. She wonders, *How can I explain that?* She can't say it was for seeing, because then Roger will know she also made an additional night trip. She also knows Roger will understand the significance behind the fact that this flashlight is only intended for underwater usage.

Roger guessed right. He says, "Still think I'm an idiot, Monica?"

She thinks, *My only hope is that he wants something more than information… something I can bargain with.* Monica's heart races to the point where the throbbing in her head pounds too loudly for her to think straight. She wonders if he can hear it. She realizes everything is on the line. Still, she exudes a serene and calm façade.

Monica might appear calm, but Roger notices the sudden flush of color across Monica's chest, neck, and ears. He's paid to notice these things. In a courtroom, his job relies on noticing and exploiting such physical clues. He registers the panic in her eyes. He salivates slightly and says, "My office. Seven tonight. Come alone. Enough toying around. You know what I want. It's time." Roger is a man not used to waiting, or being denied.

Josie walks out of the locker room to see Monica and Roger in another heated exchange. She didn't hear what was said. She doesn't need to hear. The air electrifies between the two, sending tiny prickling hairs up the back of Josie's neck. Before storming past, Josie slaps Roger hard across the face and says, "Do you have to sleep with everyone I know?"

Immediately, Josie regrets her outburst, even before reaching the parking lot. *I shouldn't have done that! But, a girl can only take so much!* Wrought with emotion, she second guesses herself. *Right? What was I supposed to do? Ugh!* She wishes her feelings could be neatly finalized on paper. *One signature and done! Like our divorce.*

Unfortunately, for Josie it doesn't work that way. Divorce doesn't make you stop loving someone. *If only it did.* Time is the only true healer.

She walks into the parking lot in a daze, wondering why some people love whom they love. *Why this person and not that one?* She would like to know the reason her heart has it all wrong. *Sigh.* She sees no rhyme or reason to her feelings. *Sure, Roger is good-looking, but that's about it. Am I that superficial?*

She massages her hand from the slap until the throbbing subsides. *Monica can have him. And Dixie. And whoever else wants him. I'm done.*

SIXTEEN

The heart has its reasons which reason knows nothing of.
-Blaise Pascal

Monica watches with great satisfaction as Josie slaps Roger. She relishes each red finger mark slowly emerging across his cheek. She thinks, *Delicious!* Monica would also enjoy slapping Roger. She hopes to one day to get the chance. For now, she waits for him to collect himself.

She watches him bristle from the slap. His reaction gives way to something else. She can't read what. She suppresses a grin, even a giggle. She thinks she detects a slight tear in the corner of his eye. She knows from the loud pop that it had to hurt. Even so, she thinks, *Sissy! Only girls cry from a slap.* Seconds go by. Finally, he looks Monica in the eye, stands confidently again, and acts as if nothing happened.

Roger says, "Well?"

Monica coolly says, "See you at seven." Suddenly, she gets an idea. She adds, "Roger, wait. Walk me to my car."

He smiles and says, "Now, that's what I'm talkin' about!" He untucks his shirt and says, "Do you have a big backseat?"

Monica says, "Yes. Big enough. One second. I left my keys on the sink." She rushes into the locker room, turns her cell phone's voice recorder on, and rejoins Roger. Monica suggests they walk through the back corridor to the parking lot. She explains, "It's the road less traveled."

Understanding, he winks. They speak softly, but their voices magnify, echoing off of the hard surface of the marble pillars and the barrel-vaulted ceiling. This hallway is an acoustic masterpiece, something Monica already knows. Roger's phone buzzes. He reads the text.

Disappointed, he says, "We'll have to wait 'til tonight. My meeting just got bumped up. I gotta go."

Monica says, "Oh, OK. 'Til tonight then. But, Roger?"

"What?"

"How will I know you will give me back my flashlight after we have sex and not turn it over for evidence?"

Roger says, "You have my word. Once we, uh, consummate the deal, the flashlight is yours. I can't promise you that if some other evidence shows up we won't use it. Ethically, we'd have to. You understand."

Monica thinks, *Your word? Ethically?* She almost bursts into laughter. There is nothing ethical about Roger Fleming. Monica says, "Of course. I trust you." She almost laughs saying the words. She says, "Did you find my black bag?"

Roger says, "We did. Very clever. You can't have that back. But without the flashlight as evidence, what I am guessing to be your story might just work for you."

Roger doesn't tell Monica that he found her blood at the scene. Nor does he mention a concierge doctor's testimony regarding a wound on her wrist from that same night. He fails to mention the story involving scuba gear that her husband told the doctor. Yes, Roger knows all about Monica's middle-of-the-night wetsuit excursion. He also knows that with the wrist injury and the blood sample, he can connect her to the scene.

With the video, remnants of the original bag, and the new evidence, Roger can prove Monica visited the scene twice and why. Roger already fits enough pieces of the puzzle together. A conviction is likely even without the flashlight. The flashlight, he muses, is merely a decoy to get himself laid: after much anticipation and in his estimation with the most exciting woman he has ever met. He hasn't stopped fantasizing about her. She haunts not only his night dreams, but his daydreams as well. Now, he intends to turn those fantasies into reality.

Monica says, "OK, but won't they miss the flashlight?"

Roger says, "Don't worry. I didn't catalogue it, yet."

Monica moves closer, runs her finger along his collar and says; "OK, but I will only sleep with you once and no kinky stuff. Just straight sex in exchange for my flashlight."

Roger says, "One hour is all I ask. I won't get too crazy, but I will keep you very, very busy for that entire hour. I promise you that." He leans toward her. His breath smells of coffee and something more sinister.

Monica pulls away and places a finger over his lips. "Patience," she says with a slight grimace. She fights the urge to vomit and thinks, *How could Josie possibly marry such a creep?* She manages a weak smile and says, "Til tonight, then."

He leers at her and says, "Til tonight and our magic hour."

Monica opens her car door. She waits until Roger reaches his car three spaces away. She checks. No one is around. She stands with one foot on her car's floorboard. With her door ajar, she yells, "Roger, wait."

He opens his car door and says, "Tell me tonight. I'm in a hurry."

"It can't wait."

He stands, leaning over the roof of his silver Tesla and says, "Fine. What is it?"

Monica takes out the phone from her pocket and replays part of their recorded conversation. Surprisingly clear, her voice recorder repeats, "Don't worry. I didn't catalogue it, yet."

Roger never loses, and he is not about to start now. He slams his fist on the top of his car, making an indentation. He slams his door closed with even greater force. He also checks. No one is around. He will get that phone no matter what it takes.

He races towards her. He knows what this recording means. Roger tampered with state's evidence and used it to blackmail Monica to sleep with him. He could lose everything.

He snarls, "Give me that!"

Monica places the phone in an outside pocket of her purse. She had planned to say more. She had planned to tell him that if she was going down, then she was taking him with her.

She had an entire speech prepared: one in which she asks whether he is ready to give up his multi-million-dollar practice, his office as President of the Florida Bar, and his carefully manicured reputation as a pristine pillar in the community.

Monica has much to say. However, delivery of her speech quickly loses its appeal as she watches Roger barrel towards her. She instinctively jumps into her car and throws the gear into reverse. Speedily, she backs out of her parking space. Roger grabs for her door handle. She screams, but the door is locked. He kicks the side of her car, denting it above the front tire. His toe breaks, but he doesn't care. He runs back, jumps in his car, and chases her.

Monica didn't plan for this. Scared, she burns rubber while exiting the parking lot. She turns a hard right.

Roger revs his engine and skips the right hand corner altogether, driving at an angle over the embankment, the vinca, the plumbego, and red mulch. He sideswipes Monica's car. Her white convertible bumps and lurches over the median and into oncoming traffic.

Roger closes in on her and rams her car from behind. She pulls hard left and misses the oncoming landscaping truck. Roger sees the truck too late. He pulls hard left also, but overcompensates with an added nudge from the oncoming truck. His car hits the curb, flies airborne, and lands with skidding thuds onto the turf on hole seven. He can't control the wheel. He bounces off of the bunker and into the water hazard. The back end of his car sticks straight out of the water like a Popsicle stick. The front end remains submerged with Roger still in it.

Suddenly, he emerges with a splash, clawing at the surface, and gasping for air in time to see Monica stepping onto the wood pilings next to the water's edge.

Roger's forehead bleeds from a large swollen gash. He treads water as he coughs out liquid. Unsympathetic, Monica holds up her phone with the recorded message on it. She yells, "Don't you ever bother me again, or I will ruin you!"

Roger swims to shore. Exhausted, he pulls himself halfway onto land, leaving his trunk and legs submerged. He rests his head and shoulders on the carefully raked white sand. Slowly, he catches his breath. He screams a mighty scream, sounding more animal than human.

Monica's detest for him magnifies. She yells, "What did Josie ever see in a pig like you?" She spits and yells, "You think I would sleep with you? Ha! You make me sick!" She begins walking away.

Duped and frustrated, Roger begins plotting. He chides himself for underestimating Monica and leaving himself vulnerable. He promises himself he will make her pay. He takes another deep breath and reminds himself that he always wins. He yells back, "You'll regret this day for the rest of your life!"

Monica turns back to retort, "Hardly." However, when she sees Roger's face, his expression sends chills down her spine. Suddenly shaken, she also begins plotting. She knows with that one look that she is in for the fight of her life. She will have to be careful.

She releases a long, slow breath. She knows with one wrong move that she too could lose everything. Roger is that kind of guy: one who crushes smaller things for the mere sport of it. Now that revenge is added to the mix, he will become even more dangerous. Instantly, she thinks of J. Paul. It surprises her that her first thought is of him and his safety. She will protect him at all costs.

The truck driver rushes to Roger's aide. Fire and Rescue and the police arrive simultaneously. Monica gives her statement to the police. She leaves out the information leading up to the crash, only telling the police officer a car came out of nowhere and hit her before landing in the lake. The truck driver gives his statement replicating Monica's.

As Monica leaves, she hears Roger giving his statement. Roger says he just broke his toe on the steps of the club moments before. He says the broken toe caused him to lose control of his car: hitting another car and landing in the water hazard. Roger knows all of the right things to say and knows what to omit. He has the policemen laughing before the end of it all.

Monica knows enough about Roger to know he will walk away from this thing with no charges. Monica surveys the scene. She estimates Roger's insurance company won't be quite as lucky. Her white convertible needs extensive bodywork to the back and side. She looks at Roger's Tesla. It slowly topples and almost completely submerges. Only part of the wheels can be seen. She's certain it is totaled.

She mumbles, "He's lucky he didn't kill himself or me."

A few blocks away, Josie leaves the tennis parking lot. She sees Monica get into her banged up convertible. She passes a landscaping truck stuck in the median. She swerves to miss a downed stop sign. She sees the wheel of a car in a water hazard. She passes the back of an ambulance in which Roger sits while getting his forehead bandaged.

Josie parks behind the ambulance. She says, "Roger, what happened? Are you all right?"

Roger holds up a finger and mouths, "One minute."

The EMT accesses Roger's head injury. He asks Roger where he lives and what his name is. Roger answers the questions before brushing the medic off.

Roger walks over and leans on Josie's open window. He says, "I lost control of my car." He points to the wheel in the lake and says, "The trampled landscaping, and the downed road signs, that's all my handiwork." He sweeps his arm in the direction of the whole scene and says, "What a mess, huh?"

She says, "Roger! That's your car in the lake?"

"Yep."

"Oh my gosh!"

"Yeah. Pretty sure it's totaled."

"Did you do that to Monica's car? I saw her driving away."

"Unfortunately. I am just glad everyone is OK." Again, he is well versed with just the right things to say.

Josie looks at the red liquid circle emerging through the gauze on his forehead. It grows increasingly larger. She says, "Are you sure you're all right?"

He points to his forehead and says, "What? This thing? It's nothing." He gingerly touches his forehead, but winces. He says, "Don't be silly. It's fine. I'm fine. Can I get a ride?"

She says, "Uh, can't Dixie come get you? Or, uh, maybe one of your tennis or golf buddies? I need to stop by a client's office on my way home."

"Come on, Jo. I live two minutes from here. You know that." It's true. She does know that. He remodeled an old Le Château mansion not too far from here.

He continues, "Besides, I don't want to wait for somebody else to get here. You're already here."

Reluctantly, she agrees. Once in the car, Roger asks her to stop. Josie pulls over. Roger opens the passenger door and vomits onto the pavement.

Josie says, "Are you sure you are all right?"

Roger replies, "Zero to sixty in 4.2 seconds."

Josie says, "I'm sorry, what?"

Roger suddenly slumps in the passenger seat. Drool pools in the corner of his mouth and forms a stringy dribble down the front of his shirt. Josie pulls over. She cradles his head in her hands and looks into his eyes. His dark pupils suddenly dilate, expanding into the pale blue surrounding them. He stares vacantly.

Josie says, "Roger? Roger, it's me, Josie. Can you hear me?"

Roger says, "ShoSho. ShoSho. Good o' ShoSho. I wuv you. Weelly doo." He passes out.

SEVENTEEN

Why is thus? What is the reason for thusness?
-Artemus Ward

Roger wakes, unsure of his surroundings. With a quick survey, he surmises that he lies in a hospital bed. However, how or why he got here remains a mystery. He recollects nothing. Dixie sleeps in a dark, faux leather recliner next to his bed.

A balloon bouquet dances under the ceiling's air-conditioning vent directly over Dixie's chair. The balloons move rhythmically as the Mylar "Get Well" messages ricochet off of each other. Roger reaches for the phone on the laminate swivel desk next to his bed. He fumbles and drops the receiver. Dixie jumps.

She says, "Roger! Oh thank God! I have been so worried!" She showers him with kisses.

He feels the bandage on his head and says, "What's this? Why am I in a hospital?"

"It's a bandage. You hit your head somethin' good. Don't ya' remember? You're at Boca University Medical Center?"

"Where?"

"The hospital. Don't ya' remember anything?"

"No."

"Nothing?"

"Fill me in."

"Well, for one thing you broke your toe, but that's not the half of it, although that's where it all started. Then, you lost control of your car. Then, you tore right through Le Château's landscaping like Starsky or Hutch and sideswiped a car or two. Then, you sunk your car into a water hazard on the golf course. Talk about a real mess! I'm sure it was a sight to behold. All that bumpin' around, you banged up your head real good along the way."

"My car. Is my car OK?"

"Well. You drove it into a lake. Decidedly not."

Suddenly, Roger receives an abbreviated flashback. He remembers answering questions for the police and medical personnel. As suddenly as the onset, the flashback fades. He remembers nothing further.

Dixie says, "Josephine drove you to the emergency room. She called to let me know you were here. You've suffered an acute subdural hematoma. Now, that's a mouthful! Say that ten times fast!"

"Go on."

"Anyway, the doctor said if you had gone home instead of coming straight here, you might have died."

Roger says, "Right. Well, is my car totaled?"

Dixie says, "You and that car. You almost died! Honestly! Is that car all you ever think about? I told you. I figure your car took the brunt of it."

"I just got that car. It's brand new!"

"I know. Don't worry, I've already done the necessary insurance paperwork."

"Where's my phone?"

"Missing."

"Right. Well, let's get packed and outta here."

She brushes his hair away from the bandage and says, "Sweetie, not so fast. You're here until doctor's orders say otherwise."

Roger drums his fingers on the laminated desk.

She smiles, kisses him, and says, "I know. You don't do 'idle' well."

He sighs and stares at the clock on the wall above the door. Neither one speaks for a minute. He fidgets. He folds the tops of his blankets down. He moves the desk and repositions it. He stares at the clock again and thinks, *Three whole minutes.* He folds the top of his blankets back up. He says, "I don't know if I can do this. I hope you brought work."

She looks at him incredulously and says, "You darned near killed yourself and you wanna work? Time for you to rest for a change, and just concentrate on gettin' better."

"I need something to do."

"Do? You can get better. That's what you can do."

"You can't expect me to just lie here."

"I most certainly can."

Roger says impatiently, "If I have to lie here, I might as well be doing something, you know, to occupy my time. Right?"

She frowns. He doesn't wait for an answer and says, "Go get some files from the office. Make sure to bring Marni's file. Also, buy me a new cell phone. Bill it to the firm. Mine is probably at the bottom of that lake. And send Josie some flowers with the words 'Thank you, Roger' on the card."

Dixie stiffens at the last request. Dixie's drawl thickens when she angers. She says, "I sure in heck ain't gonna send no ex-wife flowers. That's just plain weird if you ask me! Maybe you hit your head a little too hard. Cuz you sure ain't thinkin' straight!"

Roger says, "It's not like that, and you know it."

She stops. It's true. She does know it. Roger speaks horribly about Josie. As a matter of fact, Dixie is surprised to hear him use her real name. Usually, he refers to her as "that fat, worthless slug". He's told Dixie numerous times that Josie was the biggest mistake of his life. Many times prior, Roger elaborately shared details about what a lousy cook, housekeeper, and lover she was.

What he left out and failed to tell Dixie is that Josie was faithful, loyal, and kind. He also forgot to mention that Josie put Roger through law school and helped launch his career. As usual, Roger picks and chooses which details to share. Dixie unquestionably takes Roger's every word for fact. She idolizes him. Never before has she felt threatened by Josie. That is until these last twenty-four hours.

They spend the next few minutes arguing back and forth. Roger raises his voice. The argument gets out of hand. Dixie remembers what the doctor said about Roger taking it easy and "no excessive activity or excitement."

Quickly, she changes her tone and gives in, saying, "Fine, but I don't like this one bit. And I don't like being your errand girl! I need to be with you. Here. Taking care of you. What if you need me? Plus, you're really not supposed to be working at all."

"Don't argue with me."

"Roger, the doctor made your injury sound pretty serious. Don't you think you'd better check with him first?"

"No."

"I think you're under observation for the next few days. You're not even supposed to get out of bed unless you gotta take a whiz."

He grabs her and kisses her.

She pulls away and says, "Roger, this is serious." Her forehead furrows into a pattern of wrinkles.

Roger kisses her forehead and says, "Relax. I'll be fine. Just do what I say." He winks, nudges her towards the door, and dismisses her concern with a pat on the rear end as she leaves.

As soon as the door shuts, his mind instantly wanders back to Josie. He tries to remember. He vaguely sees the outline of her face, her car, her hands on his face, and a sign reading "Emergency Entrance". The memories prove too hazy. He can't piece it all together. He questions what is real or imagined.

Roger stands to walk to the bathroom. To his alarm, his head violently aches to the point where he thinks he might be experiencing an aneurysm. He cries out in excruciating pain and collapses onto the floor. He continues screaming high-voltage, shrilling screams. The pain reaches epic proportions, too great to bear. He feels as if two white-hot pokers jab him behind his eyes. He hears feet running. He loses consciousness.

Roger briefly wakes to find a bag hanging from his bedside. He realizes with this new bag that it won't be necessary to get up to go to the bathroom anymore. He roughly makes out the outline of a pot of peach orchids and beyond it, Dixie's face. He loses focus as the blurry images fade to black. He sleeps the hours away.

Again, he wakes. He sees files neatly stacked next to his bed, but he hasn't the strength to reach for them. He sleeps more. He remembers Dixie coming and going, some doctors and nurses fussing over him, but not much else. The memories are abbreviated with faded edging. The afternoon turns into three days.

Roger finally wakes. He sees Josie next to his bed. He smiles and says, "Jo, are we going home today?"

She says, "I'm sorry, what?"

He quickly remembers his situation and says, "I mean what are you doing here?"

Josie says, "Marni asked me to come with her." Only then does Roger notice Marni standing next to her.

Marni speaks up, "Roger, I am almost embarrassed to ask you this. I hate to bother you at all. In any other circumstance I wouldn't, but my arraignment is today. I am not sure what to do. What I mean to say is that you're here. Do I still go? By myself?"

The doctor bursts through the door. He interrupts and talks strictly business. He asks Roger questions, takes notes, nods, pokes, and prods. The nurse follows closely while taking vital signs, and changing the bandage as the doctor assesses the wound. Dixie watches, standing out of the way.

The doctor says, "I am happy with your progress, Roger. You gave us quite a scare, but the worst is over now. I'd like to keep you here another night or two, but that is strictly precautionary. You should be able to go home by the weekend."

The doctor turns to Josie and Marni and says, "Now, who are these beautiful women?" He gestures to Dixie in the background and says, "I've already met Dixie. You're one lucky guy, Roger. Three beautiful women all in the same room to see you?"

Roger says, "Dr. Bartholomew, this is Marni Schoppelmann, a client, and Josephine Fleming, my ex-wife."

Dr. Bartholomew shakes hands and says, "Josephine. Aaah. Is this the 'Jo' you've been calling out for the last three days?" He doesn't wait for an answer and continues, "Well, see you tomorrow, Roger." The nurse wheels the metal cart behind the doctor, past a seething Dixie, and out of the door.

Roger turns a brilliant shade of red. Dixie turns green. Embarrassed, Roger doesn't remember a thing. Helpless, he looks to Dixie. She offers him little support. An awkward silence envelops the room.

Fortunately for Roger, he is a master of diversion. He says, "Dixie, didn't you reschedule the arraignment?"

Similar to The Iron Giant, her search and destroy sensor heats up as she ascertains Josie as a threat. Unable to control her offensive mechanisms, they will fire soon. She will destroy Josie or anyone in her path to Roger.

Roger smiles at Dixie as she momentarily holds it together. She pulls out Marni's file from the heap next to Roger. She takes control of her emotions and says evenly, "Yes, because of Roger's, uh, situation, they've rescheduled for two week's time. Sorry, with everything goin' on I forgot to notify you. I meant to."

Marni says, "I can imagine. No problem. And thank you. For everything." She turns to Roger and says, "I'm glad you are going to be okay. No offense--and I know this is not good timing, Roger--but I would kinda like closure on this chapter in my life."

Dixie says, "Well—" Roger waves her quiet.

Marni continues, "You would not believe the nightmares I have been having. I'm scared. I don't want to keep putting it off. I am not sleeping at night. I'm having trouble keeping food down. My hair is falling out. I just want this thing over and put behind me so that I can get on with my life."

Dixie jumps in and says, "Well, it ain't like he's been sunnin' himself on the beach in the Bahamas!" She prepares to fight.

With another wave of his hand, Roger dismisses Dixie and says, "It's quite all right. I understand. There is no need to worry, Marni. As far as I am concerned, this chapter of your life is over. You can put this behind you. I just need to finish tying up the final loose ends. It would be done before now if it wasn't for this." He points to his bandage and continues, "I have evidence to back up your alibi."

"You do?"

"Yes. You didn't tell us you made a call during that time."

"What time?"

"The burglary, of course."

"Oh, right."

"You had said you were on your computer during the burglary."

"I was."

"It is a good thing we (by "we" he means Dixie) crosschecked your phone records. You were on the phone with tech support at the exact time of the burglary. You couldn't possibly have been at Violet's house. The phone call was recorded." He snaps his fingers, points at Marni's file, and says, "Dixie, do we have that yet?"

Dixie says, "Not yet. Today. Maybe tomorrow. They mailed a certified copy. I have her phone records though."

Roger says, "It's done Marni. So stop your worrying and sleep well tonight."

Marni lets out a cry. She covers her mouth to muffle more. With happy tears, she hugs Roger. She had forgotten about the tech call when her computer locked up. She speaks muffled, unintelligible words of gratitude through tears of relief.

Roger returns her hug, laughs, and says, "There, there. It's OK. I am just sorry I couldn't get our hands on the actual burglar." He thinks, *And her red panties.* He says, "We were close." *Real close.* He licks his lips at the mere thought of just how close and says, "Too bad now the trail is cold. Sorry." Obviously, his memory is not completely gone.

Marni says, "Sorry? Don't be silly. I am so, so very grateful. You saved my life!"

Roger looks directly at Josie and says, "I can understand your sentiment."

Uncomfortable, Josie shifts from one foot to the other. Dixie puts her hands on her hips and looks at Josie and then to Roger.

As if reading Dixie's mind, Josie says, "Marni, we should go now. He needs his rest. Dixie, he's all yours. Feel better, Roger."

With that one statement "he is all yours", Dixie's tense muscles immediately relax. Just like the robot in the Iron Giant, once the threat vanishes, so does Dixie's arsenal of firepower bent on total annihilation. She powers down.

Dixie says, "Thank ya'll for stoppin' by. And thanks for the ride Josie and takin' care of my old man. Y'all take care."

Josie leaves the room feeling uncomfortable. She didn't like the way Roger looked at her. *That look in his eyes. I've seen that before.*

She's seen Roger more in the last six weeks than she did in the entire last year of their marriage. Her emotions run hot and then cold. She feels both the awkwardness and the pain of seeing him, but also gratitude for him helping Marni. And while he is not her favorite person, she feels relief that the man dying in her hands a few nights before will survive and be fine.

During the entire car ride to the club, Marni positively beams so much so that it's hard for Josie not to follow. She looks at Marni and thinks, *Roger might have been the worst husband ever, but he is by far the best lawyer I could possibly have hired for her. I will be forever grateful for this.*

With the weight lifted off of her shoulders, Marni's zeal for life returns with a fervor. When she arrives at the courts, some of the day's matches are already completed. She finds Ceridwin eating lunch in the buffet area.

Marni eats a lemon bar from Ceridwin's plate and loudly says, "Make way in the buffet line ladies! If the line could please part, this is my first meal as an exonerated woman!"

Ceridwin puts down her plate and jumps up and down with tiny hops, "What? That's great! GREAT!" She hugs her.

Marni smiles and says loudly enough for everyone to hear, "You may want to get in front of me, because there's not gonna be much left behind me. I'm making up for lost time."

Josie laughs. She watches her friend take her place in the line. Joking aside, Marni has lost weight in the last few weeks waiting for her impending trial, too much weight. Her eyes look sunken, surrounded by hollows of skin and darkened by a perpetual lack of sleep. Her cheekbones pronounce themselves dramatically, and her clothes hang loosely on her new wispy frame. Worry takes its toll.

As Ceridwin orders champagne for the table, two girls in the front of the buffet line move aside, making room. They motion for Marni to cut in front of them. They might be on the opposing team, but they know Marni's story and share in the excitement.

Monica sees the newly formed opening in the buffet line and takes it for herself. She says, "Don't mind if I do." She wedges her plate between the teammates, pushes to the front of the line, and helps herself. The two girls know Monica by reputation.

One says, "Monica, what do you think you're doing?"

Monica says, "Oh, were you not giving up your place in line?"

The girl answers, "Yes, but it was for Marni."

Monica wants to say, "Marni, Marni, Marni. When will the lovefest end?" Instead, she curtly says, "I should feel bad I suppose. Especially, since this space is reserved only for Marni."

Shocked the girl says, "Yes, you should. We were making a gesture."

Monica says, "Well, this is my gesture." She flips the girl off.

The girl slams her plate down and says, "That's it! Monica, you were rude to us on the court, and now you're even ruder to us off of the court. And for no apparent reason! I don't know what your problem is, and frankly I don't care!"

Her partner says, "Yeah, and I will be making a formal complaint to the board detailing your outrageous behavior. You cannot act this way and expect to get away with it! It is simply unacceptable! You *will* be hearing from the board. I promise you that!"

Monica says, "Don't be such a whiney baby. Fine. Go tell the board on me. Tattletale!" Monica strikes a pose, mocking a terrified look, and says, "OK, whiney baby! I'm so scared! Go tell your big sister so she can come beat me up, because you're too much of a wuss to do it yourself!" Monica scopes out the deserts, never acknowledging the shocked look on the girl's face.

The girl's partner also slams her plate down. She lunges for Monica, but her partner holds her back and says, "She's not worth it! Come on, let's go!"

Monica says, "Let's discuss worth, shall we? I'm not worth any of the lowbrow crap you can dish out! It's beneath me. You see? I'm worth much more! I'm better than anything you got on or off of the court." She shakes a finger at them and continues, "You hear that? I'm better than you, and you, and your little scrawny threats!"

Both girls turn to leave. The one who held her friend back yells, "How rude!"

Monica says, "It ain't just rude, it's Boca rude, baby."

The girl says, "One day Monica, you're going to get what's coming to you!"

Monica holds up one hand as if she is testifying in a gospel choir and belts out, "Boca rude, baby. Mmmm-hmmm." She sees one of the girls has left the last piece of peppermint chocolate bark on her discarded and untouched plate. Monica holds up the chocolate delicacy and yells after them, "If this is what's coming to me, bring it on! Everyone knows I love peppermint!" She eats it on the way back to her seat. The girls leave in a huff.

Mitch sits at the next table well within earshot. He silently listens to the whole conversation. The last thing he needs is another complaint to the board regarding Monica's behavior. It doesn't reflect well on the club. He sighs and follows the offended girls to the parking lot. As he approaches the girls, he thinks of what to say and how to fix this ugly mess: yet another one of Monica's fires to put out.

EIGHTEEN

What is laid down, ordered, factual is never enough to embrace the whole truth: life always spills over the rim of every cup.
-Boris Pasternak

After lunch, Marni says, "Josie, come on. Let's hit." Feeling like her old self again, Marni anxiously wants to get back to the courts. She relishes the idea of resuming to normalcy after the arrest, especially in regards to tennis.

Josie looks at her watch and says, "I don't know."

Marni says, "Come on. We might as well get some exercise while we are here. Right?" She pats her belly and says, "Plus, I ate way too much. I should run some of this off."

Josie looks at her watch again and says, "I have forty-five minutes. I need to be on a call in an hour."

"Let's do it!"

Josie says in a less than enthusiastic tone, "Absolutely."

They change in the locker room and chat as they walk to Court Three with their tennis bags in tow. When they pass Court Four, Josie recognizes a familiar face. She stops and yells through the bougainvillea-entwined fence surrounding the court, "You need a frying pan for a forehand like that."

Todd laughs and says, "Why don't you come on out here, and let me hit you a few serves? Then, we'll see what you have to say about the way I hit."

Josie doesn't answer. Last time she returned his serves her wrist hurt for a week. Instead, she says, "Playing hooky?"

Todd says, "No, this is what lunch looks like for me most days." He yells, "Forty: Love." Todd stops his service motion and says, "Sorry. Josie, Marni, this is Stephen Conrad."

After they exchange civilties, Todd adds, "Stephen owns the music store off of Glades by the mall."

Stephen says, "Josie, your brother tells me you are an excellent accountant. He didn't mention how beautiful you are, too. I was just telling him I need a new C.P.A. Mine retired. Do you have a card on you?" Josie and Stephen briefly exchange contact information before Josie moves to the next court.

As Marni and Josie unpack their tennis bags, Marni whispers, "He's kinda cute, don't you think?"

"Stephen?"

"Yeah."

Stephen looks her way and smiles. *He's got a nice smile.* As he notices Josie looking, he decides to deliver something worthy of watching. He goes for his next shot. However, in doing so, he overcooks a cross-court forehand. Miraculously, it finds the back of the baseline. He follows the shot in to the net. He glances sideways to make sure that Josie still watches.

Todd makes a desperate stab, gets a racquet on the deep ball, and defensively pops it up. The lob falls short.

Stephen rushes in and jumps in the air for a Pete Sampras-esque crushing overhead. He unleashes his racquet with maximum force to crush the ball. Overcome with enthusiasm, he overruns the ball. He tries correcting his positioning midair. The effort results in overcompensation, throwing his body further off balance. He completely whiffs on the ball with such impressive velocity that he slams into the net, racking himself with the end of his racquet on his follow through. He moans, and crumbles into a heap.

Josie and Marni wince simultaneously. Josie says to Marni, "Oooph. Hope he's okay."

"Wow. Well, he's still got the cute part going for him. However, you two may never have children."

Stephen howls several obscenities and then whimpers.

Josie frowns and says, "Yeah. Not feeling it."

Marni says, "What? Not feeling it? That's it! Give the guy a chance. He just might be boyfriend material."

Todd runs for ice. Stephen vomits. Mitch arrives by golf cart with an icepack. Together, Todd and Mitch help Stephen into the cart.

Josie says discreetly, "I didn't know getting racked could make you vomit."

Marni says, "Yeah, poor guy. It can. From the pain. It shoots an urgent message up the spermatic plexus into the abdominal cavity, causing nausea, and sometimes vomiting."

"Geez, you're such a geek."

"Thank you."

"Spermatic plexus?"

"Mm, hm."

"There are so many questions running through my head right now, I don't even know where to start."

"Like about the origin of medical terminology? Cuz it's so easy to break down, you know. It's easy to figure out from the Latin roots, well, the meaning of any medical word, really. Cool, huh?"

"No. Besides, my questions were geared more toward an entirely different direction. Like, what's on your night table? JAMA? And when in your lifetime would you ever need to use the term spermatic plexus?"

"Excuse me, but I just did. Anyway, to give you an example: spermatic plexus. If you break down the word spermatic to—"

"Please stop."

Stephen says in a significantly higher pitch, "Todd, grab my phone, please? Can you call my Mom? She's on speed dial one. Ask her to come pick me up. I don't think I can drive."

Marni quietly teases Josie, "Whoa. Speed dial one? You just gave him your contact info, right? Maybe you could work your way up to Speed Dial 2. Eventually."

"I don't even care to be three or four."

"Maybe you could go on a date with him. And his Speed Dial One Mom."

Josie says, "Wait. What happened to Miss Sympathy and he 'just might be boyfriend material?'"

"True. He might be. And his Mom might be a nice lady. Just sayin'."

"Ugh."

Marni hits solid groundstrokes alternating between Josie's backhand and forehand, and says, "Maybe she's a good baker."

Mitch puts the cart in gear and the three guys sputter off. Josie mixes in a few slices and says, "Or an ice pack maker."

"He does seem to need an ice pack. You never know. She could be your Mom away from Mom."

"True. She could be the designated driver in the three-way relationship."

Marni hits a high roller and says, "It would be nice to have a designated driver for your dates."

Josie says, "Yes, and she could carry a mini pack of tissues for us."

Marni comes in for some volleys and says, "You never know when you need a tissue."

Josie hits an approach shot and jogs to the net. She says, "Never."

Marni and Josie oscillate between opposite ends of their service boxes, taking the ball out the air while volleying the whole time. Marni says, "Seriously though, I do know of someone who is certifiably boyfriend material."

Josie says, "Does he come with a stamp?"

"This guy doesn't need one."

"Expiration date?"

"Doesn't need one of those either."

"OK, so when are you going out with him?"

Marni approaches the subject carefully and picks her words with even greater care. She failed miserably on her last three attempts to set Josie up on a date. She says, "Actually, I was kinda thinking of setting him up with someone."

"Are you looking at me? Don't look at me."

"It's time, Josie. It's been almost two years."

They trade groundstrokes for several minutes. Finally, Josie says, "Yes, it's been *over* two years. And I'm still not ready."

Marni says, "You don't have to be ready. Just dip your toe in."

"You sound like Todd."

"So, listen to Todd. Listen to me."

"Nope. Not ready." Josie remembers the last date she went on, over two years ago. It was right after her divorce was finalized. She would rather forget that date with Billy Rollins, the neighborhood bachelor and not by choice. That night still haunts her.

She drank far too much and made out with Billy at the local bar. The kissing started nicely enough, until Josie began calling him Roger in her drunken stupor.

The final straw for Billy resulted from Josie insisting they start couple's therapy, even going so far as to pull out her phone to dial her therapist. She doesn't remember, but learned later that she called her not-so-thrilled therapist at one o'clock in the morning. While doing so, she dropped her phone, bent to pick it up, knocked her head on the bar, and passed out cold on the sticky floor.

Billy took this as a sign from God and ran. Josie woke to her throbbing forehead being stitched in the emergency room. She was too inebriated for painkillers. Luckily, the wound only needed four stiches. *That night was a total crash and burn.*

Marni says, "Hello? I asked 'so will you'?"

"Oh, sorry, I was just thinking. And no thanks."

Marni moves into the middle of the net for volleys. She says, "Just go out with him as a friend, a companion."

Josie says, "Why don't you go out with him if he is so great?"

Marni moves back to the baseline and Josie stays at the net for some volleys. Marni says, "No way. My sister dated him."

Simultaneously, they both say, "Ew."

Marni says, "She's moved on. She's dating someone new, but my whole family misses him. It's too bad. If she hadn't have dated him, I probably would have."

"OK, now that's saying something. Cuz, you're so picky!" Josie thinks for a minute. *I do want to see a movie coming out. It would be nice not to go alone.* She says, "OK. One date and that is it. And it has to be Dutch."

Too excited to continue playing, Marni says, "Great! Well, gotta go." She doesn't want to give Josie a chance to change her mind and back out.

Josie looks at her watch and says, "Wait. Where are you going? We still have twenty minutes."

Marni says, "I know. Sorry, but I have to go."

Josie has repeatedly refused being set up. Everyone has tried, everyone from Vivian to Violet to Ceridwin and back again. Marni can't believe Josie finally said "yes".

Marni doesn't wait to pack up her things. She doesn't want Josie to catch up with her. She scoops up her gear in one giant heap and hurries to her scooter. She calls Scott, her sister's old boyfriend, before leaving the parking lot.

By the time Marni reaches her driveway, Josie has a first date set for Friday night. Marni giggles. She wants more than anything to do something good for Josie. Josie has done so much for her. She smiles, throws her keys on the counter, and mumbles, "Scott is a nice guy. Nice with incredible good looks. Even if nothing comes of it, Josie will enjoy just looking at him." That she is sure of. In Marni's opinion, no one deserves to have fun more than Josie.

❧

Friday night arrives quickly. Josie fidgets on her sofa, flipping channels and glancing at the clock. She's been ready for over an hour. It's not that Scott's late, it is just that Josie is early. Extremely early. And nervous. As Scott pulls into Josie's driveway, the lights from his high beams briefly announce his arrival across her living room walls.

Suddenly, a moment of regret washes over Josie. She takes a small ornamental pillow off of her sofa and wrings it. For a brief second, she considers not answering the door at all. *What was I thinking? I am not ready for this.*

Scott knocks on the door. Josie covers her face with the pillow and doesn't answer. Scott rings the doorbell. Still, Josie doesn't answer. Scott knocks on the door again. Finally, Josie opens the door to a bouquet of bright yellow tennis balls on long stems and a dimple just above the right corner crease in Scott's lips. The cleft chin and curly blonde hair leave her speechless. *Marni didn't say I was dating Abercrombie and Fitch.* He flashes a smile, and Josie forgets about ever canceling this date.

Scott says, "I believe you like tennis." He thrusts the bouquet forward.

Josie smiles and says, "Uh, tennis." *Uh, Tennis? Nice. Smooth. Ugh.* She thanks him, takes the bouquet, and says, "Please come in." She pulls the door all of the way open, forgetting to move her foot. The door hits her foot, bounces back and hits Scott in the shoulder.

Scott says, "Ow."

Mortified, she tries humor, "Oh, sorry, but there's more of that to come. Turn your head for one second and bam!" They both laugh: albeit, his laughter sounds more nervous.

He rubs his shoulder and says, "I'm glad Marni arranged this. I've been wanting to see this movie."

"Yeah, me too!" It's the reason she accepted the date in the first place. Instead of saying so, she says, "I heard they're already making a sequel." Unsure of what to do with a bouquet of tennis balls, she decides on an elegant eighteen-inch oval vase. She fusses with the arrangement. *Hmmm. Water or no water?*

Amused, Scott smiles when Josie fills the vase with water, but he doesn't say anything. She leans over the counter to arrange the stems. A wisp of wavy brown hair loosens from her swept back hairdo and falls onto her cheek. Instinctively, Scott moves forward and gingerly places the strand behind her ear. He grins. He likes what he sees.

There goes that dimple again. She shyly looks away. She doesn't know how much more of that dimple she can take. *It's magical or something.*

Scott says, "I definitely will have to thank Marni for this one." He brushes her cheek with the back of his hand after releasing the strand.

She says, "Yes, the reviews are fantastic. I haven't seen a good movie in so long."

"I wasn't talking about the movie." He grins at her again.

A rosy pink blushes over Josie's cheeks, down her neck and up to the tips of her ears. Josie makes an excuse about being late and rushes out of the door. The door closes behind her. Scott scrambles to keep up before it completely shuts.

Josie walks straight to his car and grabs the door handle as if it were base. She doesn't trust herself. *Gosh, he's cute! If he flashes that smile again, I don't know what I'll do.* They arrive for the movie a full forty-five minutes early.

Scott looks at his watch, shrugs, and says, "It's a beautiful night. Want to go for a walk? Uh, we have time."

They leisurely stroll around the lake in front of the theater. The sun sets as they begin their walk: casting yards of gold, magenta, and feathery clouds of violet light. After the sun finishes its final glory, the rising moon shines, not yet at its apex. It beams, painting glittery marks across the middle of the lake as it flicks the tips of small rippling waves.

At the water's edge, the breeze rustles through an expanse of Banyan trees, swaying their dense leaves, and brownish-red tendrils. Their waxy, green, elliptical leaves peacefully *swish-swish* in the late afternoon. The cane toads bellow a rhythmic throaty call in the distance. A spoonbill crane answers with an almost humanlike shriek.

Scott says, "What was that!"

"Spoonbill crane."

"Noisy little suckers."

'Uh-huh."

"A little unsettling."

"Yeah. The first time I heard one I thought someone was caught in the lake."

"I could see that. It sounds like it's in trouble."

"Exactly, but that's a normal call."

Carefully, Scott sidesteps a banana slug slowly marching across the sidewalk. The slug leaves a sticky opaque trail in its slow-moving wake. Scott picks up a fallen palm frond, gently scoops up the slug, and places it at the base of a tree.

He says to the slug, "Lotsa people out walking tonight. This sidewalk is not a great pick for your little stroll."

Josie says, "I know someone who steps on slugs on purpose."

"Seems pointless."

Not everyone is kind. "Especially, from the slug's point of view."

"What?"

She says, "Uh, nothing." She swats a mosquito on her arm, grimaces at its remains, and says, "That's about the only living thing I make an effort to squash."

Scott says, "Uh-huh. Mosquitoes suck. And we have our fair share of them, don't we?"

"In South Florida?"

"Yeah."

"Yeah. I should've brought bug spray."

"I just read in the paper that my county spent over ten million dollars last year in mosquito control."

She whistles and says, "No way. Ten million. Are you kidding me?"

"Nope."

"You think ten million is really necessary?"

"I don't know. Not sure. No point of reference. Did you know a couple of hundred years ago Florida was considered uninhabitable because of those tiny little buggers?"

She shoos a mosquito away from his face.

He smiles and says, "I'm sorry. I promise on our next date I'll bring my Encyclopedia of Entomology."

Next date? She smiles back. She says, "It's OK. It's hard not to talk about mosquitoes when they are swarming all around you."

"And you thought we were alone on our date."

"Ha-ha. Yeah. Maybe people were smart a couple of hundred years ago to avoid Florida." She slaps another mosquito off of her arm.

"It's different now. We can live here in relative harmony with the mosquito."

"That goes back to that ten million?"

"Yeah, I guess harmony isn't the right word. Nowadays, Florida is not so, uh, so itchy."

"Yeah. A few bites aren't going to hurt anybody."

"I dunno about that. Ever hear of yellow fever, dengue fever, or malaria?"

"Sure. I remember reading about the yellow fever epidemics Florida had in the eighteen hundreds, but that was a long time ago."

"Exactly. Guess why?"

"Uh, back to the ten million?"

"You guessed it. Mosquito control."

"OK. Sure, but what about the Native Americans? The Seminoles? They thrived in this area long before our ancestors arrived. How could they live here if mosquitoes were so, uh, horrible?"

"They were smart, using their local resources. They pounded the root of Goldenseal, mixed it with bear grease, and used it as a repellent lotion. They also smeared parts of the yarrow plant over themselves. Sometimes, they burned fringed sagewort. The smoke was said to repel mosquitoes so well that even their horses would stand in its smoky path, avoiding the wrath of those tiny vermin."

"Bear grease?"

"Bear grease."

"Is that what I think it is?"

"Yep."

"That couldn't have smelled very good."

"That's the whole idea behind repelling."

"Yuck. We still have mosquitoes."

"Yep. And mosquito control. Top Florida tourist destinations battle the little beasts so visitors don't have to and can enjoy their surroundings. Case in point, I don't think I've ever seen a mosquito at Disney."

"Seriously?"

"Yeah. Never. Not one."

Scott walks between two red hibiscus topiaries to reach the last Banyan tree in a long row at the water's edge. Josie follows. The Banyan's knotted branches form a perfectly scooped-out seat in the tree's hollow. It's well worn. Obviously, many moonlight nights have housed the seats of untold couples.

Scott brushes off the seat, sits in half, and offers the other half to Josie. Another couple walks slowly past along the meandering path.

The man says to his date, "They got our seat." He asks Scott, "How long are you going to be there?"

Scott says, "Not long. Our movie starts in a few minutes."

The woman swats a mosquito off of her date's arm. The guy says, "Ow. What was that for?"

She says, "Mosquito."

Scott says, "Too bad you don't have any bear grease!"

The couple looks at him oddly.

Josie adds, "We could burn some fringed sagewort for you."

The guy gives them a sour look, ushers his date quickly past, and scoffs, "Druggies!"

Scott says to Josie, "You really should do something about that."

"About what?"

"Your sagewort problem."

Josie chuckles and leans forward to brush a fallen leaf from her lap. The unruly hair strand falls loose again. Scott takes the strand, and places it tenderly behind her ear. He rests his hand there before gently cupping the back of her neck and leans in for a kiss. From the far side of the lake, the bell tower chimes. One by one, the chimes count off each hour.

It's been years since Josie kissed anyone, especially someone so attractive. She doesn't trust herself to fully give in to the kiss. She slightly opens her eyelids to study his face. *It is difficult, but I must avoid the irresistible power of that dimple!* He opens his eyes also and smiles. She can't believe just how irresistible.

Scott rests her head in the nook between his shoulder and elbow, and kisses her again. He lets his kiss linger. He looks into her hazel eyes and mutters, "I really must thank Marni." He kisses her again.

As the tower finishes nine consecutive booming bells, Josie unexpectedly jumps from her seat and says, "Nine. Did I count nine?"

Scott falls backwards out of the tree. For a brief second, only his shoes are visible. When he reappears, he looks disoriented.

Josie says, "Sorry. Oh. Gosh! I am so sorry." She brushes the banyan leaves and red mulch from the back of his shirt. She continues, "It's just that our movie started at 8:50. Nine. That was nine bells. That means it's nine o'clock. We're late. Oh. Are you hurt?"

"No. Karma."

"Karma?"

"It's just that's what I get."

"Get for what?"

"Kissing you. I promised Marni this would be just a platonic date. She made me promise, but I just can't help myself." He shrugs and smiles.

That dimple. She kisses him, giving in to it fully. With great difficulty she stops herself, regains composure, and says, "We'll miss the previews, but maybe we can still make the movie." Avoiding any further eye contact, she walks off the path directly through the grass and makes a beeline for the theater. *Don't smile. Please. No more dimple.*

Scott catches up to her and asks, "Where's the fire? Hey, maybe we should skip the movie."

"What?" She is certain that moments alone with him will only prove increasingly difficult to maintain her integrity. Looking at the ground, she says, "But we both want to see this movie."

"Yes, but just look at that tree. It looks so, so lonely." He grins again.

She grabs his hand and says, "Come on. We're late." *And for heaven's sake, please stop grinning.*

NINETEEN

Laughter is the sun that drives winter from the human face.
-Victor Hugo

After the first big action scene, Scott leans over and says, "Good flick!"

Josie smiles and nods. Reentering the dating world proves easier than she expected. *Why didn't I do this before? I wasted too much time.* She makes a promise, *Never again will I let a break-up break me.*

She chews on her popcorn, chocolate goobers, and sour gummies. She drinks from her forty-two-ounce soda. In the concession line, Scott had jokingly said, "You sure you don't want the nachos? It's the only thing you didn't order?"

She replied, "Sorry. I am making up for lost time." She hasn't been to the movies in years.

She plops a handful of the popcorn and chocolate goobers into her mouth. The mixture turns into a velvety clump. *Mmmm.* She vows tomorrow she will play three single's sets to burn off the extra calories.

Scott opens a box of Lemonheads and drinks his Vitamin Water. He would like to hold her hand, but she doesn't have a free one.

She whispers, "Great action."

Scott says, "Better than the one in the tree?"

"You're still thinking about that tree?"

"Yep."

Despite herself, she chuckles. When she does, a clump of two partially chewed chocolate goobers cemented with wet popcorn and mashed gummies move from her palate to the back of her throat.

Reflexively, she coughs. When she does, the now unrecognizably wet, gooey ball flies out of her mouth and lands squarely on Scott's beautifully pressed, light blue, windowpane shirt. The mess sticks to the right of his collar with impressive staying power. Scott doesn't notice and continues watching the screen.

Aghast, Josie stares. It truly is a horrific sight: a matted and slimy dark ball. *Much like the oily remains of an invertebrate. Ew.* Disgusted, she places her hand over her mouth. She can't believe that came from her.

Occasionally, and at the right unseen opportunities, she blows on the mess, hoping to dislodge the glob from its starchy, cotton home and send it into the murky depths beneath the theatre's stadium seating. Unsuccessful, she reformulates her plan. She decides to knock the goo off in the parking lot somehow before Scott gets in his car. The movie ends, and the lights turn on. She jumps back. It's more grotesque than she thought.

Scott talks, but she doesn't hear. She can't take her eyes off of the oozing ball of goo on his shirt. The chocolate and buttery grease stain spreads, creating an oily halo affect around the chewed piece lodged firmly on Scott's fine cotton shirt.

Scott says, "Are you all right? You look as if you've just seen a ghost."

"Worse. I mean I'm fine. It was just an exciting movie that's all. Twist ending with a gooey mess."

"With a what?"

"Er, never mind. Do you mind if we take a shortcut to the car?" Anxious to rid Scott's shirt of the mess, she points to the side exit.

He says, "Sure, but do you mind if we make a pit-stop first? I need to visit the bathroom." She nods. He grabs her hand and leads her through the congested hallway. She waits by the door. He says, "Back in a flash."

Shortly, he returns from the men's bathroom as the hallway clears. Josie notices a large watermark where the ball of goo once clung. Scott says, "Sorry it took so long, but I had the most disgusting thing stuck on my shirt. And I mean stuck on, like cement. It took some real elbow grease to get it off."

She opens her mouth to explain the goo, but nervous laughter erupts instead. She feels obliged to confess that the offending goo came from her.

Scott asks, "What's so funny?"

She says, "In the movie—" and erupts into laughter all over again.

Scott says, "Hmm. I didn't think the movie was funny at all. The hero loses his mentor and the love of his life."

Josie says, "I know. It's not that. It's—" She pictures the goo and the mess and how awful it all is. She curses her bad luck and the fact that she would accidentally spitball not only the best looking guy in the entire theater, but also her first date in years. It shouldn't be funny, but somehow the absurdity of the situation catches her off guard, and she giggles again uncontrollably.

Scott hugs her, tickles her, and says, "Did they spike that forty-two-ounce soda of yours? Or is this some sort of sugar rush from your concession stand extravaganza?"

She attempts explaining again and says, "It wasn't the soda. It was the mixture of goobers, popcorn and--" Embarrassed, she giggles again. The laughter starts in her belly and works its way up. It doesn't occur to her that he might not find it funny. She holds her stomach, but cannot contain the laughter. Her side aches under her ribs.

He holds her hand as they walk towards the parking lot. He says, "Come on Giggles. Let's get out of here before I run into whatever it was that left that mark on my shirt. I *never* want to meet the creature that thing came from. Disgusting!"

Sobering thought. It hadn't occurred to her that he might find *her* disgusting, not just the goo. She decides to remain mute on the subject for now.

Only a short car ride away, they arrive at her front door. She doesn't invite him in. She can't. *I don't trust myself. If he smiles again and flashes that dimple, I am lost.* He delivers one of the best kisses in her lifetime, making it even harder to say goodnight.

He asks, "When can I see you again?" They make plans for the following Saturday.

৵৵

Saturday arrives quickly for Josie's second date with Scott. Every few minutes she checks the clock above her kitchen sink. She checks again and reads the time. *Nine forty-five.* Scott said to be ready at ten o'clock a.m. He wouldn't say where they were going; only that she should wear a bikini.

I haven't worn a bikini in years. Nervously, she fidgets with the strap in the back of her new black halter-top. She checks the fit of the two-piece in the foyer mirror one last time. She poses and turns, poses and turns. Her stomach muscles define themselves. The sinewy muscles in her legs ripple as she turns. Still, not completely comfortable, she mumbles, "Bikini, huh? Not my favorite thing."

She pauses as it occurs to her; she stood in this exact spot two years earlier, equally unsure and uncomfortable. Todd had dragged her out to Le Château for the first time. Back then she donned a plus-sized tennis shorts ensemble. She turns again. Gone is the double chin. She sucks in her stomach and turns sideways. No longer does she slouch.

She rips the size six tag off of the bathing suit. She slips on her white gauze cover-up, slides on her black flip-flops, and grabs her oversized straw sunhat. The shade from the large hat will more than cover her shoulders. Still, she packs sunscreen as Scott suggested.

The doorbell rings. Scott gives her a breezy kiss on the cheek and quickly ushers her to the car. They drive forty-five minutes before turning right off of Interstate 95.

Josie says, "Still not going to tell me?"

He smiles and says, "Nope. It's a surprise. Besides, we are almost there." A short drive further and a little more than one mile south of Sailfish Marina, Scott parks his car on a slab of coquina. They walk around to the back of what looks to be an old historic one-story stucco house. The details look ancient: light walnut stained doors, Key West style shuttered windows, and an old brick and mortar style back deck with built in seating. A grand old Poinciana tree stretches its mighty orange flower-laden branches over most of the house's roof, generously cooling the sweltering temperatures underneath by many degrees.

Scott walks between two sweetly aromatic, white-blossomed camellia bushes and through a covered walkway. The entire back of the house features floor-to-ceiling windows facing the water. Scott sees a note with his name stuck on the sliding glass doors.

Reading it, he announces, "Shoot. We just missed them. I wanted you to meet them."

"Who?"

He walks back through the camellia bushes again and unlocks a narrow wooden side door. Josie peers inside through the door's small window. The window features tiny bars with an iron leaf and vine motif. Scott works the key and opens the door into a small mudroom. He scribbles on the back of the note and leaves it on the counter next to a massive stainless steel utility sink.

He takes two similar keys from a leaf and vine iron rack. Josie helps carry supplies from his trunk to the boat dock. Two jet skis sit waiting. Scott packs a portable grill and a small bag of charcoal on one side of the first Sea-Doo. He then packs a portable cooler under its hood. He packs two collapsible chairs on the side of the second Sea-Doo.

Josie says, "Won't the owner get mad?"

"Not if the owner is my Mom and she suggested it."

"Your Mom rides Sea-Doos?"

Scott laughs at the picture in his head and says, "Not exactly. She's on her boat that is usually docked there." He points to the empty spot off the dock. He continues, "My sister and her family are here from Naples. They all went out on the boat earlier. We just missed them by twenty minutes. I guess they couldn't wait. Anyway, they won't be back until tomorrow or maybe the next day. The Sea-Doos are mine and my sister's."

He gives her a run-through on how to operate the Sea-Doo. Next, he instructs her on what to do when wakes from passing boats collide with them. He says they won't travel fast due to the weighted load he packed.

They arrive at a small, private island in the middle of the Intracoastal Waterway just before noon. Scott unpacks their beach chairs and sets them next to a round pit in the sand. Next, he sets up the portable grill. They walk along the beach until Scott spots what he searches for. He wades into thigh-high water until he stands next to an old fisherman.

Scott asks, "What's in the bucket?" He points to the water filled bucket behind them on the beach.

The fisherman says, "Two black grouper and one red snapper."

"What do you want for the snapper?"

"Not for sale."

"The black grouper?"

"You can have the smaller one."

"Ten bucks?"

"You can just take it."

Scott thanks the fisherman, and hands him the ten bucks anyway. They chat for a while about the area, the best bait to use, places to fish, and the fisherman's gear. Finally, Scott carries the flopping fish back to where the coals are now smoking hot on the grill.

Scott hands Josie corn on the cob from the cooler. She seasons and wraps it in aluminum foil before placing it on the grill. She finds a small piece of driftwood with a flat spot in the middle. She uses it as a table between their two chairs. Scott quickly and expertly fillets the fish. He adds a pat of butter to the pan on the small grill then adds the lightly salted and peppered grouper fillets. The fish sizzles upon contact against the cast iron skillet, emitting a clean succulent aroma.

More and more people arrive by boats as the day unfolds. The tiny beach fills. Josie and Scott eat, swim, and snorkel. After a few sun-soaked hours in the water, they recline in their beach chairs and while away the hours relaxing. The shade from a palm tree overhead partially blocks the sun's rays. The ocean's rhythmic waves roar, tumbling into white frothy foam just before hitting the shore. The seagulls caw pleasantly in the distance. Josie hears shouts and laughter from the boats and water nearby. The salt air tingles her nose and leaves a slightly gritty film on her skin. She digs her feet into the warm sand and reclines further into her chair.

Relaxed and full, Josie falls asleep while watching a school of dolphins emerge and re-emerge in the distance. Josie wakes as a volleyball rolls into her foot. A young boy apologizes, retrieves the ball, and rejoins his game.

Scott says, "Hey, sleepy head. Glad I'm so exciting."

"Sorry, I was up late finishing a file. I guess too late."

He grins and says, "No problem. I could watch you sleep all day."

"Did I miss anything?"

"Nope. But I've been waiting for you to wake up. Ready to leave?"

Josie stretches, yawns, and nods. They pack their Sea-Doos in the late afternoon sun, just as the beach reaches nearly full capacity. Taking several trips, they weave between sunbathers, a beach soccer game, and sand castles as they repack their Sea-Doos before heading back.

Once at the house, they swim in the pool, ridding themselves of the remaining beach sand and sea salt. Slightly sunburned, they change into dry clothes and drive to Sailfish Marina for drinks just in time for a vibrant orange, crimson red, and golden sunset.

As the sun sets Scott leans over and kisses her. He says, "I've been waiting to do that since the last one when you knocked me out of the tree."

She blushes.

He plays with the one wavy loose strand of hair framing her face, gently twisting it around his finger. He smiles. His dimple never ceases to amaze her. He says, "It was worth the wait." They finish their drinks and feed the rabid amberjack darting back and forth underneath the pier.

Not wanting the day to end, Scott says, "Look, that grouper was good for lunch, but it just wasn't enough for me. I know this great place not too far from here. It's a small place in an unassuming strip mall called the Food Shack. They have a butternut squash encrusted hogfish to die for. Want to go?"

Not wanting the day to end either, Josie says, "Of course, I want to go. I have to see what a hogfish looks like."

❧

They sit on old wooden barstools in front of the galley kitchen and the bustling chefs. Josie orders the sweet potato encrusted tilefish. Scott orders the butternut dill hogfish. They split half and half, trading delicious morsels.

Josie says, "Incredible. All ten thousand of my taste buds thank you." She takes another bite and says, "Mmmm. So good. How did you find this place?"

Scott says, "Old hangout from my younger days. I guess I never grew out of it. Hope I never do."

Josie takes another bite and says, "Some things you should never outgrow."

"I make the drive up here at least once a month. I hope the next time I do that you'll consider going with me."

Before she answers, Scott kisses her. She says, "Best dessert ever." This time, he blushes.

Stuffed, they walk along the beach, talk, stop, and kiss every few steps. A sliver of moon illuminates the beach enough for them to see that they are not alone. A lone sandpiper runs back and forth, foraging with its beak along the wet sand. Its tiny brown spindly legs carry it quickly from one spot to the next, darting back and forth as the water ebbs and flows with each rushing wave.

The piper's small tufted white belly matches the white sea foam it expertly avoids. As the sea foam rolls onshore, the sandpiper moves away, always keeping the same distance between itself and the moving line of foam. It creates a perfectly synchronized dance, as if some magical string exists between the edge of the foam and those tiny spindly legs. Occasionally, the piper stops and smoothes its brown speckled feathers with its pointed beak. Mirroring Josie and Scott, the bird walks and stops, and walks and stops. But for Josie and Scott, the stops involve kissing, a lot of kissing. It's after one in the morning before Scott drops her home alone.

Sleepily, she touches her lips, warm from the slight sunburn. She thinks of Scott and his sweet kisses as she drifts off into her first dream of the night.

TWENTY

By perseverance the snail reached the ark.
-Charles Haddon Spurgeon

Marni wants to hear all about the date. She says, "Power of the Dimple? I guess he does have a pretty cute smile. So, did you succumb to the Power of the Dimple?"

Josie says, "Ok. I already regret ever telling you about his dimple."

"Well? Did you?"

Josie says, "We kissed. Just hit the ball, would you?"

Marni says, "A kiss? That's it? What are you? Born-again virgin?"

"Very funny."

"OK, then what's stopping you?"

"From what?"

"From enjoying yourself for once!"

"Values. They're called values."

"Uh-huh. And what about the Power of the Dimple?"

"Shhh. Do you have to say that so loudly?"

Their opponents ask them to pipe down. One says, "All of this chatter has got to stop. We're trying to warm-up here."

Marni rolls her eyes and says in a whisper to Josie, "You could have at least invited him in for a night cap."

"No. I couldn't. That would send him the wrong message."

"No, it wouldn't!"

"A divorcee inviting a man in at one in the morning? I don't think so. He would definitely interpret that as an invitation, and you know it."

"I'm sorry. Did you say something? I fell asleep over here."

"Sorry not to paint a more sordid picture for your selfish entertainment."

"Not selfish. I am willing to share the info with anyone willing to listen."

"Hilarious. But seriously, who wrote the rules anyway? Is there a manual for post-divorce dating? Does it say that you have to put out? Is it expected just because I've been married before? Why can't I take it slow? Besides, he told me that you told him to keep it platonic."

"I meant for the first five minutes."

Josie says, "I see."

Marni hits a cross-court forehand and approaches the net for volleys. She says, "If we lose today, it's because you lulled me to sleep with stories of your dull, dull, *very* dull dating life."

Josie bounces a ball off of Marni's leg. Josie says, "Well, wakeup and bring it. I want to get done early. I have a report to finish before five. Besides, if we lose today, I'm blaming it all on you."

"Pressure, pressure."

"Yes, and the joy of playing doubles."

"What? You mean that nothing is ever your fault?"

"Never is. Well, that is unless we win. Then, that is entirely my fault."

At the end of the warm-up, Josie and Marni meet their opponents at the net. They spin Josie's racquet, deciding who serves first. The other team wins the spin and decides to receive instead of serving first.

Before each team returns to their respective places on the court, one of the opponents says, "I hope you girls don't talk this much during the match. If you do, I will be using the hindrance rule against you. It will cost you points. Consider that your warning." She stares directly at Josie.

Josie meets her gaze and says, "Let's keep it fun, girls."

Marni says, "Don't worry. We won't be talking much. Josie hasn't anything interesting to say." Then, she whispers to Josie, "Homework. You have homework to do. And I will be grading every juicy detail!"

Despite herself, Josie laughs.

Josie and Marni finish the two set victory in a crushing forty-seven minutes with a score of 6:1; 6:0. They shake hands with their opponents at the net.

Marni says to the opponent, "Too bad we didn't talk much. You could've used that hindrance rule to help you out. Either that or maybe a real forehand."

The opponent drops her racquet, and yells, "How rude! You don't have to rub our noses in it!" She balls up her hand into a clenched fist. She gets her full weight behind a punch that lands squarely on Marni's soon-to-be bloody nose. It is lights-out for Marni. Unconscious, Marni falls backwards as if into a deep slumber onto a lush, feathery mattress. However, her landing is anything but soft and feathery.

"Marni!" Josie screams. She lifts Marni's head off of the clay. She shouts at her opponent, "What is wrong with you!" The girl stares in shock. Her partner runs for help.

The girl says, "I-I-I…"

Josie brushes the clay out of Marni's hair. She says to the girl, "You'd better hope she is OK. If not, you just ruined the rest of your life over a little lighthearted ribbing from one of the nicest people you'll ever meet."

The girl starts crying and says, "I didn't mean to! It was an accident!" Her cries turn to sobs as she says, "It was just a reaction. You know. After such a horrible and hu-humiliating loss and everything. I lost my temper for a m-moment. That's it, just a b-brief moment! She had to g-go and make a j-j-joke about it and all. I-I didn't mean it! Oh my God! I h-hope sh-sh-she's OK!"

Josie says, "Accident? Yeah, right. This was no accident. You punched her right on the nose!"

The girl stops sobbing and quickly turns angry again. Marni comes to just as the girl says, "It's just that she provoked me! That's all! She was nasty to me. Rubbing my face in it and all! I am not normally like this. She egged me on. It's all her fault. It's her fault!" She points at Marni as Marni slowly regains focus.

Marni says groggily, "What happened?"

Josie says, "Marni, you were hit and you fell. You hit your head on the ground. You Ok? How many fingers am I holding up?"

The girl says, "It wasn't my fault! I didn't want to hit her!"

Marni says, "Three." Marni holds up her middle finger towards the girl and says to her, "How many fingers am I holding up?" The girl walks off in a huff.

The girl's partner returns and says Mitch is on his way. She whispers to Marni, "Sorry, but you have to understand. She isn't normally like this. Her hormones are all outta whack. She's menopausal."

Marni says, "That's impossible. What is she? Thirty?"

"Thirty-two."

Josie and Marni begin to reply simultaneously, but the girl runs off to catch up to her partner.

Mitch arrives as Josie applies a towel to Marni's bloody nose. He applies an ice pack to the swelling on the back of Marni's head and says, "Is the whole world going crazy? Can't we just have a normal day where normal people play normal tennis?" He inspects Marni's nose and the bump on the back of her head. He shakes his head and says, "Marni, did she really hit you?"

"Yes, as far as I can recollect."

He says, "Unbelievable." Mitch smoothes the furrows in his forehead and says, "OK. I will take care of this. Do you allow me to speak on your behalf?"

Marni says, "Knock yourself out."

Mitch yells at the girl before she catches up to her partner and completely out of earshot, "Wait up!" He orders her to wait in his office. Her coach, Thomas, intercepts her in The Breezeway and guides her through the maze of hallways to Mitch's office. They sit in the office chairs across from Mitch's desk and wait.

All local pros know each other. Thomas and Mitch prove no exception. Besides running their leagues, they've played each other in their club's pro events for years.

Thomas knows Mitch is a pushover off of the court. Thomas plans to use this knowledge to his advantage. While Thomas waits with his player in Mitch's office, he strategizes. He has time. It takes a while for Marni to get to her feet. As a courtesy, the other courts suspend play until she stands and walks. They clap when she finally starts moving again.

When Mitch opens his office door, he's ready to take someone's head off. However, he doesn't get the chance. Thomas launches into a verbal assault before Mitch gets a word in edgewise.

Mitch gives the time-out sign and says, "Hold on a second. I know what you are doing, but you owe it to me to listen." With that one statement, he disarms Thomas. Mitch vents first at the girl and then at Thomas. Thomas didn't see this coming. He's never seen Mitch with so much fight off of the court. He recalculates his strategy.

From the dialogue, Thomas soon realizes his girl will never play tennis at Le Château ever again. Further, she won't be allowed to play in the league, but Thomas takes heart knowing that she won't get sued—a favorite Boca past time. Like Thomas, Mitch wants to avoid as many lawsuits as possible involving his club and its members. Not surprisingly, the girl readily agrees.

By the end of the conversation, they all reach an agreement. The girl can still play in the league. However, she may never set foot on the grounds of Le Château ever again. Further, she must agree to pay Marni's medical bills and to issue a written apology.

Thomas asks for one last stipulation: if Marni's nose isn't broken then the girl can still play at Le Château. Mitch and Thomas argue. Mitch quickly moves for the close. He thinks of Marni's bloody nose and refuses to give another inch.

Mitch says, "Let's come to terms. Look, we don't want to get our lawyers involved, do we? I'll call Fran in to finalize."

While Mitch calls his secretary to his office, Thomas argues another point.

Mitch cuts him off and says, "Unfortunately, this is not the first time something like this has happened. Thomas, we have to set an example so future events like these won't happen again. Stop fighting me on this." His secretary fills in the necessary blanks on the form document, making only minor adjustments to the legal wording. She notarizes the signatures and promptly leaves.

Fortunately for Marni, Mitch knows his way around a legal agreement. As President of Tennis at Le Château, he sees more legal disputes in a year than most lawyers handle in a lifetime. Mitch finally relaxes once the ink dries on the documents. Satisfied, he feels he did well enough. As Thomas and the girl will soon find out, the punch deviated Marni's septum. Fixing a deviated septum is not cheap.

After the girl leaves Mitch's office, Thomas lingers. He makes one last ditch effort to negotiate a better deal. Desperate, he says, "I'll play you for it." Thomas hopes to return as a hero to his club's board with a better deal in hand.

Mitch says, "For what?"

Thomas hatches a plan to beat Mitch off the court. He'll tear him down and then go in for the kill on the court. He says, "I win and the paperwork goes away. You win; everything you want you keep, and I'll give you a grand out of my own pocket." Thomas doesn't really plan on digging into his own pocket, but he hopes Mitch takes the bait. His club will pay any out-of-pocket expense, especially to make an ugly mess like this go away. Besides, Thomas banks on his plan to win by beating Mitch off the court first. By the time they walk onto the court, he will have reduced Mitch to an emotional pile of ruble. He need only be on the court long enough to sweep up the remaining pieces.

Armed with the knowledge that he has never lost a match to Thomas, Mitch doesn't see the point. Besides, he doesn't want to take advantage of an old friend by taking his money. Mitch says, "Sorry, Thomas. Even if I wanted to, I couldn't. Back to back lessons and meetings the rest of the day."

Thomas says, "Come on, I think we both know that any pro finds it hard to pass on a challenge. We are wired that way. One pro set?"

Mitch hesitates, but only momentarily. Determined not to capitalize on Marni's misfortune, he says, "As I said--"

Frustrated, Thomas cuts him off and says, "Yeah, yeah. I know. Your dance card is full. You shouldn't take your job so seriously, Mitch. It's just tennis."

"Just like your player didn't take it so seriously?"

Mitch says, "I'll drive you to the hospital, Marni."

Marni remembers the last time she caught a ride with Mitch, they were left stranded on I-95 until the tow truck arrived. She says, "I thought you had lessons. Besides, Josie already offered. Thanks though."

Josie carries Marni's gear to her car. As Marni eases into her passenger seat, Josie says what she has been waiting to say, "You should sue that girl for punching you like that!"

Marni says, rather nasally, "Nah. Mitch got everything worked out. Besides, I'd just as soon spend as little time as possible with lawyers or in a courtroom, especially after what I've been through. Legal stuff is nasty no matter how right you are. And exhausting."

Josie thinks of Violet's burglary and says, "But you were innocent. It was just a matter of time before the truth came out."

Marni thinks of the hard, cold cell she sat in not so long ago and considers herself lucky. She flips down the visor.

Josie watches her friend access the damage in her passenger mirror: the dark half circle forming under one eye; the crusted blood under her nostrils.

Marni winces as she dabs at the dried blood under her nose and flips the visor back up. She says, "Ow."

Josie says, "Let's turn the car around! We should find that girl. Teach her a lesson!"

Marni says, "Oh, she'll get one all right. Medical bills are not cheap!" Marni cleans the dried blood off of her hand and says, "She obviously has no sense of humor."

"That's for sure."

"Mitch says she will issue an apology in addition to paying for fixing this mess."

Josie says, "That's good. Anger management classes might help, too."

Marni mumbles, "Or hormone therapy."

"What a mess."

"Yeah. You know this is a mess. You're right. Maybe I shouldn't have egged her on."

Josie rolls her eyes and says, "What? How is this your fault? Don't go there. This is tennis in Boca! If you can't take a little ribbing then you're in the wrong place!"

They drive out of the club's parking lot, unaware of what happens on Court One just a few hundred feet away. Ceridwin runs for a drop volley. She slides into the shot. She hits a dry patch of clay. Her shoe digs in and wedges to a jarring stop. The sudden stop lodges her shoe firmly into place while the rest of her body continues in forward motion. Her ankle rolls over her shoe. A loud crack erupts from the tendon and ligaments in her ankle. She cries out, tumbles to the ground, and stops just short of the net. She tries, but cannot stand up or put the slightest bit of weight on her foot. Her ankle swells to two times its normal size right before her eyes.

Mitch drives his golf cart over the embankment and onto the court. He lifts Ceridwin into the cart and elevates her foot. He examines it, before placing an ice pack on it. They both look worried.

Mitch thinks Ceridwin's ankle might be broken, but he doesn't say so. He doesn't want to upset her anymore than she already is.

Ceridwin says, "Sorry, Mitch. I know this has been one heck of a day for you."

"Sorry? You're the one in pain. Don't worry about me." In truth, there's nothing worse for any coach than losing his star player.

Ceridwin knows her team was tied for first place. Marni is out with what is probably a broken nose. And now, Ceridwin will be out with an injured ankle for who knows how long. She knows Mitch will miss out on the season ending bonus that he clearly deserves.

Mitch watches helplessly as the swelling continues and two purple welts suddenly spring up. He frowns. He doesn't like what he sees. He pats her shoulder and says, "Let's get you to a doctor. I know of a great sports med guy. I'll call and get you in right away."

She says, "The swelling is pushing against my shoe. Can you take it off?"

Mitch says, "Better to leave it on to help contain the swelling until we get you to a doc. I'll pull my car around. Keep the ice on."

Ceridwin says, "I have a podiatrist. Let me call her first." She calls her podiatrist and books an emergency appointment.

Mitch says, "I'll drive you to your podiatrist." He looks at her mushrooming ankle again and says, "Your husband isn't going to like this one bit. Want me to call him and break the news? It'll be easier coming for me. It'll prepare him first, before he sees that." He points to the bulbous ankle now riddled with multiple ruptured blood vessels resembling purplish-red bee stings.

Ceridwin doesn't tell Mitch that her husband is away on business, or that she plans not to tell him until he returns home next week. By that time, the ankle should look better, much better. She doesn't want to alarm him. She reasons that there's nothing he can do from that distance anyway.

Luckily, her left ankle is the one injured. So, she can still drive with her right. She doesn't tell Mitch that she plans to do so. She knows he would argue. She lifts her foot in midair and surveys the injury. She says, "Yuck! It's ugly, and it's throbbing!"

Mitch hands her two ibuprofen capsules and a bottled water. He knows it's going to take a few minutes for her to feel any pain relief, and much longer before she can play tennis again. Mitch will have to bump everyone up a position to cover the hole in the lineup that her absence will create. Still, there is no replacing Ceridwin. This will further weaken his Elite team's hope of ever winning the season ending title. He sighs. Again, Mitch offers to drive Ceridwin to the podiatrist.

Again, she refuses and lies, "Violet is taking me."

Violet looks wide-eyed at her over Mitch's shoulder, before remembering the last time she caught a ride with Mitch. His car's door handle came off in her hand. Ceridwin gives her the zip-it look. Ceridwin would rather drive herself.

Back in his office, Mitch rubs his forehead. He talks on his phone with a ball machine repairman. Through his office window, he sees Ceridwin hopping to her car. He mutters, "I knew it! I told her I would drive her."

The repairman says, "Told who?"

Mitch wonders aloud, "Why does no one want me to drive them anywhere?"

Confused, the repairman says, "Uh, I have a car."

Mitch says, "Not you. Sorry. Yes, we need it fixed. It won't run on anything but random. Can you have someone out today?" The voice on the other end speaks, but Mitch only partially listens.

Preoccupied, Mitch hangs up. He knows the bonus he hoped for--and worked so hard for--is now only a pipedream. He'll never max out on his bonus from his Elite division's year-ending win, not with two key players gone.

He opens his desk drawer and removes the new automobile brochures, dumping them into the trash. He rubs his forehead, asks for his secretary to cancel his remaining lessons, and meets his rusty beater in the parking lot. He needs to be anywhere except here for a few hours.

TWENTY·ONE

'Tain't worthwhile to wear a day all out before it comes.
-Sarah Orne Jewett, *The Country of the Pointed Firs, 1896*

Mitch won't budge. He says, "I know I told you that you would never have to play with her again, but that was before I lost Marni and Ceridwin both on the same day. You have to play with Monica. I'm sorry, but that is just the way it is."

Josie says, "Vivian? How about Vivian? Put me with her."

Mitch rubs his forehead again, changes his tone and says softly, "Not you too, Josie. There was a time when I could count on you. You would play anywhere and with anyone who I asked you to. Don't turn into another diva. God knows I already have plenty of those."

She pauses and then says, "Well, is there really nobody else?"

"No one. Otherwise, I wouldn't be asking."

"OK. I guess I could do it, but just this once."

"Fine. Marni will be back next week. You'll play with her then. It's only this once."

"OK. And I'm sorry. I don't mean to be difficult. It's just that when I play with Monica, I feel like I have three opponents instead of two. I feel outnumbered."

Mitch says, "I could understand that. Here's what you do; play your game, even when Monica gives you advice or directives. Nod in agreement, but stick to what you know works for you. Just play your game. Play to your strengths and to the ball coming at you. Block her out. Don't let her in."

"I don't want to be rude."

"I am not saying be rude, but turn a deaf ear. In other words, it is possible for you to enjoy your tennis, play well, and still not let her into your head. It can be done. Don't let her dictate your mood or your actions on the tennis court. Stay Josie."

"OK. I will try." *But this is Monica we're talking about.* A pleaser at heart, Josie has never learned how to not let other people ruin her day.

Mitch says, "OK?"

"Um, OK."

As it turns out, it is not OK. Monica tells Josie to isolate the weaker player. Josie nods as Mitch instructed, but instead of playing the weaker player, Josie plays the ball instead. Monica tells Josie to poach. Josie nods, but doesn't poach. She reads the ball, stays put, and deflects a reflex volley for a winner. Monica doesn't care that it was the right move. She wants Josie to listen.

She tells Josie to stay back for the next point; however, when the opponent hits the ball short, Josie reacts by following the short ball to the net.

Monica fumes and says, "Get with the program, Josie." Monica's dictatorship has been questioned, and she doesn't take kindly to dissension. Finally, Monica calls for a timeout.

One opponent says, "Timeout? For what? You can't call a timeout! This isn't football."

Monica says, "Fine. I am calling an injury timeout. Take ten, ladies."

The other opponent says, "An injury timeout? For what?"

Monica looks at her incredulously and says, "For the pain I am feeling in my ass."

The opponent replies, "Well! I never! Really! Come on Cynthia." The opponents walk off for the entire ten minutes allowable. They don't want to see or be anywhere near Monica.

Monica uses the full ten minutes to berate Josie. Josie stays in her calm place. That is until it shatters into oblivion: about three minutes into Monica's barrage. Josie sobs uncontrollably into her hand towel. Her embroidered name covers with a gooey clear mess from her running nose.

Monica winces, "Ewww! Josie, you're not a pretty crier."

Josie's eyebrows furrow. Her nose and forehead wrinkle into countless folds. Her chin recedes and trembles.

Helpless, Mitch and a bandaged Marni watch from the courtside.

At the end of the tirade, Monica admonishes Josie. She says, "Pull yourself together, Josie. You are representing Le Château after all. You'll give us a bad reputation! You look, well, pathetic. We still have tennis to play."

They lose 7:5, 1:6. 0:6. Josie skips the team's luncheon and takes a steam shower instead. She soaks under the nozzle until the skin on her fingers and toes wrinkle into raisin-like folds. She shampoos her hair and wonders why she didn't stand up to Monica.

She rinses her hair as she peers through the skylights above. A rainbow fans into a vibrant semicircle through the remnants of a distant shower. She stands up straight. *That's it! After every storm, there is a rainbow.* She turns off the showerhead and towels off. She looks in the mirror and slouches again. *Wait. There is no rainbow after the storm that is Monica. Maybe this life lesson is one I will never completely understand. Maybe Monica is the Category Five I will never fully recover from.*

Josie knows they should have won today. That is not what bothers her. *I seem to have somehow lost my spine in the divorce. I thought I was stronger. I just shouldn't take it. Tasha doesn't take it. Neither does Ceridwin, or Violet. Not even sweet Marni puts up with Monica.*

Mad at herself all over again, Josie takes another towel and dries her hair. She wishes she could act more like Marni or Ceridwin, drawing the line in the clay and enforcing it. *Sigh.* Replaying the situation over and over in her head doesn't seem to help.

She combs through her wet hair and begins blowing it dry. *Maybe I can't change Monica. And maybe I can't change myself.* She concludes that some personalities clash. *Monica and I just do not mesh.*

She applies gel and slicks her hair back into a low chignon. She slings her tennis bag over her shoulder and pushes open the locker room's exit door. She steps out of the locker room as a hand catches her bag and sets it down. She turns to find herself face-to-face and eye-to-eye with Scott.

She says, "Scott!"

"Yes. Surprised?"

"What are you doing here?"

Scott says, "I drove all the way here to do this." He brushes a loose strand of hair from her face and kisses her. The kiss is anything but a peck. He kisses her--a soft sweet slow rolling kiss--both tender and powerful at the same time. They stumble backwards. He catches their fall against the locker room door. The kiss leaves Josie breathless.

Scott says, "I know this sounds crazy, but I have to go back to work now."

"What!"

He looks at his watch and says, "I have a client arriving any minute. I have to go."

"Now?"

"Like right now."

"But you just got here." This time she kisses him. Someone pushes on the door from the inside. Josie yells to them, "Out of order! Use the other door!"

Scott looks at his watch and says, "I will call you later."

"You drove all this way just to kiss me?"

He blushes and says, "It was worth it."

She flings her arms around him and jumps, wrapping her legs around him too. Again, they fall against the locker room door with a heavy thud. She finds his tongue. Finally, she takes a breath. She says, "If we weren't in public—"

He smiles and places his finger over her mouth and says, "Shhhh. My, my Miss Josephine. I sure do like the way you talk."

Marni rounds the corner and says, "*This* is why I can't open the door!"

Embarrassed, Josie says, "Oh, sorry." She jumps down, straightens her shirt and says, "We were just, uh, talking."

Scott says, "Hi Marni."

Marni waves and gives Scott the once over. His hair shoots out in all different directions as if he just finished wrestling a bear. His untucked shirt hangs in a rumpled mess. Josie looks equally disheveled.

Marni says rather nasally to Josie through the bandages, "No, no. It's me that is sorry. I was just leaving. Carry on, er, talking." She turns on her heel. Josie hears Marni mumble down the hall, "Now, that is the kind of homework I was talking about."

Scott says, "I've got that dinner thing tonight. I won't see you. Unless, that is, you want to go with me?" He looks hopefully at her and adds, "We will be talking business. You might get bored, but it sure would be nice to have you with me."

Josie's biggest client meets with her early in the morning. She looks at her watch. Mentally, she does the math. If she goes home now, she might be able to finish the last document in time to go to dinner with Scott. She nods.

He says, "Is that a 'yes'?"

"Yes."

Scott doesn't wipe the grin off of his face the entire drive back to his office.

Josie passes the front desk on her way to her car. Mitch waits behind the desk. He says, "Josie, hey! I've been waiting for you. I want to apologize. You were right."

Josie touches her lips, still warm from Scott's kisses. She says, "About what?"

Mitch says, "About playing with Monica."

Josie positively beams from her recent encounter with Scott. She says, "Monica who?" She doesn't wait for his answer. She saunters across the parking lot, opens the hatch to her car, and tosses her tennis bag inside. She hears her name, and turns to see Roger Fleming walking towards her.

Roger says, "Do you have a sec?"

"No. Not really. I'm in a hurry."

"This won't take long."

"Roger, I really don't have time. Can I call you tomorrow?"

"This can't wait."

"What is it?"

"Jo, I miss you."

She blinks and stares at him.

He holds up his hands in mock surrender and says, "I know. I know it sounds crazy, but I miss you. I really miss you. I think about you day and night. Ever since I bumped my head, I've been seeing things more clearly."

"Is this some sort of joke?"

Roger shakes his head and says, "No. I wish it were. It would make things a heck of a lot less complicated. Believe me. I was wrong. I was wrong about so many things."

"Did you just admit that you were wrong about something? Roger, maybe that bump really did do something."

"Very funny."

"You should see your doctor. I have to go."

"Wait! I was wrong about us. The problem wasn't you. It was me. I wasn't ready. I wasn't ready for the type of relationship we had."

"If you weren't ready to be married, then you shouldn't have asked me."

"Hear me out. You see it wasn't you. It was me. You held us together all those years, and I threw away the best thing that ever happened to me. You were a great wife, a great lover, and a great friend. I just wasn't mature enough to handle it."

"Oh, so is this the apology? You ruined my life and everything, because you were immature?"

"Yes! Exactly!"

"Please. This *is* a joke, right?" *There is no way I could have seen this coming, not a chance.*

"Believe me, I wish it were. Then, it would be over. Jo, I am not OK. I feel sick all of the time. I can't sleep. I can't eat. I lose focus at work. I miss you. I am miserable without you."

Josie wants no part in this conversation. She wants him to go away, vanish. She gets in her car and starts the engine. She says, "Well, you legally left me because you *didn't* want to see me anymore." She shuts her door and puts her car in reverse.

He knocks on her window with the back of his knuckle and motions for her to roll it down. He says, "I know it sounds crazy, but ever since I hit my head, I've been seeing things clearly. It's you. It's always been you. I need you."

"What are you talking about?"

"I thought I could live without you. I even thought I didn't love you, but I do. I absolutely do."

One thing she has learned over the years; a hidden agendum lurks behind every remark Roger makes. Josie says, "OK. I have no time for this. Tell me what you want?"

"Nothing."

"Really?"

"Can we start over?" Hopeful, he sees the look on her face and quickly adds, "As friends?"

"Roger, you're the worst friend ever. I've moved on. I can't be your doormat any longer."

Roger says, "And that's the problem. Don't you see? You didn't stand up for yourself, Jo, and I walked all over you!"

Angrily she says, "Oh, so your bad behavior is my fault? Is that it? Well, allow me to clarify something; in a relationship, I don't want to have to stand up for myself, Roger. On the contrary, I want the other person to have my back. You were awful to me. Why doesn't it surprise me that you would blame anyone but yourself for that!"

"It takes two to make a marriage crumble. No one wants to be married to a doormat. Of course, they take them for granted. Of course, they treat them subpar."

"*Subpar*? How about sub-human!"

"I know I treated you horribly, and I'm sorry for that."

Josie looks shocked. *Did he just apologize again?* Never once in their many years of marriage did he ever apologize for anything. On the contrary, his sense of entitlement pushed new boundaries. Once, he even asked her to wipe his behind after he went to the bathroom. It was an all-time low for her and one of the few times she said "no" to him. She can't hear anymore of his nonsense. She steps on the gas.

He says, "Hey, wait! Just wait! One second!"

She hits the brake and yells, "I wasn't a doormat, Roger! I was a good partner and worked hard at being a good partner. My Dad once told me that in a marriage if you both gave one hundred and ten percent, then your marriage would be successful. I gave one hundred and ten percent." She looks at the clock on her dash. She needs to go. She yells at him, "How much did you give!"

"But that's just it! I don't *want* a doormat. I want a partner. You weren't an equal partner. You gave too much! You're different now. Somehow."

She looks incredulous. She says, "Oh, I see. I should have given the least I possibly could and taken the most, just like you? Right? Is that it?"

She grips the wheel and fights the urge to run him over. He looks unruffled and almost pleased. He says, "See? Now, we are talking. Now, we're getting somewhere. Would you consider going to counseling with me? I mean we are both in a better place. Look at you, and look at me. We should talk this thing out."

"There is no *thing* to talk out, Roger. What we had is long gone. Where there is a *you*, a *me* cannot exist. You crush me. You suck the very life out of me. I'll never go back to that place." *I can't. It would be the end of me.* She decides to finalize this once and for all and says, "It will never happen, Roger. Never."

Roger realizes he will not get what he wants, for now. Never one to walk away empty-handed, he aspires to win a smaller victory. Ever the tactician, he says, "I'm not asking you to change your life, but wouldn't it be nice if we could be friends? We see each other all of the time. We run in the same circles. Wouldn't it be nice if it weren't awkward when we saw each other? If we actually got along?"

She says, "I'm fine with the way things are between us. Better yet, I'm fine with the way things are with myself. Now, take your hands off of my car. I have to go."

He says, "Go where? To see that boyfriend of yours."

So, that is what this is about. She says, "How did you know about him?"

"I came here to talk with you today, and I saw you two kissing in the hallway. So, I came out here and waited for you."

"Well, don't wait for me anymore. I am not looking to be friends or anything else with you. You hear me?"

"Sure. You say that now, but you sure were nice to me when you needed a favor."

"A favor? Are you talking about Marni? If I remember correctly, you got something out of that: a ruthless new no-alimony agreement. So don't act all altruistic!" She guns her engine and leaves the parking lot. She grumbles to herself the entire drive home. No one gets her blood boiling quite like Roger Fleming.

Roger smiles while watching her drive away, and mutters, "I like the new Jo."

Josie watches as his image grows smaller and smaller in her rearview mirror. She takes in a deep breath, glad for the increasing distance between them. Confronting Roger takes a heavy toll on her each time. It's complicated. Part of her still loves him and always will. Before turning out of the parking lot, she looks back one last time. The other part leaves her stomach churning, culminating into a sharp reflux of bile production. She swallows hard, but still belches.

As Roger's image fades, his shirt remains in her thoughts. *It's the same dark blue button down he wore on our last day together.* She remembers that day all too vividly. Over their morning coffee, she mustered the courage to confront him. She remembers how nervous she felt before she spoke, as if the rest of her life depended on her next few words.

She said, "Roger, I've been wanting to talk with you. It's just that I-- well, I-I-I am not sure what is happening here. You know between us. I miss you. I miss us. I don't know what I've done, or why things have changed." She began crying softly. She managed to pull herself together enough to say, "I want to fix this. I know we can fix this. I would like to."

Roger said nothing in response. Disappointed and with her determination fading, she boldly aimed for the heart of the matter and said, "I know something is wrong. Y-y-you haven't touched me in so long." She waited for him to say something: a word, a syllable, anything.

Roger continued sipping his coffee. He did not feel the need to look up from his newspaper or address his wife's concern. Josie remembers how heavy the air felt between them, as if the weight might suffocate her and crush all she holds dear. She patiently waited, surveying the top of his perfectly coifed light brown hair protruding inches above his newspaper. More minutes lapsed.

Deflated from no response, her desperation grew. Now, she cringes as she remembers what she asked next. She said, "How about a hug this morning before you go to work?" She doesn't know why she asked. *Stupid. That was a stupid thing to ask.*

She glances in her rearview mirror. *Glad I can't see him. A hug of all things.* She remembers his response. Finally, Roger folded his newspaper and placed it neatly next to his breakfast plate. He avoided looking directly at his wife: her shoulder-length wavy chestnut hair, her soft pink semi-sheer nightgown, and her hopeful eyes. Once his newspaper rested on the table and with every last sip of his coffee consumed, only then did Roger acknowledge his wife's presence. He stood to leave for work, and simply said, "Now, why would I do that?" He briskly walked past.

She doesn't want to remember more. She arrives home. *I'm done crying.* Mad at herself all over again, she says, "Why do I let him get to me like this?" She makes a promise to herself. *Never again.* She parks her car and slams the door, leaving Roger Fleming behind for good.

❧

Josie hardly walks through her door when suddenly her phone buzzes. She forgets about Roger instantly when she sees the message from Scott. She starts up her computer while reading his text. He wants to talk. She smiles and texts back, "We got in trouble for talking earlier."

She sits at her desk and glances at the clock. If she hurries, she can finish this file before meeting Scott for dinner. She knows it won't be easy. She'll have to rush. She won't be able to so much as look up the next few hours.

Scott texts back, asking whether he can call her now. He insists they need to talk. She smiles and texts back. She asks to talk tonight instead. Scott says it is important, but he will wait. Josie turns her ringer off and puts on her noise cancelling headphones. She wants no distractions. This is her biggest client. She wants the file to be perfect. She begins typing: adjusting page, after page, after page.

TWENTY·TWO

*May your service of love a beautiful thing; want nothing else, fear nothing
else and let love be free to become what love truly is.*
-Hadewijch of Antwerp

Scott arrives to Josie's home promptly at seven thirty p.m.
As she opens the door, Scott whistles. He twirls her by
the hand to get a full three-hundred-and-sixty-degree view.

She wears three-inch, wooden heeled shoes with gray
suede uppers. The shoes lace up the middle with ties ending
in tiny, golden grommets just below her ankle. A side slit
helps her fitted long gray skirt give when she walks. Her
black, silk crepe top has a mock cowl neck in the front and
an open back. With the open back, she had to rethink
wearing a bra. Limited by pasties and bra tape, she tries not
to lift her arm too high as she twirls.

Her glossy, newly straightened locks sweep back into a
sleek high ponytail. The long straight ends come to a silky
point between her shoulder blades and shimmer with each
twirl. Her gray eyeliner, soft blush, and nude lips bring out
the vibrant hazel in her eyes. Her long eyelashes almost
touch the tops of her lids. She blinks, and Scott can't think
straight.

Scott says, "Are you trying to kill me?" He braces his
racing heart with the palm of his hand against his chest. He
had something important to say. At the moment, it escapes
him. Instead he says, "You smell delicious!"

She pulls him towards her and into the foyer, shutting the
door behind him. She kisses him as she leads him into the
living room.

He says, "You taste even better." He holds her shoulders at an arm's length to get another look and says, "This is the softest shirt I have ever felt."

She wants to say, "Take it off," but is too shy. Besides, she wears the pasties underneath and is embarrassed. *With the glue and tape holding everything together, I worry sex would be more like an arts and crafts project.*

Again, he remembers he had something to say, but the facts remain overshadowed by her. He sees the clock over the sink and asks, "Is that time right?"

"Yeah, I think so."

"How long have we been kissing."

"Dunno. Fifteen minutes?"

"We gotta go."

"What? Right now?"

"Yes, now. My boss's wife is cooking dinner for us. She comes from a military family. They don't let the food sit out for more than twenty minutes before throwing it all away."

"Really? All of it?"

"Yes."

"Well, I guess that adds a degree of excitement to the meal. I've never heard of such a thing. How is that military?

"Dunno. Didn't ask. The last thing my boss told me today was not to be late. He said that if his dinner goes down the drain, then so does my career. He said no later than eight."

"Gosh. OK. I was hoping to, uh, spend more time with you, but I'll grab my purse. One sec."

"More time?" He smiles, accentuating his dimple.

Josie bites her lip. Restraint is something she normally has no trouble with. That was before she met Scott. Her impulsive desire surprises even herself. She's never felt this way about anyone. *He's just so cute.* She quickly turns on the house alarm and locks the door. He opens her car door. *And gentlemanly. Everything a girl like me likes.*

They arrive three minutes before eight p.m. Scott rushes Josie up the sidewalk. He says, "Come on. Let's go. We have three minutes."

She laughs as her heels clunk against the sidewalk and says, "I can't run in these heels!"

They stand in front of the door. Before he knocks, Scott uses one of the three spare minutes and says, "Look Josie, I need to tell you something. I have been trying to tell you all day. This morning I found out—" The door opens before Scott finishes his sentence.

His boss extends a hand to Scott and then to Josie and says, "Welcome you two! We've been waiting for you." He introduces himself to Josie as he leads them through the living room and to the back patio. He says, "I hope you don't mind, but we are eating *out* tonight." He laughs at his own joke. He says, "Well, *out*side that is." He guffaws and slaps Scott on the back. He opens the sliding glass door to the patio and gestures for Scott and Josie to follow. It is pitch black outside, a moonless night.

Josie steps across the sliding glass door's threshold and into the blanket darkness of the backyard. Scott follows. Suddenly, a deafening roar erupts accompanied by the sudden lighting of what she now sees to be a patio structure and a massive garden jam-packed with people. As more lights flicker on, people burst forth from behind shrubs, chairs, a grill, trees and columns. They collectively yell, "SURPRISE!" Blaring horns sound, party favors toot, confetti streams, and balloons fly up into the air all at once.

Instinctively, Scott jumps. Josie slightly wets herself: not enough to notice, but enough that she will need to excuse herself at the earliest convenience to visit the restroom.

The look of shock quickly turns to appreciation on Scott's face. A mariachi band starts up. Scott laughs, grabs Josie by the hand and begins to salsa. He twirls her, stops, clasps his hands together and yells to the crowd, "You got me!" His words do not carry through the din; so he mouths the words "thank you" to everyone. Josie claps along to the music until she reads the signs:

Good Luck Scott

We'll Miss You

Don't Forget to Write

She whispers in Scott's ear, "Are you going somewhere?"

His smile disappears. He says, "That's what I have been trying to tell you all day."

She's been out with him every night this week. He didn't mention anything before now. A thought occurs to her, and her heart skips a beat. She asks, "When? Where? For how long?"

"Bangkok. Most likely two years. I leave Monday."

She doesn't understand. She says, "B-but how?"

"It's a two-year contract with a premier Asian firm. It's an opportunity of a lifetime, a big promotion for me. I can finally make a name for myself. Farber was supposed to go. He just found out today his wife is expecting. He backed out, which leaves me. I tried telling you."

She thinks back to his text messages, the conversation when he picked her up, and just before his boss opened the door. She says, "Yes, I guess you did." She can't think of what else to say. Finally, she says, "Congratulations," before bursting into tears, running into the house, and locking herself in the powder bathroom.

Scott catches up to her and knocks on the door. He says, "Hey, come on now. We need to talk. Please, open the door."

Josie says, "No. I need to collect myself. Please, give me a minute. I don't want to say something stupid I will regret later." She faces the mirror and wipes the mascara smears away.

"Say something stupid. Say anything. I don't care. Just talk to me. Trust me." He wants to tell her that he has never felt this way about anyone before. He wants to tell her that he wishes he could take her with him. He knows they haven't dated long enough--not quite three weeks--to make that idea truly feasible, but he can't suppress the thought. He assumes he would sound like a complete idiot for even suggesting it. They haven't even used the "L" word yet.

"Yeah, right. I can *trust* you to leave. You're moving to China in three days."

He corrects her, "Thailand."

"Fine. Thailand! Whatever. You're leaving. Did you even think about me? Us?" *How can you leave us when we are just getting going? I thought I found love before with Roger, but not like this. I thought--well, it doesn't matter what I thought now. This might be the broken heart I never get over.*

She weeps. She weeps for the love she'll never make to this man, for the children she'll never have with him, and for those soft, wavy, blonde curls that she'll desperately miss. *And the dimple. Oh, that dimple.* He is the love of her life, no matter how brief. She feels certain of it.

Scott hears her crying and says, "I can't reach my arms through the door, you know. Open up."

She stares at the handle. She begins to reach for it when she hears Scott's boss. He says, "The man of the hour! There you are! I've been looking all over for you. I want you to meet Benjarong. He will be your Thai liaison." Josie hears their voices trail off. She makes one phone call before crying herself to sleep on the bathroom's cold marble floor. She wakes to knocking.

A voice through the door says, "Is anyone in there? Hello?" Another voice says, "I think it's locked from the inside, dear."

Josie opens the door to see a surprised host and hostess with a bobby pin trying to pick the lock on the door. Josie excuses herself, darts between them, and exits into the street where Marni waits with her car engine running. Scott chases after her, but runs into the street only in time to see the tail end of Marni's car grow smaller and smaller before disappearing altogether around the corner.

Marni—in a bathrobe and with a green mask on her face—says, "I got here as fast as I could."

"Thanks."

"What happened?" Marni listens. Josie tells her everything from the beginning to the end, leaving nothing out. Afterwards, Marni cries along with her. Marni says, "This is just so, so horrible! It's all my fault. I'm so sorry, Jo."

"Wait-- your fault? How could this possibly be your fault? He's going to Thailand."

"I know. I know. But I set you up with him. If I had just left well enough alone, maybe none of this would have ever happened."

Josie pats her hand and says, "Yes. I see why you would blame yourself. It's all your fault. Didn't you know that no good deed ever goes unpunished?" They both laugh, and then they cry again.

Drying her eyes, Josie says, "Seriously though, it's not your fault. It's not anyone's fault. It's just the way love works for me, always has. I seem doomed to only find love as long as it comes with a whole lot of hurt. I give up on it!"

"On love? That's a bit rash! You can't give up on love."

"I think I just did."

"Thailand is not the end of the world."

"It's on the edge."

"Oh, come on. You could visit. The food is incredible and it's beautiful there."

"You've been?"

"No. But I read a lot of the travel blogs. Look, don't give up on him. This is an obstacle. I'll give you that, but for God's sake, don't give up. What if he is the guy for you?"

They drive in silence for a few more minutes before Josie says, "Thailand of all places."

Marni shakes her head and says, "Yeah. I know. Sucks."

They arrive at Marni's house. Marni says, "You're staying in my guest room tonight. No argument. We are not leaving you alone."

Josie says, "We?"

"Yes. We, in the collective."

Marni parks in her garage. She opens the door and holds it for Josie. Josie squeezes past storage boxes and Marni's scooter to enter a full house. In the kitchen, Ceridwin mixes cocktails. By the kitchen's island, Violet stirs a Crockpot full of dark hot cocoa and lines up mugs with chunky homemade marshmallows. Tasha pops popcorn. Monica sits on a barstool and sips a cosmopolitan slowly.

Vivian holds three remotes as she curses the DVD player into action. She says, "Whose idea was it to give the dinosaur in the room the newest tech gadgets?" The DVD player pops open, ready for a disc. She says, "Ha-HA! I got you now you little sucker!"

Ceridwin says, "Just use the little remote and go to Apple T.V."

"What, now? No way! I just got the DVD door to open!" Vivian notices Josie and announces, "She's here!"

Everyone stops what they're doing. Smothered by hugs, Josie says, "Is this some sort of party?"

Monica doesn't bother to hug Josie. She remains seated on her stool and says, "Yes. A pity party. Oh, joy."

Ceridwin says, "Ignore her," and whispers, "one too many cosmos!"

Vivian raises a glass and says, "Tonight we cry."

Marni says, "Here, here!" Everyone clinks glasses.

Violet says, "That's right! We get it all out."

Tasha says, "That's right! Out with the old and in with the new. Tomorrow, we open a new chapter in the life of Josephine Fleming. A fresh start."

Vivian says, "Now, I have the tearjerkers to do the job." She holds up the DVD selection and says, "Which do you want to start with? *Romeo and Juliet*, the 1968 Zefferelli version? Or maybe the 1934 classic, *In Love with Life*? *Brian's Song*? *Beaches*? Aah, I have just the one, *An Affair to Remember*!"

Vivian starts the DVD player. Everyone finds a seat. Josie plops herself in the middle of the couch. Marni hands her a blanket, a tissue box, and a bowl of popcorn.

As the movie starts, Josie looks around the dimly lit room as the screen flickers light across the faces of these busy women. Humbled, she realizes all of them dropped what they were doing tonight just for her. She smiles and spreads out her blanket, covering herself and all it will reach

She sips the hot chocolate: grateful for its sweet warmth, grateful for this group of friends, and grateful not to be alone. She tries not to think about Scott, the going-away party, or what finality Monday might bring between them. Little does she know that only a few miles away Scott sits on her front porch with his head in his hands, waiting for her. He, like she, worries what Monday will bring.

TWENTY·THREE

We don't receive wisdom; we must discover it for ourselves
after a journey that no one can take for us or spare us.
-Marcel Proust

Josie arrives home Saturday morning at six. She enters through the garage, never noticing the note on her front door. She showers, changes, eats breakfast and arrives at her client's office by seven: an hour early.

Her phone buzzes. She sees the text is from Scott. She has no time to respond. She will be delivering the biggest presentation of her career in a short while. She turns her ringer off and places her phone inside her pocket. She wants to speak with Scott, but not now. She will have to wait to say the things unsaid.

She sets up her displays and checks her AV equipment. She makes sure her file is compatible before arranging the bagels, fruit, and coffee on the reception table. She runs through her presentation one last time, adding some last minute changes before stopping by the restroom. She adjusts her hair, makeup, and sticks a nametag on her lapel.

The boardroom begins filling with executives fifteen minutes before start time. They trickle in by ones and twos. She chats with the executives she knows and introduces herself to the ones she doesn't. She drinks coffee, waits until everyone finds a seat, and delivers the fiscal year-end numbers presentation.

Previously, Jim Hartling, the C.E.O., had asked her to forecast next year's sales numbers based on new raw data he provided. She found a gap when doing so.

Based on projections, the current manufacturing facility would become obsolete within the year, not able to keep up with rapid growth from the forecasted demand. Josie first noticed the discrepancy when running and then rerunning the numbers.

When she called Jim with the news, she also proposed what manufacturing capacity will most likely need based on the projected growth. She found no way around it. A new manufacturing facility needs to be built or bought by year's end. Jim responded by asking her to save the information and share it in the meeting.

As Josie speaks, a board member interrupts and asks what will happen if they do either: keep the facility or build a new one. She provides scenarios for both and how each might affect the bottom line. Other than her slide discussing depreciation, most board members appear engaged. However, the applause at the end catches her off-guard. She shakes hands, gives Jim a hard copy of her work, and says her goodbyes. Before she reaches the parking lot, Jim catches up with her.

Jim says, "Josephine! Wait. What's the hurry?"

Josie says, "Sorry. Did I miss some questions?" She takes her finger off of the speed dial button for Scott's number. She drops her phone back inside her pocket.

Jim says, "No. On the contrary, I wanted to thank you for your insight today."

"But, I already shared the info with you weeks ago."

"I know. It's good. Important. That's why I wanted you to present the findings yourself. The board agrees with your decision."

"Oh, that's good news."

"You've been a big help over the years, and I just wanted you to know that."

Never great at accepting compliments, she says, "Not a problem. Just doing my job."

Jim says, "Next year could've been a real mess without your recommendations. I hope you realize that."

She says, "Glad to help. You've built a great company."

Jim says, "Pretty and bright."

"Er, OK. You've built a pretty and bright company."

"I wasn't talking about my company. I was talking about you."

Uncomfortable with yet another compliment, Josie blushes.

Jim disarms her with a laugh and says, "Sorry, get me fifty feet out of the office, and I become completely unprofessional. My apologies."

"Apology accepted." He's never given her any reason to do otherwise. Jim is the consummate professional. *Except for that day when he returned to work after his wife passed away, but who could blame him? He spent most of that day crying on my shoulder. Poor guy.*

It all started when they met at the water cooler, and she politely let him fill his cup first. He began to say, "Thank you," but the floodgates opened before he got the words fully out. Unsure of what else to do, Josie grabbed his cup and filled it for him. When she handed it to him, his hands were too shaky to hold his own cup. She felt embarrassed for him.

Jim's despair struck a chord with her. Instinctively, she put her arm around him, guided him to his office and let him talk it out and cry until both the words and the tears flowed no more. Although they've always worked well together for years, that day forged a special bond between the two.

Jim says, "Thanks again for coming in on a Saturday morning. This is the only day we could get all of those hotshots together. And thanks for making it so early. Everyone has tee times later this morning."

"No problem."

Jim says, "We were wondering if you could do the same presentation for our investors this coming Monday at nine a.m."

She'll have to skip practice, but work comes first. "Of course," she says without hesitation.

Jim says, "Josephine, you've been with us since the beginning, since we were a fledgling start-up. Your guidance has meant so much. Maybe I'm repeating myself here, but I just want you to know that."

She laughs and says, "Glad I didn't help run it into the ground or something."

"Didn't your mother ever tell you that there are times to just say 'thank you'?"

"Fine. Thank you."

"You've always been there when we've needed you. Like the time I was going to make a staffing cut in order to make year-end numbers. You showed me how that was only a short-term fix. If I just hung in there a little while longer, a few big-ticket items would be coming off the books and the numbers would right themselves. Remember that?"

"Yes."

"You suggested that we needed to actually increase staff in order to keep up with demand. Who knows what would have happened if I hadn't taken that advice. I might have folded if you didn't tell me that. You know that?"

"I don't know about that."

"I do. A lot of things were possible, because you helped me. Big things. I lost sleep over that firing decision, you know. Did I ever tell you that?"

"No. You didn't."

"Yeah, I couldn't do it. We are a family here. I was so happy with the information you gave me. You have no idea. It gave me such tremendous relief. You work hard Josie, and you're a good person. You have been able to do everything I have asked of you. And the not-so-strange thing is that I knew you could." He smiles, "Did you?"

Josie tries to laugh off the compliment. She says, "Well, it's sort of like my forehand in tennis. You just hope it shows up on the day you really need it."

He smiles at her.

She says, "OK. Thank you."

Jim winks and says, "Don't ever sell yourself short, Josephine. At Monday's meeting, I am recommending as part of our growth initiative for next year that we hire a full-time C.F.O. I hope you don't mind if I put your name in the hat."

Stunned, Josie realizes what this means. This position will give her a fulltime income. *OK, I'm going to try to remain calm, but YEA!* Roger doesn't pay alimony, and the house was initially bought based on his income, not hers. *I can make my mortgage payments now, no prob. Double YEA!*

She knows this job could alleviate much of her financial struggles. Besides a bump in pay, it would also mean corporate medical insurance, and a matching 401K: things she can't afford on her own. She knows these benefits could change her life for the better. What she doesn't know is that Jim knows all of this, too.

Much business transpires on the golf courses of Boca Raton, Florida. Over the years, Jim has played golf with a myriad of local professionals. One of the biggest mouths around town is none other than a hotshot lawyer: Roger Fleming.

While golfing, Roger has a habit of passing out business cards, drumming up deals, and bad-mouthing his ex-wife. More than once, Roger has bragged about screwing over Josie; how he hid money from her, and set up the divorce so she got nothing except debt. Roger laughed when he told the guys how he drives a new Tesla, and Josie drives an eight-year-old Mini. He said she got stuck with the old house and he bought a new one double in size in a better neighborhood.

Jim remembers the last time he played golf with Roger. Roger had the audacity to blame Josie for their divorce and for "being just plain stupid". Roger bragged how he started cheating on Josie right under her nose only months after their wedding. He joked about how the only thing he gave her in the divorce was a house that she can't afford and will most likely lose.

Jim thinks, *Yes, Roger Fleming has told everyone who'll listen about how he pulled a fast one over on his ex-wife whom he loathes.* What Roger didn't say, in Jim's opinion, was the truth: that Josie is beautiful, smart, compassionate, and competent. Jim thinks, *The real loser in this scenario is Roger, not Josie.*

Jim can't tell Josie these things. It would be unprofessional. He also can't right the wrong that has been dealt to her at the hands of a guy like Roger Fleming. What he can do is make her life a little better, and he intends to try.

Jim says, "I hope you will consider the position. I mean it still has to get approved by the board and everything first."

Josie tries not to sound too eager. She says, "Is it OK if I let you know Monday at the meeting?"

Jim says, "Of course." They shake hands.

Josie starts up her car, but leaves it in park. The air conditioning blows through her hair, cooling the thin line of perspiration starting to form along her forehead. She phones Scott. He answers on the first ring.

He says, "Where did you go last night?"

"I stayed at Marni's."

"You didn't say goodbye. I was worried."

"Oh. Sorry." *Wait! Why am I apologizing? He's the one moving to Thailand.*

"I've been want--," he pauses midsentence, "*trying* to talk with you. When can we meet?"

She can't stand the pain of seeing him again. Besides, she doesn't trust herself alone with him. She is afraid that with one smile and that dimple, she will sleep with him. She wants to sleep with him. She knows she can't do that. It would mean too much to her and only break her heart more when he leaves in two days.

Josie makes a legitimate excuse and says, "I am working today. I can't." She tears up as she says the words. Rejecting him proves more difficult than she ever imagined.

He doesn't say anything for a few seconds. Finally, he says, "Well, you've got to eat, don't you?"

Afraid the trembling in her voice will give her away, she doesn't answer. *I won't be a bumbling, crying buffoon.* She wants to say into the phone, *Don't go, Scott. Please.*

Scott says, "My sister and nephew are driving in from Naples today. She is staying at my place to finalize everything that I don't have time for, given the short notice and all. There's a lot to do, like renting out my house."

Josie doesn't want to hear about finalizing arrangements. *Can we talk about something other than your leaving?* She starts crying. This time, the sound is clearly audible.

Scott's tone softens. He says, "Hey. Listen, this is not the end. It doesn't have to be. Don't think of it that way. We need to talk."

When? You're leaving.

When she doesn't say anything, Scott continues, "Look, I know there's not much time. I'm going to take a break from running errands all day and take my sister and nephew to dinner. Reservations are for six at Max's Harvest. If you care about me at all, you'll be there."

Josie says, "I can't promise I will be there. I just can't." She hangs up. She grabs the steering wheel with both hands and cries uncontrollably. She waits for the pain to go away. It doesn't. She wasn't prepared for how much this would hurt. *I guess maybe I really do love him. Love hurts.* She knows friends who would argue otherwise, but, for Josephine Fleming, love hurts.

She stays that way in her car, crying with her head on her steering wheel. Twenty minutes pass. She doesn't see the concerned face peering through the third story window from above. She doesn't notice Jim leave the window and walk into the parking lot to check on her. She doesn't notice him approaching when she puts her car into drive and motors away. Through blurry, tear-filled eyes Josie drives home, accidentally veering over her jasmine hedge before parking in her garage.

She walks down the driveway. The hedge is completely crushed. She throws up her hands and walks inside. *Great.*

Josie dries her eyes and sets up shop at her desk. She plants her MP3 player, and a steamy cup of her favorite tea—one Irish breakfast and one mint tea bag, topped with a heaping scoop of vanilla ice cream--next to her computer. She stirs most of the ice cream into the tea, leaving part floating on top. The heat of the tea and the coolness of the ice cream mix together, forming a refreshing froth in her mouth. She licks the froth off her upper lip.

She opens the file for the local bait shop, and begins balancing their books. By four p.m. the books are finished along with her tears. She has nothing left to cry. What she has left is anger.

Josie drives to the tennis courts, checks out the ball machine and makes ball after ball pay for Scott's move to Thailand. She pauses and leans on her racquet. Slowly catching her breath, she towels off her face, arms, and neck. The heavy humidity mixes with her sweat, soaking her through.

She arrives home, checks the clock over her sink, and hopes it is too late to make the dinner date with Scott. *5:03. Ugh. I have time to shower, get dressed, and meet him.*

She sits at her desk, pulls out a blank sheet of paper, and draws a line down the middle of the page. She titles the top: Seeing Scott Tonight. She lists all of the cons in one column and all of the pros in the next column. She adds up both sides. The pros outweigh the cons. *Sigh. No regrets.* She showers, changes, and arrives at Max's Harvest by six fifteen.

Scott flags her down, "Over here!" He holds a chair for her and says, "I didn't think you were going to make it! I am so happy!"

He leans in for a kiss. She turns and gives him her cheek instead. He looks crushed.

His sister looks nothing like him except for the unmistakable crystal blue eyes. Scott says, "This is Susan, my little sister. And this is William, my three-year-old nephew."

William jumps into her lap and says, "Josie, I can say that!"

Josie says, "Yes, you can. And you say it very well!" She high-five's him. He hugs her and looks up. She sees William also inherited the stunning family trait. *Adorable baby blues.* William smiles. *And the same dimple as Scott, too.* Josie is immediately smitten. Scott orders her a drink, and excuses himself to the restroom.

Susan instantly puts Josie at ease. They share much in common. Susan works part-time as an accountant, mainly during tax season. The rest of the year, she devotes her time to mothering William.

Susan says, "I just started tennis this season for the first time. I want to lose the last ten pounds of the baby weight." She grabs the small tire around her middle. "Well actually, it's been three years. So, I don't know if I can still call it baby weight. Anyway, I hope tennis can help."

Josie says, "Tennis is a great way to get in shape. It helped me. I'm sure it can help you, too."

"Scott says you're a phenom on the court. Mind if I pick your brain?"

"Shoot." *But tonight you may need less of a pickaxe and more of a toothpick.*

Susan asks Josie about grips, swings, coaches, everything: including the best sneakers for Har-Tru. Josie and Susan talk through the meal and well into dessert. Josie could talk tennis all night. They are discussing the best way to move back for an overhead when suddenly Scott kicks Susan under the table.

Susan says, "Owwww, oooh, wow!" She glares at Scott. His look registers, and she says, "Look at the time! Uh, William missed his, uh, afternoon walk. I'd better take him or he'll never sleep tonight. Be back in around forty-five minutes. Forty-five is good?"

Susan looks at Scott. Scott nods. She says, "Yes. I think forty-five minutes should do it." Rubbing her shin, she smiles uneasily as William says, "But I don't want to go. I want to stay here with Josie."

Scott says, "Yes, but Kilwin's has bubble gum flavored ice cream."

William's eyes grow larger. He says, "Bubble gum? Bubble gum in ice cream?"

Scott leans forward and says, "Yes. I've had it, and it's fantastic!"

"Fantaskit! Ooh, goody! I like fantaskit!"

After William and Susan leave, Scott talks with Josie. They sit in the back corner under the soft candlelight. Sarah Vaughan sings *Pennies from Heaven* on the outdoor patio's speakers. Tempted, he restrains from kissing her. The waiter seems to pick up on the vibe that they wish to be left alone. He rarely visits their table.

Time doesn't run in excess for Scott. He leaves in less than forty-eight hours. He wastes none of it. He says, "Just because I am leaving doesn't mean I don't feel the way I feel about you. And I think we both know how I feel. It's obvious. You can't get mad at me. You can't just cut me off. I mean what am I supposed to do? Not take the promotion? It's my job. And I can't ask you to go with me. We haven't even been dating a month." He thinks, *Not even long enough to tell each other that we love each other.*

She says, "Why do you have to leave?"

"I just told you why. I can't help it! It's just unfortunate."

Unfortunate? He makes it sound so trite. She says, "It's a malicious act of fate. What if I don't want to be unfortunate?"

"It's not our choice to make. It is beyond our control."

She sighs. She's tired of misfortune. *When it comes to love, I seem to be the Queen of Misfortune.*

Unwilling to accept this fate without a fight, she musters up her courage and says, "Scott, what if this is love? I mean I don't know about you, but this feels very real to me."

Scott says, "I think you do know about me."

She continues, "Some people live their whole lives and never find love. I think we've got a real shot at it here."

He reaches for her hand.

She adds, "What if you leave and we never find out? What if you get delayed on another Asian contract and two years turns into ten? What if we never get a chance to see this thing through? You know see what it will turn out to be?"

"Believe me, I've thought about that."

"Well then, wouldn't that be a travesty? At the very least, a regret? I mean I think a person is lucky to find what we've found, no matter how brief. To find something like this and not accept it, or to treat it like a frivolity, wouldn't that be a huge mistake?"

Scott says, "That was a lot of what-if's. What are you asking me to do?" He wants to hear her say it.

"I am not asking you to do anything." She wants to hear him say it.

"Yes, you are. You are asking me to make a choice: a choice between you and my job."

"If that is what I am asking you, then what are you saying? Wait for me for two years when or if you come back?"

"I am not asking you to wait for me."

She blushes and feels like a fool. *Then why am I here? Why are we talking? You want nothing from me? What is there left to discuss?*

He realizes he offended her. He says, "Would you?"

She throws her napkin on the table and says, "You're not asking me? Really? You're not asking me, but *would* I? I'm too old for games, Scott." She heads for the door.

Scott says, "Wait!"

Josie turns and says, "I am not some what-if, Scott."

He looks perplexed and says, "I didn't say you were."

She says, "What if your what-if just walked out the door and what if you'll never know what your what-if could've turned out to be?"

He raises his eyebrows, wrinkling his forehead and says, "I'm not sure—I'm sorry. What?"

"Ooooph! Never mind!" She storms out of the restaurant.

The waiter approaches the table and motions to Josie's dessert plate. He says, "Is the lady done?"

Scott mumbles, "Unfortunately, I am afraid so."

TWENTY·FOUR

Success is to be measured not so much by the position that one has reached in life as by the obstacles which he has overcome.
-Booker T. Washington

The arrival of Monday morning proves bittersweet for Josie as she prepares for the investor's meeting. Today, she will potentially gain her dream job and loose her dream boyfriend. Normally before an important meeting, she would be typing away and finessing the numbers one last time: double-checking her math, conclusions, and projections. However, today she blankly stares at the computer screen, not truly seeing it.

Instead, she sees Scott, sitting in an airplane seat. She opens a new tab and looks up his flight. *Wow. His flight to Bangkok takes three legs before he finally arrives. That's a lot of time sitting in airplane seats.* She looks at the clock. *His plane is taking off right now.* She imagines his initial ascent, leaving Miami's International Airport en route to New York's La Guardia.

Unable to focus, she walks to the kitchen and uses the instant hot water tap to make her favorite tea. She says the ingredients out loud as she adds them, "Twenty-ounce mug. Check. One bag of Earl Grey and one bag of lavender tea. Check. Eight ounces of, *ouch*, hot water. Check." In a separate mug, she heats six ounces of milk in the microwave. Then, while using an electric whisk to froth the milk, she drizzles honey into its whirling center.

She continues, "One heaping tablespoonful of Tupelo honey. Check." She throws away the tea bags and adds the mug of steamed milk into the half-full mug of tea, carefully folding in the foam on top. She sprinkles in vanilla and says, "Creating a delicious distraction. Check."

She returns to her desk with her frothy concoction. Again, she struggles to focus on the numbers before her. She still can't rid her mind of Scott. Mindlessly, she types. She stops, and reads what she typed: Scott + Distance = > and > Josie. She deletes it, sighs, and starts over.

Josie packs her computer bag, and texts Jim, letting him know she will arrive shortly. He texts back, asking whether she wants the job. She responds that she does. He texts back that they should communicate verbally after the meeting, but for now he needs to "go have a few key conversations." *Key conversations?* She wonders what that means, but doesn't ask.

She arrives at the office thirty minutes early. She unpacks her case as her mind wanders back to Scott. She sets up her equipment in the AV room for the presentation.

Jim Hartling walks into the room. He helps set the refreshment table and says, "Come here a second. Did you dress yourself today, or what?" He chuckles, fixes her inside-out collar, and then says, "Oh, you forgot this thing." He makes a rolling motion in front of his lips.

Josie grabs her phone and looks at her reflection. She sees an outline of much-too-heavy lip liner with nothing filled in. She says, "Oh. Thanks. Be right back."

He says, "I thought maybe it was one of those special, read-my-lips, speaker tactic things."

"No, uh, I just forgot my lipstick." She grabs her purse.

When she does, Jim notices something off with her gait. He looks down at her feet, chuckles again, and says, "What is up with you today?" He points to her shoes.

She looks down and sees that she is wearing one black flat and one navy. She says, "Well, they do look similar. Anyone can make that mistake."

"One has a buckle and the other one has at least a half-inch higher heel. Don't you feel the difference when you walk?"

"Not at all." She takes the lipstick from her purse and walks with a slight bob in her step to the restroom. When she returns her presentation awaits, completely set up. Board members and investors file into the room. She smiles at Jim and mouths the words, "Thank you."

He smiles and flexes both biceps into a muscle man pose. She tries not to laugh.

After she concludes her presentation, Josie patiently takes questions. She glances at the clock over the doorway: 9:45 a.m. *Scott's plane should be descending into New York's La Guardia airport at this very moment.* She wonders if he thinks of her while she thinks of him. *By now his seat and tray table should rest in their upright position.* Scott's first of three legs on his lengthy journey is nearly complete. She does the math in her head and calculates his total travel time. When all is said and done, he will have traveled close to twenty-seven hours in total. *How do you keep yourself busy for twenty-seven hours on airplanes and waiting in airports?*

"Josie?"

"Yes?"

An investor says, "I asked if you have a hard copy that I might keep."

"Yes, sorry. Of course. I made enough for everyone." She passes the folders around the room. She fields more questions and explains how she derived at certain numbers and projections. When the questions become more personal, she realizes that this is also her interview.

She shares her background information, and career goals. She sees heads nodding. *This is more relaxed than I expected.* It feels as if it is more of a get-to-know-you session rather than an intense executive interview.

Josie wonders why everyone in the room acts so kindly towards her and goes so easy on her. *Not that I'm complaining.* Their questions seem to be almost scripted, setting her up for one easy answer after another. She looks at Jim. He smiles, crosses his arms, and leans back in his chair.

Josie takes her time, answering each question concisely and to the best of her ability. The last question catches her off guard. She asks for the question to be repeated and turns to see who asked it.

J. Paul says, "I only need to know one thing and that's it. Can you set up a budget like you set up your forehand?"

She hadn't noticed J. Paul Mooney before now. He sits in the back, partially obscured from view.

She laughs and replies, "Hi, J. Paul. I didn't see you there."

"It's OK, I'm used to it. Most women don't notice me." He nudges the guy next to him.

The guy says, "Don't feel bad J. Paul, it's not that women don't notice you."

"Thank you, Carson."

'It's simply that *nobody* notices you."

All of the men burst into laughter, even J. Paul.

The laughter subsides and Jim says, "Don't worry J. Paul, you can take his weekly twenty-five dollars on the golf course again today. Maybe then he'll notice you." The laughter erupts again as light-hearted insults fly.

Josie waits to speak. *I guess trash talk is not limited to the tennis court.* Josie might have been surprised to see J. Paul here, but she shouldn't be. J. Paul sits on the board of three South Florida business firms and invests in several more. Retirement hasn't slowed him down. As a stalwart in the community, he lends a hand to not only the local business community, but also to the philanthropic one as well.

Although, possessing a reputation as a successful venture capitalist, his true passion leans more toward charitable interests. In turn, South Florida has honored his efforts. Telltale signs appreciating J. Paul's generosity dot the South Floridian landscape. His name graces a multiplex community sport's center, a downtown park, a library, a nature preserve, and a major boulevard running through the center of Boca Raton. Here, the name of Jackson Paul Mooney will live on in history.

When Josie finishes speaking, Jim stands and says, "OK. Everyone satisfied?" Everyone nods. "Any more questions?" No more nods. "Josephine, do you mind waiting outside for a few minutes? We old windbags need to let out a little hot air. It won't take long."

"Of course." She looks at her watch: 11:14 a.m. *Scott should be making his way through the La Guardia concourses and changing planes to Cathay now.* In less than three hours, he will leave for the second leg of his trip.

Josie hears talking through the door, but the words prove too muffled to understand. If she could hear, she would know that Jim argues to hire her full-time. She would also know that J. Paul argues against hiring her full-time.

J. Paul argues for Josie to continue strictly on a consultative basis. He lists reasons, but the last reason he keeps to himself. Josie will still be able to play club tennis. He realizes the absurdity of his motive. Still, he considers this suggestion a gift for Monica. He can't wait to tell Monica how he saved one of her teammates from nearly having to quit her team.

Another investor interjects, backing J. Paul's decision. He argues that Josie does the work already. He reasons, "So, why should we pay more, offering her a full-time salary for work she's already doing? It doesn't make sense."

Jim anticipated this argument. He argues, "Josie is worth her weight. Trust me. She will more than pay for herself. If we don't hire her full-time then we may lose her to the competition. I cannot emphasize enough that that is something we truly cannot afford to do. We need to cement this business relationship with Josie today, before we lose her."

In the next twenty minutes, the momentum in the heated debate waivers back and forth. Jim feels the momentum shift and fights with added gusto to garner more support.

J. Paul relents. He likes Josie. He realizes this means that he won't see her around the club anymore. Still, he decides to consider what truly is best for his investment. He hopes Monica will understand when he tells her that Josie won't be available to play tennis any longer. He considers this a loss, not just for Monica's team, but for the club as well. He may be here today as an investor, but he also sits on the club's board. Josie fits the profile type that the club has been pushing to recruit: young, talented, and doesn't make waves.

Suddenly, J. Paul hatches a plan. He makes one last ditch effort to block Jim. He says, "I propose we hire her on a contract for five years. That way we get the stability Jim needs, and we make her sign a non-compete so we can't lose her. We bump her salary to make the offer more attractive and semi-permanent."

J. Paul slows his speech for emphasis, "However, since she is not on the books as a full-time exec, we save on health insurance, sick and vacation days, and any other perks we might have had to pay out for a full-time C.F.O. position." He realizes the ridiculousness behind his motive; he wants to make his wife happy. He adds, "She can put in her work hours and still have a flexible schedule." Meaning, she can still play team tennis for Le Château.

This is not the deal Jim envisioned for Josie. He has relied on her for years. Her hard work and good counsel served him through the worst of times over the last few years. He thinks, *She deserves better.* He stands and says, "I still say full-time. Not only is she competent, but you have no idea what a pleasure she is like to work with. I am telling you, what she adds to this company is simply not quantifiable. Her ripple effect impacts this entire office. You can't put a price tag on that!"

An investor seated next to J. Paul says, "Why are we wasting so much time on one potential employee? Don't get me wrong, and I realize she is a good hire--consultative or full-time--but who cares? A good hire is a good hire. And all good hires are replaceable. You just have to find the next good hire. See what I mean? Offer her the lowest amount."

Jim says, "I think everyone sitting around this table is surprised by how fast we've grown. I know I am. This company is successful because of its people. We're a real family here. I need more good people. Why replace one we are lucky enough to already have?"

The investor says, "I wasn't saying replace her. I was simply stating she *is* replaceable. No sense giving away so much on someone who will obviously take less."

Jim asks, "And if she doesn't?"

The investor says, "Find someone else."

Jim frowns. He likes it when good things happen to good people. He argues for more, but it's an uphill battle. J. Paul wins the final point.

As the support swings J. Paul's way, Jim feels as though he failed Josie. This is not the offer he hoped for her. Still, he takes some heart in knowing that Josie's salary will increase significantly. He might not have gotten the package deal he wanted for her--or that she deserves—but at least he got her something better than what she currently has. For now, this will have to do.

Jim says, "All agreed?" Everyone mumbles a "yes" or nods. "Okay. I will get her."

As he turns the handle, Jim gets an idea. He opens the door and says privately before he ushers Josie inside, "Go for a two-year contract instead of five." He doesn't want to wait five years to bring her onboard full-time. He continues, "Also, mention that you will be losing valuable business if you take on more here. Go for an extra twenty K. You'll get it. Oh, and an annual grant of thirty thousand shares. OK? Got it?"

Nervously, she nods.

He says, "Don't forget. Thirty thousand shares."

She nods again. Josie says exactly what Jim instructed. She walks out of the boardroom with the best deal of her career.

J. Paul stops her and shakes her hand. He says, "Nice last minute counter, Josephine. I'm impressed. I didn't know you had it in you." He smiles and pats her on the shoulder.

"Thank you." *I didn't either. I have to thank Jim.*

She gets her chance when Jim walks her to her car. She says, "Thanks for your help back there. I would never have thought of those things to say. I almost feel guilty asking for so much."

Jim shrugs it off and says, "No big deal. You earned it. Honestly, you deserve more." He pauses and says, "There is something else that has been on my mind. Mind if I ask you something?"

She opens her car door. Before she gets in, she says, "What?"

Jim says, "I hope I am not out of line here, but I couldn't help but notice you left here upset last Friday. I just hope it wasn't anything I said. I'm really good at offending people and never even knowing it."

A rosy tone flushes across her cheeks and down her neck. She says, "What? No. You didn't. And, you're not." She thinks back to last Friday. She remembers her phone conversation with Scott and the half an hour bawling session in her car and cringes.

Jim says, "I saw you in the parking lot."

She says, "You saw that?"

"Yes. And I noticed you barely made it to your car before breaking down. I hope it wasn't anything I said."

"No. Oh, no, of course not. You've been great. Everything is fine. Really."

"So, why the crying? That is if you don't mind my asking."

"I got some bad news that I'm still trying to process. Nothing to do with work. I assure you."

"You are OK, then?"

"Yes, of course."

He doesn't say anything for a few seconds. Then, he hugs her. It catches her off guard, but she doesn't pull away or feel threatened by the hug. It just feels good. Finally, he says, "Just in case you needed one of those."

Surprised to find herself not put off by the hug, she says, "OK. Uh, thanks." She smiles.

Jim says, "I know that was probably unprofessional, but we've known each other for a long time now. So, I hope it is OK."

"It's OK."

"I consider you a friend. I've never said anything before, but you really helped me out when Abby died. It was hard to make it through a full day at the office. You picked me up more than just a few times. You're a true friend. I couldn't let last week go by without repaying the favor and making sure you were OK."

"Thank you, but I'm fine. Really."

"OK, but I am just letting you know there are a lot of people who care about you here. If you ever need to talk--" Awkwardly, he lets the words hang in the air. He never has been one to talk about feelings.

She fills in the rest of his sentence, "I'll know where to go." However, she has no intention of telling Jim anything about her private life. *That would be so unprofessional.*

"Exactly."

Now, that he knows it wasn't something at work, Jim assumes Josie's ex-husband caused her parking lot meltdown.

After a long pause, Josie says, "OK, well, thanks again."

Jim smiles and says, "Sure."

"Yep."

After another awkward pause, Jim says, "OK, I'll call you once I have the contract written up."

"Great."

"Great."

After yet another awkward pause, she says, "Ok, and thanks again. For everything."

"Stop thanking me. It's nothing. You earned it, Josephine."

She glances at the clock on her dashboard: 12:30 p.m. *Scott leaves in just over an hour for the second leg of his trip.* She drives home. As she passes the front of her house, she sees a box sitting on her porch. *Finally, my office supplies.*

She pulls into her driveway and presses the remote on her visor. The wooden garage door lifts open. She parks how she sleeps: on the left side, leaving space for one more. *Old habits…*

She walks down the driveway and hops over the smashed jasmine hedge. She smiles. She knows with the new position that she can afford to replace the crumpled mess.

She walks up to her front porch and surveys the front doors as she picks up the box. Todd nailed them back together as best he could after he broke through them with a crowbar two years ago. *I will be able to afford to fix those, too.* She smiles again, knowing that she will be able to take care of the very house that only yesterday she was unsure if she would keep.

She opens the front door and a white piece of paper flutters to the ground. She puts the box down. She sees her name imprinted on the front of the paper and picks it up. The note--left wedged between her doors for two days-- already looks yellowed and weathered from the Florida humidity and heat. Without opening the note, she instantly knows who wrote it. She turns it over in her hands, takes a deep breath, and unfolds it. The letter reads:

Dear Josie,

You broke my heart tonight. I didn't want you to go. I have been sitting here on your porch all night, waiting for you to come home. I guess I really blew it at the Max's, huh? I'm really sorry. I never meant to hurt you. I have so much to say to you, and I am running out of time to say it. Call me. We need to talk face to face before I go. I want you to know something.

Scott

She repeats the last words aloud, *"I want you to know something."* She holds the letter to her heart. *He must have waited all night for me when I stayed at Marni's.* She checks her watch. It's almost one o'clock p.m. She knows Scott boards again soon. She takes a chance and dials his number. He answers.

She takes a deep breath, and says, "Scott?"

"Josie? Is that you?"

"Yes. I found your letter on my porch just now."

He says nothing.

She wants to ask him what it was that he wants her to know. Instead, she says, "I'm sorry. I didn't see it before. I didn't know this is how you felt. I didn't mean to break your heart. I didn't-- don't want to."

He says, "It's OK."

"Why didn't you say these things to me Friday night?"

"Yeah. Well, uh, never been great with words. But, uh, I guess you could already tell that from our dinner conversation the other night. Not surprisingly, you're not the first girl I've sent running out of restaurant." He hears soft laughter. It's a wonderful sound. He presses the phone closer to his ear.

Josie says, "Do you think you'll come back. You know, to visit? Or will you stay there the whole two years?"

"There's a training seminar in the fall. Late August, I think. I'll be back for that. Three weeks long."

August? But that's months away! She tries to sound positive and says, "OK. August. Maybe we can try to pick up where we left off?"

His cell phone drops the connection. He calls her back. Before she says 'hello', he says, "I had the same idea. I mean we came this far, didn't we? It's been about that same amount of time. Right? Three weeks?"

She searches for something more to hold onto. She says, "Yeah. So, should we date other people?" *Say no.*

Disappointed at what he thinks is her suggestion to do so, he says unenthusiastically, "Sure. I guess. I mean we'll be so far away, and it will be a while. So, OK, yeah."

Disappointed that he doesn't want to date exclusively her, she says, "Oh. OK. If that's what you want."

Scott's cell phone coverage falters, but doesn't fully disconnect. He doesn't hear her say, "But I don't want to." The connection fizzles again.

He says, "I guess it would be silly not to, you know, so far away and all," before his cell phone drops completely.

He moves up and down the concourse's corridor until he finds more bars on his phone. He thinks about what she said, about her wanting to date other people. It's not what he wants. Still, he doesn't want to upset her anymore than he already has. When she answers, he avoids the dating issue altogether and says, "I think I can get texts, but I am not sure. I know we can email and Skype. I will try texting you when I land."

"Oh, OK. Great!"

He says, "We're boarding." His cell phone drops again. He calls her back and says, "Me, again."

She says, "Have a great trip! And Scott--"

"Yes?"

She gathers her courage and says, "I know the distance will make things hard., but that is something we cannot change. I also think dating other people will make things harder, but that is something we can change. I was hoping you didn't want to." She waits for him to say something.

Finally, she says, "Scott?" He's gone. She is not sure how much he heard. She's also not sure if she will have the courage to repeat what she said. It's not easy for her to be vulnerable and say how she feels. She needs trust for that. Coming off of a bad relationship with Roger, trusting again does not come easy.

Josie carefully and neatly folds the note back into a square. She places it in her top dresser drawer. She'll take the letter out and read it many times over the next several months.

TWENTY·FIVE

Blessed is the influence of one true, loving human soul on another.
-George Eliot

J. Paul Mooney arrives home early from his morning meeting. He surprises Monica with a bouquet from the flower truck off of Yamato Road. Monica coos over the exotic vibrancy: bright orange birds of paradise, chartreuse orchids, deep indigo lilies against a backdrop of pale green fronds and tiny white pinwheel flowers. She leaves the computer to find a vase.

J. Paul yells after her, "I hope you don't mind if I jump on for a second? I want to check scores from yesterday's matches." He turns the screen toward him.

Monica hurries back into the office and says, "Wait! No! Wait! Just one second." She quickly closes the webpage: a little too quickly for J. Paul's taste. He makes a mental note to check the computer's cache and history later, but makes no mention of it now. He helps Monica find a vase.

J. Paul says, "You will never believe who I helped hire today?"

Feigning interest, Monica says, "Who?"

"Josephine Fleming."

Monica's interest suddenly piques. Cheerily, she says, "Oh, that's the best news I've heard all day! Assuming that means she won't be able to play tennis for the team anymore, of course." Monica plans whom she will call first to spread the news.

Surprised, J. Paul says, "Not so fast, Hot Rod." He pulls her in for a kiss. "It's consultative. Her schedule remains mostly her own. She can still play tennis. Besides, isn't that the good news?"

She lets her tongue linger around his earlobe, and says, "What would it take for you to hire her full-time, say eighty hours per week?" She gently bites his ear.

He says, "I thought you would be happy. After all, I helped keep one of your teammates on your team."

"Too bad I couldn't pick which one."

"What does that mean?"

"Nothing."

"Did something happen between you and Josie that you aren't telling me about?"

She only wants to talk about Josie if it involves kicking her off the team. She kisses him long and hard. He barely catches his breath: that's exactly her plan. She purposely won't let him up for air, silencing all conversation. She doesn't want him to know how awful she treated Josie, or how she crushed her game from the inside out. Monica caresses him and kisses his neck, his ear, and then his mouth. She straddles him in the office chair. Breathless, she says, "So glad you're home."

He knows what she is doing. He knows she uses kisses to distract him. He just doesn't know why, but he knows enough. He understands that Monica derails him from a scent of some trail he must have picked up. Still, J. Paul leans back in his chair, completely vexed.

He might adeptly control numerous deals in the boardroom; however, the deals at home often prove more challenging, albeit more enjoyable. He returns her kisses with interest.

While enjoyable, J. Paul wishes sex between them didn't come with a price tag or agenda. He longs for sex between them to be honest; where vulnerability renders a mutual act of beauty, and is not considered a weakness. He craves that degree of intimacy from her. He wants to tell her that this cat-and-mouse game is unnecessary. She has already won him.

Monica says, "I could sweeten the pot a little if you work her seven days a week with no time for tennis friends, or a life whatsoever."

J. Paul says, "I am not saying I will do that, but you don't have to sweeten the pot. *We're* a team." He kisses her and realizes his mistake right away. Wary of trust and vulnerability, Monica loathes the type of relationship where either party lets their guard down, even momentarily.

J. Paul knows all this, yet he still hopes to some day share a relationship built on exactly those two virtues. He knows it will take time and considerable patience. He willingly waits and methodically builds something he hopes to last.

She pulls away and says, "Don't be such a wimp. It's such a big turn-off."

He has been with Monica far too long to be shocked by her callousness. He sees the sting for what it is, and he knows how to keep her in check. In his opinion, that is exactly what she needs: someone to keep her in check. As she kisses him, the tips of her blonde angled bob softly brush against his cheeks. He looks into her piercing blue eyes and makes a mental note to do just that, keep her in check. However, her kisses distract and mesmerize him, simultaneously. Weakening, he changes the tactic and decides to play out the hand dealt. It's not a bad hand, he reasons. He knows it will take many years before she comes to him as herself, free from all pretenses. He will wait and hope, continuing to love: patient, true, and forgiving.

J. Paul says, "Tell me what you had in mind, and I'll let you know."

She whispers in his ear, "Why don't I show you?"

He says, "Aah, magic words." He hoped she might suggest that very thing. Thirty-seven wonderful minutes later J. Paul lays down the law. His mind is completely blown, but he knows better than to say so. Monica wouldn't take it as a compliment, but rather as a sign of weakness; something she loathes.

He says, "Sorry luv, you'll have to do better next time. Don't get me wrong. I loved every second, but it's not enough to sway me."

Secretly intrigued by his seemingly impenetrable armor, Monica says, "You're joking." She gets up to turn the ceiling fan on high.

J. Paul swivels his chair, watching her walk completely naked to the wall switch. He rests his hands behind his head and brings up the previous issue. He says, "Besides, Josephine is a sweetheart. What do you have against her, anyway?"

"Ugh! Not her again. Do we have to talk about *her*?"

"She's been nothing but kind to you. Why can't you two become better friends?"

"You're kidding, right?"

"No, I'm not. That's the kinda girl I would like to see you hang out with more. I think she would make a loyal friend for you."

Monica pouts, but secretly loves the fact that she can't manipulate him. His strength draws her in. Never has she met such a man: so strong and yet so kind. She thinks, *Josie, Josie. Why is everyone always looking out for Josie? What's so special about her anyway? In my country, she would never have made it past adolescence: gone the way of the Dodo bird. Big stupid Dodo Josie!* Instead of stating what she thinks, she says with added droll, "Loyal? Yes. She is the regular Golden Retriever of friends. The standard for all other Golden Retrievers to follow."

J. Paul says, "Oh, come on. Don't be angry with me. Besides, you deserve a good friend."

She thinks, *I would rather get a Brazilian wax then listen to Josie and her incessant good-natured rattling. Please. Boring!* Again, Monica refrains from saying her true thoughts and says, "*You* might have to sweeten the pot before that ever happens. Besides, Tasha is my friend." She sits on his lap again, resting her head on his shoulder, entwining her fingers into his.

J. Paul is not a fan of Tasha's. He kisses Monica's forehead and says, "It's already sweet."

She smiles. She knows she doesn't deserve this man leaning over her, loving her. He truly is the most decent human being she has ever met and the only man able to keep up with her. Monica stares at the computer again and decides to check the weather. The same screen pops up from before. She jumps, quickly closing it.

J. Paul didn't get the wording, but he saw that it was an email. He knows the relative size and shape of the graphics. He also knows from Monica's reaction that he was not meant to see it. He will find the email later. He rubs her shoulders while she types. He kisses the top of her head before taking the newspaper to the lanai for his afternoon nap. He yawns. He finds holding a tiger by the tail exhausting.

Hours after his nap, J. Paul escorts Monica to a benefit dinner. It takes them well over one hour driving time to arrive at the Viscaya Museum and Gardens in Miami. The sun sets while they park. They walk passed a myriad of broad fanning exotic plants, an elongated coquina water fountain, and a lighted limestone path as they wind their way toward the entrance. The line at the entrance far exceeds capacity with more than two hundred persons waiting. The guard at the gate lets one person in for every single person leaving.

J. Paul grabs Monica's hand and guides her around to a side entrance. He flashes his V.I.P. badge at the uniformed guard standing under a sign reading "Musician's Entrance". J. Paul slowly leads Monica through the ancient, uneven limestone walkways and around the side patio towards the back of the old mansion. She walks on her tiptoes, avoiding wedging her heels into the various crevices of the aged limestone tiles.

They find the dance floor packed on the back patio that faces Biscayne Bay. The offshore breeze carries the outdoor music to the expansive grounds. Printed pink banners and small lights stream from the third story overhead balconies, softening the dark skyline. On the dance floor, bright green, pink, and yellow lights flash as the oversized speakers pulsate with heavy bass. The massive crowd moves in rhythmic beat with the Latin pop music. Waiters--donning white jackets, black Bermuda shorts, and bow ties--pass hors d'oeuvres along the bustling crowd's perimeter. The cash bar divides into two lines flanking either side of the glass doors that lead into the early twentieth century, lush interior.

J. Paul flags down a gondola that takes passengers from the back patio to the old stone barge just a few watery feet away.

The gondola's operator says, "Sorry sir, the breakwater barge is only for V.I.P. guests this evening." J. Paul flashes his badge. The operator helps Monica onto the gondola first and begins poling his way to the elaborate stone barge lined with Tuscan Italian statues.

J. Paul says, "Take us all of the way around first, would you?" He signals his finger in a looping motion and points to the estate property.

The young man continues poling in the direction of the barge and says, "My apologies, but the small canal around the property is closed this evening. I am only allowed to take you to the barge."

J. Paul hands the man something from his wallet and says, "If it doesn't get you into too much trouble, I think my wife would enjoy the tour all of the way around. She's never been here."

The young gondola operator looks at the bill in his hand. His eyes grow large. He says, "Yes, sir. No trouble at all." He guides the small boat along the side of the property to the small intimate moat-like canal surrounding the mansion.

The incoming briny water from the bay laps against the side of the stone, moat-like walls and the gondola as it navigates the tight turn. J. Paul sits behind Monica and wraps his arms around her. She leans back against his chest.

He says, "All that's missing is a little music." He asks the gondola operator if he would sing a tune.

The gondola operator replies, "No tip in the world is big enough to make me do that sir. I honestly cannot carry a tune."

A Green Heron noisily click-clicks in the background as a golden sliver of a moon emerges from behind a night cloud. Monica kisses J. Paul.

Inspired, J. Paul stands in the gondola. The sudden movement gently sways the boat. He begins singing in a robust tenor *Un Amore Cosi Grande*.

Embarrassed, Monica implores, "Stop it! Please. People will hear you! Sit down!"

He smiles at her mischievously and says, "I can't. My heart is filled with a love that truly is so deep and so great."

With added vigor, he belts out the second verse. People emerge from nearby maze gardens to witness this magnificent rendition of a romantic classic.

An older woman sees J. Paul in the gondola. She points, grabs her husband's hand, and says, "It reminds me of our honeymoon in Venice. Remember?"

Her husband kisses her hand and says, "How could I forget?" They applaud as the gondola floats by them.

Monica firmly grabs the rim of the boat on both edges and rocks it violently. She says, "I'm begging you. Please stop!"

J. Paul grins, holds on for balance and digs in deep for the finale. He eloquently finishes the undulating performance, holding the last note for what Monica thinks must be some new record. Monica leans back and crosses her arms.

She says, "Honestly. You would think a grown man in a tuxedo would know how to act." She rolls her eyes as bystanders line the water's edge and clap for J. Paul's stunning performance.

Monica says to the crowd, "Don't encourage him!" Then she says to J. Paul, "OK Mr. Andrea Bocelli, are you happy now? You've made a spectacle."

J. Paul humbly bows to the crowd and says loudly for all to hear, "Only one thing could make me happier." He grabs Monica's hand and pulls her to a standing position. He wraps his arm in hers and pulls her to his chest. He kisses her passionately and whispers, "Yes. That's happier." Again, the crowd applauds along with a few whistles. He dips her. The boat wobbles.

She grumbles, "For heaven's sake." She reaches her free hand out to the biggest bystander in the crowd. The bystander extends his hand back to Monica. He pulls her off of the boat in one fell swoop, whisking her onto the limestone walkway. The slit in her fitted long red dress gives way for the giant leap off of the boat. One finely toned leg peeps out all of the way up to her thigh. Her black heels click the limestone walkway upon contact. She turns and smoothes her dress, and then smoothes her completely slicked back gelled hair. She raises an eyebrow and waves as J. Paul and the gondola float away towards the bay.

J. Paul watches Monica. Her beauty stuns him. As the gondola enters the bay, he begins losing sight of her. He registers a faint outline of her smile and fading silhouette. He leans over the boat in time to see the last few sparkles from her Harry Winston large diamond hoop earrings and open lattice bracelet completely fade into the evening darkness. J. Paul begins singing *'O Sole Mio* at the top of his lungs.

One of the bystanders in the crowd says, "Who was that guy?"

Another says, "Not sure, but he's amazing!"

Despite herself, Monica giggles. She winds her way through the crowd and disappears. It takes J. Paul over an hour to find her dancing on the barge. Before taking another gondola to join her, he rests his elbows on the stone railing, watching her. She dances alone in the middle of twenty or thirty people.

TWENTY·SIX

L'esperienza di questa dolce vita.
-Dante Alighieri

A familiar voice approaches J. Paul from behind and says, "Enjoying the view?"

Recognizing the voice, J. Paul turns and says, "Wouldn't you?"

Jim Hartling extends his hand and says, "Yes, and I can see why. What a piece of work."

"Yeah. She's put together OK."

"OK? She's better formed than those Grecian statues next to her on that barge."

"Hey, that's my wife you're talking about."

"I know. And what she's doing with a lug like you, I'll never know."

J. Paul laughs, shakes hands, and says, "Good to see you, Jim. Glad you could be here tonight."

They both watch the crowd on the barge. Jim says, "It's a good night for the Cancer Institute."

J. Paul says, "Yep. It was well planned. Wonder who the caterer was? Food was incredible."

Jim says, "Yeah. Perfect night. I heard they made their magic number, too."

J. Paul says, "Enough for the expansion?"

"Think so."

"That's great. Where's your date?"

"What date?"

"The date you would obviously bring to a beautiful event like this."

Jim changes the wording slightly and says, "'O solo mio."

"Ha! You heard that?"

"Yes, as did half of Miami." Jim nudges him and adds, "You're so dreamy!"

"Asshole."

"Yep."

"That was for my wife."

"Wuss. Seriously though, best rendition of '*O Sole Mio* I've heard in a long time."

J. Paul tries to gauge whether he is kidding or not, before saying, "Thanks."

"I downloaded it to YouTube already." Jim turns his phone on, points, and says, "Twenty-eight hits. Not bad." They both laugh. Jim continues, "Who knew you were such a crooner." He starts reading the comments out loud, "Love this! I got goose bumps from this hot Italian tenor! He--"

"OK, you can shut up." J. Paul looks across the water at Monica dancing and says, "Glad at least somebody appreciates my effort."

"Twenty-eight somebodies, to be exact."

"I'm only interested in one."

Jim follows the direction of J. Paul's gaze, gives a wry smile, and says, "I see."

J. Paul changes the subject and says, "So, what are you doing here by yourself?"

"I'm always by myself. I am the office monk."

"I knew that."

"Then, you also know that I rarely leave work except to sleep. No time to meet women."

"Yeah. There was a time when all I did was work, too. Work, eat, sleep. That was my mantra. It ruined my first marriage."

"Yeah, that mantra sounds familiar. It plays in my head all the time. You know, I wouldn't even be here tonight, if--" His voice trails off. He swallows hard, pushing away the pain.

Jim doesn't need to finish his sentence. J. Paul understands. He knows Jim's wife died of breast cancer a few years ago. He also knows that Jim wouldn't be here at all, if it weren't in her honor.

J. Paul and Monica often saw Jim and Abby at the same events over the years. J. Paul remembers Abby well. He puts his hand on Jim's shoulder and says, "You married a great lady. It's a beautiful night. She would have been dancing out there with Monica."

Jim nods, sniffles, and pushes away a tear with the back of his hand.

J. Paul says, "I hope you don't mind if I offer you some fatherly advice. I am an old fart. Old enough to qualify you know."

"I have a feeling I already know what you are going to say, but go ahead."

"OK. Now that the business has grown, it's time for you to take a small step back. Let the baby learn how to walk a little on her own. You know what I mean? You're entitled to a life. Balance."

"Balance is overrated."

"When you start blurring the lines between work and play, you lose yourself."

Jim thinks, *How can you lose yourself when there is nothing left?*

J. Paul continues, "You lose life and what's important. Birthdays and holidays go by and they feel like regular workdays. It feels OK at first, but over time losing those meaningful moments adds up. Before you know, everything feels the same."

"The same, but only the date changes."

"It's like eating bland toast everyday for the rest of your life. You miss color, texture, and the richness that only those special moments bring. It's that set of special moments strung together over time that adds up to a life worth living, no matter how important you think your job is. It's not what matters most."

"Uh-huh. Says the guy who doesn't know how to retire."

"Guilty. But at least now I take the holidays and the weekends. They're there for a reason, Jim."

Since his wife died, Jim has been absent from the South Florida scene. He looks around at the lights, the moon on the water, the beautiful grounds, and the opulent decorations. He listens to the laughter from the dance floor. He knows Abby would have loved a night like this. His eyes well up again.

As if reading his mind, J. Paul says, "She wouldn't mind you being out, you know. You don't need permission. She would have wanted you to live your life."

Not a fan of talking about Abby in the past tense, Jim quickly changes the subject. He says, "Hey, isn't that Ceridwin?"

J. Paul says, "Where?"

"There."

"It is. And Marni, and Violet, and Josephine."

Jim knows how much the tickets to this event cost. They dropped a pretty penny to be here. He says, "It's nice of them to show their support."

"Yeah. Marni's mother has had breast cancer twice. She's a survivor."

Jim looks at his feet and says, "How is she, you know, now?"

"Cancer-free for three years now."

"That's great to hear." Jim's voice borders on melancholy. What he and Abby would have given to have three more years together. Although genuinely happy for Marni's family, it's difficult for Jim to hear stories about others granted something so cherished, so longed for, and denied to Abby.

Josie spots Jim and J. Paul leaning against the railing. She walks over and leans her elbows against the railing in between the two. She notices the sullen look on their faces and says to them, "Is this a good time? Now, about those year-ending numbers." J. Paul grabs her in a bear hug while Jim gives her nuggies. She laughs and says, "Was it something I said?"

When J. Paul releases her, Jim says, "Wow! I really messed up your hair. Hold still." He licks the palm of his hand and smoothes down the poof on the crown of her head.

She says, "You didn't just do that."

"Sorry. Had to be done. Besides, gives it a nice sheen."

"Eww."

Ceridwin, Marni, and Violet walk over to join them. Violet says, "Beautiful night," and flashes a smile. The bright white smile brings out the richness in her chocolaty-hued skin. Her high neck dress has a keyhole cutout in the front and gathers behind her neck with a large marcasite clasp. The sleeveless peach baby doll frock accentuates her toned arms and tapered legs. She bends over, adjusting the buckle on her gray T-strap high heels. A guy walking past stops and whistles. Ceridwin rolls her eyes and tells him to keep moving.

J. Paul says, "Even better on the barge. It's a little cooler over there with the breeze. Why don't you all join us over there?"

Violet says, "We would, but I think you have to be a V.I.P to dance on the barge."

J. Paul and Jim flash their V.I.P. badges simultaneously. Once they reach the barge, Jim offers a hand, helping all of the girls onto the ramp. As they walk up the landing, a tall elegant woman--stationed at the entrance and wearing a beauty queen sash--hands them stuffed bags with various promotional gifts inside.

They join Monica in the middle of the dance floor. The breeze from the open water gusts more heavily over the barge than under the sheltered patio. Marni holds down the full skirt from her vintage 1950's, champagne and navy, Chantilly lace overlay dress. She kicks off her navy pumps and freak dances Monica.

Monica turns to Ceridwin and says, "Can you please tell June Cleaver over here to get a grip."

Ceridwin smiles as Marni cuts a wild caper in her vintage getup. Ceridwin says, "Sorry, but there's no stopping June once she gets going. Besides, aren't you tired of dancing by yourself?"

Monica's shellacked-back hair proves windproof. As a matter of fact, it's hurricane proof. Prepared for the elements, her tight red full-length dress also stands up to the test. Flawlessly put together, she coolly turns from her friends and dances alone again.

Violet says, "Someone doesn't like us."

Marni says, "Clearly, the 1950's doesn't get the respect it deserves."

Ceridwin says, "Should it?"

Violet says, "They didn't call it the Golden Age for nothing. Maybe June's on to something."

Ceridwin points over to Josie, who's dancing the robot, and says, "OK, but what about the eighties?"

Violet covers her mouth and mumbles, "Can't help you there."

While Ceridwin dances, she adjusts her strawberry blonde locks as the wind shifts her coif from one direction to another. Though heavily weighted by the dense green tartan fabric of her native Scottish Drummond clan, the skirt on her strapless dress billows in the whirling gusts.

Marni soon tires and follows Josie toward the bar. They order drinks as the five-piece band near the rear of the barge suddenly switches tempo to a slower song. A hand reaches through the crowd and firmly rests on Josie's shoulder. She turns. A good-looking man--approximately in his late twenties--emerges from between the two people behind her.

He says, "I don't suppose you want to dance?"

Josie says shyly, "No, thank you. I'm here with friends."

"One song?"

"I couldn't possibly."

Marni grabs Josie's drink from her hand and pushes her towards the dance floor. Marni says, "Yes, she possibly could. And she will."

Marni almost immediately regrets her insistence. The man pulls Josie in uncomfortably close and muscles his arm around her waist too tightly. Josie tries, but she can't push him away. He leers at her and whispers something lewd in her ear. His hot breath reeks of alcohol and cigarettes. He rests his other hand too low on her hip. Josie pushes his hand away as it drops even lower, but she can't wrest away from his other arm pinning her to him.

She says, "I don't like this. Please let go of me!"

The guy says, "Give me a chance. You'll like me after you get to know me better, if you know what I mean."

Josie says, "No. I don't. I won't. Now, let go of me!"

The guy says, "You're not leaving me standing on the dance floor. You'll have to wait at least until this song is over."

Abruptly, the strong arm lets go of Josie. Suddenly, no longer looking at his face, she looks eye-level to his chest. Jim picks the guy up from behind and holds him a foot off of the ground.

Jim says, "Actually, now is good." Jim asks Josie if she is all right before escorting the drunken guy to the nearest gondola. The guy's feet never touch the floor until he sits in the back of the gondola. J. Paul follows and instructs the gondola's operator to escort the guy off of the premises.

Before the gondola leaves, Jim says to the guy, "Don't come back until you learn some manners."

The guy shouts some slurred obscenities. Jim turns, and walks towards the gondola. The guy shuts up and helps push the gondola off of the barge.

Marni says to Josie, "I am so sorry I made you dance with that drunk loser! Are you all right?"

Josie brushes off her arms as if wiping away an invisible string of cobwebs. She says, "That was gross. Ugh! Apology accepted. It's not your fault. I am just a loser magnet."

Jim returns from the gondola and asks again, "Josie, are you all right?"

Josie nods and observes Jim's clothes after the altercation. She fixes his deep blue and gold bow tie. The mishap left it and his hair askew. She notices that Jim's white shirt with blue pinstripes is rumpled and halfway untucked. She also notices Jim is missing a button from his navy blazer. Also, his grey pants have a small tear at the pocket from the brief resistance the guy mustered.

She smoothes down the creases in the fabric across Jim's shoulders and smiles at him. She says, "What? No muscle man pose this time?"

He shrugs and says, "Muscle man? Who? A guy like me?"

She frowns. *A little rumpled.* She looks down at his feet and smiles again. *His shoes are completely out of place.* Jim follows her stare and blushes.

Josie says, "Yes, a guy like you: a hero."

"Uh, pretty sure heroes don't wear fisherman sandals."

"Fisherman sandals are very versatile. Think Roman Gladiator without the unnecessary leather strapping. Think Hercules."

"Wow. Now, there's something. Maybe you're stretching here. Hercules in a bow tie?"

"Yes. And well, anything spectacular along those lines." She hugs him and says, "Thank you."

As the night wears on into the morning hours, the conversation shifts multiple times. Thoughts of the drunken guy move further and further from everyone's mind. Spent, the band listlessly plays the last few requests. Josie stops dancing and leans against the railing. Even the wind tires to a low murmur.

An hour before the event closes J. Paul asks the bartender to serve coffee to his Boca Raton friends. He wants everyone sober for the trek home.

Monica falls asleep in the passenger seat on the way. J. Paul wakes her as they pull into their driveway. He says, "Come on sleepy. It's three in the morning. We're home."

Tired but restless, J. Paul lies awake in bed. Monica--her hair still perfectly gelled back atop her pillow--sleeps soundly next to him. Something from earlier in the day eats at him. He can't erase the picture of Monica quickly closing the webpage from his mind. Too tired to investigate now, he decides it will have to wait. He rolls over and promises himself to look into it in the morning. He sighs and wonders, *What has she gotten into now?* He can only imagine.

Last summer, he caught Monica posing as a jewelry broker, buying wholesale jewelry, and selling items to her friends at a premium. In September, he caught her cashing in part of his carefully planned portfolio and buying gold bullion with it. With great difficulty, he traced the gold to a safety deposit box where she hoarded it. Upsetting as these things might be, J. Paul handles them all calmly, cleaning up mess after mess. Last month, he finished unloading a timeshare at half of its original cost. Monica bought it on an active fault line in Iceland of all places. Why Iceland and why does she do the things she does? He'll never fully know.

Learning from each mishap, J. Paul puts the applicable roadblocks into place, making it harder for Monica to get away with anything new next time. He doesn't blame her completely. He understands that her childhood is partly at fault. She makes many decisions based on the hard times she experienced in her past, not always thinking things through, or so he believes.

For example, she hoards necessities. He remembers the time when he opened the hallway closet looking for masking tape. Out fell a tower of toilet tissue: twenty-seven multi-packs to be exact. When he asked her why there was more toilet tissue in the closet than they could possibly hope to use in an entire year, her answer confounded him. She said, "Toilet tissue never goes out of style."

Later in that same week, he went into the attic to wire speakers for the den. As he unfolded the attic stairs and climbed onto the landing, he pulled the string to the overhead light. He found himself surrounded by canned foods stacked waist high. Again, her answer confounded him. She simply stated, "I ran out of room in the kitchen cupboards." He spent no small amount of time pondering these curiosities. He finally concluded that Monica, deprived of basic necessities in her youth, harbors anxiety associated with doing without.

J. Paul feels compelled to help. He hopes with time and continued stability that he might rid her of all worries caused by any childhood trauma. He recognizes the importance his role makes and takes it seriously. He commits to provide consistency and stability in her life. He meticulously plans for Monica's healing and future. He knows that he is all she has. Meanwhile, he works the nearly impossible feat of keeping her out of trouble. He wonders what tomorrow will bring, and what mischief she might get into. He chuckles, and falls asleep holding her hand.

Hearing the sprinklers sputter on, J. Paul wakes before dawn. He reminds himself to speak with the yard crew about running the sprinklers at such an hour. He tries, but cannot return to sleep. Quietly, he slips off the covers and shuts the bedroom doors behind him.

He leaves the office light off, but turns on the computer and begins searching. He finds nothing. Frustrated, he gets up and quietly walks to his closet. He lays out his tennis clothes, undresses, and jumps into the shower. While washing his hair, it occurs to him, *The email trash folder.* He remembers seeing one message not yet deleted. Soaking wet, he tiptoes through the bedroom again and enters the office.

He clicks a few keys, and there it is: one lonely message awaiting automatic deletion. He takes a deep breath before clicking on the icon and mumbles, "Here goes nothing."

Puzzled, he reads a generic "thank you" form letter from tennistowels.com. He mumbles, 'Why wouldn't she want me to see this?" The purchase totals less than twenty dollars.

He previously set up an automatic sweep that deletes the emails in his trash folder every twenty-four hours. Luckily, this one is still here. He removes the email from the trashbin and makes an extra copy. He can't put his finger on it, but he somehow knows that this seemingly insignificant purchase of a single tennis towel is anything but. He reads the letter again and mumbles, "Standard." It thanks her for her purchase back in October. It offers her twenty percent off of her next embroidered towel purchase of thirty dollars or more before the month's end. He mumbles, "Embroidered towels. Embroidered towels." Unsure why, this resonates with him. Then, spurred on by a hunch, he pulls his chair in closer and begins typing.

The computer locks up. While it reboots, he leaves to change into his tennis clothes. He returns and breaks Monica's account password in three tries. He looks up her order history and finds the towel she ordered back in October. He looks at the yellow towel with the name "Marni" printed in pink Lucida Calligraphy. J. Paul knows enough about Violet's burglary case to understand the significance of this towel and this purchase. He hits the print button again, making a copy of the order.

His eyebrows furrow as he stares at the copy. Suddenly, stomach acid shoots into his esophagus. He swallows the rancid taste and mumbles, "This will not do, even for my Monica." He wants this to not be true. He needs it to not be true. He knows in his gut it is, and what he has to do.

He looks up as Monica softly raps on the office door. Already dressed in her tennis clothes, she says, "Good morning, sunshine! How long have you been up?" She sees his face and instantly knows something is wrong. She says, "What is it?" He doesn't answer. She repeats, "J. Paul, what is it? You look as if you've just seen a ghost."

J. Paul turns the computer screen around so it faces her. He says, "How could you?"

"But—"

"This is too much, Monica. This is going too far, even for you."

"B-b-but she got off. Everything is fine. It's OK. Really. I would have made amends eventually. I would have! J. Paul! You've got to believe me!"

"She's a good kid. I can't let you get away with this one. I won't!"

He walks out of the office. She grabs his arm and says, "Wait! Listen!" Her hand slips. She grabs hold of him again.

He pulls his arm away, brushes her hand aside, and says, "Let go of me! What you did is beyond belief." J. Paul has known Marni Schoppelmann since she was a third grader whose family moved into his New York neighborhood. J. Paul's daughter from his first marriage was Marni's best friend growing up. He feels an almost paternal instinct towards her. He says, "You can't mess with people's lives like that, Monica. This might be the last straw!" He throws his tennis bag over his shoulder and walks toward the door.

She grabs his arm yet again. She says, "No. J. Paul, please! Wait! Just listen to me! *Please!*"

He pulls himself free again and opens the door. Desperate, she lunges for him. She grabs his shoulders firmly and says, "*Please*, just listen!"

J. Paul says, "This is it!"

"But, don't you love me?"

"Love? What does love have to do with *this*? Let go!"

She whimpers, "J. Paul! Don't leave me! I can't--I can't live without you! I can't! I'll do anything! *Anything*! Just please! Wait! No, no, no. *No!* Just please don't leave!"

He says, "I said let go of me!" He swings his arm upward and out, releasing her hold, accidentally clipping the edge of her chin in the process.

She falls backwards against the wall. Hopelessly, she pleads, "J. Paul?" She begins crying and asks, "Are you leaving me?" What scares her the most is how calmly he answers.

Before he walks out the door, he says, "There are always consequences for your actions, Monica. You should have thought this thing through." He might sound calm, but on the inside his heart races. As a matter of fact, J. Paul feels as though it might leap out of his chest at any moment. He knows this might be the one mess that even he cannot clean up.

J. Paul slams his tan Turismo into drive. He looks left, then right, then left again before punching the gas. He leaves a billowing trail of smoke and a pungent burnt rubber smell in his wake. His chest hurts slightly. He massages the center where it hurts on the short drive to the tennis courts. Once on the court, he unpacks his gear, stretches, and joins his partner. J. Paul starts profusely sweating even before warm-up begins. Deep into the first set, he vomits. His partner insists that he sit down.

A few courts away and unaware, Monica begins her tennis match. Tasha introduces their opponents. She explains that one of the girls used to be her roommate. Tasha goes into an elaborate story about how they met. Monica can't be bothered with such trivialities when her marriage is falling apart. She thrusts her hand towards the girl and says, "Nice to meet you. I don't want to hear about how you two met. *Now*, can we play some tennis?" The girl looks uneasily at Tasha. Tasha merely shrugs in response to Monica's rudeness.

Frazzled, Monica cannot pull herself together. Monica hits the first of many balls either out or into the net. Tasha has never witnessed Monica rattled. Monica typically remains cool and always in control.

After Monica frames another ball into the net, Tasha says, "What's got you all worked up today? And what happened to your chin?"

Monica gives Tasha the brush off and says, "Don't talk to me right now."

Tasha says, "You're my tennis partner. Who am I supposed to talk to?"

Randomly, Monica points to Tasha's old roommate and says, "Her. How about her? Now, shut-up."

Tasha smiles, erroneously thinking she understands why Monica suddenly becomes curt with her. She interprets Monica's behavior as jealousy.

Monica ignores Tasha. Her mind races back to this morning's event and to J. Paul. To get off of the court as quickly as possible, Monica intends to take her first dive ever. She needs to talk with J. Paul. It can't wait. Somehow, she needs to make him understand. In her mind she forms her words, preparing what to say.

In the second game of the match, Tasha turns to Monica and asks, "Really? You don't know the score? Since when don't you know the score? You *always* know the score. What's up with you today?"

When she sees Monica struggling to remember, Tasha's friend shouts out the score and readies herself to receive Monica's next serve.

Again, Tasha says to Monica, "I can't believe you didn't know the score. This is a first."

Monica can't be bothered with such small talk when her world is falling apart. She says, "Next time, ask your stupid friend over there and keep a lid on it. She seems to know the score. And don't talk the rest of the match. I am not in the mood for chatter."

Again, Tasha smiles while thinking, albeit incorrectly, that she now knows for certain what bothers Monica. Normally, Tasha wouldn't put up with such rude behavior. However, today she merely smiles and plays her game. Still, Tasha's patience is not enough to make up for Monica's pitiful performance.

Mitch watches from courtside. He stops taking stats after a while. Curious, he crosses his arms and tilts his head. He knows a dive when he sees one. At that exact moment, Jeffrey, a groundskeeper runs up to Mitch. Frantically and with waving arms, Jeffrey explains something to Mitch with such animation that the girls stop playing to watch. They can't make out exactly what he says, but it looks urgent.

Jeffrey grabs Mitch by the arm excitedly, pulling him. Together, Mitch and Jeffrey run to the middle courts. Less than two minutes later Jeffrey returns. This time he runs onto Monica's court and stops play. Out of breath, he motions for Monica to follow him. She refuses.

She says, "Get off my court. We're playing."

Jeffrey says, "You must run! *Run*! Follow me!" She doesn't run. Finally, he says, "Your husband."

Her eyes grow large. She drops her racquet and outsprints him to J. Paul's court. She arrives simultaneously with the emergency vehicle. Deeply winded, Monica drops to J. Paul's side. She grabs his hand and squeezes.

She says, "J. Paul?" His eyes stare vacantly, unfocused. She says, "J. Paul, can you hear me?" His eyes roll halfway back under his eyelids. Monica screams, "J. Paul? J. Paul!"

Mitch says, "He fainted, Monica. Let the EMTs through."

Two EMTs quickly perform a series of diagnostic tests on J. Paul. While the first EMT checks the pulse, J. Paul stops breathing.

The first EMT says to the second, "We lost him."

The second one checks the electrocardiogram. He says, "Ventricular fibrillation."

The first EMT cuts open J. Paul's shirt. He places one gelled defibrillator electrode on J. Paul's upper right chest area above the heart and one on J. Paul's lower left chest area below the heart. He adjusts the joules and delivers a charge. J. Paul gasps and begins breathing again.

The second EMT checks the electrocardiogram again and says, "OK. Let's go! Go, go, go!"

Mitch helps Monica into the back of the ambulance. She sits next to the stretcher and holds J. Paul's hand. On the way to the hospital, she answers the EMTs series of questions, starting with J. Paul's age, height, weight, health, and medical history.

While the EMT works on J. Paul, she asks, "Is he going to be all right?" Tears fill to the brim of her eyes and begin spilling down her cheeks in a steady stream. She adds, "He is. Right?"

The EMT says, "We'll do our best to make sure that he is." It's the best he can offer.

TWENTY·SEVEN

The best and most beautiful things in the world cannot be seen or even touched. They must be felt within the heart.
-Helen Keller

Hours pass before the doctor walks into the waiting room where Monica faces the window, cold and alone. He introduces himself to Monica and says, "Hello, Mrs. Mooney. I am Dr. Dozier. Your husband is in stable condition." He sees that she has been crying.

"When can he come home?"

"Rest assured that the worst is over, but we'll need to keep him for a few days. He did have a significant blockage. The angioplasty we performed was effective. He is responding remarkably well. We expect him to make a full recovery."

For the next twenty minutes, Dr. Dozier answers all of Monica's questions. She diligently takes notes while he speaks. He says, "No need to write that down. Here's a pamphlet. It may also answer some future questions. If not, call my office. I would like to see Mr. Mooney make these dietary and lifestyle changes." He takes a pen and marks a section in the pamphlet. Monica realizes she has some serious studying to do. She thumbs through the brochure's key points. Some of the changes aren't little. Quietly, she makes a promise to learn all she can about J. Paul's condition and to implement these new lifestyle changes for his sake.

Monica plans to dedicate herself to making sure this never happens to J. Paul again. In the months to come, she will learn about the best exercise programs and dietary supplements to incorporate into J. Paul's new daily life. She will also learn everything she can about the procedure he had and the best doctors in the country for his continued care.

Although Monica has confidence in Dr. Dozier, she will leave nothing to chance. She will read about other patients with similar conditions, and what worked and didn't for them. In short, for J. Paul's sake, she will become an expert.

Dr. Dozier asks, "Any more questions?"

Monica says, "Yes. When can I see him?"

"He is in recovery right now. He is experiencing a mild case of nausea, which is quite normal. The nurse will call you as soon as we move him to his private room. I do want to emphasize one thing; it is imperative that you keep his environment as stress-free as possible, especially for the next few days."

Monica says, "Yes, of course." She thinks back to this morning's events.

Dr. Dozier says, "Anything else?" He prepares to leave.

"Yes, this may sound odd, but we had a, uh, disagreement this morning. Do you think that caused his heart to break, uh, malfunction?"

"Mrs. Mooney, his heart did not *break*. He had an M.I. You did not cause his carotid artery stenosis. That is from years of smoking and unhealthy eating habits. You are not the problem, but you can be part of the solution. I understand he recently quit smoking."

"Yes. That was a long battle I finally won."

"Congratulations. Smoking cessation will definitely speed up his recovery, but many lifestyle changes need to coincide. Just read the pamphlet, it explains how. Your role in implementing these changes is vital. A healthy partner can be key in behavioral modification. Forgive me Mrs. Mooney, but I must go. I was due in surgery ten minutes ago. Any last questions?"

"Did he ask for me?"

Dr. Dozier pats her hand and says, "Not yet. As I said, he is battling nausea. The wife is always the first person they ask for though. So, don't worry." He smiles and reassuringly puts his hand on her shoulder.

She mumbles, "But what about a wife he doesn't want around anymore?"

Dr. Dozier says, "What did you say?"

"Nothing important. Thank you for helping my husband."

"My pleasure."

J. Paul sleeps through the rest of the day and through the night. The next morning, he stirs, but doesn't wake. Monica never leaves his side. She hears a faint knock on the door. She answers. To her surprise, Ceridwin, Marni, Violet, Josie, Vivian, and Tasha peek their heads through the door.

Monica says, "What are you all doing here? Come in!"

Ceridwin explains, "We don't want to come in. We know J. Paul needs his rest. We just wanted you to know we were thinking about you. And J. Paul, of course." She hands Monica a soft blanket and some tennis magazines.

Monica hugs the blanket and says, "Oh thank you! There's been an unruly draft in here."

Vivian says, "And I want you to know we all are only a phone call away. If you need anything, that is."

Visibly moved, Monica hugs Vivian.

Tasha hands Monica a hot coffee the way she likes it: black with a double shot of espresso. Tasha says, "We all know how you can get without your coffee." Everyone laughs. Vivian hands her wrapped butcher paper from her favorite bagel shop.

Monica opens the paper and says, "Way Beyond Bagels? My favorite."

Vivian says, "Yep. Toasted rye with veggie cream cheese."

The bagel's warmth seeps through the wrapping and into her hands. Though it smells delicious, Monica knows she won't eat it. She can't stomach anything until J. Paul finally wakes. Until then, the queasy feeling in her stomach will keep bubbling up. Still, she doesn't say so. For once, she minds her manners.

She says, "Smells delicious. Thank you!" She hugs them all and thinks, *I guess this is what J. Paul was talking about. He wants me to have nice friends. Maybe I already do.* She contemplates the wisdom in J. Paul's advice as she looks at each girl's smiling face. She truly does feel better. She manages a genuine smile. A microscopic crack forms in the hard shell around Monica's heart.

Josie thrusts a bouquet through the door and says, "Flowers. From all of us! A little bit of sunshine to brighten the room." She tiptoes in, placing the vase on the sill and tiptoes back.

Touched by the gesture, Monica briefly grimaces. Not fully understanding why, she feels conflicted. A pang deep inside her heart aches. Unused to kindness with no strings attached, she suddenly feels overwhelmed with the urge to cry. She thinks, *These women give of themselves so freely and with no demands from me.* She keeps waiting for the catch. Slowly, it sinks in. There is none.

Monica says, "The sunflowers are simply gorgeous! J. Paul will love them! You know he planted sunflowers in the yard last year along our--" Without warning she starts crying, unable to finish her sentence. She apologizes after she gathers her composure.

Violet says, "It's Ok, Monica. Let it go."

Monica says, "I've never cried so much in my life! The crazy thing is, I know he is going to be OK. So, I don't know why I am crying." She wipes the tears away.

Ceridwin says, "It's a lot to go through."

Vivian adds, "For anybody."

Tasha says, "This is no easy thing."

Josie says, "Yeah. This was probably very scary."

Ceridwin sees Monica start to lose her composure again and quickly changes the subject by saying, "So, he likes sunflowers?"

Monica smiles and says, "Yes. Last time he grew them, he woke up every morning, brought his coffee outside, and drank it while walking among them. He said he liked how they turned their happy faces to greet the morning's sun." She starts crying again before quickly pulling herself together. "He will be so happy to have them in the room. Thank you!"

Ceridwin says, "I downloaded a bunch of tennis clips and sent them to your email address. I also sent you a download of performances by my favorite comedian, Brian Regan. He will crack you up!"

Violet chimes in, "Oh, he's very funny! He'll make you laugh for sure. Laughter is great medicine!"

Monica quickly wipes a single trailing tear away. A woman of control, she feels uncomfortable with so much emotion.

All of her teammates know not to ask about J. Paul's condition. They don't want to make Monica any more upset than she already is.

Violet says, "I hope you don't mind, but your maid let me into your house. Here's your mini iPad, toothbrush and toothpaste, change of clothes, and," Violet holds up the deodorant, "something I think we all can agree on."

Despite herself, Monica laughs. It feels good to laugh. The tension in her shoulders suddenly subsides.

Monica thinks, *Oh, the irony in you forcing your way into my home.* However, she says, "Thank you Violet. I know. I could use this. I am still in my sweaty tennis clothes from yesterday. You all are awesome! And I am sure the staff here will appreciate this even more than me!" She opens the bottle and rolls the deodorant on immediately. They all laugh.

Violet asks, "Here's the rest: makeup, toiletries, you name it. I hope you won't be mad at your maid. I have to give her credit. She really didn't want to let me in. I had to force my way in!"

Monica stops and thinks, *Force my way in.* Then, she pictures throwing the brick through Violet's plate glass door. She jumps as if she actually hears it shatter.

Violet says, "Are you all right?"

Monica collects herself and says, "Yes. Just tired. Anyway, that's Rose for you. She is a tough lady. Tough as they come. And no, it's no trouble. I truly appreciate this."

Violet says, "OK. I just didn't want you to think I broke in or something."

Monica says, "Eh, ha-ha. Who would ever think that, right?"

"Yeah, tell Rose thanks and not to worry. I'm not some low-life, just a harmless do-gooder."

Violet's words cut Monica deeply. Another flashback hits her. She sees herself throwing the bag of Violet's precious belongings into the water hazard. She grabs for the wall, steadying herself from instant vertigo. The brace is not enough. She falls against the doorjamb.

Josie catches her and says, "My God! Are you sure you are all right?"

Monica quickly dismisses the question, "Yes. Sorry. Just a little woozy from lack of sleep, I suppose."

Marni says, "Poor thing! You must not have slept a wink last night. We should all be going. I will leave you with this. If you can't sleep, this will keep you company. It's a book of my favorite poems by Pam Ayres. I love reading her work. It's always a great pick-me-up. Witty. Funny. I hope you like it, too."

Monica hugs Marni tightly and says, "Sorry. I am so very sorry, Marni."

Marni looks confused and says, "Sorry? For what? Why would you be sorry?"

Monica says, "Oh. Uh, forgive me. I meant to say 'thank you'. I'm just tired. That's all."

Josie says, "Understandable. You should rest. We're going to go. Promise you'll get some sleep?"

Monica hugs all of them once more and says, "Promise." This friend experience is new to her. Hesitant to trust it fully, she ponders this newfound gift. Though cautiously processing what it all means or how it will change her life, she genuinely appreciates the bright, sunny faces at the door. She knows that in order to let people in, you have to be vulnerable. She distrusts vulnerability. She looks at each friend's face again. Wary as she might be, she's not going to write it off just yet.

J. Paul wakes while Monica showers in his hospital bathroom. He doesn't know where she is, and he doesn't ask as the nurse walks in. His first thoughts are not of Monica, but of his lawyer and longtime business partner, Howard Gibbons. By the time Monica finishes blow-drying her hair and applying her makeup, Howard's car arrives in front of the hospital.

A fog of heavy steam rolls out from the bathroom door as Monica exits. J. Paul sits upright with an "L" shaped table pulled in front of his chest. He works with notepad and pen. He finishes his third page of notes. He looks at her over his bifocals.

"J. Paul!" Monica lunges in for a hug. "Thank God!" She pulls back to look into his eyes. She says, "I have been so worried!" She bursts into tears and buries her face into his chest. Relieved beyond belief, she sobs uncontrollably.

Gently he pulls her back and says, "I know this is hard for you. It's hard for me, too." Before he finishes explaining, Howard walks through the door.

Howard says, "Found it. I left it in the car." He hands J. Paul a portable desktop scanner.

Monica says, "Howard? What are you doing here?"

Howard says, "Hello, Monica. Where did you come from?"

"The shower." She points to the steaming bathroom.

Howard asks J. Paul, "Are you sure you are feeling up to this?"

J. Paul says, "Yes. I feel a little lightheaded, but otherwise OK."

Howard looks at J. Paul's desk, the notes, and the telephone resting in front of him. In the few minutes it took him to run back down to his car, J. Paul has created an impressive body of work. Howard says, "Are you sure you should be working? I don't know about this. Shouldn't I come back in a few days with these?" He takes the file out of his computer bag.

J. Paul motions for him to put the file on his desk and says, "I have a few immediacies that don't care if I am in the hospital or not."

Howard makes a *tsk-tsk* noise under his breath, but hands over the papers.

With a dismissive wave of his hand, J. Paul says, "Don't worry so much. I haven't overdone it. And, I won't." He opens the file and says, "Unfortunately, this can't wait either."

Howard shoots an uneasy look towards Monica as J. Paul opens the document and glances through it.

J. Paul asks Howard, "Everything like I asked?"

Howard says, "Exactly. I worked on it all day after you called me from your car yesterday morning. You may want to double check, but I think I have everything in there."

J. Paul says, "It's OK. I trust you." He can. Howard has the memory of an elephant and pushes the boundaries of perfectionism. He's one of a handful of people whom J. Paul wholeheartedly trusts to do a job as well as he would do himself, possibly even better.

Howard looks awkwardly at Monica and then to J. Paul. He fidgets and changes his weight from one foot to another. Impatiently, Howard says, "Perhaps, I should step outside for a moment. That is, if you like."

J. Paul says, "That might be a good idea. I'll call you back in when we need a witness for our signatures."

Howard looks relieved to make a hasty retreat and shuts the door quickly behind him.

Immediately, Monica stops crying. She says, "Signatures for what? J. Paul, what is going on?"

J. Paul says, "Monica, these are our divorce papers."

"What?" Monica cries again.

Her mouth hangs open in shock. This time the tears steadily stream down her cheeks. Her newly applied mascara ebbs and flows with each pooling teardrop. She bites her bottom lip to control the sobbing. The truth is that she never believed she deserved a man like J. Paul. She thinks, *I always knew this day would come. Fairy tales don't last forever. So, why would this one? This is the end.*

J. Paul continues, "Read it, but these are the terms. I will divorce you. You forfeit all alimony and former prenuptial agreements. You formally apologize to Marni Schoppelmann and explain exactly what you did down to every last detail. I want her to know. She *deserves* to know what really happened to her and why. We settle out of court with her. You *will* right this wrong. Understood?"

She nods.

He continues, "You owe yourself and Marni that much. Lastly, I have another prenuptial agreement. We will be remarried sometime next year once you have fulfilled your part of this agreement and executed all requirements as detailed. If at anytime I am made aware that you purposely and maliciously meddled in the lives of innocent people again, I will have the right--and no choice--but to dissolve all agreements. Understood?"

With wide eyes, she nods again, and says, "Wait."

He's been anticipating this moment: worried that she might wrangle her way out of doing what is right. That's why he had Harold draw up the legal agreement. That, and he wanted to see whether underneath all of her scheming, she really does love him. She is about to pass the test or fail it. If she signs, then he knows without a doubt that she loves him. If she doesn't, then she walks away with half of everything he owns, and he walks away with a broken heart. He takes a deep breath.

He says, "What?"

"Before I sign, I need to know one thing."

"Yes?"

"Do you still love me?"

"God help me, yes."

She flings herself across his chest and smothers him in kisses. His heart aches again; this time it has nothing to do with his arteriosclerosis.

Howard listens through the cracked doorway. He can't believe Monica signed. She could've walked away as a free woman, not to mention an incredibly wealthy one. Instead, she willingly gave up all of her rights to half of everything. He never liked Monica, always assuming she was in her marriage for the wrong reasons. After the signature, he now knows that not to be the case. She loves J. Paul for himself and not for his worldly possessions.

TWENTY·EIGHT

A hypocrite is a person who—but who isn't?
-Don Marquis

When the Mooney's and their lawyer meet with Marni Schoppelmann, she takes the news rather well; that is, as far as outward appearances show. Omitting the fact that Marni's mouth hangs wide open for much of the conference, her emotions and body language give little away.

Marni remains speechless as her lawyer does most of the talking. The Mooney's lawyer, Howard, shares every last detail regarding how and why Monica set Marni up for Violet's burglary. Monica holds J. Paul's hand throughout the meeting and only occasionally glances in Marni's direction.

When J. Paul first called Marni to set up the meeting, she declined having a lawyer present. That was before she knew any of the details. J. Paul insisted on her hiring one. Now, hearing the news in its entirety, Marni is forever grateful he did. This is beyond her comprehension.

J. Paul intends for this meeting to end with a neat and tidy bow: one that's tied into a tight knot of finality. Not only did J. Paul insist on Marni having a lawyer present, but he also insisted on several other key details. It's obvious he thought this meeting through, leaving nothing to chance. Among the demands, he insists on Monica writing a formal apology letter to Marni and another to her parents.

Monica objects, "To her parents? Why her parents?"

J. Paul silences Monica with one look. It's been years since J. Paul has lived in New York, but he still keeps in touch with Marni's parents.

He explains to Monica that when you harm friends' lives intentionally, you must make amends no matter how painful the consequences. He further explains that the Schoppelmanns are his friends: good people who deserve respect along with a full resolution.

He intends for Monica to apologize for any embarrassment this fiasco may have caused them. After all, Boca Raton is really just another New York City borough. Word gets around. Anything that happens in Boca is news in NYC as well. In good conscience, he could not neglect making amends with Marni's whole family. Monica sighs, but knows better than to argue.

Once the settlement's details rest neatly into place and Marni's initial shock subsides, J. Paul ensures that a permanent non-disclosure agreement, a NDA, remains in place. The NDA is for Monica's sake. It stipulates that Marni and her parents may never utter a single word about what truly happened the day of Violet's home burglary. Further, they may never discuss Monica's extensive cover-up or seek legal recourse.

Feeling as though she waits in the principal's office, Monica sits up straight and intently listens to the terms J. Paul lays out. She nods, and nervously fidgets with her fingernails, biting her cuticles one by one. When Marni finally acknowledges Monica's presence, Monica feigns remorse. She knows it is expected of her. As the meeting progresses, her idle nervousness eventually gives way to sheer boredom with the droning, legal rhetoric.

The out-of-court settlement comes with a hefty price tag paid entirely by J. Paul. Howard shakes his head at the mere mention of the ridiculous sum. Previously, J. Paul and Howard argued over the absurd amount with heated debate. J. Paul had reasoned that it was cheaper than a divorce under the original prenuptial agreement. Howard countered, calling the sheer magnitude of the number "fiscal lunacy".

For J. Paul, he couldn't take the risk of making too small an offer. He needs the Schoppelmanns to accept the offer. He told Howard that he didn't want this thing to "heat up and bounce around any longer".

If Marni didn't accept the offer and decided to seek legal recourse, Monica could go to jail. For him, that's not an option. It's not just about the money. He wants not only to right the wrong, but to also walk away with his wife in tact.

J. Paul knows with this pricetag, Marni's chance of accepting the offer is one hundred percent. She would be foolish not to do so. At the end of the legal conference, all parties sign the paperwork as expected, and J. Paul writes the check.

J. Paul remains calm in his manner and speech throughout the meeting. However, Monica picks up on subtle clues that he is anything but. She notices his face and neck suddenly turn a brilliant shade of red as he signs and pushes the check across the long mahogany table towards Marni.

Monica suddenly wonders the depths to which she has embarrassed him. She hadn't thought of that before now. Regret washes over her. She squirms in her seat. She wonders just how much humiliation J. Paul must feel. Knowing it's all her fault, she sighs, realizing the lengths he went through to give her this second chance. She makes a promise to herself not to blow it.

As quickly as it manifested, the shame disappears, giving way to joy. She looks at J. Paul and smiles broadly as she thinks, *He must really love me*. The look catches J. Paul off guard. Ruffled, he momentarily pauses before finishing his sentence. She doesn't care, and she smiles again. She thinks, *Yeah. He loves me. He has to after all this rigmarole.* She couldn't be happier. Marni catches the exchange and looks at her awkwardly.

After the meeting, Monica waits by the exit. She stops Marni and says, "Thank you so much for the Pam Ayres book of poems. I am sorry I haven't gotten a 'thank you' note out to you yet."

Marni says nothing. Monica laughs and says, "Well, with all the business--crazy Monica terrorizing Boca--who has time for correspondence, right?" She laughs again.

Again, Marni doesn't answer. She is rendered speechless. She merely glares at Monica.

Unnerved, Monica attempts to break the ice again. She says, "The limericks were my favorite. You should recommend that author to Ceridwin. I bet she would love her. You know with her being from Scotland and all." Monica thinks now that the paperwork ended with a nice tidy bow, so should any ill will between them. She doesn't stop to consider that emotions don't always work the same way as paperwork.

Unable to contain herself, Marni practically spits the words at her, "Limericks are English, going back to the eighteenth century. Perhaps, if Ceridwin were from England and not from Scotland, she might give a care!"

"England. Scotland. It's all the same thing really. I mean, ha, the UK is the UK after all. Right?" She nudges Marni playfully.

Marni says, "Tell that to a Scotsman or an Englishman. And don't touch me again. Ever."

Marni briskly walks past Monica. Monica doesn't let it go. She doggedly trails behind Marni. Monica wants to immediately put into action her faithful pledge to J. Paul. It's a struggle for Monica, but she intends to become a model citizen starting right here, right now with Marni.

Monica says cheerfully, "You have to admit. Limericks are a great way of delivering a message."

Marni stops in her tracks and says:

> You say a limerick is what you wish,
> So be it; a limerick I shall dish,

But what your just dessert,
Not suited for lips pert,
But better suited by foot to derriere-ish.

Monica clasps her hands together and says, "Wonderful! How fun that-- wait! Are you saying you would like to kick me in the pants?"

Marni opens her car door, sits, and revs the engine. She says in an expressionless tone, "Why would I say that?" Her car barely misses Monica's foot as she wheels it into reverse.

J. Paul rolls his eyes while watching the fiasco unfold. He walks up from behind Monica and says, "Give it time."

Monica pouts, "I don't need time. I need a massage. Nice is exhausting."

J. Paul puts his arm around her and says, "Time heals all."

Monica pats his chest, leaning into him and says, "You know I am no good at this nice thing. Nobody is ever going to believe it. Not even me."

He laughs and says, "Yes, they will. Time. You'll see."

೩೦

At the next day's pre-match meeting, Monica feels the sting of Marni's biting anger once again. Monica repeatedly tries small talk, but Marni wants no part in it. She remains curt, when not ignoring Monica altogether. Monica remains dogged. She continues just as J. Paul suggested. Monica tries again and again to be the new, nice, gregarious person so completely foreign to her. Not used to opening herself up, Monica wonders how long she can remain vulnerable, and how deep Marni will cut.

However, with Marni's hands tied, Monica needn't worry long. According to the settlement agreement, Marni is limited to what she can say. J. Paul thought of everything to protect Monica from any backlash or social upheaval. However, one look at Marni's hate-filled stare, and Monica doesn't feel completely safe from reprisal.

Monica doesn't like the way it feels to be on the receiving end of venom. She would much rather deliver the sting than receive it.

Monica sighs. She hates making herself a vulnerable target. She mutters, "Pushovers are losers and this nice thing is overrated." Being nice might prove to be the hardest thing she's ever done.

When Monica finally walks onto her tennis court, Tasha stands ready and waiting. Tasha takes one look and says, "What's wrong with you? I've never seen you be such a social butterfly! You said 'hi' to almost everyone you passed on The Breezeway. Are you running for Miss Le Château?"

Monica says, "Nice to see you, too. Oh! Look who it is!"

Tasha looks at their opponent and whispers, "It's the big-boobed boob again."

"Yeah, I know."

"Are we playing her today?"

"Guess so."

Dixie unloads her gear courtside. She puts down her tennis bag and sets a three-tiered Tupperware tray on the table. While she lathers her face and upper torso with sunscreen, Dixie says, "Hi y'all! I was a crazy woman in the kitchen this morning! I baked way too many cupcakes. So, I brought the rest here." Dixie pats her completely flat stomach and says, "Roger likes me trim." She laughs, "You ladies understand. Thankfully, most of them got eaten on the walk to the court. I only have a few left. Y'all want some?"

Tasha says, "No. Thank you. Really, I couldn't. I just ate breakfast an hour ago." She notices the coconut in the frosting and says, "Is that one German Chocolate?"

Dixie says, loudly enough for Monica to hear, "Why, it sure is! The rest are all German chocolate. Well, that is, except for that one. That one is my last peppermint chocolate chip cupcake left."

Monica walks back to the table. She says, "Did you say peppermint?"

"I sure did. Peppermint chocolate chip."

Monica picks it up and says, "I absolutely love peppermint! It's my favorite."

Dixie hands Monica a napkin and thinks, *I know*.

Monica moans as she bites into the moist cupcake and mumbles through a mouthful of crumbs, "Scrummous! Wu weally need to give me 'is wecipe! Ummy!"

Dixie says, "Of course, I will." She grins and thinks, *Special, indeed.* In truth, it is the only peppermint chocolate chip cupcake Dixie baked. She had planned for this moment weeks in advance: ever since Monica came out of Roger's office leaving a toppled chair in her wake, and Roger Fleming looking like a helpless, hopeless puppy. Yes, Dixie will gladly share this family recipe: all except for the one key ingredient added especially for Monica. Dixie stifles a giggle as Monica licks every last finger. Dixie begins counting minutes on her watch. *Tick, tick, tick.*

After Monica enjoys every crumb of the cupcake, she works on her model citizenship skills. She says, "Dixie, just to clear the air, I am not interested in your, uh, boyfriend, and nothing ever happened. I know things didn't look great in his office the other day, but that's the truth. I am sorry if I gave you the wrong impression."

Dixie remembers the way Roger looked at Monica. That's a look she thought he reserved exclusively for her. She closes her eyes and remembers the closed blinds, Roger's bleeding lip, and the toppled chair. Try as she might, she can't rid her mind of the way Roger looked at Monica. Dixie hasn't been on the receiving end of that look since Roger met Monica. She opens her eyes, sticks her chin out, and thinks, *Yes, you are a threat Monica, but not for long if I can help it.* Dixie musters a smile and says, "Oh, yes. I am sure that meeting was strictly business."

Thinking she detects sarcasm, Monica says, "It really was."

Dixie says, "Of course, it was." She keeps looking at her watch. *Tick-tock, Monica.*

The match starts slowly and slows even further into the middle of the first set, almost to a standstill. Tasha says to Monica, "My, aren't we the calm one today? Never have I seen you let somebody dictate the match using such blatant stall tactics. I thought for sure you would have blown your stack by now or, at the very least, reduced Dixie to tears."

Monica doesn't reply. She doesn't say a word for the first few games. Finally, Tasha can stand no more.

Tasha asks, "OK. What's up with you?"

"Nothing."

"Really? Cuz, we are only into the fourth game, and it's taken fifty-four minutes. Any slower and I'll start napping between points."

"Come on. It's not that slow."

"Usually, we're at the business end of the second set by now. How can you take this?"

Monica thinks of J. Paul and her promise to turn over a new leaf. She forces a steely smile and says, "Patience. Let's give Dixie the benefit of the doubt. Everyone has those days."

"Are you on sedatives?"

"No. Don't make fun of me! You should be nicer."

"Really? *Nicer?* When did you turn into Saint Monica? I can't stand one more second of you like this. Where's the real Monica? I can't play like this. Drop the act and let's kick butt." Play resumes.

Dixie drops the ball over and over, spending more and more time retrieving each runaway ball. She forgets the score repeatedly. She argues about obvious and routine line calls, and she returns service faults with out-of-the-park returns. Monica calmly chases down each ball. Dixie uses every possible tactic to slow down the match and keep Monica on the court as long as possible.

Normally, Monica would have reduced Dixie to a pile of rubble by now. The old Monica would never let Dixie get away with this behavior. Feeling the weight of the so-called new leaf that J. Paul gave her, Monica smiles patiently, but silently digs her fingernails into her palms. She wants to scream. She forces herself to breathe deeply. She counts to ten in her head, pleasantly smiling all of the while. She hopes she can make it through the match without crucifying Dixie. "For J. Paul sake," Monica tells herself, "for J. Paul's sake."

Dixie pokes the butt of her racquet into the limb of a perfectly manicured ligustrum tree next to their court. She says, "Silly old me! I can't believe I hit another ball out of the court. And, this one! This one right into a tree!" Dixie climbs the tree in search of the tennis ball.

Tasha drops her racquet on the court with a loud clang and says to Monica, "You've got to be kidding me. Now, she's tree climbing?"

"Patience."

"Is she for real? If you don't say something, then I will. I can't take anymore of this crap." Tasha walks over to Monica's bag and opens a new can of balls. Since Monica buys most of Tasha's gear anyway--and Tasha hasn't paid for a can of tennis balls in months--she feels comfortable helping herself. She knows Monica will replenish the supply.

Tasha says to Dixie, "Look, even your partner is getting impatient. I opened a new can. OK? We'll just play with these. For heaven's sake, get out of that God-forsaken tree. You look like a pelican perched up there. Can we *finally* play some tennis?"

Dixie climbs down, taking her time. She brushes the leaves from her skort and retakes her position on the court. She laughs and says, "I haven't climbed a tree since I was just a little squirt! Sorry to take so long. It isn't as easy as it used to be. That's for sure. Now, where were we? Anyone remember the score?" She throws her arms into the air with fake exasperation.

Monica plasters a smile on her face again and says, "Yes, of course. It's 15:40." Suddenly, the moment Dixie has been waiting for arrives. Monica grabs her stomach. It gurgles loudly enough for her opponents to hear.

Tasha says, "Are you OK? You look green."

Monica starts to answer, but says, "Awwwrgh," instead. The cramp takes her by surprise and doubles her over. She gasps before catching her breath.

Tasha hears a slippery, wet squirt. Monica reaches for the back of her formerly white designer tennis skort. Her hand comes back a gooey brown.

Monica says, "What? Oh!"

Tasha watches Monica run courtside. Tasha sees the huge brown stain with streaks running down Monica's legs. Instantly, Tasha smells the stench. She gags, heaving cupcake remnants onto the HarTru.

Dixie thinks, *And Tasha, too? Bonus. My work here is done.*

Monica wraps her towel around her skort and runs frantically to the locker room.

Dixie smugly walks over to her chair while swinging her racquet and thinks, *Aaah, it will be a long time before people stop talking about how Monica Mooney ran down The Breezeway in broad daylight with poop streaking down her legs. That box of laxatives was worth every last penny, one hundred fold.*

Dixie can't wait to tell Roger about Monica's unfortunate intestinal issues. She mutters, "Let's see how much he likes her then. Nobody wants to get hot and heavy with a Miss Dirty-Squirty." She giggles.

Dixie says to Tasha, "Is this a forfeit? I have to get confirmation before we leave the court ya' know. Sorry. Rules are rules. I surely hope that doesn't sound too callous."

Tasha looks bewildered. She wipes off her mouth, swishes with water, and says, "What do you think? Of course, it does."

In the days to come, Monica--working on a hunch that Dixie set her up--will do some reconnaissance work. She will call friends who also ate Dixie's cupcakes. She will ask them whether they too felt sick afterwards. Unfortunately, she won't ask which flavor they ate. If she had asked, she would have realized that she was the only one given a peppermint cupcake and the only one to get sick. This might have led her to the correct conclusion; Dixie set her up. Instead, she doesn't ask, and her hunch doesn't pan out: as was all part of Dixie's plan.

Monica concludes that her sickness had nothing to do with the cupcake and chalks it up to an unfortunate stomach bug, very unfortunate. For years to come she will be known as Miss Dirty-Squirty behind her back. She will endure vague references and double entendres thrown her way: an outsider, and a joke.

TWENTY-NINE

We can learn even from our enemies.
-Ovid, *Metamorphoses*

Monica phones Josie.

Josie answers, "Hello?"

"Josie. It's me, Monica."

Josie attempts to sound pleased to hear from Monica and says, "Oh, hi. How are you?"

"Fine. We need to talk. It's important. Can we meet after tennis today?"

Josie doesn't want to meet with Monica after tennis today or any day. Josie says, "Can't we just talk on the courts? I have a deadline. This afternoon isn't great for me."

Monica insists, "How about a coffee? Just fifteen minutes of your time. It really is important. The Bean Stop on Glades Road?"

Reluctantly, Josie says, "Fine, but if you don't mind, I prefer Saquella off Federal. That's the best cappuccino in Boca." Josie thinks since she can't look forward to seeing Monica, at least she can look forward to drinking a well-made cappuccino. Then Josie thinks about Saquella's rustic blueberry and pear tart. *Mmmmm.* Maybe she will manage the fifteen-minute meeting after all; if not for Monica, then for the cappuccino, and more importantly, the tart.

After tennis, they meet at the small unassuming restaurant. Josie listens to the whirring background noise of her cappuccino foaming into perfection. The cappuccino promptly arrives with a frothy heart afloat in the foam.

Josie orders a rustic tart and Monica orders a strawberry Napoleon. They sit and sip and take tiny bites of their confectionery treasures, making them last.

Josie asks, "How's the coffee?"

"With a double shot of espresso, what's not to like? Yummy. I have to remember this place. I've probably driven past here a dozen times and never bothered to stop." She daintily wipes her mouth, and gets to the heart of the matter. She says, "You're probably wondering what this is all about or what could possibly be so important that we have to meet right away."

"I'll admit I am stumped."

Monica says, "I'm making amends with all of my friends that I have wronged over the years. Turning over a new leaf. You are one of the first people I thought of, you know, making amends with. I want to apologize for the way I've treated you in the past."

Josie looks around and then says, "Is this a joke? Are you kidding?"

Monica says, "I know this is hard to believe, but I truly am sorry. I didn't take your feelings into consideration, and I was exceptionally cruel to you. I was only thinking of myself."

Josie says, "Wow."

"I know."

"Why now?"

"Let's just say, I made a pact with someone special. This is part of it…of that pact."

"I don't know what to say."

"How about 'apology accepted'?"

"OK, apology accepted."

"Really?" Monica clasps her hands together.

"Yes."

"Oh, thank you. I wasn't sure if you would be willing to forgive me. I was so horrible to you. You don't know what that means to me! If we ever play tennis together again, you will see. I am serious. You will be treated differently. I promise."

"Whoa. OK. I mean, great. Great. OK. Er, thanks."

"Yes, and I am going to be making amends with everyone else I offended at the club."

Josie finishes her cappuccino. *That's going to be a lot of coffee.* She says, "Why the pact?"

"I had a life-altering experience that brought me in check; it made me realize how short life is, and what truly matters most."

Josie says, "Are you moving?"

"No."

"Cancer?"

"No. Nothing like that. As you know, I almost lost someone dear to me. I'm a different person now because of that."

Josie thinks of dear, sweet J. Paul. Then, she thinks of a Homer Simpson quote. *People do change. They change quickly and then quickly change back.* She says, "This is nice, Monica. Good for you. Somehow, this suits you. I hope you fulfill your, uh, pact. Do you think this change will be temporary?"

"Why would it be temporary?"

"I don't know. Change can be elusive."

"Not if I can help it."

"Well, good. Good for you!"

"No hard feelings?"

"Good as gone. Clean slate." She hugs Monica. She has one last lingering question. She says, "Monica, I've often wondered. What is your accent?"

Monica doesn't feel the need to share everything. She simply says, "Does it matter?"

"No. Just curious. Your accent is so slight. Almost gone. It must be a good story how you wound up in America."

Monica says, "All immigrants have good stories." Monica is prepared to change her life here in America and dig deep to better herself for the sake of her marriage. However, she is not prepared to rehash her painful past for mere casual conversation.

Only J. Paul knows that part of Monica's life, and she will keep it that way. Before Josie can ask any more questions, Monica says, "Well, thanks for the girl time. We should do this again." She kisses the air next to Josie's cheeks and quickly leaves.

Josie plops the last bit of blueberry tart into her mouth. She says, "Mmmm. Why not."

❦

Josie begins working on her computer soon after arriving home. By three-thirty in the afternoon, she reaches the halfway mark in a lengthy document. Her Skype icon bounces in the corner of her screen. She clicks on it. She sees Scott is online. Thankful for the much-needed break, she clicks on the "call" button.

They talk about tennis, about the different local Thai foods he's tried, about his lingering jet lag, and his lack of sleep. They run down the list of day-to-day stuff. She looks at his image and would like to touch his blonde, curly hair. His blue eyes fill with mirth as he recants a story from work. He smiles, and his dimple makes her forget what she was about to say.

That dimple! Josie remembers and asks about the food.

Scott says, "I eat rice bowls for breakfast pretty much every morning. Don't get me wrong; I like rice. It's sorta the oatmeal of the eastern world. It's just that the rice here often comes with meat in it."

"That's a problem?"

"I'm not talking USDA ground."

"I don't understand."

"Okay. Let's just say this; no meat is my new motto."

"Oh. You became vegan?"

"No, but a few more rice bowls with parts in them that I don't recognize, and I might consider it."

"Eww."

"Yeah. What I wouldn't give for a juicy American hamburger. Or maybe a pizza. I don't normally eat KFC, but I hear there is one twenty minutes away. I haven't been out much because of the typhoon, but I may brave the weather. I just need something American to eat. I don't care what and fried chicken sounds fantastic!"

"Wait-- typhoon?"

"Yeah, we aren't anywhere close to the eye. We're getting some tough bands though. Really crappy stuff. Some of the winds are crazy. Yesterday, I had an umbrella with me, but I still got soaked through anyway. The water came in sideways. The umbrella was for show."

"Wow. Maybe you should rethink going out until that storm subsides, KFC or not."

"You don't understand. I'm desperate. I would swim floodwaters for an original two piece with mash potatoes and gravy."

"Isn't there normally flying debris in a typhoon? Won't you get hurt?"

"It would be worth it."

"I wish I could send you something from here. Are there any American hotel chains nearby?"

"Yeah, there is a Marriott downtown."

"Maybe they have some American menu items."

"Like pancakes? Waffles? What I wouldn't give for a big, hot, blueberry pancake with maple syrup oozing all over it."

"I am just looking it up now on TripAdvisor. Yep. Looks like you can get an omelet, and a pancake. Waffle. Sausage. Bacon."

"What! Are you kidding me?"

"Nope. Looking at it right here."

"I will definitely investigate this firsthand in the morning. I could kiss you!"

She smiles. *Wish you could!*

They talk like this day after day, week after week. It's part of their daily routine. It doesn't matter that it is usually in the middle of the night for Scott. Still not completely used to the time change, his body wakes at odd hours. He eagerly anticipates her Skype calls. He looks haggard and tired, but otherwise adorable to Josie. She tells him about the new job she will soon begin, starting with her boss, Jim Hartling.

He says, "Jim Hartling? I know Jim. We play golf in the same league. Or we did. When I was there. Nice guy. Talked about work incessantly."

She smiles and says, "Yeah. That's Jim."

"Which part? Nice guy? Or talking about work?"

"Work. Well, both really."

"I heard his wife died six years ago. He was a real mess afterwards. We didn't see him on the golf course for a while and when we did, he didn't say much. Kinda kept to himself. Cried a few times just driving the cart around. Sad shape. Pulled himself together though. Must have been tough with his wife and all. Some sorta cancer thing. Diagnosed and then dead within the year."

Josie says, "Tough on anyone, I suppose." She doesn't divulge any of the information Jim shared with her about his wife over the years. She doesn't talk about his dark days, when he arrived to work unshowered and unshaven for days in a row. Or about how sometimes he slept in his work clothes at his desk, because he couldn't bear going home to his empty house. She doesn't mention those things. Just as she doesn't mention his first day back to work after the funeral when she ran into him at the water cooler, and he had a complete meltdown.

She remembers that day as if it were yesterday. Jim wiped the tears away in embarrassment, only to have more follow. He apologized profusely. Josie--moved by seeing this big bear of a man rendered so helpless--hugged him. Realizing she crossed some invisible personal space line, she in turn offered an apology. He made a joke about suing her for workplace harassment. She laughed. With relief, she watched his tearful face turn into a smile as he joined in her laughter. They bonded that day: no longer just coworkers, but friends. No stranger to loss, Josie provided an ear for Jim in the weeks and months to come.

Scott says, "Earth to Josie. I said it must have been tough on him."

"Sorry. Lost in thought. Yeah. Loss is tough, especially for the person left behind."

"Yeah. Jim was a real mess. We didn't see him on the club course for a solid year. Heard he buried himself in work."

"Everyone copes differently."

"Yeah. That's tough. Poor guy."

Josie sees a woman walk behind Scott. She asks, "Who is that?"

Scott looks behind him. He yawns and says, "Hey, Sophia!" The girl lifts her arm to wave back. When she does, the T-shirt lifts enough to show the edge of her black-laced underwear. Next, she rubs her eyes and mumbles something about coffee. She is petite with wispy brown hair, olive skin, and seems to be wearing an oversized T-shirt. Scott turns back to the computer screen. His reaction to the girl is minimal.

Josie's response is anything but. Josie says, "Who is Sophia? Is that your T-shirt? What is going on?"

He looks back at the girl walking through the kitchen behind him. He says, "No. I don't think so." He yells to Sophia, "Is that my T-shirt?"

Sophia says, "I don't know. I found it on the top of the dryer."

Scott turns back to the screen and says, "I forgot to tell you; I can buy your tennis racquets here so much cheaper and bring some back for you in August, almost half price!"

Josie watches Sophia in the background. Sophia makes coffee in a small press and sits on the counter while she drinks it.

Josie says unenthusiastically, "Gee. That's great."

"I know, right?"

Josie says, "I'd like to talk about Sophia."

Scott says, "Why?"

"*Why*? What is she doing there in the middle of the night?"

Scott finally connects the dots and says, "Oh, right. OK. Remember when I told you I was moving into a bigger building. Well, this is it. This is the bigger building. Our old rooms were too small for even our luggage to fit into them. I am not kidding. They were the size of an American walk-in closet. I could barely turn around without hitting a wall. Anyway, we found this place. Six of us from my office stay here. It has large private rooms and private baths, but a communal kitchen and workspace. Which is fine; most of us eat out anyway."

"What about Sophia?"

"Yeah. She eats out, too."

"No, I mean. Why is she there?"

Scott says, "She is one of the lucky six. She is from our Florence office." Scott thinks, *Geez, talk about jealous.*

Sophia yawns, stretches, and slips off of the counter.

"Do I need to be worried?"

Scott sighs and thinks, *Says the girl who wants to date other people.* He says, "What? Are you kidding? I work, sleep, and Skype with you. That's it! I don't have time for anything else. I haven't even gone out, except to eat." He grins.

That dimple! Josie begins to soften. "OK, but imagine what I see. I have a computer screen with you on it and a young girl in a-a-a t-shirt. You can't expect me to not draw some lines here."

Irritable from lack of sleep, he rubs his eyes and says, "I Skyped you because I miss you. I told you that nothing is going on. What do you want me to say? You know what? Fine. Draw lines. Draw squares, circles, or a boat if it makes you happy! I am going back to sleep!" He mumbles something unintelligible about cake and eating it too, then he hits the off button and the screen turns black.

Josie blinks, staring at the blank screen. *No. I Skyped you! You didn't Skype me!* She crosses her arms and says to her reflection in the empty screen, "That went well. Very romantic. *Do I need to be worried?* Why did I say that?" She opens a screen to her latest work file and begins typing. She struggles to focus, fighting to push all thoughts of Scott at bay.

✛

That night, Josie doesn't sleep well. In the morning, she arrives to practice a few minutes late. She remains a step behind the entire time. After practice, she sits at the bistro table towards the end of The Breezeway. People pass and wave. She waves back. Some stop, sit, and chat. Josie doesn't know why she sits here wasting time. She needs to go home to finish her file from last night. *It is Due Day after all.* Still, she finds no motivation to stand or walk for that matter.

Another familiar face pulls up a chair and joins her. Enthusiastically, J. Paul shares a new product idea for Jim's company. He runs the product details and then the financial information by Josie. They talk about the cost of R&D, manufacturing, marketing, and product launch details. For a brief moment, she forgets about Scott and her aching heart.

J. Paul says, "Well? What do you think?"

Josie says, "I just worry that a significant amount of cannibalism will incur from the new product over the current one." She explains why—including the potential short and long-term affects--when suddenly Mitch walks by to hand J. Paul sunglasses.

Mitch says, "Excuse me, but I think these are Monica's. She left them on the table by her court."

J. Paul says, "I recognize those. You may still be able to catch her. She and Tasha just walked to the parking lot."

Mitch says, "Sorry. Can't. Meeting with the board right now over the new parking garage plans."

J. Paul says, "OK. No problem. I'm skipping that meeting. Josephine, will you walk with me so we can still finish our conversation? Monica likes to drive with these. I may still catch her in the parking lot if we talk while we walk."

He and Josie take the shortcut through the alley behind the clubhouse and around the row of dumpsters. J. Paul recognizes the sound of Monica's car engine starting before he and Josie actually see it.

J. Paul says, "I think we're in luck. There she is."

With the tire on Tasha's scooter flat, Monica had offered to drive her home. Monica starts her car. Tasha buckles. Tasha's knees hit the glove box.

Tasha asks, "Where's the seat button to move the seat back? I can't fit my legs."

Monica explains, but Tasha finds the wrong button. She moves the seat up and down, but never back. Finally, out of frustration Monica leans across Tasha and feels for the button. She pushes the button back until Tasha's knees visibly separate from the glove box.

Monica says, "There. How's that?"

Tasha says, "A little more please."

Monica leans over again, feeling for the button, but what she finds instead surprises her. Tasha wraps her left arm around Monica and cradles Monica's head with her other arm. She caresses Monica's hair as she kisses her. This kiss is so out of the realm of possibilities for Monica that it takes her a second to register what is actually happening. Tasha misinterprets this momentary hesitation as condonement and locks lips for a heavier kiss.

At that precise moment, J. Paul opens the driver side door and says, "Hey, sweetheart, you might need--" He drops the glasses and says, "What the--?"

J. Paul steps back, accessing the situation. Monica looks at him helplessly. Tasha's jaw drops open. Josie's jaw drops open. Monica's jaw begins jabbering at a steady pace.

J. Paul picks up the glasses and throws them on her dashboard and says, "That's it!" He storms off.

Monica pleadingly says, "J. Paul, give me a chance to explain." She turns to Tasha and viciously says, "Who paid you to do that? Tell me now."

Tasha says, "You did."

"What are you talking about?"

"I'm talking about the expensive club membership you bought me. The matching outfits, lunches, shoes, racquet, tennis balls and tennis lessons you bought me. Doesn't it all add up?"

"It most certainly does not!"

"Everything comes with a price, Monica. You can't tell me you were just being nice! Any nicer and you'd be broke."

"The money is *not* for this."

"I thought this was it. I thought this is what you wanted. Didn't you know I was a lesbian?"

Monica wipes her mouth with the back of her hand and says, "I had no idea!"

Tasha says, "Then why were you in such a jealous rage that day on the court when you met my ex-partner, my ex-lover?"

Monica thinks back to the girl across the net a few weeks ago. She vaguely recollects that she was Tasha's old partner. She spits the words at Tasha, "I wasn't jealous! I was preoccupied! I was having problems with J. Paul, you idiot! I'm in love with your tennis, not you! Now, look what you've done!" Monica points at J. Paul. She glares at Tasha and says, "You give 'lesbian' a bad name!"

Monica runs past a speechless Josie in the parking lot. She catches up to J. Paul as he climbs into his car. She grabs his arm. He wrestles it free, closing the car door and locking it.

Monica shouts through the car's window, "Come on J. Paul! You know that's not me! She read me wrong! It's not what you think! Let me explain! *Please*!" He nudges his car forward, but she won't move out of the way.

She yells, "Don't go!" She jumps onto his car. He nudges his car further. She straddles his hood and stares at him through the windshield.

He cracks the window and says, *"How do I know that's not you?* Rather, how do I know it was you? Because I saw it with my own eyes! I'm done, Monica. Get off my car." He's furious with her, but mainly he is furious with himself. He's tired of being her patsy. He yells at her, "You played me. You used me to finance your romance with Miss Legs over there. I should have known. I'll never let you play me again."

She digs her fingernails into the rubber under the windshield wipers and shouts, "No! I am not letting go! Listen to me!"

J. Paul says, "Have it your way." He rolls his window back up. He sees her jaw clench and then start jabbering. He wants to hear none of what she says. He blares the radio. He drives at a snail's pace the entire way home with his soon to be ex-wife on the hood of his car. Cars honk and pass him. He smiles and waves and sings along with Axl Rose's "Sweet Child O' Mine".

When Josie leaves the parking lot, she sees Monica already walking back to the courts. Monica kicks a small coconut as she walks, mumbling to herself. She looks as if she has aged fifteen years in the last fifteen minutes since Josie has last seen her. Josie ducks as low as possible in her driver's seat and avoids eye contact. *Too late.* Monica sees Josie's car and runs over the median. She flags Josie down and jumps into the passenger seat.

THIRTY

A harbor, even if it is a little harbor, is a good thing…
It takes something from the world, and has something to give in return.
-Sarah Orne Jewett

Monica says, "Please don't tell anybody about what happened with Tasha!"

Josie says, "You mean The Kiss?"

Clearly uncomfortable, Monica says, "Uh, yeah. Please don't."

Josie thinks of the two women who routinely sit at the juice bar and gossip about anyone and everyone who walks by. She says, "Who would I tell?"

Monica gives her an are-you-serious look and says, "Please."

"OK."

"Promise?"

"Uh, OK. Promise."

Monica says, "My life is in shambles." She gives a 'poor me' pitiful look and says, "I don't know how I got to this place."

Josie remains mute on the subject, but only with a great degree of difficulty. *I don't know, maybe Karma? Or maybe, the fact that you dump on everyone around you? Or, that you only care about yourself?*

Monica grabs Josie by the arm. She intends to hug Josie. However, after seeing The Kiss, Josie instinctively pulls her arm away.

Crushed by the rebuff, Monica says, "I only wanted to hug and thank you for picking me up. You're such a good person, Josie. I know I've treated you horribly. I know we talked, and you forgave me; but it's times like these that I truly see how wrong I was. I regret it, you know; how I treated you."

Josie says, "No thanks necessary. It's no big deal. Really. I am just driving you a mile down the road to your car."

"But I don't want to go to my car."

Confused, Josie says, "Um, OK. Then where? Your house?"

Monica says, "No. J. Paul locked me out. How about somewhere fun?"

Josie looks nervous. She says, "Sorry. Can't. I have to go home and work on a file due by tomorrow."

"Perfect. We'll go to your house."

"Monica, I have to work. I can't have company. I don't have time. I have a deadline. I will be locked in my office until late."

"I won't make a peep, I promise. Please. Just for an hour or two until J. Paul comes to his senses."

"No."

"Yeah. OK. I understand. You can just drop me at my car."

Josie pulls into the parking lot and lets Monica out next to her car. Josie adjusts her rearview mirror. As she drives away, she sees Monica fall to pieces. Monica rests her head on her arm and leans against her car. She sobs. Josie sees Monica's body shake with each sob; it's a hard, end-of-the-world kind of shake. Josie relents. She turns her car around and pulls up next to Monica. She says, "Come on. Get in."

Hopeful, Monica looks at Josie and says, "I won't forget this, Josie. I swear I won't. And you won't regret it! Thank you. I really need a friend to just be there. Thank you."

It's almost midnight before Josie looks up from her work. She stretches, yawns, and walks to the kitchen to fill her glass with water. She sees the television playing. *Strange. I don't remember leaving that on.*

Forgetting about Monica, Josie finds the remote. It's next to Monica, sleeping soundly on the sofa. Josie turns the television off and finds a comforter in the hallway closet to cover Monica.

Next, Josie places a pillow under Monica's head. Then, she leaves on a small accent light in the kitchen. *If Monica wakes in the middle of the night, she'll have enough light to get her bearings.* She crosses her arms and looks at Monica sleeping. *How innocent and sweet Monica looks!* However, Josie knows the truth. *Hmmm. Innocent and sweet don't really belong in the same sentence with Monica.* She is anything but.

❧

Josie wakes early to the deafening crack of lightning. Seconds later, she hears the roll of thunder and then another deafening crack. Judging by how closely the thunder follows the lightning, she guesses the storm to be only a few miles away. She looks at the clock: 6:32 a.m. She hears Monica in the kitchen making a pot of coffee. When Monica sees Josie, she pours another cup.

Exuberantly, Monica holds the cup out for Josie and says, "I made this. I found all of the stuff, and I made this for you. Usually, Rose makes our coffee for us in the morning, but I wanted to do something nice. I found everything."

"It smells delicious."

Monica beams.

Josie takes a sip and finds something chewy in her drink. She sees coffee grinds floating at the top. *I guess you didn't find the coffee filters.* She says, "Thanks. I guess tennis is cancelled for today."

Monica watches the storm brewing through the window. The palm branches heave to and fro, heavy rain pelts the glass, and another round of lightning snakes through the dark blanket of clouds. Josie sees Monica has been crying and—out of courtesy--avoids eye contact.

Monica says, "Yes. It looks like the bottom should fall out at any minute."

"Some storm. We should get you home. Who knows how long this will last and you might get stuck here."

Monica stands, but not sure or deliberate in her actions. She picks her mug up and then sets it down without taking a sip. She says, "If you say so." Terrified to confront J. Paul, she bites her cuticles one by one.

Josie doesn't bother putting on her shoes. There is no need. She will drop Monica off and return home in less than ten minutes.

They arrive at Monica's house. What they see surprises both of them. Monica's labeled belongings are packed into bags, crates, and boxes. All are neatly stacked on the front porch.

They wait for a break in the rain and make a run for the porch. Josie nudges Monica past the boxes and says, "Ring the bell. Go ahead. Talk to him. Ring it."

Monica turns to Josie. She fights back tears. She says, "I can't. I can't take any more hurt right now. I just can't. What if he refuses to talk with me? I couldn't handle that."

"Well, then what are you going to do?"

Monica shrugs and says, "Start packing boxes into your Mini."

Josie looks at her watch. She needs to meet with Jim at 8:30 a.m. It's almost 7 a.m. She says, "Look. You can put the boxes in my garage for now. You can stay in my guest room until this weekend. By then, you and J. Paul should have plenty of time to sort this thing out. OK?"

This time Monica cries tears of gratitude. She nods and says, "I'm sorry I am so emotional lately. It's just that J. Paul means everything to me." The sky darkens further as they load the boxes and bags into Josie's Mini. Finally, the sky opens up with a terrific flash of lightning.

Josie feels the reverberations from the thunder against her feet as the ground and sky rumble. She says, "That was too close! Let's get a move on."

Hurriedly, they manage to pack the remaining few boxes just as the rain begins to drive, soaking them through. The thick musty humidity weighs down the air. This heaviness, coupled with their wet clothes, adds to their arduous efforts. They cram the last box into place. Arriving back at Josie's house, they unload Monica's belongings into stacks in the garage's open space. Josie plugs in a fan to help Monica's belongings air out and dry.

Josie says, "We'll get your car later after the storm passes. You can park it here in the third spot. I just need to move my bike." She hands her a remote for the garage door and says, "You'll need this."

Monica usually possesses more than her fair share of words. Today, she possesses few. She meekly expresses gratitude and little else.

Josie notices Monica's unusual silence and says, "You know Monica, leaving difficult emotions bottled up creates problems in the long run. Believe me, I know from past experience. You wanna talk about it?"

"No. Thanks though."

Josie says, "OK, but I heard your conversation with Tasha after J. Paul walked away. I know what happened. Just explain it to him. Don't let it fester. Talk to him. He'll understand. Things like this are just a big misunderstanding waiting to be cleared up. You gotta talk with him."

Monica says, "I tried last night and this morning. He won't answer my calls. He wouldn't listen to me yesterday."

"Try again."

"You heard what he said. He's done with me. He left me on the hood of his car the whole drive home. I mean come on. He locked me out of the house. I think it's pretty obvious how he feels. He doesn't want me. He won't listen. There's nothing left to talk about."

"He can't listen if you don't give him a chance."

"He needs time."

"I disagree with you. I think time is the worse thing to give him. He needs to know the truth. And not later, but right now. You should've knocked on that door when you had your chance twenty minutes ago. You knock, and you keep knocking on that door until he answers and listens. You owe it, not just to yourself, but to him."

"You don't understand, Josie. I was already on my last chance with him. He's had it. You heard him. He's done with me. I'm not worth his trouble."

"How can it be a last chance when it is only a misunderstanding?" Josie tries to make light of the situation and continues, "Granted, a shocking misunderstanding, but a misunderstanding nonetheless." Monica doesn't laugh. Josie says, "Sorry, maybe it's too soon for humor. But how can any finality come from a misunderstanding so easy to clear up? Think about it. I think you're giving up too easily. I'll go pour some more coffee." Josie discreetly throws away the batch with grinds in it and makes a new one.

Monica watches the rainfall down Josie's brick driveway and pool into the street's gutter. She mumbles, "I know, because I never deserved him. That's how."

Monica looks far away over the deep gray sky and into the approaching expanse of black, ominous clouds. The banyan trees move violently, swaying their heavy branches into the wind. She would like to believe Josie. She wishes Josie's words to be true. Instead, she listens to the voice in her head. She mumbles, "Things are as they should be: as they inevitably would be. I am destined to be alone. How could anyone love me?"

A mighty gust of wind enters the garage, blowing her trailing tears into a backward angle across her cheeks. The storm moves directly overhead. She sits on a box full of expensive wet shoes. The booming thunder muffles the sound of her crying.

৽৵

It's just after five p.m. when Josie returns home from her meeting. Pulling into her driveway, she sees the unexpected. With a bottle of tequila in one hand, Monica precariously sits perched on the roof with her legs dangling over the edge. She's wearing the same top from yesterday, neon pink underwear, plaid wellingtons, a terry robe minus the belt, diamond chandelier earrings, and a tiara. Monica vomits over the side into the bushes before waving "hello" to Josie. Josie slams her car into park and rushes to the side of her house, looking up.

Josie shouts, "What are you doing up there?" She doesn't wait for an answer and yells, "You could kill yourself! Get down! Right now!"

Monica points to the horizon, swirling the bottle in the process. She says, "I thought I could schee my houz from here! Hiccup! But all I schee are zum topz of tees! Ha-ha-ha! I mean trees! Ha! Tees. Like golf course. Tees. Get it? Hiccup! *Tees*."

Josie, trying to establish an air of calm, says slowly, "Why don't we take a drive there. You and me. You could schee, I mean see, your house up close. Now, come down and we'll go."

Monica says, "Nope. Nnnnot comin' dow'. He locked me out! He canceled my cred-hiccup-it cardz. He hatezzz me! He won't answurrr door. Hiccup. He blocked my e-mails. He hatezz me! Hatezz Monka!" She motions in the direction of her house. This time the swirling bottle spills liquid over the roof's edge and onto Josie.

Monica says, "Zzzorrry!" She drops the tequila off of the roof, looks down at the broken bottle, and says, "Oopzzzy." While she looks down, she loses balance, and falls off of the roof and into the jasmine hedge.

Frantically, Josie rushes to her side. She untangles Monica's blonde locks from the hedge, brushes the twigs and leaves off, and helps her up. Josie says, "Are you all right? Can you stand? Anything broken? Bruised? Hurt?"

Monica bleeds from a few minor scratches. Other than that, she appears OK. She says, "Juzz my heart, Josie, juzz my heart. Zzzzorry Josie! I know yooooo juz got dem bushez replazed." She holds onto Josie as they walk into the house. She barfs on Josie's newly restored front doors. She says, "Can I get 'nother bottle tequila?"

Her rancid breath bathes Josie's nostrils in an extraordinarily foul affront. Monica rattles on about how all she owns in this world is in the garage in boxes. She wants to throw it all away, except the jewelry. Josie tries turning her head, breathing in the other direction as they walk. Monica says she intends to sell some of her jewelry and pay Josie rent.

Rent? Alarmed, Josie wonders if Monica thinks she is staying. She gets Monica settled on her couch with a mug of coffee, a blanket, and the remote. She makes an immediate call to J. Paul. She stresses the urgency, before discreetly leaving the house to meet with him.

J. Paul doesn't want to talk about Monica. He interrupts Josie at every point. The first few minutes continue this way. Finally, he relents and listens half-heartedly. Josie tells him what really transpired with Tasha, and what he missed that day after he walked away. She also paints the picture as to the exact state of mind Monica presently resides.

He starts out defiant, and then he looks sullen. By the end of the conversation, he looks pained and concerned. He asks more about Monica. Josie shares every last detail.

J. Paul says, "What! She fell off of the roof? Is she OK?"

"Yes, thankfully. I've had to hide the liquor bottles and her keys. She is on a self-destructive binge."

"Uh-huh." J. Paul doesn't speak for a few minutes.

Josie breaks the silence and says, "J. Paul, she really needs you. If you knew how much she loves you, you wouldn't still be sitting here. She's a mess. I don't know what to do with her."

J. Paul says, "Leave that to me. Mind if I follow you back to your house? I'll speak with her."

Speak with her. Exactly. "Yes! Sure. Great!"

"I hope she hasn't been too much trouble for you."

"No, but I'd be lying if I didn't say she has kept me busy."

J. Paul says, "I know Monica can be a handful." Suddenly, his features soften and he chuckles. He says, "She has a mischievous streak in her a mile wide that makes me laugh at times. Other times, it gives me an exploding headache the size of a cannonball." He shakes Josie's hand and says, "Thank you for watching over her these past couple of days. Josephine, she needs a friend like you. She is a hard nut to crack, but what's inside is solid and good. I promise you that."

"With all due respect, J. Paul--and maybe I haven't seen enough of what's inside--but she's been pretty horrible to me, especially on the tennis court. I haven't seen too much good at all."

He sighs.

Josie frowns and says, "She did ask me to meet with her last week for coffee. She apologized for everything she has ever done. Says she wants to be friends and be nicer to me."

"She said that?"

"Yes."

"I can't believe it."

"Yeah. And she said she is going to make amends with everyone else she has offended."

J. Paul's eyes light up. He says, "Come on. Let's go get her."

"Let's go."

When Josie opens the front door, she finds a more sober Monica sitting on the kitchen counter with her feet in the sink, trying to drink white wine vinegar.

Monica spits the mouthful into the sink and says, "Yuck! You hid all the real liquor! This stuff is disgusting!" J. Paul enters the room behind Josie. Monica sits straight up, speechless. She drops the vinegar bottle into the sink. In one scoop, J. Paul picks her up and carries her to his car.

Monica says, "Not so fast, Mr. Mooney. I did everything you asked, and you still blew me off. I am not going home with you. Not now. Not after all the heartache you've caused me. No way!"

Josie yells after them, "She didn't mean that!" She shuts the doors, locks the bolt, and leans her back against the door. She slowly takes in a deep breath and lets it out even slower.

J. Paul sets Monica in the passenger seat and buckles her. He smiles, too happy to say anything. Monica points to the garage. She says, "My belongings, my clothes. They're all in there."

J. Paul says, "You won't be needing clothes anytime soon." After the short drive, he parks in his garage and carries her into the house. They kiss in the hallway. She no longer tastes of vomit thanks to the cleansing rinse of white wine vinegar. He could care less.

For Monica, the kisses are bittersweet. She says, "You left me."

"I'll never leave you again."

"It could happen."

"Nope. You belong with me."

Monica places her hand on her chest where her heart hurts. She says, "It still hurts. I cannot survive another one of these."

J. Paul grabs her hand and puts it on his chest above where his heart rests. He says, "As long as I am alive, you will always have a home right here."

She feels his heart beat under her palm. She whispers, "Your heart is racing."

J. Paul says, "I know. This is why." He leans forward and kisses her tenderly.

She gives all of herself into his kiss. She tastes him, feels his hair, his skin, smells his neck, and tastes his tongue deeper. Every inch of her melds into him. Not so much as the tiniest of air or space separate them. This man, this vulnerable breathing flesh and blood, brings her more joy in this lifetime than anything else she has ever known or hoped for before. She clings to him, needy. She knows nothing in this lifetime lasts forever, and she may not be allowed to keep this man until the day she dies. She silently prays. She thanks God for this not-so-small miracle of love, making her once broken and miserable heart whole.

THIRTY·ONE

Those who know how to win are much more numerous than those who
know how to make proper use of their victories.
-Polybius

Josie says to Mitch, "What? Why am I playing with
Monica? Who is Tasha playing with, and why aren't they
playing together?"

Mitch shrugs and says, "They wouldn't play together.
Don't ask me why. They wouldn't say. I mean go figure;
after all the pushing and pulling they did to play together,
and now they demand to play apart. I've given up trying to
understand women. Anyhow, Tasha and Marni are playing
line two. You and Monica are playing line three."

Josie says, "Oh, come on! Why did I get the short straw?"
She has more than a sneaking suspicion as to why Monica
and Tasha will no longer play together, but she says nothing
about it to Mitch. *The Kiss shouldn't mean I should have to play
with her! It's not my fault they shared an awkward moment.*

Mitch says, "Don't fight me on this. I have it straight in
my head. One more change and my head might explode like
a pressure cooker full of minestrone with too loose a lid."

With a wry smile, she looks at him and says, "Pressure
cooker full of minestrone?"

He smiles wryly and adds, "I had it for dinner last night,
as did some of my kitchen walls."

You cook? Really? "I see. Well, as long as you've got it
straight in your head, that's all anyone should care about,
right?" Josie walks out of the office.

Mitch says, "That and my kitchen walls."

"Not funny. I won't play with her."

He thinks, *That's new.* He yells after her, "More Josie and less diva, please!" She yells something unintelligible back as she walks out of sight. He mumbles, "No more divas. No more divas. No more divas. Please."

∽✌

Josie passes J. Paul. He wears street clothes and carries no tennis gear. She says, "No tennis today?"

He says, "Not today. I'm here strictly in a supportive role, well, and as eye candy."

"Eye candy?"

"Yes, I keep hoping that Monica will look past the gray and wrinkles and see the real me. But she's superficial like that. See? Watch." He yells through the fence, "Look, Honey!"

Monica stops hitting volleys and yells, "What?"

Standing a good two inches shorter than Josie, J. Paul flexes his best that-way-to-the-beach pose.

Monica yells, "Good God, what are you doing? I'm playing tennis here!"

J. Paul says to Josie, "See? It's exhausting being an object of desire."

Josie says, "Yes. The level of your pain is imaginary. I mean I can only imagine your level of pain."

"Excruciating. Really. Anyway, enough about me, good luck today!"

"Thanks. I am playing with your wife."

J. Paul says, "Yeah. I know. Have fun!" He pulls up a chair.

"Thanks. See you on the other side." *Fun? Yeah, right. Hardly.*

Monica hits volley after volley with her opponents as Josie enters the court. Josie says, "Thanks for keeping them busy until I got here. Guess you're stuck with me today."

Monica says, "Not stuck. I asked to play with you."

Great. I suppose I should be flattered.

Monica continues, "I've decided it's more important to enjoy myself on the court than to win."

Josie coolly replies, "I see you've already warmed up your backhand. It's looking particularly wicked."

Monica says, "What? I've only hit volleys so far."

"I mean that left-handed compliment was a bruiser."

"Ooh. Sorry. Yeah, you're right. That didn't come out right at all. What I meant to say was I'm trying not to take my tennis so seriously and just have fun. Ugh, that didn't come out right either. Don't worry; I am still going to try to win. I mean I know you will, too. That's not what I'm saying. I think we will, uh, win, but I know we will have fun, too. Uh, winning that is. That's what I meant. Fun is the most important thing, right? Ugh, I'm not making any sense."

Josie sighs, accepts her fate, and begins warming-up. *Fun, fun, fun.* By the time the match begins, perspiration dots her collar. The humidity adds an additional five degrees to the heat index. Josie dabs her neck with a tennis towel and whispers a word of thanks to the grounds crew as they deliver a bin of water bottles immersed in ice.

One of her opponents says, "I think it must be well over one hundred and five degrees. If it is, league rules say we can reschedule. What do you girls say? Want to?"

Monica pulls an outdoor thermometer from her bag.

Josie says, "You carry a thermometer?"

"Always prepared." She says to the opponents, "It's one o' three. Looks like it's on, ladies. Besides, I like the heat in Florida. I'd rather be in moist heat than dry heat any day. I was in Scottsdale for a tournament last summer. It was a very dry one hundred and twenty degrees. It was so hot, I had to use a hand towel to pick up my sterling silver Tiffany tennis ball can. Can you believe that?"

One opponent rolls her eyes and says, "How ever did you manage?"

"Evian face spritzer, Black Ice personal cooling device for my neck, and an all white ensemble."

The opponent smirks and says, "I went to a tournament last weekend. It was so hot that they passed out paper fans at the entrance. But I think the paper was from Kate's Paperie in New York City."

Not realizing the girl is making fun, Monica says, "Now why would they pass out fans? Did you know that fanning actually generates more heat than it dissipates? Fanning simply doesn't work. Only if you have someone fan you, not do it yourself. Anyway, I'll take our humidity any day. Keeps my lungs moist."

No one comments. It's simply too hot to argue or poke holes through Monica's ridiculous statements. Josie gathers the hair sticking to her neck, and sweeps it into a ponytail. She chews on a piece of ice as she prepares her service motion. She double faults her first service away; not surprisingly, since she normally starts out slowly. She wanted to serve last, but Monica told her to serve first. *Some things never change.*

Expecting Monica to berate her for double faulting the first point of the match away, Josie pauses before serving again. She braces herself for a verbal barrage.

Monica turns and says, "What's the matter? Everything OK?"

Josie says, "I thought you were going to say something."

Instead of punishing Josie with a string of insults, Monica says, "Oh, yeah. Right. Take a deep breath, and take your time."

Wow. Josie takes a deep breath. *Didn't see that coming. That was actually nice!*

At the changeover Monica hands Josie a terry wristband. She says, "Here. I noticed you forgot yours today."

"Thanks. I'll wash it and return it."

"No need. Keep it and we can match. I have an extra shirt like this one too. They make the cutest tops. Don't you think? I'll bring it next time."

"No thanks, Monica. Don't be that girl."

"What girl? What do you mean?"

"Some friendships are better earned and not bought."

Monica blushes. She doesn't know how to have a true friend. Hurt, she stammers, "Right. I was just tr-trying to show you. That's all. Because it's different. Or it will be. For you. And me. That didn't come out right, again. Sorry. Like I told you before, I am turning over a new leaf. That's all. I am trying to be a better person. You know, a better friend."

Josie doesn't comment. She doesn't want drama. She sees her opponents watching with piqued interest. Josie doesn't like much chitchat on the court. She prefers to focus on strategy or simple mechanics.

For Monica, tennis is about much more than simply hitting the ball. She thrives on social interaction. Monica knows Josie remains skeptical, and maybe even a little annoyed. Still, she thinks, *It's going to be different, Josie. You'll see.*

At the changeover, one of the opponents teases Josie, "Nice service game, Josie. A little shaky, but you held it together in the end, didn't you?"

The other opponent laughs and says, "Yeah, by a thread."

Josie doesn't reply. She knows that getting rid of pregame jitters plagues the beginning of almost every one of her matches. *Ugh. Can we not go there?* She also knows trash talk is simply part of the game. She knows that she shouldn't let it get to her, but sometimes she can't help it. *I should be less porous. I let everything in. Less like a sponge.* She was raised not to backtalk and that lesson has spilled over into all other aspects of her life, including tennis. Josie despises the trash talk in tennis, even when it's sugarcoated as today's remark is. She remains civil, doing her best to do another thing she was taught: turn the other cheek.

Monica, on the other hand, looks at the snarky comment as an open invitation for hunting season. She views trash talk as a lethal weapon on the court, much like a killer forehand.

Monica stares her opponents down, glaring at the one laughing. She knows she promised J. Paul she would be good, but she can only bend so far.

Monica reasons to herself, *This girl asked for it. He can't possibly mind if I stick up for Josie. Josie hasn't the spine to do it herself. Someone's got to step in.* She only hopes J. Paul will understand.

Monica says to her opponent, "Oh, I know, I know. She was a little shaky. We all are. That is except for you." Monica bends her back, pushes her stomach out, pats it, and then points to the mouthy girl. She says, "And good for you! I see you are not shaky at all and I can see why. When you have a full stomach, it calms the nerves. Doesn't it?" The opponent puts her hands on her hips.

With added exaggeration, Monica pats her stomach again and adds, "As a matter of fact, I'll bet you never get nervous: rock solid under pressure every time! That is, with the help of a plateful of carbs always at the ready." Monica points to her tennis bag, "I have some snacks in my bag in case you don't make it until lunch or all the way through the match." She lets the comment soak in. Monica winks at Josie before taking her usual place for the service return.

The girl sucks in her paunch. She bounces the ball three times before serving. She possesses an unusually high toss. It's a windy day. In Boca Raton, an easterly wind from the beach often picks up around ten thirty a.m. A gust shifts the ball midair. The ball drifts left as she completely whiffs on her serve.

Monica looks at her watch. It reads ten forty-two a.m. *Come on wind.*

The opponent points at Monica and says, "I know what you're trying to do."

Monica smiles, lifts her hands in fake exasperation, and holds her tongue. The girl jogs in place with a side-to-side motion, takes a deep breath, and bounces the ball three more times again. She takes another deep breath, calming herself. She focuses on the ball and compensates for the wind by lowering her toss.

This slight adjustment throws off her service motion's rhythm. She frames the second ball into the net. She moves to the add side as she calls out, "0:15."

Delighted, Monica can't help herself. She says, "Getting a little *shaky*, are we? Not to worry, I will text in an emergency order for a double cheeseburger and fries on our next changeover. A girl of your constitution can't possibly be expected to wait until lunch. Nerves or not." Josie gives Monica an uneasy glance. Monica merely winks again in response.

As promised, a silver tray--carrying a double cheeseburger and fries via clubhouse waiter—arrives before the end of the first set.

Josie says, "You know she is never going to eat that."

Monica says, "Well, that's not the point, now is it? Besides, Mitch will. He's told me before that he's a burger a day kinda guy. Look Josie, the point is that she messed with you. As your partner, I cannot allow for that. She made a fatal mistake. She just made herself a delicious target: a big juicy half-pounder target with melted cheese. *Yummy!* I hope she plays the net. I'm going to crush her with overhead after overhead."

Josie says, "What happened to turning over a new leaf?"

"Baby steps."

"So I will be seeing the old Monica from time to time?"

"Nope. You won't. But any opponent that messes with you will."

Josie says, "I can take care of myself."

Monica bites her lip, thinking, *No. No, you can't. Not even on a good day. You are a doormat waiting to be trod upon. You cannot navigate in the simple game of life--much less this more complicated game of tennis--without becoming reduced to an emotional bowl of mush.*

As if reading Monica's thoughts, Josie explains, "It's not that I don't stand up for myself. It's just that I don't want to lower myself."

"Whatever makes you feel better."

"I try to block out the crap and just play. Less spongy."

"Spongy? What are you talking about?"

"Not soaking up the crap."

"Ah, but that is your mistake, Josie, I mean SpongeBob. The *crap* is part of it. Deal with it. A lot of tennis matches are won before you even step one foot onto the court."

"I don't want to play tennis like that, and I don't want to win like that."

"Then you're in denial."

"No, you're in denial. If you think on a whim you can become a different person, then you're the one in denial."

"Oh, is that what all this is really about? Cuz, let me tell you, I know it's hard to believe, but I've changed."

"People don't just change like that, Monica. OK. Tell me why. How."

"Haven't you listened to a word I've said? Let's just say, that a certain somebody has found my soft white underbelly. Come on, I don't need to rehash everything! Do I? You know what I've been through."

"I don't know if I do. All I know is that people don't change!"

"Richard Burton changed Elizabeth Taylor in *The Taming of the Shrew*."

"Oh, so now you're Elizabeth Taylor?"

"No. That's not what I'm saying."

"That was a movie. *Fiction*."

"Love is a powerful thing. It does things. Not just to people's hearts, but to their heads, and changes them forever."

"Oh, please. Are you trying to convince me or yourself? Please don't lecture me on love."

"You can only change people with love, never with hate. At least, not for the good."

"Actually, you can't change people at all."

"I think you're becoming a cynic, and I don't like it. It doesn't suit you."

"Well, I think you're becoming a fruitcake, and no one likes fruitcake."

Their opponent yells, "You ladies going to serve or what?"

Monica sighs, and bounces the ball six times before starting her service motion. She kicks it out wide for an ace.

Monica changes to the ad side and announces, "15:0." Trust doesn't come naturally for Monica. Other than her connection to J. Paul, she has never had a real friend. After her family died, most of her life centered purely on survival. Friendship was not a luxury afforded to her. She never cared to explore the act of extending a helping hand to anyone until now. Now, she cares, and it makes her uncomfortable.

Through the years in South Florida, Monica has amassed a considerable number of superficial friends. She never lacks for company on any given occasion. However, she never stopped to consider--let alone build--a true friendship. She plans for Josie to be her first true friend: a trusted confidant.

Josie makes the ideal candidate. Monica knows Josie will never hurt her intentionally. It's simply not in Josie's DNA. Still, the possibility of leaving herself vulnerable goes against Monica's grain. She lives in fear of emotional hurt. She sighs and thinks, *I've lived with enough hurt in my life, enough for ten lifetimes.*

Over time, she has built a protective barrier out of necessity. It took J. Paul and his lion-sized heart to break through it, altering her life forever. Now, feeling empowered and appreciating love and all of its fine beauty, she willingly accepts life's terms for it. Cautiously, she wants more. She wants to count on people and have them count on her. She wants to finally open up and become human again.

Surprised by her own transformation, she can't believe her thoughts, *I guess I'm not as cold-hearted as I believed. Still, I'm no pushover like Josie.* Like Josie, she understands the risk of hurt accompanying love. But for Monica, the risk is much more carefully calculated.

Thanks to J. Paul, Monica also knows that love brings enough joy to make all of the risk in the world worth it. Excited at the prospect of real friendship, she commits to find out everything about it.

Before she serves, she says to Josie, "I don't care what you say. I'm going to be your friend and a good one at that." That fateful claim will prove true for years to come.

೪ೲ

Monica and Josie win 7:5, 6:1. Afterward, Josie showers, skipping lunch altogether. She promised Scott she would Skype at one o'clock. If she hurries, she'll make it.

Mitch sees her exit the locker room and shouts after her with cheeseburger crumbs muffling his words, "Newt though bad tooduh."

Josie says, "Which isn't so bad? The cheeseburger or playing with Monica?"

Mitch swallows, wipes his mouth, and says, "Both."

They both smile.

Skipping out early, Josie left her opponents and Monica on the court, still packing up. Apparently, one of the opponents performs a lengthy cool down ritual after each match, involving a series of intense stretching. While she completes her post-match cool-down, her partner packs up. Her partner throws her a towel. They avoid eye contact with Monica, not that Monica looks at them either. Monica hasn't been cooling down. Quite the opposite is true. She's been sitting on J. Paul's lap and making out.

J. Paul takes a breath and says, "Congratulations on your win." He kisses her again and says, "I thought you were going to be nice today."

Monica takes her tennis towel and wipes her sweat off of his cheeks and chin. She says, "I was." Proud of herself, she crows excitedly, "Did you see *how* nice I was to Josie? I complimented her a lot. When she screwed up, I said encouraging things like 'it's OK', or 'nice try'."

J. Paul kisses her again and says, "Yes, you did."

"I like being nice. Feels good."

"It should, but what about the cheeseburger?"

Monica shrugs, "You can't expect me to completely change overnight, can you? You have to admit that I've made some real progress. Besides, did you hear what she said to Josie?"

"I missed it."

"She was making fun of Josie's nervous serve. You know how Josie gets the yips in the beginning? Well, I just couldn't help myself. She had Josie in a tizzy. She could hardly serve at all."

"In that case, you did well." They openly make-out, pushing the limits of public displays of affection and moral decency.

Her opponents leave the courts angry from losing, and angrier from the cheeseburger incident. They also leave feeling nauseated from the overt display of affection between J. Paul and Monica. One opponent says to the other, "I'm not sure which I find more distasteful, losing to the likes of her or having to watch that." She gestures toward Monica and J. Paul.

Her partner says, "I know. You can actually hear them kissing."

"Yeah, I know. Yuck!"

❧

Todd flags Josie down as she leaves the parking lot. She rolls down the window and says, "Where did you come from?"

"I had tennis for lunch today."

"Yummy. What do you want? I'm in a hurry."

"Nice to see you, too. Drop me off at work. The guys aren't ready to leave yet, and I have a one o'clock."

"So do I."

"Oh. New client?"

"Not exactly."

"Jim work thing?"

"No. None of your business."

Todd gets into the passenger seat and buckles. He says, "None of my business? Must be something good."

Josie sighs and says, "I don't have time for this."

Todd says, "It's on the way. Shut up and drive."

She gripes, "If I miss Scott because of you, I am going to kick your butt."

Todd says, "Aaah, Scott is it? I thought he was in Bangkok."

"He is."

"Then you've already missed him."

"Not if we are Skyping."

"Oh. How long?"

"How long what?"

"Is he gone?"

"Two years."

"Don't tell me you are trying to make something happen from this distance and for two whole years?" He rolls his eyes.

"I don't need your advice."

"It's not advice. It's a dose of reality. It's a long shot, no matter how much you like running your hands through his curly blonde hair."

She punches his arm.

"Owww. That one really hurt!"

She says, "Good. Two years isn't that long. Besides, some things ripen with time."

He says, "Yeah, but some things actually mildew with time. And this is South Florida, mildew capital of the world. Definitely keep your options open, and don't just wait around for two years. Promise me. That's social suicide."

"Did I ask for your advice? Anyway, what if I am waiting? What of it? Maybe he's worth the wait. You're not always right you know."

"Yes. Yes, I am. And it's because I can see into the future." Todd shuts his eyes and rubs his temples. He says, "Shhh. I'm getting something. Yes. It's a word, and it begins with the letter 'r'. Ah, I see. It's in all capitals: R, E, G, R, E, T. Yes, that's it: regret."

"You're not helping. Scott and I have a connection. This is something special."

Todd says, "I'm right, and you know it. I want to hear you say it."

She stops the car in front of his office building and says, "Get out."

He drops the smile and says, "He's not good enough for you."

"How would you know?"

"Does it matter?"

"Can you just mind your own business for once?"

He smiles again and says, "My business is to drive you crazy."

She moves to punch him again, but he's too quick. He slams the door and waves goodbye with a stupid grin. Despite herself, she shakes her head and laughs.

When Josie arrives home, she throws the keys on the counter. The clock above the sink reads 1:07 p.m. She rushes into the office, booting up her computer. By the time she places the scheduled Skype call, the clock reads 1:11 p.m. To her surprise, Benjarong answers the call. She recognizes him from the farewell party in Boca Raton several months earlier.

She says, "Hi, Benjarong."

He says, "Uh, Benji, please."

Josie says, "OK, hi Benji. I didn't expect to see you. Is Scott there?"

Benjarong says, "Yes, he is." He moves the monitor screen to his left so Josie can see. Scott sits asleep in a high-back leather office chair. His chin almost touches his chest as it rises and falls with each breath. Benjarong moves the monitor screen back to his own face. He says, "He has been up since four a.m. our time. I think he got wiped-out. He was glued to the computer screen waiting for you. He just didn't make it. Should I wake him?"

Benjarong hears the disappointment in her voice as she says, "Uh, no. That's OK. Let him sleep. Sounds like he needs it. Tell him I called. Would you?"

Benjarong says, "Sure thing. Have a good night. I mean day."

"Yeah. Thanks. You too. Have a good day. I mean night."

THIRTY-TWO

Hope, like the gleaming taper's light,
Adorns and cheers our way;
And still, as darker grows the night,
Emits a brighter ray.
-Oliver Goldsmith

Solo, Josie arrives to the year-end tennis gala. Annually, the league's board pulls out all the stops for a league-wide celebration including a dinner, dance, and award ceremony. Le Château happens to host this year's event. The parking lot floods with tennis players from all over South Florida. After circling the lot several times, Josie gives up on finding an empty parking space.

She parks under the porte-cochere. A valet attendant offers his hand as she steps out of her car. He hands her a ticket and—with the car door still slightly ajar and one foot hanging out--he motors her car away. As she teeters on black stilettos up the first flight of steps, she hears a familiar voice from behind.

Marni says, "Hey, Dateless Wonder! Wait up! I almost didn't recognize you with your hair straightened. It's getting so long: down to the middle of your back."

"Yeah. Let's just hope it doesn't rain. One drop and I am wearing a frizzy poof." They walk through the marbled corridor together to the main dining hall's entrance. Balloons and signs point the way, although Josie and Marni don't need directions on their home turf.

Marni says, "You're a brave soul for finishing out the season with Monica."

Josie says, "She's not so bad."

"Oh, she's bad! Take it from me."

"What's that supposed to mean?"

Marni's gag order prohibits saying more. Instead, she says, "Even Tasha doesn't like her. You can tell."

Josie says, "If you say so." She doesn't share her next thought. *I wouldn't say she doesn't like her. As a matter of fact, I would say she likes her maybe too much.*

Marni says, "That should tell you something. She partnered with Tasha for half of the year. As you know, when you share a court with someone you really get to know them. Now, she barely says two words to Monica." As the main dining hall fills, they've yet to see a familiar face.

"Don't read too much into that."

Marni says, "Trust me. Monica is dangerous. Stay away from her."

Josie laughs, "Dangerous? She's a Boca Raton housewife. What kind of dangerous is that?"

Marni says, "The worst kind."

"Oh, come on. She's our teammate."

"I'm warning you."

"Marni, don't you think you're being a little too hard on her? Besides, you are right. When you share a court with someone, you really get to know them. I've played the last five matches with her, and I'm telling you, she's not so bad. Really."

"Don't say I didn't warn you."

"Really, Marni. It's not like she is a deranged criminal or something."

Marni purses her lips together and thinks, *This gag order is harder than I thought it would be.*

Josie and Marni make their way through the crowd and to the bar. The roaring band muffles their conversation.

Marni says loudly over the music, "I'll be back in a minute. Going to the powder room."

"OK. What do you want me to order for you?"

"Dewars rocks."

"Geez. That's a little hard core. Don't you think?"

"No."

"You want a cigar with that? Maybe a tattoo? I was going to order a spritzer."

Marni laughs and says, "Maybe you want a bendy straw with yours?"

The bartender asks, "What would you ladies like?'

As Marni walks away she hears Josie order, "Dewars with real rocks in it and a Shirley Temple with a bendy straw."

Marni yells over her shoulder, "Wuss."

Josie points to the glass of scotch whiskey and says, "Want some nails in this?"

Marni laughs all the way to the bathroom.

While Josie waits for Marni to return, she sees Jim Hartling on the dance floor with a woman half of his age.

He notices Josie, too. He excuses himself, and walks over. Jim says, "Hey Stranger! Double fisting it tonight, I see."

Josie holds up one hand and says, "Marni's nectar of the gods." She holds up the other hand and says, "What we mere mortals drink." She takes a sip through her straw. Josie notices Jim's dance partner looking their way and says, "You're being missed."

Jim's expression softens. He says, "Well. I'm right here. How can I be missed if I am standing right in front of you?"

Josie sips from her straw, points with a free finger and says, "No. Right there. Your date. She is boring a hole through the back of your head."

Flustered, Jim says, "Er, right. I see. Well. I'll have to find a round peg then."

"Round peg?"

"A square one wouldn't fit properly."

"Fit what?"

"The hole. You know. That just got bored through my head."

"Ooooh. Right." They share an awkward pause.

Jim looks at his feet and says, "I've got to go before--"

"Yes, by all means."

"Save my head and all."

As Jim walks back onto the dance floor, his date grabs him, French kisses him, and glares in Josie's direction. Josie smiles sweetly and gives her a thumb's up. *Whatever.*

Overhearing their conversation, the bartender says, "What a douche."

"Actually, he is a good guy."

"Maybe, but talk about socially awkward. Round peg? Where did he get that?"

She shoots the bartender a look and says, "Perhaps, we all could use some more social graces."

The bartender doesn't get the hint. He says, "My five-year-old nephew has got better pick-up lines."

Josie takes another sip and says, "He's not picking me up. We're friends. Besides, better a diamond with a flaw then a pebble without."

"I'm sorry, what?"

"Confucius."

"What?"

"Never mind."

Josie sips from her straw and watches Jim line-dance by himself. His date looks bewildered.

Marni arrives and says, "Is Jim doing the Hustle?"

Josie chuckles and says, "Yeah, I think so."

Marni takes her drink and gestures toward Jim. She says, "Arguably the worst dancer I have ever seen." Jim suddenly spins, knocking drinks out of two people's hands.

Josie smiles and says, "It's good to see him enjoying himself. God knows he deserves it." Jim dips his date and a fake hair attachment falls off her low chignon, exposing a ponytail nub.

"Well, he's enthusiastic. I'll give him that!"

"Should we rescue the piece for her?"

"Nah. Look at it. It's already being trampled upon."

A lady screams, "Rat! Ah! Rat," and points to the trodden hairpiece. Pandemonium ensues.

ৡ৵

Todd enters the ballroom and finds Marni and Josie.

Josie says, "What are you doing here?"

Todd says, "Ordering a drink." He orders a *Hole in One* from the bartender.

Josie persists, "Who let you in? You're not part of the ladies' league. What are you even doing here?"

He takes a swig of his drink and does his best Sean Connery impression, "Membership has its privileges."

Marni says, "That was pretty good!"

Josie says, "Don't encourage him!"

Todd says, "Would either of you lovely ladies like to dance."

Josie says, "No way am I dancing with my brother!"

Todd says, "Here. Then make yourself useful." He hands Josie his drink. Todd takes Marni's hand and leads her to the dance floor.

Josie says to no one in particular, "Official drink holder." On the next change of music, she hands Todd back his drink and says, "I'm going outside. I need some fresh air."

Josie pushes on the horizontal metal bar, releasing the exit door with a clang. She lets the door bounce closed behind her, shutting out the noise. She enters the warm and peaceful night air. She rubs her serving shoulder--still sore from the day's match-- and follows the only light she sees in the distance.

Circling the topiary garden, she opens the gate to the pool area. Like a beacon in the night, the illumination radiates from four round underwater pool lights, twenty floating lotus candles, and a dozen or so carefully placed ground lights. The ground lights highlight a long line of Royal Palms encompassing the far end of the octagonal pool.

Josie wanders across the blue and white Italian tiles and takes off the black belt on her Dolce and Gabbana floral-print dress. She kicks off her black peep-toe heels. She sits on the rough surface of the pool's cement edge and slides in her feet. She immerses her hands and rubs her feet. *Feels so good.* As a rule, the feet of tennis players take a beating. Josie's prove no exception.

As she methodically points and flexes her feet like a ballerina, she lets a finger dangle in the water. Gently, she makes circular ripples that enlarge and expand outward into all directions. She stretches her back before lying down, hanging her knees over the side, and kicking her feet gently under the water. Her glossy locks fan out around her head, spilling along the tiles. She turns her head, side to side for a panoramic view. Other than the pool lights, the night paints a dark and cloudy backdrop, completely shading out the moon. She nudges one of the floating candles with a toe. A soft melancholy sigh escapes her as the candle gently sails away.

The water feels cool and inviting on such a humid night. She swats a mosquito and hears something rustle at the far end of the pool. Too dark too see anything, she assumes it's the usual. *Probably one of South Florida's many lizards rustling about.* She imagines totally immersing herself into the watery coolness. *I wish I were wearing my bathing suit.* Tempted to jump in, she sinks her legs deeper, dampening the edges of her hemline. She lightly splashes her arms and neck with the cool water. She hears the distant boom-boom of the bass reverberating from the party's music. The secluded pool area provides a welcoming calmness.

She thinks of Scott. It's difficult not to do so. She looks up at the starless night and wonders what his sky looks like so many miles away from her own. It's difficult to be without him. *I miss him.* She wonders if her brother was right: if she is a fool to wait for Scott. Putting her life on hold these last several months has proved difficult. *At least we have the Skype calls. We've learned a lot about each other. Better to get to know each other and not rush into anything. It's probably better that it's long distance, in the beginning.* She wants her thoughts to ring true. She shakes her head, realizing the flimsiness of her reasoning. *But, if he were here, we would know by now.* She would know whether what they have is truly something worth waiting for.

Her life on hold has become a popular subject with family and friends. Todd offers her constant and unsolicited advice at the slightest provocation. He reasons she lost years to a love that wasn't love at all, and now she loses more time to a "guy where love is only a remote possibility". Todd emphasizes repeatedly that Scott isn't in the same hemisphere. In their last conversation, Todd's words were hard to take:

> You may think you are dating Scott, but you're not. You're talking with him over your computer. It's not the same thing. That's not dating. Date people you can actually see and touch, and, for God's sake, live your life for once. Stop waiting. You're always waiting. Life doesn't come to you. You have to go to it. You can still get to know Scott with Skype. And if you want to date him when he gets back, then date him. But this video chat thing is not dating. Don't kid yourself, and don't waste your time.

Kid myself? Todd just doesn't understand. It's not that easy for me. Unlike Todd, serial dating has never interested Josie. Once her heart is set, then that is it. It's set. Todd called that notion sophomoric. *He can call it whatever he likes. I can't change my heart or who I am.*

She hears another rustle at the far end of the pool. For the first time, she notices something in a lounge chair. She hadn't noticed it before now. She sees an outline of a silhouette emerge as the figure stands and moves towards her. Uneasy, she sees the figure is a man. *A tall man.* As the figure moves closer and out of the shadows, she looks around. No one else is near. She wonders if she screams if anyone would hear, especially over the loud music. The dark figure drags something behind it as it moves towards her. *Thud. Drag. Thud. Drag.* It gets closer. *Thud. Drag.*

She screams! Again, and again, and again, she screams bloodcurdling screams at the top of her lungs as the figure draws closer. Helpless and frozen, she braces herself.

She hears, "Josie?"

Josie stops screaming and says, "Jim? Is that you?"

"Yes."

"Oh, you almost gave me a heart attack."

"I could say the same about you."

"Sorry. You scared me."

"What are you doing out here?"

"Getting some fresh air. Day dreaming. What are you doing out here?"

"I am recuperating."

"From what?"

"As it turns out, I really can't date someone almost young enough to be my daughter. I can't keep up. My toes are numb. I can't walk right. And she's still out there dancing. Maybe if I had some orthopedic inserts, or electrolyte tablets, or five espressos. I can't even lift my jacket. I have to drag it."

Josie laughs and says, "Exhausting maybe, but she is pretty."

Jim sits down next to her, kicks off his shoes and puts his feet into the cool water. He looks at her thick-lashed hazel eyes, her chestnut glossy long locks, and her rosy petite bow mouth. *No. You're pretty.* Distracting himself away from such inappropriate thoughts, he says, "Day dreaming, huh? What's his name?"

"His name is Scott. I don't want to talk about it."

"I see."

"Sorry about the screaming."

"It's OK. You have a fantastically horrifying scream!"

She bows and says, "Thank you."

"Sure you don't want to talk about Scott? I'm a good listener. Besides, I have more than talked your ear off on more than one occasion if I remember correctly. I figure I have it coming. So shoot."

"Nah. I don't want to get too personal, since we work together and all. Let's just say, I am a little lovesick at the moment, and leave it at that."

"OK. I understand. The water feels great."

"I know. I was thinking of jumping in."

"So, jump in."

"What? No! Really?"

"Absolutely." Fully clothed, he pushes off of the cement edging and slides into the center of the pool.

Josie covers her mouth, stifling a laugh.

He extends a hand and says, "Come on."

"No. I couldn't. What will people say?"

Jim motions to the surrounding darkness and says, "What people?"

Josie laughs, reaches for his hand, and slides into the pool.

Jim says, "Feels great, right?"

"Like I imagined. You're going to have a lot of explaining to do when you take your date home while soaking wet."

Jim says, "I have the corporate fundraiser next weekend. I was going to ask her." He motions to the dance party inside and continues, "But I don't think my body can take another dance-off."

"Go by yourself."

"It's not like that. There's a seating chart with the traditional boy/girl, boy/girl."

"How unfortunate."

"Truly." He looks hopeful and says, "Go with me?"

She doesn't answer.

Waiting, he loses confidence and then offers, "You know, as friends. That is, if you don't have a date with Scott or something."

"Can I get back with you?"

He kicks his feet, keeping his head steadily above the water and says, "Sure."

Curious, Josie says, "Who is your date tonight, anyway? Does she play for Le Château?"

"No. Charlemagne. Her name is Isabelle Connor."

"Oh. I've heard of her. Nice player. Good team."

"That's what she says. This is some year-end party. They pull out all the stops."

"Yeah. The committee always does a nice job. Pricey, but nice. Not that I am complaining. We all have a final vote in the gala's budget. Plus, it's nice to get out of our sweaty tennis clothes, put on some makeup, and not compete against one another for a change. Funny thing is that half of us don't recognize each other without our sweaty tennis gear, even though we just spent a whole season together."

THIRTY-THREE

All the darkness in the world cannot extinguish the light of a single candle.
-Saint Francis of Assisi

Marni finds Josie and says, "There you are! What are you doing? Look at you!"

Josie lifts up her hands and shrugs.

Marni says, "And by the way, I caught the tail end of that and I must say you *are* an ugly tennis player. No wonder no one recognizes you. I wouldn't recognize you myself, if I didn't already know you. You do clean up well. I'll give you that. Although you would never know it, because look at you! You're soaked through. Who raised you? Honestly, Jo!"

Josie sticks her tongue out.

Marni slips off her chocolate pumps and slides her feet into the pool. She teases, "As for me, I look the same on or off of the court: any time of day or night. It doesn't matter. Here! I took the liberty of putting a little vodka in your Shirley Temple." She thrusts a drink in Josie's direction.

Josie swims over and takes a sip. She coughs and says, "I thought you said a little."

Marni says, "Did you hear screaming earlier?"

Jim says, "What? No."

Almost at the same time, Josie says, "What? No."

Jim and Josie look at each other and suppress a grin.

Josie says, "Marni, this is Jim Hartling. Jim Hartling: Marni." They know each other in passing, but have never been officially introduced.

Jim swims over and shakes hands with Marni. She says excitedly, "Hear that? The bell! The awards are about to begin. Come on!"

Josie says, "What? You can't expect me to go in there like this. I'm soaking wet."

Marni says, "Suit yourself. I'm not gonna miss it! Bye, Tim, I mean Jim, right? Nice to meet you." She grabs her shoes and rushes inside.

Jim and Josie walk into the shallow end, up the stairs, and out of the pool. Marni runs back into the pool area. She grabs Josie's hand and yells, "Come on. You just won Most Improved Player of the year." She yanks Josie's arm in the direction of the banquet hall. Josie protests, but Marni will hear none of it. She thrusts open the door, parts the crowd, and yells, "Here she is! Here she is! I found her! Here's Josephine Fleming!"

Everyone begins clapping. Marni pushes Josie towards the stage. The clapping abruptly ceases as all eyes fall on soaking wet Josie. The league president collects herself and presents the trophy to Josie.

The president clears her throat and says into the microphone, "Yes, er, well. OK then. Well, it's good to have you here anyhow, Josephine. Congratulations on winning the league wide vote for Most Improved Player. Please accept this trophy on behalf of the board, and please say a few words."

Josie looks out among the crowd. Her wet hair plasters to her head and strings down her back, dripping onto the floor. The league president steps away from the newly forming puddle. Josie's mascara smudges underneath her eyes, and her soaked dress clings to her taut frame. She stands in the spotlight at the podium on the wooden stage.

The president says, "Josie?"

"Uh, yes?"

"Please, say a few words."

"Right." She looks for a familiar face and sees her teammates: Violet, Ceridwin, Vivian, Marni, and Monica in the crowd. Seeing them gives her the boost that she needs. She wrings out the hem of her dress and says, "And you thought I sweat a lot on the tennis court. Ha!"

No one laughs.

She gathers her thoughts and tries again, "But seriously, it's really great to be here tonight among such incredible talent and company. Thank you for this trophy commemorating my improvements in tennis. However, for me, it's not strictly about the tennis. I'd like to acknowledge improvements of a different sort. You see, when I was a little girl, my mom would often say, 'Show me who your friends are and I'll show you who you are.' My mom said her mom told her the same thing when she was growing up. See, she knew that friends influence your life and can make your life better. Well, I'm looking at my friends in the crowd and--" She pauses and looks into the stage lights. She tries to regain focus as she sees blue dots instead of people.

Ceridwin yells out an encouraging, "Come on, Josie!"

Josie smiles and continues, "And I am grateful. You improve my life. I know I wouldn't be standing here today without each of you." She points to them and continues, "My mom was right, but don't tell her I said so." She looks out over the expanse of the crowd again and says, "Did you know that anything can be fixed on a tennis court?" She hears a few "amens" and continues, "It's true. With the advice you get from your friends on the court, your life can literally change before your eyes. Your time spent on the court with your teammates transforms you. Your girlfriends will fix your love life, save your job, redesign your home, decide your best hair color, repair basically anything that is broken in your life, including you." Josie finds her teammates in the crowd again and says, "So girlfriends, thank you. If I've improved at all, it's because of you. This is truly an honor." She holds up the trophy and says, "To the healing power of girlfriends."

Ceridwin yells out, "You deserve it, Josie!" Applause erupts.

Josie steps away from the podium and hands the mic to the league president. As she does, Josie trips on a taped-down power cord. She lands and slips in her own wet trail towards the edge of the stage. She turns and teeters with wild helicopter arms, before falling backwards only to be lifted up by a sea of hands from the crowd.

The sea of hands supports an open-mouthed Josie. The crowd's effort instantly turns lackluster as more and more hands pull away from soggy Josie. From her angle, Josie sees the ceiling. She doesn't see the finely dressed women underneath shirking their responsibilities of supporting her as their hair and clothes dampen under their efforts. Josie drips, leaving more and more grimacing participants. One woman barks commands to ease Josie to the ground, but the coordinated effort fails.

Jim, also dripping wet, arrives just in time to see the spectacle. He doubles over with laughter. He cannot stop laughing; that is until he sees Josie drop.

He rushes to her side, but can't get through the crowd.

Marni gets there first. She sees Josie pop up in the crowd, holding a stiletto with a broken heel.

Marni says, "Oh my gosh! Are you Ok? I'm so sorry, Josie."

Still getting her bearings, Josie says, "Only one casualty."

"Casualty?"

"Yes, I just bought these!"

"Maybe I shouldn't have pushed you onto the stage. I was trying to make you have fun. I'm so glad you didn't get hurt. I should've left you in the pool."

"The pool was relaxing, but I'm glad I got to thank everyone, even if I am embarrassed."

"I'm going to stop pushing you into awkward situations."

"Promise?"

"Promise."

Josie thinks back to Marni pushing her to dance with the drunken guy on the barge. She thinks about Marni setting her up on the blind date with Scott, the heartbreaker. And now, Marni pushed her into a public speech while standing in soaking wet clothes. *Humiliating. Ending in some failed mosh pit thing.* Josie has every right to be angry. Instead, she throws her head back with laughter and teases, "Yes, please stop. Didn't you know that no good deed goes unpunished?"

Marni laughs too, hugging a very wet Josie, and says, "I'll take that as I am forgiven. Anyway, yea! Congrats! You earned that monster of a trophy! How much does that thing weigh?"

Josie hugs her back and says, "I don't know. It's killing my wrist. Marni?"

"Yeah?"

"Don't ever apologize for being a good friend."

The league president takes the podium again and announces, "Yes. Well. That was interesting. Thank you, Josie. Now, if I may have your attention again, please. Quiet. Please. Thank you. Also by popular league-wide vote, I would like to announce the next award. This year's winner of Miss Congeniality is--" She opens the envelope and continues, "Monica Mooney." Everyone laughs while applauding.

Monica--not realizing that everyone voted for her as a joke--takes the award seriously. She approaches the stage and grabs the mic firmly with both fists. The volume and speed of her speech along with the enormous size of the room causes the mic to echo: normally a problem for public speaking. However, Monica loves hearing herself twice.

She says with slow emphatic words, "Life is a competition. Or, so I used to think. I have come to the realization that there is more to life than winning. It seems that when all you concentrate on is winning, that is when you have the most to lose." She looks at J. Paul through the crowd.

He won't let on that he gets the vote was a planned league-wide joke. He also gets that while that may be the case, it's not a joke to Monica. She has made strides. That is all he cares about. He gives her a thumb's up sign.

She continues, "I am glad the league recognizes me with this trophy and my efforts to become a better person, not just on the tennis court, but in all walks of life. Can I see a show of hands of people who consider themselves competitive?"

Someone in the crowd mutters loudly enough to be overheard by most, "Duh! It's tennis!"

Unaffected by the remark, Monica addresses the sea of hands. She announces, "I see there are many of you. OK. You may put your hands down, because I am more competitive than all of you. Not just in tennis, but, also, in everything I do. I am driven to be first, numero uno. You can even tell by the way I drive here in Boca. I'll cut anyone off. I can't seem to beat out those ambulances though. Anyway, I am trying to navigate, not just on the local roads, or in tennis, but in everything I do in life with a new decorum. I am trying to be *nice*." She holds up the trophy and says, "And it's *nice* that you recognized that. Thank you."

J. Paul is the only audience member clapping. As she makes her way through the crowd, a hand grabs her arm. She turns.

Roger says, "Dixie and I are happy for you." Dixie doesn't smile, but says, "Congratulations, Miss Dirty-Squirty."

Monica says, "What did you just call me? That's not an affectionate nickname!"

Dixie says, "I said nothing."

"Yes, you did!"

"Calm down!"

Monica looks at Roger and says, "Unhand me."

Roger says, "Of course. "

She walks towards J. Paul and hears Roger yell after her, "Maybe we can talk about Bosnia sometime."

She stops frozen in her tracks. She turns to see a viciously grinning Roger Fleming wink at her. She cries the entire drive home. J. Paul can't get an intelligible word out of her until they reach their driveway.

∽◦◦∾

While a dripping wet Josephine waits for the valet to bring her car around, Mitch catches up to her. Breathless, he says, "There you are! Josie, I need someone to captain the team next year. I need someone levelheaded and fair. I need to turn in captain forms tomorrow. What do you say?"

Josephine says, "I don't want to be captain. Thanks for the offer Mitch, but I don't have the time or the stature to be an authority figure."

He laughs and says, "Come on. I could use someone like you."

She says, "No thanks." *Captain? I don't even listen to me.* "I am taking a long overdue certification course this summer for work. I won't be playing much tennis or doing much else, except working." *Besides, in eight weeks, I will be busy with Scott. Very busy.*

Josie arrives home just before midnight. Scott waits on the other end for their Skype call. Everyday, they arrange a certain time to talk. She towels off her dark wavy locks and adjusts the collar on her robe. Scott's picture pops up on her screen. First she sees his curly blonde hair, and then his boyish toothy grin. Her stomach flips. She could stare at him all day.

He says, "Where ya' been all dressed up? You had a hot date?"

She adjusts the collar on her robe and says, "Ha! Very funny. I guess you could say I went for a swim."

"Nice."

"I did have that year-end tennis gala tonight. The one that I was telling you about."

"Oh yeah, that was tonight. How was it? You look incredible!"

"Good and yeah, right!"

"I'm serious. I think you should always wear a robe. That just-out-of-the-shower look works for me."

"Ha. What about you? You look great, too! You have a hot date after work later?"

"I wouldn't call it a hot date."

You do? Stunned, she says, "What would you call it?"

"Friendship. I am taking Sophia out after work. Her husband threatened to divorce her. She's in a bad place. I think the stress of a long distance relationship is way too much for him and for her. She needs to get out. Apparently, long distance breeds divorce."

Geez, then what will it breed for us? We're not even married. "Why do you say that?"

"Because almost half of my fourteen married coworkers here are going through some sort of marital crisis, and we've only been here five months. We still have a little over a year and one half to go."

Josie's smile fades. She was kidding when she asked if he had a hot date. She didn't expect his answer to be "yes". She says, "Do you like Sophia?"

"What? No. It's not like that. We're just friends." He wonders why she recommended they date other people and then keeps getting jealous at the mere prospect.

Josie worries. She tries to sound upbeat and happy during the rest of the Skype call, but it's not easy. For the ten or fifteen minutes she gets to see Scott everyday via Skype, she wants it to be pleasant. Still, she can't help herself. At the end of the conversation she says, "And what about us, Scott? We're just dating. What does the distance do to us?"

Scott shrugs off the question, saying, "I will see you in eight weeks and three days." He grins and says, "Not that I've been counting. We can talk about it then."

The next day, they talk. Scott talks about the concert he saw with Sophia. He talks about the bar he visited with Sophia. He talks about the cab ride home he shared with Sophia. It takes Josie three days before she phones Jim Hartling and accepts his offer of a friendly date to his next corporate fundraiser. So it goes. Over the summer, Josie will accompany Jim seven more times on official "non-date" events for work-related functions.

THIRTY-FOUR

It is better to be envied then pitied.
-Herodotus

Josie answers the phone. Jim says, "Today's the big day! Are you going to pick him up from the airport?"

"Yes. Can't wait. What do you think: jeans, and strappy heels, or jeans with a t-shirt and flip-flops? Or a summer dress and espadrilles?"

"Summer dress with flip-flops and hair down."

"Understated."

"Yes. You don't need to try."

"Flip-flops, flip-flops. Where are my flip-flops?"

"Good luck. See you on Monday. And Josie, I hope this weekend is everything you hoped for. You deserve it, Jo."

"I found one! Now for the other. Thanks! You too! Have a great weekend!"

The phone rings again. Josie answers on the first ring. Excitedly, Marni says, "Not too much longer! Homework. I expect some serious homework to be done tonight. Ooh. Gotta run! Been waiting on this call." She hangs up before Josie gets one word in.

The phone rings again. Todd says, "Look. I know I said this before, but you really need to make this guy work to gain your respect. Look at the facts. He left you here. Your arrangement with him is not exclusive. What do you really have besides some Skype calls, emails, and texts?"

Josie says, "A gut feeling. Now leave me alone. I have a lot to do today."

Todd says, "Just don't--" He wants to say, "Just don't get hurt." but he doesn't finish his sentence.

Josie says, "Don't what?"

Todd says, "Just don't go into this thing head first. Stick a toe in. Make sure the water is OK. You know what I'm saying?"

"Yes. Yes, of course. Mask. Wet suit. SCUBA tank. And if you had it your way, nuclear sub for backup! Thank you. I am hanging up now. Love you." Her hair appointment is in fifteen minutes and a ten-minute drive away. Any more phone calls and she'll miss the appointment altogether.

❧

By the time she reaches the airport, Josie's hair, feet, nails, and face have all received professional treatment. After her dentist whitened her teeth yesterday, she allowed him to inject some chemical into the crow's feet around her eyes. He said the injection would smooth out her "ever-so-slight wrinkles". Today, her left eye occasionally twitches. She wonders if it might be from the injection. Several times, traffic reaches a standstill on her drive from Boca Raton to the Miami International Airport. With her brakes hot from the continued stop and go, she comes to a screeching halt as she parks in the airport's garage. She checks her watch. *Just in time to meet Scott's plane.* She enters the terminal and waits.

Excitedly, she sees Scott walk towards her. She feels as if it is Christmas and as if she might throw-up all at the same time. He sees her and drops his bag at his feet.

She says, "You came all this way from Bangkok with only one carry-on? As an avid over-packer, I am genuinely impressed."

Scott says, "It's not what I left behind in Bangkok that is important, it's what I left here that is." He wraps his arms around her and leans forward, causing her back to arch slightly. He kisses her tenderly and doesn't come up for air. People walk past and stare. Some comment. Josie and Scott don't notice and don't care.

Minutes pass before Scott takes a breather and says, "We'd better leave. I think I hear the parking meter ticking from here."

She begins walking. He grabs her hand and stops her. He kisses her again. He can't help himself. He looks her in the eye with each kiss and wonders why she keeps winking with her left eye. He whispers, "This is going to be the best night of your life."

Best night of my life? Crap! She's not sure she is ready for what she thinks that means. The last time she made love wasn't a good night at all. It was with Roger. He left her weeping and humiliated.

Nervously, she fidgets with her chandelier earrings. She prefers to ease back into this dating thing before committing physically. She continues to fidget. Just in case something actually does happen later, she speeds through a personal inventory. She breathes into her cupped hands. *My breath is OK.* She knows her hair is. She paid a pretty penny for the blowout. Her skin and nails flawlessly shine.

Josie smoothes out a wrinkle on the skirt of her dress. She wears a white eyelet summer dress with a fitted waist and mid-calf hemline. The hem on the three-quarter length sleeves turns up with sweetheart buttons holding the trim in place. The dress's light summer top has three sweetheart pink buttons down the center. She leans over and adjusts the strap on one of her tan woven leather sandals. The dress's skirt moves in a pendulum's side-to-side motion with its bell-shape.

Scott says, "Everything Ok?"

"Yes." Comfortable after her complete mental inventory, she takes a deep breath. *Everything's fine.* She only feels uncomfortable about the flashy diamond earrings that Monica made her borrow. *They're so in-your-face.* The heaviness pulls on her lobes. She drew the line when Monica suggested a Brazilian wax. *A.) I'm not ready for sex. B.) Hanging my privates in the air for some stranger to rip hair off of them will never happen in my lifetime. That I am certain of.*

Scott picks up his bag and says, "OK. Point the way."

Josie points to the parking garage through the doors and on the other side of the road. She says, "Short-term."

A girl in jeans, black wedges, and a black and white polka dot top with peek-a-boo cut-outs on the shoulders walks up and says, "Scott, we got your checked baggage. We'll drop it off later, like you asked."

Josie recognizes the girl: the highly arched eyebrows, the shoulder length wavy dark hair, the widely set exotic eyes, and thick pouty lips. Sophia appears smaller in person and, to Josie's dismay, much prettier. Josie also recognizes Benjarong walking behind Sophia. Benjarong waves while Sophia ignores Josie's presence altogether. Sophia walks past as if Josie doesn't exist.

Josie says, "Thought you packed light for noble reasons, notably me." She tries to laugh it off.

Scott says, "Technically, I did…in a way. That is, I asked them to get my checked bag so I could get to you first. I couldn't wait to see you." He grins, and she instantly forgives him for the white lie.

Since Scott's house is leased, he rents a corporate condo in Highland Beach: the same complex where his coworkers will also stay for the next three weeks. Josie and Scott arrive at his furnished new digs. Josie sits on the brown suede couch and takes her earrings off. *Aah. Better.* Scott throws his suitcase into his room. It bounces and skids before coming to a halting stop against the bed. He jumps on the couch next to her. They start kissing.

Josie says, "I have to say something."

"What? Now? Can't we talk later?"

"It's just that when we talked about dating other people, I really didn't want to. I just said that because I thought you did."

Scott kisses her neck while she talks. He unbuttons one of her sweetheart buttons and whispers, "So let's not date anyone else."

Josie sits straight up and faces him. She says, "Really? You mean it?"

"Of course, I do. Now, come here." He lightly chews on her earlobe and kisses his way slowly down her neckline.

She says, "There is something else."

"Can it wait?"

"No."

"Uh-huh." He moves lower along her neckline and kisses across it. "Sure?"

Josie says, "Would it be OK if we waited."

Suddenly, Scott sits upright. He says, "Now, there's a sobering thought."

"I'm serious. It's just that it's been a long time for me. I'm a little nervous. I was hoping we could maybe ease into things."

Scott's phone buzzes. He grabs it, but doesn't read the message, yet. He says, "*Ease* into things? When? I leave in three weeks. I've been waiting for this for months. Haven't you? I thought we were on the same page. I thought we both wanted this." He sounds angry. She looks at him, wounded.

He reads the text message while she says, "I'm incredibly attracted to you. I-I'm just nervous. I just need to get used to having you around again, I guess."

Scott softens his tone and says, "Yeah. No problem. Maybe I'm a little nervous, too. I guess the buildup has gotten to both of us. Take all of the time you need." He turns the screen of his phone towards her. He says, "I just got called to the office. See?"

"What? Now? Are you serious? You just got in. Don't they allow for jet lag?"

Scott thinks, *I guess we both have things to be disappointed about.* But says, "Not when they've got a multi-million-dollar question on the table and you've got the answer on your laptop."

"Can I drop you off at work?"

"No. That's OK. Thank you, though. I will catch a ride with Sophia and Benjarong. They have to go in, too. Can I call you tonight?"

"Sure. Will I see you tonight?"

"Not tonight. I'll work until I crash. I got four hours of sleep on the plane and that's it. How about tomorrow night? Seven? I'll pick you up."

Josie manages a meek smile, "Sure. Seven. Sounds great!" At the door, he kisses her forehead. Too depressed to go home, she drives to the office and buries herself deep into an IPO proposal for Jim's company. She hears a knock on her office door and looks up to see Jim standing in her doorway.

Jim looks around and says, "This is the most curious date I have ever seen. Are you working to impress Scott with your superior accounting skills? Because if you are, I have to recommend a different tactic."

Despite herself, Josie laughs, and then she begins to cry. Without much prodding, she explains the day's events to Jim. He listens to every detail. He doesn't judge or offer advice.

He simply states, "You're a smart girl, Jo. You'll figure out what to do. In the meantime, it's dinnertime. Let's go eat. It'll do you some good to get out."

"I'm not hungry."

"Let's go to Vietnam House. A nice hot bowl of pho? You can take home what you don't eat."

"I guess it's no good to sit around and wallow."

"Absolutely not. I forgot to mention that we have a strict company policy against wallowing."

No sooner do they leave the office when her phone rings. Josie's answers are short and interrupted by whoever is on the other end of the line.

Jim says, "Who was that?"

"Monica. She wants her Traffic Mini earrings back right away. She's wearing them tonight. I left them at Scott's. I hope you don't mind if we make a stop."

Jim says, "Sure. Point the way."

She calls Scott.

Scott says, "But I already left. I'm at work."

"Sorry, I know it's a pain., but I need them."

"My sister may still be there doing my laundry. I'll call her. She'll let you in."

"Thanks. Wait. Your sister does your laundry? You just got here? How much laundry can you possibly have already?"

Annoyed, Scott says, "Yeah. She does my laundry. So what? My maid doesn't start until Monday. I brought a lot of dirty clothes with me. I don't have time for laundry. Susan knows that."

"Oh, I see. Sorry. I can tell you're busy. Um, thanks. See you tomorrow."

Josie and Jim arrive at Scott's apartment. Susan lets them inside. Josie hugs her and asks, "Where's William?"

"He's with grandma. As a matter of fact, I'm late picking him up. I hope you don't mind if I don't chat. I have to hurry and fold this last load. Oh, I heard about the lost jewelry. Sorry, but I haven't had time to check. Look around for yourself, OK?"

"Ok. No problem. Thanks."

Josie walks around the back of the couch and reaches over its corner, retrieving Monica's earrings off of the end table. When she does, she knocks the couch cushion over. She picks it up and notices something underneath. She pulls out a silk top: not just any silk top, but a black and white polka dot top with shoulder cutouts.

Josie recognizes the top from earlier today. Next, she holds up something else: a pink thong. Both were shoved under the cushion. Susan walks back into the room after putting the laundry away. Josie quickly shoves the shirt and thong back behind the cushion.

Susan says, "Is something wrong?"

Josie says, "Uh, yes. I mean no."

"Did you find what you were looking for?"

"Yes. And then some."

"And then some what?"

Josie says, "Sorry. I mean I sure did. Thank you very much." She hugs Susan and says, "Goodbye," knowing it will be the last time she ever sees her.

When they reach the car, Jim says, "Why the long face? You want to fill me in?"

"I sat in that same spot hours before."

"Before what? What spot?"

"On that couch. That very same couch. Against that pillow. That exact same pillow."

"So?"

"So nothing happened. At least not while I was there. After I left maybe a little too much happened."

"I'm lost."

"Sophia's clothes and underwear were wedged under the cushion." Josie starts crying.

Jim holds her hand. He says, "Who is Sophia?"

"His coworker." *His very close coworker.*

When they arrive at Monica's door, Josie asks Jim if he minds running the earrings inside. She doesn't want to talk with anyone, especially Monica. *Not now.* She knows Monica will ask about Scott. After Jim drops off the earrings, he takes Josie back to her car in the office parking lot. They sit for a while, talking.

Josie says, "That could've been me. That *should've* been me. My shirt. My underwear. My heart. All lost on that couch, shoved into a corner."

Jim says, "You owe him a chance to explain."

"Do I?"

"I think so. You've spent a lot of time on this thing, and you've talked like you really like him. Shouldn't you give him a chance to explain? I am thinking more for your own peace of mind. I couldn't care less about his."

Josie says, "I can overlook a lot of faults, but cheating is not one of them. Maybe I am too jealous or insecure, or maybe both. Or, maybe it's because I've been waiting my whole life for a love I can truly believe in."

"You should still believe. Don't let—"

She cuts him off, "No. I can't. I've been on the receiving end of cheating too many times. I can't take it anymore. I can't. I can't be that person again. I'm just not strong enough." She blows her nose into a tissue and says, "Intimacy means far too much to me to have a third wheel lurking around in the background. Call me old-fashioned, but I want something real and solid between two people. And that's it. Not three or four or however many. Just two. Am I the only human being still believing in that?"

"Well. No. I mean I do. Believe that is. I think plenty of people do."

"Well, not Scott. He lied. The whole thing was a lie. A cheater and a liar. That's what he is. Not for me. He's not for me. I hate him." She sobs and says, "I just wish he wasn't so cute."

Jim looks almost as broken as she feels. He says, "What are you going to do?"

"I am tired of being on the losing end of love and always being so, so, so, uh…pathetic."

"I wouldn't call you pathetic. Unlucky maybe, but not pathetic."

"I don't want him to know he broke my heart. I won't be that person again. I won't. No matter what. I was that person far too long in my marriage."

"Confront him."

"And say what?"

"I don't know. How about how you feel? Or ask him any unanswered questions."

There are no unanswered questions. Suddenly, she hatches an idea and says, "I know this sounds crazy, but I will become him."

"Don't lower yourself."

"I won't. Hear me out." She details the plan. Reluctantly, Jim agrees to participate.

తౌ

The next night, Scott arrives promptly at seven p.m. to pick up Josie. He knocks, but opens the door himself. Jim exits through Josie's front door as soon as Scott opens it.

Surprised, Scott says, "Um, hello."

Josie briefly introduces Scott to Jim. Scott gives Jim the once over and says, "Yes, we've met on the golf course."

Jim shakes hands then excuses himself. Jim's business jacket hangs open. Scott notices Jim's button-down shirt hangs halfway untucked and is buttoned wrong. He also notices Jim's disheveled hair.

After Jim leaves, Scott sits on the couch and says, "How well do you know him?"

Josie doesn't answer right away. She reads a cocktail recipe from Kate McDonald. She mixes the ingredients for two Jenkins: lichi liquor, gin, lemon juice, honey, rose water, and lemon bitters. She shakes, and double strains the drink into two chilled glasses.

Finally, she says, "Oh, you know. He's a close coworker. I *work* with him."

Scott leans back against the couch cushion, but it won't push back all the way. He softly punches the cushion, but it won't budge. He says, "Work, huh? But what was he doing *here?*"

"We were, you know, going over some last minute figures and discussing some false expectations that could affect the bottom line, I suppose you could say." She hands him his drink and offers him a plate of Humboldt Fog cheese on thin French loaf slices with homemade fig paste.

Scott says, "Delicious. Thank you."

He leans back again, but his cushion still won't give. Josie leans all the way back on hers. Since his abruptly stops short, he sits uncomfortably upright. He notices the discrepancy. Finally, he stands, removes the cushion and gently pounds it. As he does, he notices something white where his cushion had been. He picks up the white item by two fingers and turns it. It's a pair of men's underwear.

Shocked, Scott says, "Who do these belong to?"

Josie says, "Well, they certainly aren't mine."

Clearly, Scott is upset, but before he speaks further, Josie says, "You have something in your front teeth. There's a mirror in the powder bathroom, right there." She points to her half bathroom across the hallway from them.

Scott drops the underwear where he stands and walks into the bathroom. He swishes his drink in his mouth along the way. When he reaches the bathroom, he sees nothing in his teeth. He turns his head from side to side in the mirror. *Nothing.* He thinks the swishing did its job. He picks up his glass from the counter and notices what sits beside it: a used pregnancy test. It reads negative. Scott walks out holding the pregnancy test.

He says, "Is this the false expectations you were talking about?" He doesn't wait for an answer. His rage boils over.

He yells, "You expect me to wait all of these months for you and then once I get here, you don't put out for me? Then, you put out for the likes of that guy? You expect me to be OK with that: you sleeping with someone else, but not with me? Ohhh, you're crazy, lady!"

Josie replies coolly, "Who says I am sleeping with anybody?"

"I know what underwear in the couch means. I'm not an idiot!"

"Don't you think it could mean something else? You know, some sort of misinterpretation?"

Scott shouts, "No! No, I don't! It means you had sex on that very couch, and his underwear got hurriedly shoved behind. That's what *that* means!"

OK. Strike one. Josie says, "Well, what of it. We *are* dating other people."

Scott says, "No! We are not! Didn't we say yesterday that we wouldn't date anyone else?"

"When did we say that?"

"When you picked me up from the airport!"

"That's true. We did say that. So, does that mean we were in a committed relationship as of yesterday, starting at the airport?"

"Yes."

"So, we shouldn't be with anyone else after that time."

"Correct! We had an agreement. You broke it!"

No. I only look like I broke it. You are the one who actually broke it. Strike Two. Next, she says, "What if I were sleeping with Jim all this time. Would that be OK?"

He throws the pregnancy test at her. She ducks. It misses. He yells, "Better than OK!" He changes his tone to a singsong one and says, "Because I have been sleeping with Sophia this whole time." Josie folds her arms. *Strike three.*

He laughs and says, "You and your fairytale notion of how love works. You need to get a grip on reality, lady. This ain't no Disney flick. You were lucky to have me. You're just another pretty face, and you know what? See how far that gets you! You'll grow to be an old recluse with eighty-five cats. You'll see. No one will want you. You're crazy if you think I would go two years without sex, especially for the likes of you! I have needs. I'm a man!"

"I'm sure you are."

"And I am really good in bed. You had your chance! You missed out! You could be wallowing in post-sex bliss right now. I could've made you *sooo* happy! Well, screw you! This is all your fault and your loss!" He leaves, slamming the door behind.

The once violently loud room instantly becomes calm and silent. The sudden contrast from one second to the next leaves Josie feeling numb. A thought occurs to her. She opens the front door and yells, "Remember our first date and that big pile of greasy goo that was stuck on your shirt at the movies?"

Scott says, "Yeah, so what?"

Josie says, "That was from me. My mouth! A big pile of goo chewed by me and hocked onto your shirt."

Scott wrinkles his nose and says, "That's disgusting!"

"Yeah, well, so there!"

Scott grumbles under his breath and slams his door, peeling rubber out of her driveway.

Well, that was one confession that certainly didn't feel cathartic. Josie plops onto her couch. *Eighty-five cats? That's a lot of cat litter.* She cries. Regret washes over her, overpowering any relief. *I don't have enough space for eighty-five cats.*

Scott calls from his car. He rants about how she'll live a life alone: eating cat food out of a tin can and being surrounded by cat feces. He hangs up before she responds. He calls again. She doesn't answer. She may have to change her number. She'll wait a few days to see.

Jim calls. Monica calls. Marni calls. Todd calls. Josie doesn't pick up. Instead, she sends a blanket text to all four: The text reads, "Update: It's over before it really began. I'm fine. Call you in a few days."

THIRTY-FIVE

No pessimist ever discovered the secret of the stars, or sailed an
unchartered land, or opened a new doorway for the human spirit.
-Helen Keller

Monica doesn't wait a few days. She drives to Josie's house
right away. She rings the doorbell, but no one answers.
She knows where Josie keeps an extra key, and she lets
herself in. Josie sits on the couch with a duo of strawberries
and fudge.

Monica whisks the bowls away and says, "Oh, no you
don't. Give me that, and put this on." She hands Josie a
swimsuit.

Josie says, "No."

"You'll feel better. Put this on."

"If you think putting on a bathing suit will make me feel
better, you need a reality check."

"It will."

"Oh, sure. How about I try it on in fluorescent lighting?"

"Bathing suits in fluorescent lighting?"

"Yeah, always a pick-me-up!"

"Don't be such a drama queen, and put this on!"

"It won't make me feel better. How about a fleece onsie?
Have you got one of those in your Prada tote? Now, that
might actually make me feel better!"

"Don't you argue with me!" Monica begins undressing
her like a toddler and says, "You *will* put this on, if I have to
wrestle you to do it. You need sunshine! And exercise! Now,
give me that arm!"

Josie pushes her hands away, "Please. Some decency,
please! Fine. I'll put it on."

Monica drives them to the pool as if a ticking bomb rests on her dashboard. She lays on the horn, weaving in and out of traffic on the slow twenty-five miles per hour club road. A driver makes the mistake of completely stopping at a stop sign. Monica blares her horn. At the next stop sign, a driver puts on her hazards to retrieve a small branch stuck on her windshield.

Monica rolls down her window and yells out, "Move your fat butt, lady! It's blocking all of Boca!"

The woman lets out a huff and says, "Well! I never!"

"You never what? Stop eating?"

"How rude!"

Monica yells, "Rude? That's right! *Boca* rude, baby. Now, move your wide load! Move it! Move it!" Monica blares the horn repeatedly before impatiently crossing over the double yellow lines. She narrowly passes the woman, almost brushing the car's side. Monica arrives at the pool a full thirty-two seconds sooner than normal.

That was insane! Relieved to be out of the car, Josie says, "I thought you were turning over a new leaf?"

"Yes. I am. I am just turning it over a little more slowly than anticipated."

They lay their towels on the white-cushioned cast iron chaises by the club's poolside. Unbeknownst to them, the automatic chlorine dispenser broke earlier in the day. Not used to manually chlorinating the pool, the pool attendant accidentally dumped quadruple the normal amount of chlorine into the pool just minutes before their arrival.

Monica says, "Sorry Josie, I left my extra pair of goggles at home. You'll have to be the one without goggles today. I can't possibly swim without them. My eyes are simply too delicate."

"Fine. I certainly don't want to be responsible for any harm done to your delicate eyes. Besides, I don't really want to swim anyway. I'll just lay here." *I'm still recovering from that crazy car ride.*

"You must swim. It's not an option."

But, I could be home with eighty-five cats. I'll have to start adopting now, because it may take some time to get the numbers up. Anyway, any more quality time with Monica and I might seriously consider becoming a cat lady. Josie rolls her eyes and says, "Ugh. OK, if I have to, but cats don't make you swim. They don't like water, now do they?"

"What? Did you say 'cats'?"

"Never mind."

They swim lap after lap. After almost an hour in the pool, they take a break. They lie on Monica's embroidered beach towels lining their lounge chairs. The top of Monica's towel reads "Mo' Mo". Josie's reads "Hunky-doo". Josie sets the towel aside, lies on the bare cushion, and rubs her eyes from the chlorine burn, only making it worse.

Monica says, "You should lie on the towel. More comfortable."

She says, "No thanks. Not feeling hunky-dooish today."

Monica says, "It's J. Paul's towel. I just grabbed two."

"Whatever."

"OK."

"OK, what?"

"Now, start from the beginning."

Knowing resistance is futile, Josie tells Monica everything.

Taking mental notes, Monica says, "Yes. Yes. Go on. I see. Mmm-hmm."

Josie shares every last detail.

At the end, Monica says, "You sure can pick 'em."

"That's what you have to say to me?"

"Well, it's true!"

Josie says, "Not helping."

Monica replies, "I *am* helping. Tough love, baby. You need to hear this. Roger Fleming is the biggest nut job I have ever had the displeasure of meeting. I really can't imagine what you ever saw in him. This guy, Scott, isn't much better. What a narcissist! What do you have against nice guys anyway?"

"That's just it. I think they *are* nice until it's too late."

"It's never too late, honey. You know what your problem is? Well, I'll tell you. I think you just give everyone the benefit of the doubt right from the start."

"What's wrong with that? Innocent until proven guilty, right?"

"It doesn't work like that. Think of it this way, Miss C.P.A. It's like everyone has a bank account, but you always give your customers a full credit line without making sure they have the collateral to back it up."

"It's not credit. It's just how I am. It's how friendship works."

"Hear me out. You give them way too much status, before it's due. Don't get me wrong Josie, that's one of the things I like about you. You've got more optimism and character than most of my favorite people combined."

"You have favorite people?"

"A few. Back to the matter: but, that doesn't really help you in real life, now does it? I mean, the generosity of Bank Josie is admirable, but it's caused problems for you in the past. Hasn't it?"

"Maybe, but what are you asking me to do? I don't want to be a cynic. I want to go through life as an optimist. Are you trying to change who I am?"

"Yes. If it needs changing, that is. You can't very well keep taking knock after knock, and still keep standing up, now can you?"

"Yes, I can. If I become stronger and more resilient after each knock."

"You have my permission not to live up to this impossible bar you've set for yourself. Embrace being human!"

"What's more human than love and acceptance? Besides, I'll never compromise on my character, even if it kills me. Anyway, you have to admit that I gave Scott some time. It's not like I jumped into anything. How could I? He was thousands of miles away. We dated for months and look at the results! It still turned out a mess."

Monica shakes her head, "OK, but Scott is different. Long distance is tricky." She gives her closing argument. "You built him up to be your dream guy. Easy to do, and easy for him to live up to from a million miles away. I've got news for you. Dream guys don't exist. What you're looking for is a guy *with* faults."

"I don't need to look for guys with faults. They seem to find me without any help at all."

Monica holds up her finger, motioning for Josie to hold on one minute. "The trick is to make sure you discover all those faults before you commit, and to make sure you can live with those faults. You think J. Paul and I are perfect? It may look that way."

Umm. No comment. Josie crosses her arms.

Monica plows on, "Well, let me tell you, J. Paul's not perfect. Did you know he has stinky feet? And—I can't believe I am saying this-- I am not perfect either. Well. I'm close. Anyway, our secret is that we know that about each other. We know the other person is not perfect. We get it. I can live with his quirks, and he can live with mine. That's the key. Josie, don't you see? Go in with your eyes open."

Josie rubs her eyes. She says, "I can't. My eyes are killing me."

"They do look a little red to tell you the truth. Let me ask you something. Why didn't you sleep with Jim? I mean why the farce? Why pretend for the sake of Scott? Why not make it real, or just tell Scott the truth that you caught him? You know bust him and be done with it?"

"Because I didn't want to look like an idiot. I didn't want to be played, although I was being played. And most of all, I don't want pity, especially Scott's."

"At this point, who cares what Scott thinks?"

"I remember how Roger looked at me toward the end of our relationship. I never want to see that look again. I never want to be that person. He looked at me like I was pitiful, like I was scum. That's something I can't handle. That's why I staged it. And to answer your question, I didn't sleep with Jim because I made a commitment to Scott. I know it sounds crazy, but I wanted to see it through until I was sure there no longer was a commitment."

Monica throws her hands up and says, "But he didn't honor the commitment. I mean he already broke it. What's the point?"

"The point is, Monica, even if it was just for a day and the biggest farce ever, I kept my word."

Monica shakes her head and says, "It must be hard being Josephine Fleming. I am so glad I don't live in your head."

Yeah. Me too. "I'm fine with who I am. I made it look like I compromised myself, but I didn't. I won't. I never will. Not for Scott, and not for anyone."

"How do you live up to these standards you set for yourself? It must be exhausting."

"I thought you were supposed to be supportive. Helpful."

"Sorry. I'm trying."

"Besides, I like Jim. I feel bad enough that I made him act a part in my staged craziness. I couldn't go one step further and just use him physically, too. I wouldn't use him like that. You know me. I don't sleep around. I take it way too seriously. It means something to me."

"Honestly Josie, I would laugh at you if it wouldn't break my heart to do so. Why do you have to be so noble about everything? You don't have to bleed all of the time and for everyone, you know. Right? You do know that?"

Josie doesn't answer.

Monica grabs her hand and says, "How are you feeling now? Better?"

"A little. Except for my burning eyes." Josie rubs her eyes again and continues, "I'm just glad I didn't sleep with Scott. At least I can take heart in that." She towels her long hair dry. She sighs and says, "I guess it feels good to talk about it. I thought I wasn't ready to do so, but I'm glad you made me. One thing I can always count on for you to do is to tell me like it is. I need that sometimes, even if it might be hard to hear."

Monica hugs Josie and says, "Tough love, baby. That and I've never been shy about speaking my mind. It's getting dark, and you've got work tomorrow. Let's get you home."

Josie hugs Monica and says, "Thanks."

Josie doesn't see Monica wipe away a tear. Monica--new to the world of empathy--hides her emotion. She feels overwhelmed with gratitude for this chance to do something good for someone so good.

ᏚᎯ

Josie sleeps soundly that night, feeling refreshed when she wakes. She stretches before getting out of bed. *That swim felt great. Well, except for my eyes.* She arrives for work with a mug of coffee and a bottle of Visine. Moments after she settles at her desk, Jim knocks on her door. He takes one look at her swollen, red eyes and a sinking feeling overwhelms him.

He thinks, *Poor kid, she must have been crying her eyes out all night long.* He hands her a file. She holds the file at an arm's length, trying to focus. Finally, she gets out a magnifying glass.

Jim thinks, *Wow. That bad? She really is in a state.* He doesn't want to bring up the sore subject of Scott until Josie is ready to talk. He respects her privacy even if he was part in her whole scheme. Looking at her now, he regrets his part. He simply asks, "Are you OK?"

She looks up through the magnifying glass at him. Her swollen eye expands to three times its normal size through the glass. Her impaired vision blurs her ability to register the concern in his eyes. She says, "Never better. I've hardly thought about him." He gets a good look at the protruding red blood vessels in her eyes.

Yeah, right. Jim says, "Who?"

"Exactly."

"OK. Well. Let me know what you think when you're done number crunching. I don't need that until tomorrow. So, take your time." He walks to the water cooler.

She says, "OK sure," and yells after him, "I never did thank you."

"No, 'thank you' necessary. I should be thanking you for my newly discovered talent. I'm thinking of moonlighting at a dinner theatre."

Josie laughs and says, "You should. That was quite a performance. No one shoves underwear into couches better than you do, or walks as disheveled either!"

He grins and says, "It's a gift. By the way, I want my underwear back."

Jim comes back in one and a half hours later to check on her. Josie's head rests on her arms. She sleeps soundly on her desk. Drool pools on the very paper he needs. She gave up some time ago trying to focus on the tiny numbers. Quietly, Jim tiptoes out and shuts her door. He puts a sign on her door that reads "Maintenance."

৽৵৻

Josie wakes to a knock on her door. Todd pops his head in and says, "Maintenance?"

Josie says, "What?"

"There's a sign on your door that reads 'maintenance'."

"I don't have a clue how that got there."

"Can I come in?"

"No."

"I brought you something."

"Go away. I'm busy."

"I heard about Scott. Geez, look at your eyes! Are you OK?"

"I'm fine. Really."

"I know that. Don't you think I don't know that? I brought you something to celebrate getting rid of that chump." Todd opens a duffle bag and plops on her desk a bottle of champagne, a vintage cabernet, and some Schnapps.

She frowns.

He says, "Now, I didn't know which you would prefer. So, I brought all three. Where should we start? Pick."

"No. I'm working."

"Why are your eyes so swollen and red?"

"Todd, please, now is not a good time. I have to get this done."

"We must have a toast."

"How is it that we are related?"

"I'm serious. I'll pick if you don't."

"As I said, I'm working. I could get fired for this. People don't drink on a job they intend to keep."

"Who will know?"

"Um, everyone. I'll smell like liquor."

"Vodka. I should've brought Vodka. I knew it! Vodka doesn't leave a smell. I'll be right back. Twenty minutes."

"Don't bother. I won't be drinking. I have a deadline."

Todd ignores her protests and leaves. The bottles rest on her desk. Josie sweeps them off with one hand into the garbage bin. She settles in to work, once again. Straining to focus through the blur takes its toll. Josie intends briefly to rest her eyes, but falls asleep again on her desk.

Todd returns, sees her sleeping, and opens the bottle of vodka. He shrugs and pours himself a vodka and tonic. He leaves the glass and open bottle on her desk. He doesn't bother to leave a note.

Jim checks on her again, only to find her fast asleep. Along with the liquor bottles in her garbage bin, he sees the open bottle and empty glass on her desk. He cringes.

ॐ॰॰॰ॐ

Josie doesn't wake until after six p.m. When she does, it's to the smell of vodka. *Todd.* She caps the bottle and throws it in the bin with the rest of the bottles. She wipes the drool off of her desk and scans over the finished document one last time before sending it to Jim. She stretches, yawns, and walks to her car.

Oblivious, to the rush hour traffic, Josie drives in a daze. She drives past Violet and Ceridwin. They see her, but she doesn't see them. She flushes her eyes with more Visine at the next red light. Ceridwin and Violet sit at the same red light in the adjacent lane. They motion to her, but Josie doesn't see them as she continues flushing her eyes. She takes a sip from an energy drink she bought after leaving work.

Violet says, "What is that?"

Ceridwin says, "Dunno. Something metal. A can?"

Violet says, "Yeah, maybe. A flash of metal or something."

Josie finishes her drink and grabs the small brown bag that the health store clerk put her purchase into. She gathers up the receipt and a couple of trash papers from her console. She places them in the small brown bag. She places the metal can from the energy drink in the paper bag, too. When she drops it on the seat next to her, she hears liquid remaining in the bottom. She lifts the can--still in the paper bag--to her lips and finishes the remaining liquid, tapping the bottom.

Violet says, "Oh my gosh! Is that what I think it is?"

Ceridwin says, "Yes! It is! Oh she's drinking, and driving, and brown baggin' it!"

Violet says, "A new low. I heard she had a breakup with that heartthrob she was always carrying on about, but I didn't know it had gotten this bad." Finally, they beep the horn, getting Josie's attention.

Josie pushes the button, and her window rolls down. Josie says, "Well, well. Fancy meeting you two here!" She smiles.

Violet and Ceridwin look at her swollen, red eyes heavily smeared with mascara and draw the same conclusion. Violet whispers to Ceridwin, "Have you ever seen such eyes?"

Ceridwin whispers, "Never! She's in a bad way. Only drunks have crazy eyes like that!"

Violet whispers, "Yeah. Crazy, crazy eyes!"

"We need to intervene before this gets out of control!"

"We don't want to lose her again."

"Or for this thing to spiral any further out of control."

"Remember where she was just two years ago?"

Ceridwin whispers, "Yeah. I remember. We can't let that happen again."

"Right away! Nip it in the bud right away before it festers!"

"Yes! Absolutely!"

Josie says, "What are you two whispering about? What's the matter? Why are you looking at me like that? Cat's got your tongue?" *Cats. Something to look forward to. Cats! Eighty-five of them.* She starts crying. Josie says, "I don't want to be a cat lady!"

Alarmed, Violet whispers to Ceridwin, "Cat lady? Oh, she's gone."

Ceridwin whispers back, "Completely."

Josie sees their mouths moving, but can't hear what they say. She says, "What? I didn't catch that."

Ceridwin says, "I was just saying no, nor do I. I'm allergic. We're just coming back from a night league match. Where are you going? Are you going home now?"

"Yes."

Violet says, "Good. I mean, OK. Have a good night." Immediately, they call Todd. They set up an emergency intervention in one hour's time with all those close to Josie.

In a ponytail and oversized football jersey, Josie answers the door. She takes the spoonful of Nutella out of her mouth and says, "What's this?"

No one answers. First, Todd walks in. Next, Monica walks in. Violet, Vivian, Ceridwin, Marni, and Jim follow closely behind. Lastly, some guy with a clipboard walks in. They all pull up chairs around her living room, making a circle with Josie at the head.

Josie says, "Is this one of those multi-level marketing cult-like meetings or something?" No one answers. She continues, "Cuz if it is, I am not selling door-to-door cleaning products for any of you! If it is, then I'm going right through that wall like Bugs Bunny, leaving only a cutout silhouette of myself behind."

The clipboard guy speaks up. He says, "This is an intervention. Do you often have delusions involving cartoon characters?"

The spoonful of Nutella falls from her mouth. Josie picks it up and says, "Delusions? An intervention? For what? This is my first spoonful. I promise."

Everyone gasps. The clipboard guy holds up one hand and says in a calming tone, "It's OK. Denial is normal. Let's start from the beginning. Josephine, when did you start drinking?"

Josie says, "First of all, unless I'm at work, only my Dad gets to call me Josephine. Second of all, WHAT ARE YOU TALKING ABOUT?"

"OK. Now Josie, calm down. Answer the question. When did you start drinking?"

"College. Will somebody please tell me what is going on?"

The clipboard guy begins speaking again. Todd shushes him and says, "No. It's a valid question. She deserves to know. You should have told her from the beginning."

The clipboard guy says, "I usually do. This is so last minute, that I forgot." He shows off his badge. He explains where he is from and why he is here. He's not thrilled to be here. He got called in for this emergency intervention after normal business hours. He says, "Josie, you are in a safe place, and you can talk freely about what you are feeling."

"I feel hungry, and you are freaking me out!"

He says, "Good. That's good. Get it out."

Josie says, "No. I mean I am confused as to why we are all here. I don't have a drinking problem."

The guy looks around the room at everyone and again speaks in an all-knowing and soothing voice, "Remember, denial is normal."

Josie amps up the volume in her voice. She says, "I am not about to go off the deep-end here!" She points at the guy and says, "Who put you up to this?"

Ceridwin and Violet meekly raise their hands at the same time. They talk about what they saw earlier. They talk about Josie's crazy eyes, her incoherent conversation, and the beer she was slamming in the brown bag.

After much coaxing, Jim raises his hand next. He gives her a sorry-to-do-this look before talking about her blistery red eyes, catching her sleeping at her desk, and the liquor bottles piled in her trashcan. They all talk about her erratic behavior and the recent crying fits. That is all except Monica. Monica remains mute and clearly entertained.

Josie says, "And that's it? Some red eyes and some liquor bottles and suddenly I have a problem? Clipboard guy, you can go!"

Clipboard guy says, "What? No! You just can't--"

Josie says, "Go! Don't worry, you'll be paid."

Josie stands and gestures to Monica. Everyone looks at Monica. Josie says, "Explain."

Monica shrugs and says, "Josie has red swollen eyes, because I took her swimming in an over-chlorinated pool without goggles. There. Happy?"

Josie says, "No. You could've stopped this whole circus before it started. Why didn't you?"

Monica says, "I didn't know that's why we were here. I thought we were here to talk about your lousy choice in boyfriends. Can we talk about that? I think we should."

Furious, Josie explains about the chlorine damage and the energy drink. She gets the bag and the metal can out of her recycle bin for added proof. Todd explains about the liquor bottles. Despite themselves, everyone laughs a deep, hearty belly laugh until some end up in tears.

That is everyone except Clipboard Guy. He says, "Nobody takes my work seriously anymore. Intervention is not a laughing matter!" He leaves abruptly, slamming the door behind him.

Jim speaks up and says, "Well, since there is no intervention, and everyone is here, can we all go to dinner? I'm starving."

Ceridwin and Violet politely bow out. Both are sweaty and exhausted from their tennis match. Violet still has homework to do with her boys. Vivian already ate. Todd and Marni both have prior commitments. Monica has dinner plans waiting for her with J. Paul.

Jim says, "That leaves me. That is if I can tear you away from your Nutella."

Before Todd walks out of the door, he says, "Night everyone! Jo, as far as Scott goes, I told you so."

Josie says, "That is the most childish thing I have ever heard."

"Childish, but true."

"Could you not think of something more caring to say to me in my moment of crisis, my moment of intervention?"

"Yeah, OK." Todd does a little dance and sings, "Yeah. I was right. I was right. Like always. Like always. I was right."

"That's it!" She chases him, but he's too fast. He hops into his car and locks the doors long before she catches up. She pulls the door handle to no avail. She says through the glass, "Chicken? Scared of your little sister? Wimp!"

He laughs and says, "Oh, yeah, right. Me? Scared? Bring it!"

"Ok. Get out of the car then, Macho Man."

"Not now. I have a date."

"Sissy! You're scared, aren't you?"

"No, but you will be. How about returning a few of my serves?"

"How about returning a few of my forehands?"

"Fine."

"Fine. Name a time and place. I'll see you on the tennis court. Then, we'll see how macho you really are."

He loves having everything back to normal, and he loves seeing the fight in her once again. It's something she lost when she married The Big Loser. Smiling, he says, "Eight a.m. Saturday."

"Done."

॰ঌ৶

Josie and Jim drive to Scuola Vecchia for Jim's favorite pizza: prosciutto and arugula. They trade bites. Jim takes a bite of Josie's Italian sausage and mushroom. He says, "Yummy. While tonight might have been funny, I really have been worried about you. I hate to see you sad."

"Tonight *was* funny."

"Crazy how circumstances can look one way, but be completely another. Sorry."

"Doesn't matter. How can I feel anything but good? I have all those wonderful family and friends willing to give up their time just for me."

Jim looks down at his plate and says, "Maybe they feel good. You know, just being around you or something."

She smiles and says, "You're a great boss. You know that?"

After their meal, they walk to the end of Atlantic Boulevard and take a stroll along the beach. The wind chills both of them. Jim offers Josie his button-down shirt and walks in his undershirt. They walk along the water's edge. Josie tells him every detail of what transpired with Scott. Again, Jim doesn't judge or make assertations. He lets her get it all out. He only listens.

Josie says, "I'm rambling. I'm sorry about this, Jim. I shouldn't be getting so personal. I promise I won't let this affect my work."

Jim says, "Nonsense. You're more important than work."

She looks at him, as if seeing him for the first time.

Jim says, "Did I tell you I have three older sisters?"

"Only one hundred times."

"No? Well, let me explain. I have seen my fair share of unrequited love by the numerous females in my life. If I may be so bold as to make a suggestion that is somewhat of a proven family remedy?"

"Proven?"

"Yes. Scientifically. Time and time again."

"How can I refuse?"

"To the mall then. Retail therapy awaits."

Once inside the mall, Jim insists that Josie only try on shoes. He says, "I can provide eyewitness testimony to years of success by applying this strictly shoe-trying method of therapy." He offers to phone his sisters for affirmation.

Josie says, "That's really not necessary. Besides, I think I see my pair." Standing in front of Neiman Marcus' window, Josie points to the mannequin donning a four-inch heeled pair of candy apple red, patent leather pumps. Their eye-catching sheen appears almost metallic. Under the sole rests another half of an inch of contoured platform. The heel tapers into a thin button end. *Stunning!*

Jim says, "Yes. I believe you are on to something here. Bold. Knockouts. Remarkably impractical."

"Exactly. Should I try them on?"

"Is that even a question?"

Josie tries the shoes on in front of the mirror. She turns and walks, surveying the shoes from every angle. She sees Jim's reflection in the background. She notices the way he looks at her. She pauses. *Why didn't I notice that before?*

Jim says to the shoe salesman, "We'll take them."

Josie hands the salesman her card, but Jim pushes it away and hands over his own card.

Jim says, "No need to wrap them up." He coughs when he reads the sum and signs the bill.

Josie peeks and says, "Let's put them back. That's a silly price to pay for a pair of shoes."

Jim says, "Yes, and as my personal accountant not just my professional one, you know I am unaccustomed to spending such frivolous amounts. However, you also know that I can afford it." He winks at her.

Josie stands before him. With the extra four and one-half inches, she stands to nearly his height. She looks down at her candy apple red shoes and mutters, "Dorothy in *The Wizard of Oz.*" She clicks her crazy red heels together three times, and something occurs to her. *I had the answer staring at me. It was right in front of me the whole time. Why didn't I see?*

Josie thinks about the time when Jim helped her secure the better job offer. She thinks about when Jim saved her from the drunk on the barge at The Viscaya. She thinks about how he diligently acted his part in her scheme with Scott. She thinks about the pool and swimming with him at the gala. She remembers when she was heartbroken and crying, how tenderly he hugged her. Suddenly, she is flooded with "Jim" memory after "Jim" memory.

Josie says quietly, "You love me, don't you?"

"Yes. For some time."

She kisses him and instantly discovers something hidden deep inside her heart: something long forgotten. Josie says, "I lo--"

Jim puts his finger to her lips. He says, "I want you to be sure when you say it. We have time."

She looks into his eyes. She realizes she is home.

ACKNOWLEDGEMENTS

I thank God for sidelining my tennis obsession and replacing my racquet with a pen. I thank Andy—a better man than J. Paul Mooney and Jim Hartling combined—for his continued love and dedication. I also thank the femmes extraordinaires: Julie P., Kathleen B., Katie A., and Jeannie P. A special thanks goes out to Finnegan for his loyalty and excellent foot-warming skills. Also, thank you to John T. for boldly living in the present. Thank you to Paul Casson for his graphic artistry and creating the book cover design. Lastly, I thank the original Hamlet Blue, no finer group ever was.

ABOUT THE AUTHOR

April Elaine is a tennis-playing housewife, formerly a medical and surgical sales representative. She grew up in Florida, graduating from FSU, and earning her MBA in Belgium. Postgraduate, she's completed creative and technical writing courses from UC Berkeley. She lives in the Miami area with her husband. She is currently writing a sequel to BocaRude.

www.bocarude.com

Made in the USA
Middletown, DE
19 December 2015